MALICE
Snake - Book One
Lost Souls MC

Written by: Brooklyn Cross

FIRST EDITION.

ASIN: B0BXMH468J

ISBN: 978-1-998015-09-2

ALL RIGHTS RESERVED.

Edited by: R. Mudawar and Kaye Kemp Book Polishing

Cover Art: Dazed Designs

Trademark Acknowledgements

LOST SOULS

THE LOST SOULS MC
SNAKE – BOOK ONE

Malice

BROOKLYN CROSS

BROOKLYN CROSS

WARNING

ALSO BY BROOKLYN CROSS

Lost Souls MC

(Motorcycle Club - Dark 3.5-4.5 Spice 3.5-4.5)

Malice

Surrender (Releasing May 16)

Showbiz

Handcuffed

The Righteous Series

(Vigilante/Ex Military Romance - Dark 3-4 Spice 3-4)

Dark Side of the Cloth

Ravaged by the Dark

Sleeping with the Dark

Hiding in the Dark

Redemption in the Dark

Crucified by the Dark

Dark Reunion (Coming 2023)

The Consumed Trilogy

(Suspense/Thriller/Anti-Hero Romance - Dark 4-5 Spice 3-4)

Burn for Me

Burn with Me

Burn me Down (Coming 2023)

The Buchanan Brother's Duet

(Serial Killer/Captive Horror Romance - Dark 4-5 Spice 3-5)

Unhinged Cain by Brooklyn

Twisted Abel by T.L Hodel

The Battered Souls World

(Standalone Books Shared World Romance/Dramatic/Women's Fiction/All
The Feels- Dark 2-3 Spice 2-3)

The Girl That Would Be Lost

The Boy That Learned To Swim (Coming Soon)

The Girl That Would Not Break (Coming Soon)

The Brothers of Shadow and Death Series

(Dystopian/Cult/Occult/Poly MMF Romance - Dark 3-4 Spice 3-4)

Anywhere Book 1 of 3

Backfire Book 1 of 3 by T.L. Hodel

Seven Sin Series

(Multi Author/PNR/Angel and Demons/Redemption - Dark 2-5 Spice 3-5)

Greed by Brooklyn Cross

Lust by Drethi Anis

Envy by Dylan Page

Gluttony by Marissa Honeycutt

Wrath by Billie Blue

Sloth by Talli Wyndham

Pride by T.L. Hodel

TO
AUTHOR NV ROEZ
&
YOUR GLITTERY LIZARDS
YOU KNOW WHY

ARKNOWLEDGEMENT

IT IS WITH LOVE AND
APPRECIATION THAT I
SAY THANK YOU TO ALL
THOSE THAT HAVE STOOD
BY MY SIDE THROUGH MY
AUTHOR JOURNEY.
WHO PICKED ME UP
DURING MY LOWEST
MOMENTS AND CONTINUE
TO MAKE ME SMILE.
I COULD NOT DO THIS
WITHOUT EACH OF YOU.

PLAYLIST

PAGE 1

VENOM - EMINEM
TREEHOUSE - HE IS WE
ME, MYSELF & I - G-EAZY X BEBE REXHA
BUTTERFLY - CRAZY TOWN
BAD HABITS - ED SHEERAN
SURVIVOR - NATHANIEL RATELIFF
A LITTLE BIT STRONGER - SARA EVANS
FORGET ME - LEWIS CAPALDI
BUTTONS - SNOOP DOGG & PUSSYCAT DOLLS
EDAMAME - BBNO$
STRONGER - KANYE WEST
I WANNA BE YOU - MANESKIN
BREATHE - SKITZ KRAVEN
LIMIT TO YOUR LOVE- JAMES BLAKE
RESCUE ME - ONE REPUBLIC
SHE KEEPS ME UP - NICKELBACK
NEVER GONNA LET YOU GO - ESTHERO
YOU WORRY ME - NATHANIEL RATELIFF
PEACHES - JUSTIN BIEBER
CTRL + ALT + DEL - REVE
GUNS+AMMUNITION - JULY TALK
COMING FOR YOU - THE OFFSPRING
BAD GUY - BILLIE EILISH
THE KIND OF LOVE WE MAKE - LUKE COMBS
MEMORY - KANE BROWN X BLACKBEAR
HOLD ON, WE'RE GOING HOME - DRAKE
ANTI-HERO - TAYLOR SWIFT

PLAYLIST

PAGE 2

SUGAR, WE'RE GOIN DOWN - FALL OUT BOY
CENTURIES - FALL OUT BOY
TOXIC - BRITNEY SPEARS
STEREO HEARTS - GYM CLASS HEROES
APOLOGIZE - TIMBERLAND
HERO - CHAD KROEGER
TAKE WHAT YOU WANT - POST MALONE
LAST RESORT - PAPA ROACH
I WALK THE LINE - HALSEY
BURY A FRIEND - BILLIE EILISH
NEVER LEAVE - BAILEY ZIMMERAMAN
RUN AWAY TO MARS - TALK
SHIVERS - ED SHEERAN
SOMETHING TO LOSE - LANDON TEWERS
WE WILL ROCK YOU - QUEEN
THE NEXT EPISODE - DR. DRE
STAY WITH ME - SAM SMITH
PONY - GINUWINE
SLOW HANDS - NIALL HORAN
ELECTRIC LOVE - BORNS
GLITTER & GOLD - BARNS COURTNEY
WAY DOWN WE GO - KALEO
KRYPTONITE - 3 DOORS DOWN
LOVE THE WAY YOU LIE - EMINEM
OUT TA GET ME - GUNS N' ROSES
SATELLITE - GUSTER
WRECKING BALL - MILEY CYRUS

ECLIPSE

SPECIALTY SHOTS

APPLE PIE - 1OZ SOUR GREEN APPLE,
1OZ CINNAMON WHISKY

BLUEBERRY BLITZ - 1OZ BLUE BERRY
VODKA, 1 OZ BLUE CURACAO

PEACH LIPS - 1/2 OZ SPICED RUM, 1/2
OZ BANANA LIQUEUR, 1OZ PEACH
SCHNAPPS

NIGHTCAP - 1/2OZ CREME DE
MENTHE, 1/2OZ KAHLUA, 1/2OZ
COFFEE LIQUEUR, TOP WITH
CHOCOLATE MILK

BEND OVER SALLY - 1OZ TEQUILA,
1OZ SOUR RASPBERRY LIQUEUR

FROST BITE - 1OZ COFFEE LIQUEUR,
1OZ MAPLE WHISKEY

SPANK ME - 1OZ LIMONCELLO, 1OZ
COCONUT CREAM LIQUEUR

PIG ROASTED - 1OZ SALTED CARAMEL
LEQUEUR, 1 OZ SMOKY WHISKEY

BIG DADDY - 1/2OZ CHERRY
LIQUEUR, 1/2OZ BANANA LEQUEUR,
1/2OZ BLUE VODKA

Snake

Chapter 1

Kaivan

"Where the fuck do you think you're going?"

I internally groaned as the annoying voice barked behind me. It was fitting since everyone called him Big Dog. The guy was big but he was more growly asshole than actual bite. I decided to think of him as Clifford, with his bright red cheeks, dopey expression, and overly round face that made him look like a bulldog. The bigger issue with Big Dog was that he was Red's lackey and did his bidding, specifically fetching. I was praying that was not the case today.

"Answer me, kid. Where the fuck are you headin'?"

I slowly turned around to stare at the burly man sporting the M

Clean pose. With all the willpower in the world, I kept the sarcasim off my face as I pointed toward the laundry cart I was pushing.

The laundry always smelled bad, but fuck, I didn't want to know what these assholes did this week. It reeked like rotting canned-tuna mixed with sloppy shit with the underlying scent of 'I jacked off too much'. If there was a scent you could bottle and call it Eau de Prison, this was it.

"Laundry," I said, keeping my voice even. "Why, do you have something you want to add?"

"Naw, but Red wants to see you," Big Dog said.

Nightmare initiated. This wasn't good. You wanted to avoid Red, not end up in his crosshairs. I learned that the first day I watched him and his pack of goons attack a guy who looked to be doing nothing but minding his own business. They messed him up so badly that the guards had to ship him to the hospital. That dude never came back, and Red's crew never got in trouble.

For the last six weeks, six days, and almost six hours, I'd kept my head low and under his radar, or at least I thought I had. It was a bad omen to be summoned at this time of day. He would want to see me for only three reasons, and I wanted nothing to do with any of them.

Option one, Red wanted to recruit me as part of his group. He would demand that I fuck someone up—and preferably kill them—to prove my loyalty. I had no interest in being part of his goon squad and didn't want to kill some random guy just because he told me to.

Option two, he wanted to use me as bait for someone else to get their stripes, then I would have to defend myself. I was pretty big for eighteen, and I could hold my own in a fight, but adding time to my sentence was on my Fuck-No list.

The only other option...he wanted to make me his bitch. There was no way I was letting that happen. I would rather die than let that man—a walking cesspool of disease—stick his cock up my ass. Not that I ever wanted any cock tearing my ass apart, but definitely not his. I didn't care if a dude wanted to fuck another dude, but it had never been my jam.

"No, I gotta get this to the laundry room," I said, and turned away from his shocked expression. The wheels squeaked as I pushed the cart, but I was immediately whipped around by a meaty hand gripping my shoulder.

Yanking out of Big Dog's hold, I snarled at him, standing nose to nose as I clenched my fists. "Don't fucking touch me."

Big Dog had eighty pounds on me easily, but I wasn't letting him intimidate me. This place was eat or be eaten, and I refused to be someone's meal.

"You have big kahunas, kid, but Red will knock you down a peg or two." Big Dog leaned in, but I refused to back down. "You need to learn your place."

"I think you mean cojones, and you need to learn to brush your teeth. Your breath fucking reeks, man. Get out of my face." His eyes narrowed into slits. "My place is to be left alone, and that's what I want you to do." I glared back and heard his neck crack as he tilted it from side to side.

"Oh, I'm gonna have so much fun with you." Big Dog stepped off to the side and pointed in the direction he wanted me to go. "Walk. Now. Or I tell Red that you disobeyed a direct summons, and you won't last another day."

I was fucked either way now. If I ignored him and stayed in the laundry room, I could avoid whatever Red had planned for tonight, but I would be labeled a pussy, and it wouldn't save me tomorrow. If I went...well...it wasn't like I was going anywhere for another five hundred and thirteen point four weeks, so I might as well get it over with.

Looking longingly at a pile of dirty clothes was not something I ever thought I would do, but I did now. Sad when handling men's cum splattered clothes was a better option than where I was headed.

Then again, there were many things I didn't think would ever happen in my life. Being tossed in prison to rot for a crime I didn't commit was currently sitting in first place. Hopefully, whatever Red had planned wouldn't knock that into number two.

I glanced up as we walked and shook my head when I spotted that the camera's light wasn't blinking, which meant that it was turned off. It seemed to be a conspiracy all on its own that random hallways at all hours of the day would no longer be recording. It was even more mysterious that the heads of the different groups that ran this place all seemed to know when they would be down.

I felt like I was walking the plank as we weaved through the maze that took us to the far side of the prison and the set of showers that were barely ever used, at least not for washing. I'd already spent an entire week cleaning and mopping in this section, and the constant grunting and moans coming from this disgusting tiled hole in the wall would've made you think it was filled with farm animals.

I swallowed hard as I stepped inside, and the three goons I'd seen beating the random dude were standing around with their arms crossed. All eyes turned my way as I stepped inside. My muscles flexed and twitched, ready for the fight I was sure was coming.

It was easy to spot the red-headed man whose beard matched the vibrant shade on his head. The scraggly strands looked like shit, but it made him stand out among the crowd.

Red was sitting on the counter by the sinks. I knew without him even opening his mouth what he wanted with me. Red's eyes openly roamed over my body, and I fought the urge to fidget under his stare.

"What are you in for?" Red asked as he leaned back on the counter and spread his legs wide. Any other guy, in any other place at any other time, I would've said he was simply relaxing, but that was not what was happening here.

The goons in the room began to do their slow shuffle as if I wouldn't notice them blocking my only escape route.

I didn't want to say why I was here. The fact that it wasn't true wouldn't matter. The moment I opened my mouth and the words rape tumbled out, it was game over. There was a code in prison. If you hurt women, you were an automatic target to be someone's bitch until the day you got out. But it was worse for those who hurt kids. Most didn't last a full day, and the ones who did wish they hadn't.

Red would have me bent over the counter so fast it would make my head spin. That may happen anyway, but I wasn't giving anyone here an open-season ticket.

"Armed robbery," I muttered, unable to think of anything better.

"Oh yeah? Robbery of what?"

Lifting my shoulders, I let them drop. "Whatever I could get my hands on. Why do you want to know? Are you looking to acquire something when I get out?"

"Oh, I plan on acquiring something all right."

He smirked, and I could feel my blood pressure rising. I was used to this feeling, this anticipation of bad shit about to happen. I had it so many times in foster care that I lost count. Until I got to the Collins family. Their place hadn't been a walk in the park either, but at least I didn't worry every time I laid my head down that someone would try to beat me, or worse. I was also a fuck load tougher. So if he wanted me, he was forcing it, and I would fight with my last breath before I submitted.

"I have it on good authority that you're a sick fuck and liked to diddle your sister," Red said, and then laughed. The sound echoed off the walls of the large space.

I didn't need any reminders of what had landed me in this fucking place. Raine was my foster sister, we were best friends until she didn't come home one night, and the police dragged me from my bed. They told me I was being arrested for rape and drove me to the precinct, where I spent so many hours in the interrogation room that I didn't even know what day of the week it was.

They never got me to break and implicate myself in something I didn't do, but it didn't matter. Stupid fucking public defender was a useless dick, and I ended up with a shit plea deal. So here I was with a ten-year sentence hanging over my head. I'd promised myself I wouldn't end up like my old man, but I guess some shit was simply unavoidable.

"Not sure where you heard that from, but it was a fucking lie. I wouldn't do that shit," I snarled. My muscles tensed, and my hands curled into fists as the goons stepped closer. I glared at them, sizing them up. This wasn't the first time I'd been outnumbered.

Red slid off the counter and took a step in my direction. "What a shame. I was hoping you were a freak. It would make what I plan to do to you so much more entertaining." Red got up in my personal space. "Wouldn't that have been ironic? You in here for diddling your sister, and then you get your ass tapped. It would've been a sweet circle of events."

"Apparently, our ideas of entertaining differ," I drawled.

Red smiled, but it did nothing to ease the hard lines on his face. "You have a smart mouth. I wonder how smart it will be when I have my cock shoved so far down your throat that you choke to death on it."

I inched closer and squared off with Red. There was no way I was backing down. "If you put your cock anywhere near my mouth, I'll fucking bite it off." I snapped my teeth together, the sound loud in the otherwise quiet bathroom.

Red looked behind me, and I knew the goons had moved closer. "You believe this kid?" The guys chuckled. "I kinda like you, but you're not getting out of this. Hold him down," Red ordered. "I'm going to be the first to teach your ass a lesson."

Not giving them a chance to grab me, I spun. My elbow sailed backward into Red's face with a hard crack.

"Ah fuck! You broke my nose." The sound was music to my ears.

I barely felt the impact and used the same arm to land a hard right hook along the jaw of the goon closest to me. Like a comic strip, blood and a tooth flew from his mouth.

Fighting was second nature to me. I'd been fighting for everything from the day I was born. I fought to breathe through the umbilical cord wrapped around my neck. Fought to keep my mother alive when gang members—pissed off at my father—decided to teach him a lesson by killing her. I fought for my next meal when my father forgot I existed. Fought to not be a punching bag for fucktards in the foster homes I bounced around in. Fighting to stay alive in this rat hole called life was all I knew.

The guy I hit stumbled back from the blow and left a shot open for me to get my foot up and into the second guy's gut. He stepped back and doubled over, grabbing his stomach. That blow should've laid him out flat. Damn, I wish I had my shitkickers on instead of these stupid white running shoes.

The third goon pushed his buddy out of the way and growled like a wild animal as he swung at me. This guy was the largest of the three and had more muscle in one arm than I had on my entire body. But that also made him slow. Ducking under his large fist, we danced around until I landed a solid strike to his kidneys. The goon winced and closed his eyes for just a moment; but that was all I needed. I stepped back and brought my foot up, landing a sidekick to his jugular. He clutched at his throat, eyes bulging as he tried to get air. I watched him for one satisfactory moment as he dropped to his knees.

I'd maneuvered enough to dash out the door, and I might've had a shot if fucking Big Dog hadn't stuck around. I hadn't seen him still hanging out in the entryway. I saw the man a second before I was slammed into like a battering ram. We crashed to the floor and skidded backward in a heap. All the air was driven out of my lungs, but I didn't care. Gasping for breath, I fought for my life.

Big Dog held the front of my jumper in one hand, and I raised my arms up just in time for his fist to crack down hard. The side of my face, shoulder, and arms all fell victim to his blows, despite the guard I held firmly in place. I tried to drive my knee or fist into any part of Big Dog's body that would force him to let go, but the guy was like the Pillsbury Doughboy, with just a bit more muscle. It felt like my fist was sinking in and being pushed back out.

Another massive fist cracked me across the face, and little stars exploded behind my eyes as the metallic taste of blood filled my mouth.

"Get him up," Red ordered, and I was hauled to my feet. "Put him on the counter, face down. I'm going to enjoy this." Red grabbed my jaw before the guys could drag me across the floor, and his meaty fingers dug in painfully. "I was going to break you in slowly because I was feeling generous, but..." I grunted as his fist slammed into my stomach and once more drove the air from my lungs.

"Now I'm going to teach you what it means to be in my waters. Your tight little asshole will be ripped apart by the time we all get our fill. It'll be a winking mess for longer. And if I have to teach you another lesson in manners, I'll cut your balls off." A shank pressed against my jugular, and I was tempted to jab myself into the sharp blade so this didn't happen. With my shit ass luck, they would sodomize my corpse, and I would have to hover over my body and watch. "I own your ass now, pup."

I tensed as he stepped back and cocked his fist. This time I was at least expecting it and flexed my muscles against the blows. Coughing and unable to breathe, I fought the two men as they dragged me across the floor, my sneakers squeaking like they were revolting as well.

"Fuck," I yelled as they forced me face-first onto the counter. It was cold and damp from what I could only hope was water. I kicked my legs out at anything I could and didn't care how ridiculous I looked doing it.

"Hold him still, for fuck's sake," Red barked.

Two more sets of hands joined in, each pair taking a leg and pulling them apart. My heart was beating so hard that I could hear the thumping echoing back at me through the surface of the counter. A hand gripped the back of my jumper and the panic that had been building reached new heights at the sound of tearing material.

"Look at that ass. Mmm hmm," Red said, his large hand cracking off my right ass cheek.

I snarled, and turned my head as best I could. "Get the fuck away from me. Or so help me, I'll rip your tongue from your head and shove it up your ass, so you'll know how you taste."

Red glared at me and raised his hand to strike again when a deep voice I didn't recognize boomed inside the room.

"Let him go, Red," a man I couldn't see said.

"Fuck you, Mannix. This guy is mine. He broke my fucking nose. I deserve payback," Red argued.

"The thing is, I don't see it that way." This voice was a lot more threatening than the whiny sound of Red's higher pitch. "You see, the kid here has already agreed to be part of my crew. So, technically, you're encroaching on my territory. Don't hand me some line that he wandered over here all on his own, either. We both know better."

I could make out a shadow along the wall, and I strained my neck to see who the hell this guy was. My eyes landed on the biggest man I'd ever seen. I didn't know where he came from, but I hadn't seen him before, and he was definitely someone you remembered.

The standard issue jumper looked too small and was open at the top. Even with my limited view, I could tell the guy was jacked. Tattoos covered every inch of his deep brown skin, but my attention was drawn to the reaper on his neck. His glare was focused on Red, and those eyes screamed do not mess with this guy. He also looked like the type who was used to people following his orders.

Great, now I'd been claimed by another leader. Why not have multiple people wanting my ass today? The fucking stars were not aligned in my favor.

"What do you mean, he's your territory? Where's his tattoo?" Red held his arm out in my direction.

Mannix stepped in close to Red, and I held back a smirk as Red craned his neck up to look at him.

"He was supposed to get it today after his duties in the laundry room, but he never showed up."

How the hell did this guy know my schedule? I'd never even seen his face before. "But then I heard you were down here, and I had a feeling that you were once more trying to steal something that wasn't yours," Mannix snarled. "Do I need to remind you what I said would happen if you did that again?" His voice dropped even lower. "What I would take from you?"

The tone of his voice made me shiver, and it wasn't even directed at me. The room was so quiet it was like everything, including the air, had been sucked out. I swallowed as I waited to see what way this would go.

Red stepped back, and I could no longer see him from my position. "Fuck, fine, you can have him. He's more trouble than he's worth," Red said. "Let's go," he grumbled, and the men holding my arms and legs let go like I was a hot potato.

Pushing myself up from the counter, I washed my hands and scrubbed at my face, horrified to think how many hairy asses and cum shots had landed on this counter.

Mannix casually stood as I washed. My eyes flicked to his light, amber-colored ones. Time to face the music. I couldn't delay any longer. Turning, I looked up at the man who still had a solid five inches on my six-four frame.

"Why did you do that?" I asked, wary of the answer.

"I was keeping an eye on you, and some things just can't be explained." He lifted a big shoulder and let it drop. "You're officially under my protection, but one day, you'll owe me a favor. That's how this place works." His lip curled up with a smirk. "Come on. I'll get you back to your cell in one piece. With your ass hanging out like that, hard to say what would happen." He smiled wide and held out his hand. "Everyone calls me Mannix."

"Kaivan, but everyone calls me Snake."

Snake

Chapter 2

Kaivan

I could hear Beast stomping up the stairs. He had a very particular gait, and it was called elephant. Taking a sip of my coffee, I waited on the long couch for him to emerge like some great troll out of the black hole of the stairwell.

Beast stepped into the main clubhouse area and stared around. "Where the fuck is everyone?"

"Fuck if I know." Unless needed to do a job, I kept to myself. Being in the clubhouse alone was rare, and I was taking full advantage of the silence and the fancy espresso machine. I had to admit that as much as I made fun of Mannix for having it installed, it was amazing. I would almost say I was becoming a coffee snob. Who knew I had it in me?

"I need to speak to Mannix. I heard from Chase and..."

Cutting Beast off, I growled, "I don't want to hear about it. Tell someone who gives a fuck about him and his missions. I'm not even done cleaning up the last pile of crap he decided to leave in his useless wake."

Beast huffed and marched over to the bar. He grabbed a couple of beers from the large glass fridge before making his way toward me. I knew the conversation about Chase wasn't over. Beast had been loyal to our illustrious president for far longer than I'd been in prison, so he gave the guy a break at every turn. I, on the other hand, had no reason to do so. Mannix inducted me into the Lost Souls, and two weeks and four days after my release, I had to go to some place called Ashen Springs to save a girl I'd never met. Like a fucking magic trick, Chase Mathers came back from the dead and popped out of whatever hole he'd crawled into to claim he was the rightful leader of the MC.

From that moment on, it had been one clusterfuck after another or Chase's complete absence. I did get a damn good blowjob out of his old lady while he was out whoring around. He disappointed me again when he didn't try to kill me. That would've been fun. Mannix filled me in on Chase's history like that would make me feel sorry for him and maybe shed a tear or two. Not likely. What I saw was a piece of shit who couldn't handle the crap in his life head-on and decided to hide like a motherfucking coward. I had no time for cowards, and they certainly didn't get my respect.

It shocked me every day that his old lady, Naomi, stayed with him. What she saw in him, I could never say. He certainly wasn't worth the effort she put into getting him clean after the shit he pulled. Then again, I guess that was the crazy you chose when you got yourself knocked up. Personal opinion, she would be better off raising that baby alone. Hell, even crazy-ass Ava would've been a better choice than Chase Mathers. That girl was no coward. Strange and off her rocker for sure, but no coward.

"You do know that at some point you're going to have to accept that Mathers is our Prez and show some respect, or you'll be out on your ass," Beast drawled in that lazy fatherly voice he put on whenever he thought one of us was saying something stupid. The bottle hissed as he popped the top off and settled back in the chair across from me like he was my motherfucking therapist.

I didn't need a therapist. Okay, that was a lie. I probably needed a therapist, but I didn't want to fix what was wrong with me. My wrong had me smiling wide as I slit someone's throat open. It was what had kept me alive for twenty-nine years and three glorious months.

"Actually, I don't have to do shit. Mathers doesn't deserve my respect, and he certainly shouldn't have yours," I argued and took a swig of my coffee. "I respect you, and I respect Mannix. Until that man proves he deserves to be at the helm, he can go to hell for all I care."

Beast shook his head and muttered something with the word fuck thrown in multiple times, which pulled at the corner of my lip.

"What are you drinking?" Beast asked as he sniffed the air and looked at my porcelain cup.

I looked from the large biker down to the black coffee and saw my reflection in the liquid. Time changed everyone, and it certainly changed me. Mannix would tell me something all philosophical like, 'time is but the journey we choose to take between one life and the next...and with each new journey you take...blah, blah, blah.' Mannix was always hitting me with crap like that. I didn't even know where he got that shit—probably scribbled on some bus stop.

"Coffee, black," I said, and chugged the rest before it got cold.

Nothing worse than cold coffee. Well, there were a couple of things, but it was up there on my list.

"Why you drinkin' that?" Beast looked up at the clock on the wall. "You planning on going dancing with those Weasel members tonight?"

My lip curled up, and to anyone other than Beast and a small handful of others, it would look malicious, and it was, but he also knew it wasn't directed at him. Becoming an enforcer for a motorcycle club had never been one of my life plans. Looking back, this was where I was always going to end up. That happened when your father was an enforcer for an MC and got sent away for three life sentences when you were nine years, two months, and ten days old.

"Yup. I have two dance partners who are in need of a lesson tonight," I said and stood to stretch out the tight muscles in my back. I'd spent four hours in the gym today, and my shoulders were officially telling me off.

That was something else that time had changed. I was no longer the eighteen-year-old punk who landed in prison with a smart mouth and very few skills or muscles to back it up. No, I trained hard, worked out harder, and now I was feared more than any other enforcer in all the southern states. Life goals pushed me to make sure that title spread to all corners of the great U.S. of A.

If you were on my list, you were a dead man, and I always left you looking like the spectacle you were meant to be. Why have a nice corpse for opposing members to clean up? That didn't leave a lasting impression.

"I said soon. I didn't mean you needed to go tonight," Beast said.

"No time like the present," I said, and lit up my smoke.

"But I just got here," Beast complained as I wandered over to the bar and put the coffee mug on the counter. Smiling, I shot Beast a teasing glance on my way to the door.

"Which is exactly why I'm leaving." I smirked as Beast swore.

Jogging down the stairs, I pushed my way out into the cool fall night and took a deep breath. I fucking loved Halloween, and I was going to make the most of it. Unable to help myself, I glanced at the dilapidated amusement park next door and snorted as I watched Wilder scurry around, covered in a camouflage of garbage and old stuffed toys. He looked like some creepy ass creature out of a horror flick. I actually found him highly entertaining, and the fact that he scared just about everyone made him A-OK in my mind.

Wilder moved out of sight in the darkness, but I knew he would still be keeping an eye on me. Crazy? Maybe. I think the term crazy was tossed around a little too much and a little too easily these days.

My two bikes stood out from the rest like a sore thumb, or in this case, a sexy middle finger to everyone else. Everyone here rode a sled of some sort, but I was never much of a joiner, so I went and got myself an Indian instead of a Harley. I thought Roach was going to faint the day I rode in on it. That was the second best day of my life. The top spot was held by getting my get-out-of-jail-free card stamped.

My second ride was a chopper. The midnight black paint glistened under the lights of the parking area. The custom paint job of snakeskin—which could only be seen at certain times of day—made you do a double take. When I rode, it looked like the skin was moving under the paint, making my heart pound and my cock hard.

I knew that even though Roach would never say it, he was jealous as hell over my ride. I'd seen him eyeing it up more than once, but I told him girls didn't dig insects on a paint job. A few choice words were thrown my way that day.

Roach had arrived at the pen when I reached the midway point of my sentence. I remembered the day well. I'd celebrated being on the back half by talking one of the guards into getting me a chocolate cupcake. It helped that I saved that particular guard from having his throat slit in a riot. Every year after that, on the same day, that guard brought me a small treat. Might have been a cupcake or a couple of cookies, but it was a gift, not a favor. I would find it left in my cell just before lights out. There was only one thing that I found tasted sweeter. It came with a cute smile and lips that could suck the chrome off a tailpipe.

Choosing the chopper for tonight, I straddled the girl and shivered as she fired up. I nodded to the guys running the gate as I got close and slipped out onto the dark road. This was a shit part of town, but it felt like home. Much like a rat would still call a sewer home, this was where I belonged.

As I got closer to Miami beach, the traffic thickened, and so did the number of people on the sidewalks. The wide assortment of costumes ranged from cute fuzzy bunnies to terrifying monsters and everything in between. I rolled up to a red light, and a group of girls dressed as different female superheroes squealed and began jumping up and down as they waved.

I smirked and winked at the girls. They were fucking hot, and if I weren't on the job tonight, one of them would've been fucked hard and fast, bent over my bike. I would make sure she couldn't stand before I brought her back to her friends, then maybe took another for a tour. My cock thickened in my jeans as I stared at the long legs of the stunning blonde dressed up like Supergirl. She could be my Supergirl any day.

The light went green, and Supergirl kissed her hand and blew the kiss in my direction. Being the gentleman I was, I grabbed it out of the air and pretended to eat that shit. Her face went scarlet.

The steady breeze coming off the water hit me in the face and blew my hair back. I decided a long time ago that nothing was ever going to smell as sweet as the ocean. Sitting on the beach in the middle of the night with a drink was my favorite pastime. Aside from killing and fucking, both of which I took very seriously.

My only experience with pussy before being locked up was Mrs.

Collins, my foster mother. She was decent to look at and lonely with her husband away all the time. He was a long-distance trucker and was only home two nights out of the week. I had no loyalty to either of them, so when her hand landed on my thigh one night while watching a movie, I didn't move away.

It had taken me by surprise, and I sat tense through the rest of the movie, but I learned that it was her testing the waters. She had her plan in place, and I would end up the main event. Not that I cared at the time. I needed the experience, and she was willing to fuck me as much as I wanted.

At seventeen, I was hard most of the day, and my hand became pretty boring. Now that I was a free man, I didn't waste a second of being buried balls deep inside some willing participant. More women at once were always welcome. I had two hands, a mouth, and a cock, all happy to get involved.

Pulling into one of the parking areas along the beach, I had to maneuver around the throngs of people that crossed back and forth between wanting food and drink and partying on the sand. A large truck was parked in the last spot at the end, with one of the local DJ's logos splashed across the door.

Perfect. Turning around, I slowly pushed the chopper backward until it hopped the curb, completely hidden from view behind the truck. A barricade, a large bush, and another parking lot blocked the other side. There were a lot of cameras around, but this particular parking lot had its cameras smashed a week ago. I knew this cause I was the one who had taken them out. You needed to pre-plan this shit, and it was fucking unwise to wander around killing people without a plan. For example, paying to know where these two assholes were going to be was a well thought out plan. Not having a plan would get your ass thrown back in the pen as quick as a look.

I double-checked my clip and knives before grabbing the Scream mask from the pouch on my bike. Stuffing the gun into the back of my jeans, I pulled on the Scream mask and wandered along the path of writhing bodies.

A group of partiers had opted for the painted body look over actual clothes and were rubbing all up on each other. My step paused for half a second as I considered joining them. The hard nipples of the girl painted like a butterfly were calling to me as she bounced up and down, and my mouth was watering for a taste.

"Fuck, that was hot," I grumbled as I forced myself to look away.

I spotted the bar area I was after and began wobbling on my feet like I was already drunk. Grabbing an open bottle of tequila from a girl's hand, she gave me a dirty look until I pulled her against my body and danced in a circle, grinding against her bare pussy with my leg.

She bit her lip and waved as I let go and continued on my way. Damn, I needed a raise. Passing all this goodness up deserved a bonus. The music was booming at this end with the massive speakers set up. My eyes locked in on the two men at the stand-up bar, each with multiple women pressed against them.

They were already hammered and sloppy from whatever alcohol and drugs they'd consumed. I pushed through the bodies dancing and swaying to the thumping beat. Colorful lights flashed in time to the music as the DJ on stage waved his arm in the air.

I had two choices. I could make this quick and seamless, in and out before the guys knew what hit them, or I could wait them out and make this a real party when they decided to leave.

As I glanced around the party, my eyes found the naked asses of women inches away from my fingers. It was Halloween, after all, and body paint was more common than clothes tonight. The one time of year that everyone let loose and became someone else. Someone dark and dangerous they wished they always could be.

I was already dark and dangerous, but I'd lost ten years of my life to a prison that handed us a cookie decorated like a ghost or a pumpkin on Halloween and then told us lights out. That was when we prayed that the real goblins and ghouls surrounding us wouldn't kill us in our sleep.

This was living, and this was what had been stolen from me. A sliver of bitterness uncoiled from where it lurked in my stomach. No, I was going to wait them out, and I had pretty good odds of getting my cock sucked too. That was a two-for-one special if I ever heard it.

Raine

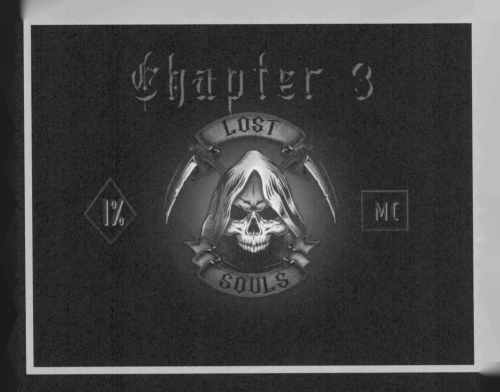

Chapter 3

Raine

The bottle twirled through the air, and I caught it mid flight before rolling the glass down my arm and flinging i across the open space to my partner. Avro had been working ba: with me for three years and was the best partner I'd ever trained. He had aspirations of making Cirque de Soleil before his knee practically exploded from some fall. He didn't like to talk about it much, and didn't want to push. I knew what it was like not wanting to share al your secrets with the world.

Alex was his real name, but he preferred to go by Avro. For whatever reason, he was obsessed with the Avro Arrow and it honestly suited him better. I couldn't picture him as Alex. The moment he was hired, we became friends. I mean, he was a guy, so I was still leery of him for a long time, but Avro had a way of setting you at ease. He had a great sense of humor, was sweet and thoughtful, and I could admit I had a crush—a little one. Okay, more than a little, but it was a go-nowhere type of crush. He was...amazing, and I was...just me.

Avro had bright blue hair this week that was spiked and stood out in all directions. I petted his head when he first arrived, joking that he looked like a hedgehog, and I was tempted to call him Sonic all night. If Sonic had been that hot, I probably would've played a lot more video games.

He jumped up, grabbed the glass, and—in a move that would've broken my back—flipped through the air to loud applause before sending the glass back. I tossed him three bottles next. He rolled them up his arms and over his back. We had two smaller bars set up with other bartenders, but people loved having their drinks served by one of us, so I filled glasses as quickly as I could in between performances. I'd been fascinated with the movie *Cocktail* as a teen. I couldn't even remember how many times I'd made Kaivan watch it with me.

My smile faltered at the thought of him. He was the one person I'd trusted in this world, and he turned on me just like everyone else in my life. You couldn't trust anyone, not really. Sometimes I didn't even know if I could trust myself. You never knew what was lurking below the surface. Even with Avro, I'd relaxed around him more than once. Fantasizing about what his lips would taste like and wondering if his shoulders and abs were as firm as they looked. I squashed those thoughts as quickly as they started.

I'd learned the hard way that everyone had their own agenda. The key was to figure out what they were after so you could stay ahead of the fallout.

The crowd was jumping tonight, and as the song switched to a mash up of a fun dance song and "edamame" by bbno$, the cheers got louder. Drinks waved in the air, and I couldn't keep from wiggling to the music.

I fucking loved this job. It was the only time I got out of my head and felt like a person, not a victim or loner, who stayed locked away in her small ratass house. The large bell on the wall rang, and all the regulars knew what was coming. With skill that only came from a shit ton of practice, Avro and I raced to get the tall stacks of shot glasses laid out along the bar.

I punched my arm in the air as the clock counted down to the start of the game. Avro stood at the far end of the bar and smiled as I stuck my tongue out at him. The sound of the buzzer was loud, but it still got drowned out by the roar of the rowdy crowd. Grabbing two bottles off the shelf, I started pouring shots. They were always something of our own creation and the only free round we offered the crowd, or at least those who could fight to get close enough.

It was amazing how excited people got over the prospect of two ounces of alcohol, but they did. They would push and shove and get into fights to be one of the few who would get the shot for free.

"Woohoo!" I screamed as I managed to pull ahead by one shot. We met in the middle, and whoever got there first forced the other person to do a specific trick or task or, in Avro's case, a dance on the bar.

This was not a new idea, but when you freshened it up, made it a competition, and offered free shit, people would keep coming in like the place was the bloody Field of Dreams. The little test glass in front of me was filled with a combination of green apple and cinnamon. I called this one my Apple Pie, and it was a bar favorite. By the bright blue color of Avro's drink, he was doing Blueberry Bomber, which was a combination of blueberry vodka and Blue Curcacao. The owner hadn't been overly excited to give away free alcohol, but he quickly changed his mind when he saw how many extra people it brought in, who then spent way more than the small freebee.

Now that ass got his picture taken for social media posts about the most popular spots in Miami, and Eclipse was quickly rising to the top of the scene. I guess I couldn't complain. I got to keep all my tips, and he gave me a two-thousand-dollar bonus for the idea, which I squirreled away for a rainy day.

"Yeah," I cheered and did a little twirl as I finished filling my last shot and held up the bottles.

Avro finished filling his and offered me one of his drinks as he conceded his loss. I drank it back and held the glass in the air.

"Go," I yelled above the music, and hands struck out like a bunch of vipers and snatched the glasses off the long bar. I wiggled backward and pointed to Avro and then the bar. "Dance, dance, dance," I chanted and got the crowd involved as my face was plastered on the massive screen, flashing the word 'dance' in neon colors.

Avro lived to dance, so this was never really a punishment. If he could, he would be on a stage somewhere full-time and not here slinging drinks with me. With a nifty maneuver, he leaped up on the top of the bar and swayed his ass back and forth, sending the women into a wild frenzy.

The guy was so smokin' hot that you'd burn your hand just touching him. Not a part of his body wasn't cut and ripped to perfection. He always wore contacts that stood out against the color of his hair, and he had the best smile. It was warm and friendly but also said, 'I would strip you naked and lick your body in all the right places.'

He was the kind of hot that made straight men in the crowd second-guess their sexuality. I'd seen more than one man who'd come in with a woman have to adjust themselves. Avro slowly peeled his T-shirt off and put it between his legs like he was riding it. A woman in the front screamed and collapsed as Avro winked at her.

I nodded to the bouncer and pointed to the woman on the floor. Not that anyone paid attention while Avro was on the bar. He ran and slid only to end up on his stomach, and even though I'd seen him practice this and knew what was coming, I couldn't peel my eyes away from the Magic Mike move. He looked like he was fucking the bar as he easily held himself up for all to see his hips working.

Yup, definitely the best job in the world.

It was three in the morning before the bouncers managed to get the last stragglers out of the bar and lock the doors.

"Is it just me, or are the crowds getting more insane?" Avro said as he thumbed through the wad of cash he made. "Fuck, five grand! Damn, at this rate, I might be able to afford that place I was telling you about."

"Only you make that kind of cash. That little move..." I thrust my hips like I was fucking the side of the bar and made him laugh. "Does them in every time."

"True, but you could make this too if you showed them a little more. You know, maybe put a cute bra-type top on under your tank so you could take it off."

Grabbing a towel and the cleaner, I squirted the sanitizer all over the bar and turned my back on Avro. He had no idea why I wouldn't want to do that, and I had no intention of letting him find out. Some scars were better left hidden.

"Just not my thing, but I'm happy for you, Avro. You're fucking good at this, even if it wasn't what you set out to do." I shot him a smile.

"Thanks. Oh, I had a few ideas for some new moves. They are a little trickier than what we normally do, but I know we can do it, and the crowd will love it."

I shrugged as I kept moving so we could get out of here. "Sure, you know I'm always open to learning new routines."

We chatted happily until our portion of the cleanup was completed. Then we changed out of the clothes soaked in alcohol, and only God knew what else. Pulling the hood up on my sweatshirt,

I searched through my backpack and pulled out my cell. I had a dozen missed calls. Putting the pack on, I followed Avro out the door and unlocked my phone.

"You want a ride home?" Avro offered. "I promise no drive-thru, no detours, and I'll only take the route you say. You can even keep the window down," he teased.

I smiled, embarrassed that he knew me so well that he was already prepared for me to refuse the offer. I'd gotten many rides from him when we finished late at night, but I always had to talk myself into it. It was stupid, and I hated the fear that crept up simply because I was trapped in a small space with a man.

"That would be great. I hate walking home this late," I said.

The simple black sedan with blacked-out windows was nice but totally opposite to his personality. Avro was always over the top with everything. It made me wonder what his home looked like. Even though we'd worked together awhile now, I'd never once seen his place; and it wasn't for lack of trying on his part.

I didn't know if he was interested in me or used the friend hangout excuse to get me alone. Just the thought of going over to his place sent fear racing through my body and choked off my air supply. It was horrible that one incident ten years ago still had me terrified to be alone with a man, but it was the truth. Kaivan had been my best friend, and I thought I knew him. Not in a million years would I have ever thought he would hurt me, but he did.

Avro put on the radio and described what he wanted to do for the new routine. It was so normal and so us that I relaxed. In a blink, he pulled up to the front of my shoebox.

Hopping out, I leaned on the open window. "Thanks, and I love those ideas. Wanna arrive an hour early tomorrow, and we can practice?"

"Fuck yes." He held out his fist for me to bump, making me laugh. "I'm not leaving until you're inside safely," he said.

He was probably a great guy. It wasn't like I thought all men were evil or anything. I just didn't know which ones were, and I didn't trust my instincts to tell me when I was in danger.

Waving to Avro, I closed the door and locked it before making my way into the kitchen and sitting down to listen to the messages on my cell.

"Raine Eastman, I'm social worker Harvey Johnson. Can you give me a call when you get this message?" I jotted down the phone number, confused about why he had called me. I hadn't spoken to a social worker in many years.

I hit the button to go to the second message. "Hi there, Raine. This is Harvey calling again. This is not news I wanted to leave in a message, but I feel you should be aware that Kaivan McMillan was released today. If you need anything, please call me at..."

I didn't hear anything else left in the message as the phone fell from my shaking hands. Jumping up, I ran to the cupboard and grabbed the bottle of anxiety meds that I'd managed to stop taking.

"Oh, no," I cried out as the stubborn lid flew off the pills and the bottle dropped from my shaking hands.

Dropping to the floor, I curled up in the corner by the sink and pulled my knees to my chest. "No, this can't be happening. No."

Please, dear God, don't let him look for me. Please let him have forgotten all about me.

Raine

Chapter 4

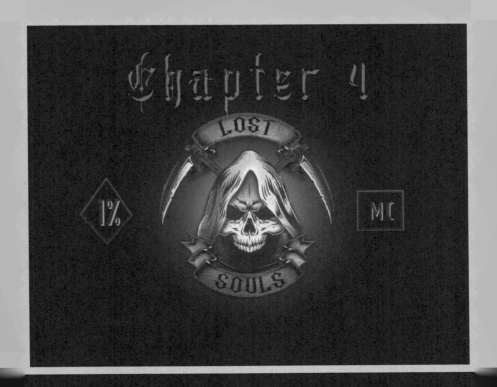

Raine

My fist hit the heavy bag over and over until my arms wouldn't lift, and I was breathing so hard that I had to step away to catch my breath.

"Not bad. Your stamina is definitely improving," Carlos said grabbing his water bottle and handing me mine.

"Thanks, it feels better," I said, drinking a few large gulps of the cool liquid. After I'd learned that Kai was free and could appear at any time, I was ready to make a run for it. The question became where the hell would I run?

I had no friends aside from Avro, and family wasn't something I'd ever had, so technically, I could run anywhere that seemed appealing. I could have closed my eyes and placed my finger on a map and just left, but this was my home. It may not be great, and I'd certainly had a ton of shit go down here, but it was also the only place I knew. So after crying my eyes out and hiding in my closet all night, I decided to train and learn to defend myself—a decision I should've made years earlier.

All through foster care, I'd been pushed around, picked on, beaten up, and the ultimate low was being assaulted and left for dead. Living the way I had been, with constant fear hanging over my head, perpetuated the feeling that I was a victim and could be again. Was it still possible? Sure, but now I had skills I could use, and more than that, somewhere in the process of learning to fight, I found the backbone I never knew I had.

I couldn't decide on which discipline I liked until I tried MMA. It was the freedom to use so many techniques that I preferred. My first fight was last week, and even though it was entry division, I walked out of there with a win. It was a shot of courage in my arm.

"Do you have any more fights coming up that I could enter?" I asked and grabbed the towel that Carlos tossed my way.

"Maybe. I'll take a look around and see if there is anyone in flyweight over the next couple of months. I'm sure we can find something for you to enter," Carlos said. "You good to train on Sunday morning?"

"No, I better not. Saturday night is our biggest night at Eclipse, and we're expecting a VIP that will make the place extra busy. Probably won't get home until like eight or nine in the morning."

"Damn, okay. Wanna let me in on who the VIP is?" He smiled, but I'd been sworn to secrecy. The agent of Grimhead Crew had made it clear that he wanted the appearance of his client and the impromptu concert to be a complete secret until they arrived.

"All I can say is that you will want to stop by and make sure to do it early, or you won't get in at all," I smiled wide.

"Damn, that big, huh? I'm in. It's my girl's birthday, and I promised that I had something special planned. My bad that I didn't get something figured out sooner, and this will make me look like an awesome boyfriend." Carlos laughed.

"Your girlfriend won't hear it from me. Just remember to arrive early and get close to the large bar area, and I'll be sure to hook you up with a couple of free drinks," I said, pulling the hoodie over my head.

I needed to get home and get ready for work. Apparently, there was a lot to prepare for when a celebrity came. I'd been given a massive list of musts and only two more days to get it done.

It would be easier if I just showered here, but stripping down naked in strange places was still on my 'No' list. I'd managed to start showering after my shift when it was just Avro around. He never made me feel uncomfortable or did something like test the door. I don't know why he would, but of all people, he was the one I secretly wished had tried. Some fantasies were just too big.

The juice bar had my green sludge ready for me and waiting on the counter. Smiling, I took a sip and held up the drink that, in reality, made me want to vomit.

"Why do I drink this?" I mumbled as I wandered down the street.

I couldn't believe it was already Halloween. It wouldn't be long until Christmas was here and then New Years, and just like that, another year would be gone. Another year older, not sure about wiser, but it felt like I was racing against a clock I couldn't see. A group of kids excitedly screamed as they ran past in their costumes, their parents trailing behind. A real smile graced my lips as I watched the little angel and the pirate run, holding hands. This time of year always made me think of Kai. Halloween was his thing, and I'd fallen in love with the day just as much because of his enthusiasm.

I hated how everything still made me think of him, wonder about him, and worry about him finding me. It didn't matter that over a year had passed since his release, and he hadn't magically appeared on my doorstep. The nagging concern was always there. The worst part was that I missed him. I hated him, and I missed him. How did those two things work?

"Come on, put it on. I spent all my savings to get these costumes for us," *Kai said, his smile wide like a child.*

"You do realize that we are too old for trick-or-treating?" I asked, holding up the Cat Woman costume. I hated to admit that it looked cool. Cool and I were not exactly on speaking terms. I was more punk/grunge mixed with total geek and a dash of loser, which was not a sexy combination.

"I'm not saying we go and collect candy, but I know of a couple of parties we can crash. Or if you don't want to do that, the beach will be wild, and before you say it, I know we can't buy any drinks." He held up a pirate's hat and snarled at me. "Argh, matey."

Bursting out laughing at the ridiculous look, I nodded my head. "Okay, fine, you win, but only if you promise never to do that again."

"Aw, come on, I need to be able to do it for at least the rest of the night. I mean, I have to remain in character." I lifted a brow at him and crossed my arms over my chest as I held firm. If I didn't, that was all I would hear all night long, and he would do it twice as much just to annoy me. "All right, fine, I promise."

An hour later, I felt like everyone we passed on the street to get to the beach was staring at me. "Why did you have to get the boots so tall? I can barely walk in these," I complained as I tried to walk in the teetering heels that added four inches to my five-foot-four height.

"Stop complaining. You look amazing, and all the guys are staring." Kai smiled like this was a good thing. I didn't like people staring. In fact, I did everything I could to avoid the very reaction that made Kai puff out his chest.

"I don't like all the guys staring," I whispered and inched closer to Kai as a couple of guys walking toward us openly gawked at my outfit.

"Ignore them. You're here with me."

I knew he didn't mean it like a date, but my heart sped faster in my chest, and I bit my lip as he wrapped his arm around my shoulders and gave it a quick reassuring squeeze before taking his arm back. I didn't want him to. I wanted him to continue to walk like I was his girl and not just his pal or the annoying foster sister.

Just like he said, the beach was crazy with people of all ages. You could easily tell the college groups from everyone else. They were far sexier and a whole lot wilder. A guy ran by and almost knocked me over as he chased a football.

"Hey, watch where you're going," Kai called out, his face dark as he glared at the guy. Kai stepped in close with his back to me, and I could smell the cologne he wore. Unable to help myself, I sucked in a deep breath and sighed. He was always so tough and abrasive, like he needed to take on the world, and yet under the hard shell was this sweet guy. I never told him that. He would probably have a heart attack if anyone thought he was sweet.

"Sorry about that," the guy said. I stepped out from behind Kai, and instantly the new guy's eyes roamed over the skin-tight leather. "Damn, do you want to party with us?"

I shook my head no as Kai suddenly grabbed my hand. "Not a fucking chance. She's with me."

The guy licked his lips and then lifted his muscled shoulders in a shrug. "Suit yourself. It's your loss." He jogged off and tossed the ball to the group of guys waiting.

It felt strange to have Kai touch me like this. That was twice very close together. We'd been staying with the same foster family for five years now, and other than a handshake when I first arrived or the fist bumps that were mandatory after a particularly good round of Call of Duty, we never touched. I looked down at our joined hands and could admit it felt nice. I had no idea how to make him see me as more, but every time he touched me like this, a jolt of excitement shot through my body.

Kai was a couple of years older, and next year, he would head off to college, and I'd be left behind. It didn't sit right. I detested the idea of him leaving for whatever college he chose. He'd already started to take off most weekends to go see the campuses. Kai was smart, much smarter than my C+ grades, but he never applied himself. He was too busy playing games and talking about how much ass he was going to get while away at school with his friends.

His new thing was street fights. I didn't like them. They were dangerous, and he always came home late with a split lip or a black eye. I'd even seen a large purple bruise that wrapped his side when he was pulling on a shirt, but he didn't want to talk about it. I was too young, or as he put it, he wanted to protect me, but I didn't need his protection. What I wanted, he had no interest in.

I'd gone out on a movie date, and as soon as Kai found out, he miraculously showed up at the theater with his friends and a couple of girls. I was furious. Not only was he there to keep an eye on me like an annoying brother, but all the jealousy I ignored when I saw him with girls reared its ugly head. The entire situation was a disaster, and I apologized to my date and said I wasn't feeling well, then took off for home, fuming the whole way.

We'd always promised to be each other's best friend, but it felt like it should be so much more. Yet, he was at home less, talked less, and it felt like he was already gone and pulling away. I was fifteen, and he was seventeen, and I knew that the closer he got to his eighteenth birthday, the more I looked like the dopey foster sister hanging onto his shirt and begging for his attention.

At least, that was how it felt. As soon as the guys moved far enough away, Kai let go of my hand, and the little pitter-patter in my chest crashed and burned.

"*Fuck, guys like him are annoying. I should've laid his ass out,*" Kai said.

"*Right. You and who exactly? That guy was huge,*" I said, and Kai turned his head to look at me.

"*I'm ripped,*" he argued, his dark brows furrowed, making his blue eyes more intense.

"*Uh-huh,*" I said and walked toward the quieter area of the beach.

I left him to either follow or not, but I needed to sit down before these tall boots were the death of me. There were still beach chairs left out from earlier in the day that had been missed during clean up. I dropped down on the chair that doubled as a lounger, groaning, and kicked my feet up.

"*What does uh-huh mean?*" Kai parked himself in the chair beside mine.

I rolled my head in his direction. "*It means that you might be, but he's still a college guy with a bunch of friends, and you're...well, you're just you.*"

"*I'm hot,*" Kai argued and then turned himself so he was sitting like I was.

"*I'm just sayin', you're seventeen, and that dude was like twenty-five.*" I had no idea why he was angry, but I could feel the tension rolling off him. The breeze off the water felt nice as it hit my face.

"*Yeah, and the guy is also a perv. He was going to take you to his friends and want to do all sorts of things that you're just not ready for,*" Kai argued.

That bristled my anger. "*Oh, really? And who says I'm not ready? Maybe I want to be ready. Maybe I wanted to be ready with him, and if so, that is my business,*" I bit out. Who the hell did he think he was? Telling me I wasn't ready for sex. He didn't get a say in the matter. No one but me did.

"*Fine, whatever. You want to be a college guy's slut. Who am I to tell you differently? Just remember that they can be charged with rape. You're still a minor." The way he said minor hurt. It was like he was purposely picking at the fact that we were growing further apart every day.*

We were silent for a long time, the strange tension between us just sitting there. I didn't know what to say and didn't want to argue with Kai. He was my only friend.

"I wouldn't, you know," I finally said.

"What?" Kai turned his head to look at me, and I felt him staring at the side of my face. I couldn't look at him, the earlier nervousness was back, and my stomach felt all weird.

"I said I wouldn't. I mean, sleep with that guy. I wouldn't fuck that guy. There, I said it." I scowled at the ocean like it was the water's fault for making me feel this way.

"Good. I didn't want to have to kill him," he said.

I did look over at Kai then. I couldn't tell if he was serious or what his tone meant. His face held no emotion and gave none of his thoughts away.

Unsure what to say about the murderous announcement. I decided he was simply joking and asked the next best question. "You ever wonder if people who don't celebrate Halloween come here and wonder what the fuck is wrong with everyone? I mean, can you picture getting off a plane and everyone outside the airport is dressed up like this?" I pointed to my Cat Woman outfit and smiled.

It took a second, but the impish grin returned to his features, and the hard stare from a moment ago disappeared. "Can you imagine if they saw the pair of guys dressed up like a toaster and a condom back there?"

We both laughed, and just like that, the awkward tension burst, and once more, we were simply two best friends hanging out.

I finished the last of my disgusting healthy drink just as I reached my front door. A honk from the road made me jump and turn. My heart rate tripled for a second until my eyes found Avro, who'd pulled up in his car.

"Fuck girl, you're running late. Hurry up, and I'll give you a ride to work."

"Okay," I called out and pushed open the door. Nervous energy made me shiver, but it was time that I put Kai and all the shit he put me through in the past. I was done letting the memory of him control me any longer. Taking a deep breath, I turned around again.

"Did you want to wait in here?"

"That's okay. I know you won't be long, and I have a couple of calls I need to make," Avro yelled back and picked up his phone.

The lone butterfly that always flitted around when Avro was near floated to the pit of my stomach. Now that I wanted him to come in, I was hurt by his refusal. Was I ever going to stop being a confused mess?

I'd officially banished Kai McMillan from my life and my mind, and yet the lasting effects continued to touch all corners of my life.

Snake

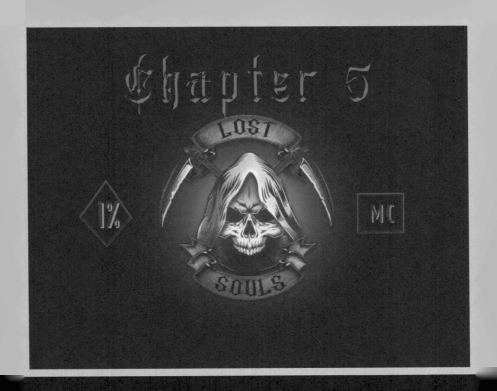

Chapter 5

Kaivan

It was times like this that made me wonder if the universe decided on the day I was born that no matter what I chose to do with my life, this was what I would end up doing.

Enforcer in a motorcycle club wasn't a bad gig. I got paid well for my duties and didn't need much. It all got put away for...I had no idea what for, but that didn't matter. I got to hang out with Roach and Mannix, and in another six months, Hollywood would be free. I slept when I wanted, ate what I liked, and fucked at least once a day. Really, what more did a guy need?

Had I always had what it took to watch the blood drain from a body and the life dim in their eyes? Had I always been able to feel nothing as they begged to live or screamed in pain as I did unspeakable things to them? No, of course not. I wasn't a psychopath. But could clearly remember a handful of times growing up when murdering someone had piqued my interest. Usually, that was because some dick was staring at Raine.

Now, finding Raine, wrapping my hands around her throat, and slowly squeezing the life out of her body had been an ongoing fantasy throughout my time in prison. I'd lain in bed many a night and dreamed of that moment over and over. How times had changed.

I'd created a calendar that counted down the days until I was free. This was nothing unusual, but what was unusual was that at the very end, all I put was RE. When the guards asked what it stood for, I said, 'rest and evaluate what to do with my life now I am free.' The parole board had been very impressed with that answer. Bunch of idiots.

It stood for Raine Eastman, the girl who ruined my life. Finding her and making her pay had been my singular goal for so long, but once I was free, I'd been too busy. I joined the Lost Souls officially, and only a few short months after my release, Mathers left a path of murder and destruction in his wake as he got high on the shit we were supposed to sell.

I'd spent almost every waking hour since that moment cleaning up one disaster after another for fucking Chase. This included killing innocent people who'd seen him do it because his sloppy ass made them a liability. I didn't mind killing. In fact, I enjoyed it most of the time now, but to have to shoot a grandmother of three because Mathers couldn't keep his head screwed on straight was not my idea of a good time. I mourned for her. I didn't want to fucking mourn anyone. I hated him all the more for turning me into a full-fledged monster. For turning me into my father.

I missed a lot while I was locked up but spending the little bit of time I had in a day to hunt down Raine and make her pay was not as enticing as it once was. Secretly, a part of me worried that I would have nothing left to keep me going once she was six feet under. Roach would've laughed his ass off at me if I had told him that.

I made the mistake of mentioning Raine to Chase one day, and he offered to take care of the bitch for me. I almost punched him out. I didn't know what to make of the strange emotions, but for now, I didn't want that chapter of my life to end. She changed me, made me into the man who could rip another's heart out without blinking. I hadn't even decided if what happened had been the best story ever written or the worst that could've happened. That was what Raine was to me, a story waiting to be finished, and I needed to decide how I wanted it to end.

I took a moment to look around at my work and smiled. Blood coated the floor and decorated the walls like I'd tried my hand at abstract art and just happened to be using red paint. It was truly amazing how much blood was in the human body. It was equally impressive how it flew when you were cutting someone up.

The Weasel Legionnaires used this warehouse to store their overflow. It was a fair distance outside of the city and not manned unless they needed to get something. These two asswipes were supposed to be on guard duty for Halloween while the rest of the club was out partying. I still couldn't get over the fucking name. Who the fuck wanted to be part of a motorcycle group with that rat shit name? Weasel Legionnaires? What idiot came up with that?

I glanced over at the man screaming like a little pansy in the corner. His eyes were filled with terror as he stared at the severed head in my hands. Surprisingly, his screams could barely be heard over the movie *Saw*, which played in the background. It was a little dramatic, even for me, but it seemed fitting. Besides, I liked it, and having it playing was sick, psychological warfare. I wished with all my heart that I could be a fly on the wall when this club of assholes found their two members and cleaned up this mess.

A really sick part of me hoped they didn't show up for a couple of days, so it would give the flesh time to rot in the heat.

I'm a sick fuck, but I loved it.

The first guy was already dead. Cutting him up had taken some work, even using the table saw in the corner. It would've helped if he hadn't been alive and trying to escape, but the living gave me much better screams.

Now those parts decorated the empty warehouse and hung from the rafters with rope, like bloody, crimson snowflake decorations. I was surprised that the guy had as much fight in him as he had, considering the massive quantities of alcohol I'd watched him consume. He'd done more little white lines off the bar than I could count, which made it impressive that he could stand, let alone scream and fight while I slowly chopped him up.

The second man—Mutt, was his name—screams reached all new levels as I ripped the two eyes out from the severed head and threaded the rope between the sockets like I was making a cranberry string.

"Oh fuck, oh fuck, oh fuck," Mutt said, then leaned over to heave for the eighth time.

I had no idea how he still had that much puke in his system. I'd asked Mutt earlier if the other guy's name was Jeff, but he didn't get the joke and said, 'No, it's Vic.' No one watched good comedy these days or had a fucking sense of humor.

"Snake man, I'm so sorry. I'll tell you whatever you want to know. Name it, and it's yours. Just please don't kill me," he said as I tossed the head like a ball over the steel beam and tied it off so that it swung slowly back and forth like a grotesque piñata. This had been a lot messier than planned, but when I got them here, and they had a saw...I mean, who can resist that? It was fucking kismet.

"Why?" I turned around to face Mutt.

"W-why w-what?" he stammered.

"Why shouldn't I kill you? I mean, I already know when your guns arrive if I wanted them. I already know it was your crew that tried to hijack our last drug shipment, and..." I held up a bloody finger. "I also know that you've been trying to take over areas that used to be the Reapers' and then claiming that it had always been yours. Those belong to the Lost Souls, and we are not fans of thieves or liars." I smiled wide and made sure to curl up the corners of my mouth like I was the goddam Joker. The wide-eyed look as the guy pissed himself was exactly what I wanted.

The movie was just getting to the good part, where the guy cut off his own foot, and I stared at the screen for a moment as those screams filled the room.

"I swear to you, I had nothing to do with any of that. I mean...I was part of the crew that tried to hit your shipment, but I only did that cause I was ordered to. You know what it's like when you have a boss you need to answer to," he pleaded. "Come on, man. I didn't want to. In fact, I told them it was a stupid idea."

Mutt wasn't wrong. He was mid-level at best, and not following orders would've been a death sentence. But he chose to be in an MC and do their bidding, which was the other side of the coin. If we planned on taking over the Weasels' network and area, I would've gone after the leader, not Mutt. We just needed them to know that we saw the crap they were pulling, and we wouldn't take any shit. Attacking and taking over areas caused other issues you never saw coming. It was better to keep the devil you knew as your neighbor than the one you didn't know at all.

"I believe you," I said, and he slumped against the wall and smiled. "But it doesn't mean I'll let you live either."

Mutt's face paled once more. "What if you keep me alive so I can give Rip a message for you?"

"A message? What is this high school? You wanna pass a love letter for me while you're at it? Maybe draw dicks and tits all over it."

Mutt looked confused. It was official. I was never going to make it as a stand-up comedian.

"I just thought I could relay the message not to mess with you guys or your shit, and I can be the voice of reason at meetings. Or I can join the Lost Souls. I mean, I never wanted to be a Weasel," he offered, nodding his head enthusiastically.

I marched across the floor, weaving my way around the puddles of blood, and with each step, Mutt shook harder. Shake, little Mutt, shake. I lived for that look now. Roach said that Chase had set loose the devil inside of me, and he was right. After fifty, I lost count of just how much blood I'd spilled in the name of the Lost Souls. So much that I craved it a little too much.

In all fairness, I'd been on the path already. A few people in the pen met their fate at the end of my blade. No matter the group or the member, they gave me a wide berth when I walked down the hall. I remembered all too well the day I killed Red and forced Big Dog to lick my shoes. Those were memories that warmed the furthest reaches of my blackened heart.

Squatting down, I stared at Mutt, his eyes wide and frozen in place like a fucking gecko. I waved my hand toward the far concrete wall.

"So what you're saying is, using your blood to write the message, don't fuck with L.S., isn't going to cut it?" I leaned my elbows on my knees and felt the blood dripping off my hands. "Hmm?"

Mutt swallowed, his Adam's apple bobbing as he did. I could almost see the mice in his brain running on little wheels as he tried to think of something to say.

"I'm waiting for an answer," I drawled. "Preferably, one in the next minute."

"Um...they aren't very good at reading." Mutt accentuated each word slowly.

My lip curled up before I laughed, and Mutt followed suit. His tone was more tense, with good reason.

"You know, that is the funniest shit anyone has ever said to me. Probably accurate too."

Technically, I didn't have to kill both. I didn't even have to kill Vic. My orders were to scare The Weasels into backing off—the how was left up to me. I glanced at the glowing red clock near the television, surprised to see it was already ten in the morning. After they left the beach, it took me exactly four hours and twenty-two minutes to capture the two men and kill Vic. Even with a hard night of drinking, the club would be coming around soon, and as much fun as a shootout with them would be, it wasn't the brightest idea.

The seconds ticked on as I thought. Mutt's eyes followed me like a wary, beaten animal. I pushed to my feet and marched over to the industrial sink with the harsh-smelling orange soap. Washing my hands and scrubbing under my nails before I wiped off my leather jacket. At least it was the morning after Halloween. Riding home looking like I was part of a horror movie would seem normal. Drying my hands off, I made my way to the exit.

"Where are you going?" Mutt called out.

My brow arched in his direction. "What? Do you want me to stay?"

"Um...no, but are you coming back?" His voice was hesitant.

"Do I have a reason too?"

"Nooo," Mutt said, drawing out the 'o' and making me smirk.

"Then I guess you answered your own fucking question. Make sure you hold up your end of the deal. Rip better step back and leave the Lost Souls' areas, or I will be back, and I won't just make a spectacle of one of you. I'll slit every single one of your throats while you're sleeping."

Mutt nodded. "Um, can I ask one thing?"

Wow, this guy didn't know when to quit. "What?"

"Can you cut me loose? They aren't going to be here for a few days," he said.

I groaned. Why did he have to say that? Why couldn't he just keep his mouth shut? Some people didn't know when not to look a gift horse in the mouth. Now I was tempted to kill him again.

No, be good. Go home. Get fucked. Get some sleep. My inner voice chanted as the part of me that loved to kill sat up and grinned wickedly in my mind.

"You know, Mutt, you owe me one." I turned to face him. "One day, I'm gonna collect a favor from you because that is how this life works. When I do, you'll do exactly what I ask when I ask you to do it, or you will end up worse than your buddy, Vic. Do you understand?"

Mutt nodded; his lips pressed tight together. I walked over to where I'd piled their crap, grumbling to myself the entire time. Snatching up the phones, I made my way around the blood to Mutt and laid them down. Mutt's hands were tied behind his back, but he could still reach the phone. It would take him a few tries to get it open, kind of like a game.

At least he was smart enough to keep his mouth shut this time as I marched for the door and pushed my way out into the sun. A few sweetbutts would be in early, getting the club ready for later. My cock had a date with one, and then I needed some sleep.

I was getting too old for these all-night parties.

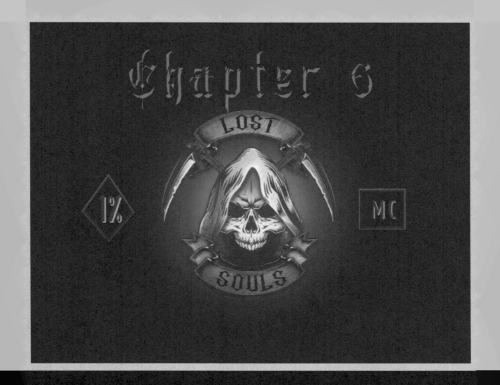

Chapter 6

Avro

"I can do this," I mumbled and got out of the car. "You're just asking her to go to the beach as a friend. Nothing wrong with that."

Other than the fact that you're completely in love with the girl, the annoying voice in my mind retorted.

No one asked you. I grumbled to myself.

Wiping my hands off on my track pants, I stared at Raine's front door. It was a pretty shade of blue, with little pots of flowers outside—nothing too much or overstated, like her. The lawn needed some tending unless she was going for the dirt look.

We'd been working together and friends for four years, and all that time, I managed to keep my feelings under wrap. Raine reminded me of a deer. If you moved too quickly, she would startle and take off. I knew that sensation all too well. If it weren't for Jace, I would still be like that.

"You've got this. Just act like your normal self," I whispered under my breath as I knocked hard on the door.

I heard the sound of feet on stairs, and Raine called out that she was coming. The thin curtain beside the window moved, and my heart skipped a beat when my eyes locked with Raine. I smiled and waved.

Okay, that felt stupid.

The door swung open, and there she was, looking like she belonged somewhere other than Florida. She wore a thick sweater and yoga pants like it was freezing outside when it was almost ninety, yet she pulled it off and was as stunning as ever. Her big blue eyes shone, and her short platinum-blonde hair looked adorable. I was staring at her lush lips as she nibbled on her bottom one and had to force myself to look up into her eyes.

"Avro, is everything okay? Nothing is wrong with the bar, right?" She peered out the door like she could see the place from here.

"No, no, everything is fine. I just stopped by to see what you're doing today. I mean, other than work later?" I swallowed the lump in my throat and prayed that it didn't sound as lame as it did in my head.

"Um...well." She crossed her arms. "Not much. I have to pick up a few groceries this weekend."

"Great. Do you want to go to the beach with me?" Her face blanched. "Just to hang out. I hate going alone. I mean, I will, and I've done it before, but I was hoping to have someone go with me for a change. They have a belly dancing festival going on. I thought it might be cool to check out," I said in one long rambling breath and promptly wanted to smack myself on the forehead. Could I sound any more lame?

Raine sucked the lip she'd been nibbling on into her mouth, and I stuffed my hands in my pockets to keep from wringing them.

Please say yes, please say yes.

"If you don't want to hang out with me, then..."

Her face morphed into a horrified expression. "No, it's not that. People and I don't exactly get along, and that sounds like a lot of people."

My brow lifted, and I couldn't help the laugh from escaping. "You do know what you do for work, right?"

A vivid shade of pink spread across her cheeks, making her look more adorable. Raine was this unique combination of sexy and adorable. She had no idea what the hell she did to me.

"Okay, I guess one day won't kill me. Come in, and I'll go grab my stuff." Raine took off upstairs. I stepped over the threshold like it was the holy grail. This was the first time I'd ever been inside her space. In all this time, we'd never been to one another's homes. Until a year ago, I couldn't even get her in my car, and she still turned me down more than she accepted.

"Mind if I look around?" I called up the stairs.

"Knock yourself out. There isn't much to look at," she yelled back.

There was a moderately sized television in the corner, a long grey couch with a matching recliner, and a single coffee table. There were a couple of pictures on the wall, but my brows knit together when I realized they were the ones that came with the frames. The only personal item was a picture of Raine outside the club when the addition was completed and we held the ribbon cutting ceremony. I knew she wasn't close with her foster family, but that was all she said. It bothered me that she didn't want to open up, but then again, I hadn't told her about everything in my life, so who was I to cast stones?

The kitchen was just as small, but it wasn't the size that bothered me. The lack of anything that screamed this was Raine East-man's place did. It could've been any Airbnb along this road.

"I'm ready," Raine called out, and I spun around to see her as she reached the bottom of the stairs.

My mouth fell open at the sight of her, and I had to snap my mouth shut. She wore a cute pair of shorts and a tank top with a bikini underneath. Sandals on her feet and a large beach bag slung over her shoulder completed her look.

"Why are you staring at me like that? Do I look bad?" Raine went to the hallway mirror to inspect herself, but I shook my head.

"No, you look amazing," I managed to say before making things awkward.

I could be so smooth at work because it meant nothing to me. It was acting, and I'd done that all my life, but when it was real, I always got tongue-tied. It was as if my brain didn't understand what words were anymore.

"Oh, okay, great. Thanks." Raine cleared her throat. "I brought clothes so we can head straight to work after. I was going to arrive a little early to make sure I didn't forget anything on the list from the Grimhead Crew's manager. I mean, who asks for freshly sliced oranges on a sugar-rimmed glass that is half full of ice cubes and gummies?"

I smirked at her annoyed expression and how her nose wrinkled up like she was smelling something gross. Did I tell her now that I knew the lead singer? In fact, I knew him better than anyone else in my life.

"And don't even get me started on the fresh, green matcha tea that needs to be made during intermission by a professional tea maker. What is a tea maker? I didn't even know such a thing existed until I had to hire one for this event. There are so many requests that I'm starting to wonder if this manager of theirs is only asking for this stuff to see if we will do it."

Raine wasn't far off the mark with that one. Jace had complained more than once about how Allen loved to screw with venues like that. The band would always take the stuff and hand it out to fans if it wasn't used, but Jace thought it was stupid and needless.

"Are we going to get going?" Raine asked, opening the door.

Okay, tell her later it was. It wasn't as simple as saying, 'oh, by the way, I know him.' Nope, that statement always came with a ton of questions, and I didn't want to answer them right now.

It wasn't even ten in the morning, and the sun was so hot that I felt beads of sweat already forming. Weather like this had a special place in the go fuck yourself part of my heart. Every shitty thing that happened to me over the years came when we had one of these intense heat waves that would undoubtedly get worse before ending in a torrential downpour.

It rained like God was trying to cool down the earth, but it was useless. Instead, everything became extra muggy, and the driving force of it tore up crops and flowers, caused leaks in your roof and snakes to show up in the most terrifying places. So yeah, this weather was fun for a day at the beach, but I would be looking over my shoulder for the inevitable shitstorm that followed.

"The nice thing about the festival is that it's only a couple miles from the club, so there's a good chance that we will be extra busy tonight," I said as we got into my car.

"That's true, and the tips will be flowing."

We sat in comfortable silence, but I had the biggest urge to grab her hand and kept glancing at her from the corner of my eye. She wore oversized sunglasses that were all the fashion and looked like a supermodel. All she needed was a fancy convertible to complete the look.

It didn't take much to find the festival. The beach was swarming with people in some form of skirt and bikini top. As usual, when something fun was going on, there was not a parking spot to be had. I ended up parking quite a ways down the road.

"Hope you're okay with walking?"

"Doesn't bother me at all. Although, if we want a quieter spot later, this is nice to come back to," Raine said, pushing open the car door.

My mind raced with all the possibilities of being alone with her on a quiet stretch of beach. I couldn't keep my feelings from her anymore, and Jace spontaneously coming to town and wanting to meet her forced my hand. The question remained, would she run or not?

Raine hid well under her humor and big personality while working. The moment you took her away from the bar, the unease shone through. I knew without asking that she'd been through something traumatic. All this time, brick by brick, I'd been putting pieces into place to make sure she knew she could trust me. I might have been able to push faster if I were Jace, but I wasn't, and it was only around a year ago that I started to see her open up and not be as guarded around me. I was terrified she would go back into her shell if I said the wrong thing or pushed too hard.

We walked along the beach toward the ever-growing crowd of people, and I made sure to walk close enough that our fingers would brush every few strides. If she noticed, she didn't say, but more importantly, she didn't move away. I kept the victory smile to myself.

A large group of guys ran past, all shouting about something exciting. They looked to be from the local campus, most likely frat boys. I suddenly felt very old thinking that. I wasn't that much older than they were, yet it seemed like we were worlds apart.

There were only three things that could make frat boys run that fast. The first was free alcohol and lots of it. The second was anything to do with sex. The kinkier, the better. The third was a fight, especially if it was brewing for a while.

"What do you think that's all about?" Raine said as we closed in on the large group of guys, all holding phones and cheering. "Maybe someone famous?"

"Not a hundred percent sure," I said. The question was answered a moment later when some girls arrived and whistled loudly, calling for more space to be made. The sea of bodies parted, and my mouth fell open.

There, parked on the beach, were three pickup trucks with their tailgates down. That on its own wasn't unusual. There were always tailgate parties along this section of the beach that went unchecked. What was mind-numbingly shocking were the six girls naked from the waist down, sitting two per truck bed with their knees spread open. As soon as a girl was free, a new guy would step up and stick his fingers in her pussy to take a selfie.

"Do they even know or care where those fingers have been?" I was unable to stop myself from asking the obvious question. Raine looked up at me. "What? It's unhygienic."

Raine laughed, a smile breaking out across her face that made the rest of the madness fade away.

"All I know is that I will not be hopping up there to join them. The last thing I want is my kitty plastered all over social media for the rest of my life. Thanks, but no thanks."

The crowd was getting rowdy with the alcohol flowing. With the overly testosterone-infested situation, there would be a fight yet. I could feel the charge in the air.

"Over this way." I nodded toward the shoreline, where fewer people gathered. We veered in that direction. "I can tell you one thing for certain. I wouldn't want to be the cop sent here to shut this down."

"No kidding," Raine said.

Movement caught my eye. Some guy was running in our direction but not looking. A football soared through the air, and there was no way he would get to it in time. I instinctively wrapped my arm around Raine's waist. She tensed but didn't jump away as I pulled her away from the torpedoing ball. I smacked it out of the air and glared at the guy that almost ran into us, my muscles ready for impact.

"Oh shit. Sorry, man," the guy said as he bent and picked up the ball. I cocked a brow at him as I told him to get the fuck away from me with my eyes.

I hadn't always been tough. In fact, one would say that I used to be the nerdy kid who got shoved in lockers and books knocked out of my hands or money stolen at lunch. The only thing that saved me from any of those things was Jace. We were polar opposites when we first met, yet we became fast friends. He only needed to look in an asshole's direction, and they would run the other way. I hadn't mastered that yet, but I was getting there.

"Thanks, I didn't even see that coming," Raine said when the guy jogged away.

"No problem." I kept my arm around her waist and counted down in my head till she pulled away. She was tense at first, but I couldn't contain my smile as she relaxed into me.

"What are you smiling about?" Raine asked.

"Just enjoying the beautiful day with one of the best people I know," I said, dancing around my words carefully.

"We're almost at the festival. Did you want to remove your sandals and walk in the water?" I suggested.

"Sure."

It felt like a race to get them off. As Raine picked up her shoes, and I gripped her hand, making her squeal as we ran for the water.

"Oh my god, nooo," she said. The protest was half-hearted as she laughed and squealed when the next wave crashed into our legs. We were soaked to our knees in a blink. She glared up at me, smiling with fake anger. "Jerk."

"I wanted to get you wet," I said, and her face turned every shade of pink before her eyes flicked away from mine. "Do you like to swim?" I quickly asked.

"Not really, at least not in the open water like all those people." Raine pointed to the large group of swimmers floating on inflatables, splashing, or playing water volleyball. "I do like pools, though. Less likelihood that I'm going to run into something creepy."

I smirked. "I guess that depends on the pool."

We looked at one another as that comment filled our minds with whatever terrifying images we conjured, then laughed hard.

"It's great to see you smile for real. You have a beautiful smile," I said.

My lips tingled with the urge to kiss her, but I held myself in check. Today was already a big win and a step forward. I had plans to push more tonight and hoped that she would be thinking about today when tonight finally came. Everything inside me was a jittery mess with the thought of Jace and Raine in the same room. I wanted this to go well.

No, I needed this to go well.

Raine

I wasn't sure what had gotten into Avro. I was shocked when he showed up at my door, but I couldn't say no to a day out with him. He was like a supermodel and could have posed for any magazine or book cover.

Yet, as we walked along the beach, he seemed completely oblivious to the stares he got. Could he be interested in me? No, that was a ridiculous thought. Or was it? Did I want him to be? I was nervous to admit that I did. It felt like I was setting myself up to be hurt if I let him in and created this whole idea of what we could be, only to have him laugh and say, 'I only meant as friends.'

The meter other people had to tell them that someone liked them was all skewed in my head. Mine spun in confusion all day long. We stopped and watched the long line of professional belly dancers. I wiggled to the music while Avro tried to match them, and of course, he was freaking amazing at it. Once again, I wondered why the hell this guy stuck around here, working in a club as a bartender when he was so talented. I tripped over my own feet while walking. He probably knew ballet. I'd been terrible at sports in school, while I knew he loved basketball and had been offered a full scholarship because he was that good.

Everyone clapped as he joined the line, earning heated stares from those watching. A tug of jealousy bloomed in my chest. It had flared before at work, but it was part of his job to flirt with the patrons and keep them buying drinks. Out here, he was sort of with me. At least, that was how it felt. This feeling was something I hadn't had for a very long time. Annoyed with myself, I swept it aside. There was no point in fantasizing about something that was never going to happen.

I couldn't stop smiling, and for the first time since I was a teen, I giggled as he danced toward me. My whole body felt like it was on fire with each step closer. He was wearing aqua-colored contacts today that matched the water at my back, but it was the intense look in his eyes that had me squirming.

"Wow, that is a lot harder than it looks." He looked over his shoulder and waved. "Thank you for the dance," he called out.

"Any time," came the reply, and I ground my teeth together as I glared at the girl.

"Did you want one of those slushies?" Avro pointed to a stand selling an assortment of cool treats along the boardwalk. "I could really use something cold."

"Yeah, sounds great." I didn't expect him to take my hand again, but when he did, I nibbled on my bottom lip and tried not to look as giddy as I felt. He was the first person in so long that made me feel a hundred percent safe and comfortable.

Nope, there was no place for Kai on this lovely day, and I dusted those thoughts to the side.

"Why don't you stay here? No need for both of us to stand in that long line in the sun," Avro offered as we stepped under the shade of tall palm trees.

"Are you sure?"

"Of course. What flavor do you want?"

I smiled wide. "Surprise me."

"Oh, I plan on it," he said and jogged away, but the glint in his eye and curl of his lips made me feel like we were no longer talking about the slushies.

More of the crowd from down the beach filtered up this way. Either they had gotten their fill, or the trucks had been shut down. I was staring down at my sandals, thinking I needed a new pair, when a hand grabbed my ass.

Yelping, I jumped forward and spun around to find a guy I'd never met.

"Damn girl, that is a damn fine ass. It would look amazing bouncing on my cock," he said, his blue eyes glazed with alcohol while his blonde hair waved in the breeze.

My relationship meter might be broken, but my creep-o-meter worked just fine.

"Don't touch me."

"Oh, you're feisty. I like it." He stepped in my direction, so I mirrored and stepped back. My hand balled into a fist while my other one gripped the handle of my bag tighter. The first thing Carlos taught me was anything could be used as a weapon.

"Don't be like that. I know you want this." Of course, the drunk asshole had to grab his cock. Why did guys do that? Did they actually think we liked it? "I mean, I'm Dennis Copland. No one can resist me."

He took another step, and I backed up once more. I would hit him if I needed to, but I preferred he just went away. An assault charge was not what I had planned for my Saturday.

"I don't care who you are. Back the fuck up," I said. I kept my tone even, but if looks could kill, he would've been dead.

"Oh, come on. You must know who I am. Everyone around here does." He cocked his hip and smiled. I was sure that had fooled some poor girl who thought pretty-boy looks and frat-boy swagger was impressive. That was not me.

"Nope, never heard of you, and I don't want to. Now, are you going to move along, or am I?"

Dennis continued to stand there and stare at me like that would somehow get me to change my mind.

"Fine, I'll move," he said, backing up a few steps. Dennis rolled his eyes and crossed his arms over his chest.

Figuring that was far enough away, I turned around to find Avro when a hand clamped onto my shoulder.

"No one turns me down, especially not some washed-up bitch like you," Dennis snarled.

Moving on instinct, I spun and knocked his arm away before stepping in close and driving my knee up into his crotch. The pain registered on his features instantly. Shoving him hard, he landed on his ass in the sand.

"I said, don't touch me," I growled at the jerk as Avro stepped up beside me.

I jumped a little when his arm brushed mine, and I immediately hated that I did.

"I was going to come over and kill this guy, but it looks like you have it all taken care of," Avro said casually. I looked up at him as he held out the slushie.

"Bitch, I think you broke my dick," Dennis groaned, still in the fetal position on the ground.

"Consider yourself lucky that's the only thing she broke, asshole. Don't touch my girlfriend again," Avro said, his voice as hard as steel.

Excited energy fluttered in my chest at the word girlfriend. Of course, just like another time in my life, it was said to get rid of a scumbag, but I couldn't help feeling that this time, it meant more. I took the red drink from his hand, and Avro immediately put his arm around my shoulder as he guided us away from Dennis and the crowd he was drawing.

"Why did you say that?" I asked.

He shrugged. "Unfortunately, guys like that only respect one thing, and that's a bigger, meaner guy. Sexist? Yes, but it doesn't make it any less true. Besides, you already embarrassed him in front of all those people." Avro leaned closer to my ear, and a shiver traveled down my spine. "And, if I stayed any longer, I was going to punch him. No one touches you..."

My mouth ran dry, and I quickly sipped on the cold slushie. It almost sounded like Avro was saying that I was his. My body heated all over, and it felt like a million degrees.

"And then everyone wonders why I don't people," I said and looked over my shoulder, but there was no sign of the jerk. Sighing, I played over the interaction and decided my mistake was turning my back on him. No matter how stupid I looked, I shouldn't have taken my eyes off him.

"Hey, are you okay?" Avro asked as the silence stretched on between us.

"Yeah, I'm just not feeling the fun beach vibe anymore. I'm sorry, that guy gave me the creeps, and I keep playing it over in my mind, trying to figure out what I could've done to avoid it altogether." I glanced up at him, and he was frowning.

"Raine, there is nothing you should have to do. That's the point. He shouldn't have touched you at all, and that's not on you." Avro pulled me closer, and I sighed, feeling completely relaxed with him around.

God, that felt good. To be touched and not be afraid. I didn't want the day to end, but I'd lost the mojo.

"Would you mind if we just headed to the club now? I really should make sure everything is set for tonight."

"Of course, but, Raine...try not to let that loser get to you. Jerks like that are a dime a dozen, and they win if you let them stop you from doing what you want. Don't give them that kind of power."

Avro smiled, but there was sadness in his eyes. Was he just sad about the day ending early, or was there more under the hooded stare? I suddenly wanted to know everything about him. Things I'd never asked to keep myself from falling more than I should. Wrapping my arm around his waist, I hugged him.

"Thanks, I needed to hear that, and thank you for an incredible day."

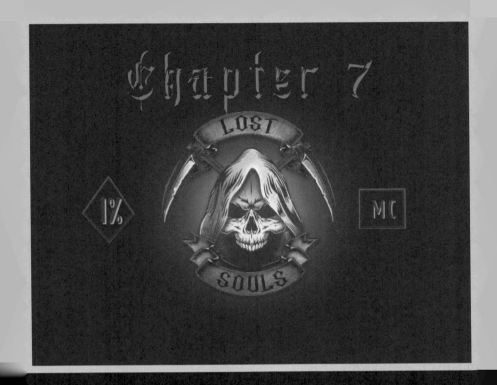

Chapter 7

Kaivan

"Wake the fuck up, man," Roach's annoying ass voice penetrated the furthest reaches of my sleep-induced brain. I kept my eyes closed and prayed that he would go away. His boots stomping up the stairs to my bedroom echoed through the old house.

"Hey, Snake, wake the fuck up. We need to get ready to go," he hollered, louder this time. I sighed as my bedroom door slammed open and rattled the walls that needed repair. "Dude, are you deaf? Let's go."

Rolling over, I blinked as I looked out the window. It was light out, but the sun was in the wrong direction. I grabbed my phone to check the time and saw that it was six o'clock at night.

"What the fuck do you want, man?" I asked, dropping the phone onto my chest and closing my eyes again.

"This girl is going to be the death of me. I swear I'm gonna have to lock her ass up in a cage somewhere," Roach said, like that comment was supposed to make sense. Something landed on my face. I grabbed it and stared at my T-shirt.

"What the fuck are you doing?" I glared at Roach as he rifled through my closet. "Come on in, why don't you? Go through my shit, why don't you? Did you even bring me any fucking coffee?"

"Here." Jeans sailed in my direction, and I caught them out of the air. "Coffee and pizza are downstairs. We need to go soon before they open the doors and don't let us in. You can eat on the way."

"Is someone dying?" I asked as Roach continued to stomp around my room like a cave dweller. I was expecting him to scratch his dick and grunt at me.

"Not yet, but I may be before the night is through," he mumbled, making me shake my head.

"Am I getting to kill someone?" I still didn't know what the fuck he was talking about, but I pulled the T-shirt on over my head, thankful I'd taken the time to shower when I got in.

"You really need to paint or something. This place looks like hell," Roach mumbled and tossed me a pair of socks from my drawer.

"I'm not going anywhere until you explain what the fuck is going on. You're not making any sense, and get out of my drawers. Shit, man, what are you, the warden?" I growled at my friend, and he slammed the drawer shut.

"I'll tell you when you get downstairs," he said, disappearing out the door.

"Hey?" I called out.

"What?"

"Is this a dress-up or get-bloody type of party?"

"I don't know. I guess dress-up. I don't expect anyone to get bloody, but with this girl, anything is possible," Roach grumbled as he stomped down my stairs.

Nothing like being woken up by the Tasmanian Devil. The guy was aptly nicknamed cause he was as annoying as any insect I'd ever come across. Holding up the jeans, I glared at them and wondered how Roach knew I liked these. It was creepy that he knew me that well. I couldn't have gone into his room and picked out an outfit that fast.

Yanking the jeans and socks on, I gave myself a once-over in the mirror. Then I strapped on my stylish leather cuffs, dropped my silver chain around my neck, and ran a hand through my hair. Guess that was about as dressed up as I got. The bathroom was next, and the fucker was just gonna have to wait.

Five minutes later, I wandered into my kitchen and watched Roach pace the floor.

"Shit, man, that took long enough." He spun around and looked at me. "Meh, you look okay, I guess. I can always bribe the bouncers."

"Break into my home, wake me up, and insult me. Keep it up. You're on a roll." I snatched the coffee off the kitchen table and popped the lid. It smelled like burnt tires. "Where the hell did you get this?"

"The gas station down the street," Roach said, pulling a piece of pizza from the box and stuffing his face with it. He was chewing so fast I would've guessed he was in a food-eating contest. Walking to the sink, I poured the coffee down the drain. "Hey, I got that for you."

"Yeah, you're trying to fucking poison me is what you're trying to do. I don't drink that shit. If you want me to go anywhere with you, then two things need to happen. The first is we hit a coffee shop of my choice on the way, cause I need the caffeine. Second, you tell me what the hell is going on."

He was jittery, like he'd taken something, but that wasn't Roach.

He smoked and drank but steered clear of drugs, so I knew this was all him.

"Can we get going first?" he said and held out the box of pizza. One look at the black olives with four different meats and extra cheese had my stomach turning.

I held up my hand. "No thanks."

"What, you watching your figure?" he mumbled around the mouthful of food.

"Do you want me to come with you or not? Cause I'm very tempted to tell you to go fuck yourself and go back to bed."

He licked his fingers and dug around in his jacket, pulling out his truck keys. "Fine, coffee and tell you what's what. I got it. Now let's go. We're taking my truck."

I grabbed my clean leather jacket, locking the door on my way out, while he jogged to the shiny black vehicle. As always, I glanced over at the amusement park between my house and the club property. I didn't like the idea of living there with everyone. Maybe it was cause for ten years I had to live with too many fucking people I didn't want to. Living here, on this old farm with a couple hundred acres to myself, was nice.

Besides, I had a great view of Wilder's crazy-ass antics, and that made me smile. There was no sign of him tonight, but that didn't mean anything. He was one of those types who could be standing right in front of you, and you wouldn't see him unless he wanted you to.

"Are you coming, Grandpa?" Roach called out, and I cracked my knuckles.

"I'd kill him if he wasn't such a good friend." Stomping down to the truck, I hopped into the passenger side and stole one of his cigarettes from the pack on the dash. Lighting up, I took a pull and blew it out the open window as we drove down my long driveway to the road.

"All right, out with it. What are we doing and why?"

"I need to keep an eye on Lane," Roach said, and I cocked an eyebrow at him. "She's going to this bar tonight. She got word from the other sorority sisters that some famous band would be there singing, and she decided to go. So we need to go. No group of horny band guys is getting their hands on Lane."

"Are we talking about Lane as in Hollywood's sister?" I was trying to keep up with his train of thought.

"Yes, who else would I be talking about? I only know one Lane," Roach said.

"You know, I really want to stab you right now," I grumbled, and took another pull on the cigarette before tossing the rest out the window. This cutting-back thing sucked ass.

"Why exactly are we stalking Hollywood's sister now? He asked you to look out for her, not turn into her personal bodyguard. Next thing you know, you'll be singing Whitney Houston songs about love," I said, and batted my eyes at Roach.

"Fuck you. It's not like that. I'm just taking my role seriously. Would you want to be in charge of a college girl while her brother trusts you to keep her safe? Especially after what Hollywood has already been through?"

"I guess not." I yawned and wished we were doing anything but going to some bar, club, or whatever this place was. "So, where are we going?"

"Do you listen to anything I say?" Roach looked over like I was a four-year-old who hadn't done my chores.

"I try really hard not to."

"So funny. Eclipse, it's down by the beach, you know, the one with the fancy lights on the patio area?"

"No, actually, I don't," I said.

"I don't get it. Why can't she be some geek that likes to be a hermit and stay in her room? And why does she always have to go out looking like she's ready to fuck everything? If someone so much as touches her, I'll cut off their hand."

Crossing my arms over my chest, I stared at the side of Roach's face and his twitching jaw muscle.

"You like her," I said, and his eyes snapped to mine.

"No, I don't."

"Yeah, you do."

"No, I fucking don't. The last time I wasn't making sure she stayed out of trouble, I found her at the clubhouse taking her shirt off." Roach gave me his full attention, his eyes wide. "Do you know what Hollywood would've done to me if he found out that she fucked one of the guys at the club? I'd be a dead man. D.E.A.D, man."

"Dramatic much? First, none of the guys were going to fuck the girls, at least I don't think, but I'm sure she fucked a ton of guys before her big bro put the chastity belt in place." Roach narrowed his eyes, and I couldn't resist poking at him. "Look at her. She's a smoke show and totally fuckable. We could've given her a good old roasted spit job that night if you hadn't chased her off," I said and waited for it.

"Don't you dare fucking touch her. You lay one finger on her fucking head, and I'll blow your dick off," Roach growled, his eyes murderous, which made me snort and then laugh.

"Yup, you don't like her at all," I said.

"You're a prick. I'm only fired up 'cause Hollywood is my bro, and if roles were reversed, he would look out for my sister. I can't let her get hurt or into trouble."

"I didn't know you had a sister," I said.

"I don't."

I shook my head and tried to right the insanity train. "Okay, fine, so you basically want me along for babysitting duty. Check. I now understand what we are doing and why. Next question, how far away is this place?"

"Dude, it's Eclipse. Fuck, do you pay attention to anything? We pass it almost every day. It's like twenty from here," Roach said as he wheeled into the coffee shop he knew I liked. I had no clue why he didn't just come here in the first place if he planned to try to bribe me.

I'd heard of this bar, but it wasn't my type of hangout. I preferred the quieter and a whole lot seedier spots or just stayed at the club-house. These popular bars were all the same. A million fucking people rubbing up against you, but with way too many clothes on. Jerks who thought they were tough when they had no idea what it was actually like to kill someone, and the booze was always way overpriced.

"Is this going to be a regular thing? The whole stalk her all over Florida?"

"If the girl would learn to stay put, then no. I really should invest in that cage. Do you think I could get away with putting her in a cage? Hollywood would be fine with it if it kept her safe, wouldn't he? I could give her pillows and food, and she would need a toilet," Roach mumbled as he tapped his chin. I didn't know if he was actually asking me this ridiculous question, so I stayed quiet. "Hollywood gets out in six months. I could make it work. College kids go MIA all the time to party, and I could force her to keep her studies up."

No, he didn't like this chick at all. Totally normal fucking reaction. I rolled my eyes at Roach. Maybe he didn't see it, but you would have to be blind not to see how he felt for this girl.

"I say no to the cage. Hollywood is not going to like his sister in a cell like he is," I said.

"Hmm, you may have a point."

I stared out the window as the sun set. There was only one girl I'd ever loved or wanted for more than getting my cock wet, and now I hated her.

Pushing the thought of Raine from my mind, I sighed and focused on the road, no longer paying attention as Roach talked. One of these days, I was going to miss something important, but that wasn't tonight.

Roach pulled into the beach parking lot and immediately swore as we watched a group of girls wearing so little it could pass as beach wear walk by the truck. Roach ducked low as Lane looked over and waved.

"Smooth, man. Totally suave. She didn't see you at all," I mocked and pushed open my door.

"Shut up, man," Roach snarled back and swore as Lane held up her finger to her friends and reversed course. She was heading straight for the truck, and I leaned against the hood, loving every fucking second of this.

Roach couldn't have looked any guiltier if he had tried as he slipped from the driver's seat and met the cute little blonde as she stepped up to the truck with her hands on her hips.

"Cole, are you following me?"

My brows lifted at the use of Roach's real name. He didn't tell many people what it was unless forced to, but I couldn't picture her having to force him to do much of anything. He looked more like he was ready to dissolve into a little puddle at her feet for a taste. Pathetic.

"No, of course not. I heard that there is a special headliner here tonight, Grim Man Garbage Bag, you know…." Roach stopped and looked over at me, but I wasn't helping him out of this mess.

Lane looked completely unimpressed as she lifted an eyebrow at Roach. "You mean Grimhead Crew?"

"Yeah, them. I was only joking. Ha, ha." He pretended to laugh.

I smirked at how ridiculous Roach was acting, earning a dirty glare from him. If this was his 'I'm acting totally cool and aloof routine,' it seriously needed work. Given even a sniff of opportunity, he would have this girl in the back of the truck fucking her hard. Oh, Hollywood was going to love that when he got out. I smiled wide. Okay, this night was making me feel a little better.

"Whatever. Look, Cole, I know that Nate has you watching me. My brother is such an ass. Of course, my brother would send his friend to spy on me. You don't need to. I'm not going to do anything stupid."

"Define stupid," Roach said.

Lane made an angry huff sound and stomped away.

"Wow, you are slick, just like butter on a hot summer day," I drawled, smiling at Roach. This night was far more entertaining than I initially thought it would. Watching Roach humiliate himself was a sport for me.

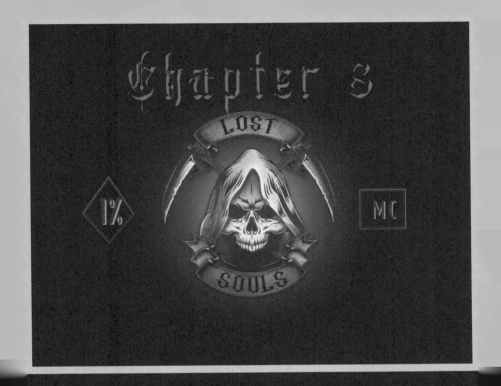

Chapter 8

Raine

Damn, this place was insane already, and Allen, the manager for Grimhead Crew, was a complete dick. I got it he wanted the best for his client, but this was their stupid idea in the first place. It wasn't like I asked them to come here and turn the bar upside down. We spent our normal prep time rearranging where the stage was and then finding chairs that Jace, the pompous leader of the group, found comfortable to sit his royal ass on.

"Fuck, I'm so excited for tonight," Avro said, and I looked up at him as I wiped down shot glasses.

The line outside was wild, and we had to call in all our bouncers. Plus, ask the temp company to send over more to make sure the crowd was under control. I had no idea how the news of Jace and his band being here had leaked to social media, but there were posts a over the place announcing the secret location of the impromptu concert.

"Why? This looks like it's gonna be a hell of a night, and not in a good way. If we're forced to call the cops once, we'll be lucky," I mumbled, my eyes going to the stage where Jace was in the middle of his sound check.

"Because that is Jace Everly. I mean, come on. I know you're not that oblivious. Look at him. He is a steak dinner ready to be devoured," Avro said and licked his lips.

"Sure, whatever you say," I mumbled, but a hint of jealousy crept through my system.

Avro was openly bi-sexual, and we'd never dated or been intimate on any level. Today at the beach was the most non-work interaction we'd ever had, and it was very PG. Yet, the fact that he was staring at Jace like he was food, and Jace was openly staring back, bothered me.

I continued to take in the rock star with his mop of shock-white hair, part of it hanging in his eyes. I hated to admit it, but he somehow pulled it off, and it looked great on him. His matching silver eyes practically glowed under the spotlights. It made me wonder if they were contacts or somehow a trick of the light that was all him. He had that air of arrogance that all those who found popularity had. I hated that attitude. Just because you became famous didn't give you the right to treat people like dirty pieces of toilet paper stuck to your shoe.

Jace looked over, and he smiled as our eyes locked. Forcing my stare away, I pointedly looked up at Avro, who seemed more flustered than any of the girls outside.

"Okay, fine, the guy is hot. You planning on leaving me here to run off with the circus?"

Avro's lips curled up as his eyes found mine. He was wearing all black tonight that matched his dyed black hair in a sexy gothic way.

He even put in cat-eye contacts that made his intense stare seem more unnerving than usual. He leaned against the bar, staring directly into my eyes.

"What is that I smell?" I looked around and down at the glass before sniffing my black tank top. He laughed at my confused look. "I mean, is that jealously I detect in your voice?"

My face heated, and I kept my eyes trained on the next shot glass I picked up. "No, of course not. What would I have to be jealous over?"

"Absolutely nothing unless...you wanted there to be," he said. The sultry tone had shivers racing down my spine.

I cleared my throat. "I'm just concerned I need to find a new bartender," I said, giving him a pointed look.

"Are you sure about that?" he asked, leaning in a little closer.

We'd worked together for a long time, and it had taken me a while to accept that I was genuinely attracted to Avro. The thing was, I hated the idea of dating. Others loved the thrill of getting dressed up and going out for the night with someone, but I liked comfy clothes and a movie. More unnerving was that I hadn't had sex since my attack. That was eleven years ago. Forget a duster. I needed a whole cleaning company to remove the cobwebs in that cave.

Shit, I'd practically hidden in my house this entire time. I wasn't even sure how to flirt with Avro. Was that something people even did anymore? Should I shoot him a text—when and where to meet—and then we could sit and stare at our phones? That seemed to be the norm now. We worked together, and...he was my only friend. Dating and sex could ruin that, and then what? Emotions were far too confusing.

"I'm sure that I want to get this done before those doors open," I said, pointing to the tall stack of shot glasses still needing to be wiped down. I loved it when they first came out of the kitchen, all clean. They were warm to the touch, and something about that fresh smell comforted me, but I hated the little spots that would dry on them if we didn't wipe them.

"You can't fool me, Raine. I saw that tough exterior crack for a little while today, and very soon, you're finally going to let me in," Avro said.

I bit my lip as it felt like he was talking about things far more intimate than the words that came out of his mouth.

"I'll be right back. Get those cleaned and ready. We don't have much time left before that swarm outside is all over us."

"I know what I want all over me," Avro said as I walked behind him.

As I glanced over my shoulder, he looked at me and then at Jace before finding my eyes again. Oh, I knew what he was thinking, and now I knew he'd stepped out of reality to wander around in fantasy land with candy canes and gumdrops.

Shaking my head, I wandered into the back and down the short staircase to the downstairs storage area. There was no point in one of us leaving the bar to get the extra cases of our most popular in the middle of the shift. We had runners, but I'd yet to find one that didn't make me want to follow them around to make sure they didn't destroy the place. We had more glasses and alcohol wasted when runners touched them than at any other time. Flicking on the bright fluorescent bulbs, I searched the shelves until I found the bottles I wanted.

Grabbing the clipboard off the rack for the aisle, I marked down what was taken and picked up the case, moving it to the bottom of the stairs.

I wondered why all these places put the storage in the booze cache area. It did help keep the stuff cool, but it wasn't like you wanted to party down here. The supplies were heavy, and it was irritating to lug them up and down all the time. A short escalator leading directly to the bar would be amazing.

I walked back to the farthest aisle to grab the next case when I heard someone coming down the stairs.

"Avro, you can take that first box up. I'm going to grab a few more of the faves," I called out as I grabbed an empty box to fill with various extra bottles.

Bending over, I reached to the back of the bottom shelf and pulled out the last case of tequila we had. That wasn't good. It must have been missed on the previous order. Pulling open the top of the box, I counted twelve bottles and sighed. There would be enough for tonight, but I would have to change my specialty shot for the challenge. Straightening, I turned and yelped when I saw Jace leaning against the shelving.

"Jesus H, you just scared the shit out of me. Are you lost?" My voice dripped with sarcasm to cover my initial fear.

I tried to ignore the burning in my gut like I'd just taken a shot. Up close, I could see his eyes, and the fact that they weren't contacts and filled with heat that had me stepping back before I forced myself to stop. I was no longer that same teen who was assaulted, and I knew how to defend myself. I proved it earlier, didn't I?

"Only in your eyes," Jace said, and my mouth fell open a second before I laughed.

"Does that actually work on anyone?"

"Usually, it has people panting at my feet." His brows furrowed, and he crossed his arms, pulling the T-shirt he wore tight across his chest.

He was built a lot like Avro. They had that same tall, athletic body, with broad shoulders and a narrow waist. I could almost picture the hard abs under the shirt, but I kept my eyes firmly on his face.

"Ah, well, I'm not most girls," I said and went to walk around him, but he stepped into the way and grabbed the box I was carrying.

"I'll take this," he said, pulling it from my hands.

Instead of turning and walking toward the exit, he placed it on a high shelf that I would need to get the step stool to reach. I opened my mouth to give him shit when he stepped into my personal space, and I found myself backed up against the shelving unit. His hands gripped the shelf on either side of my waist as he leaned in close enough that I could feel the demanding heat from his body as it pressed into mine.

"What are you doing?"

I knew it was a stupid question. My heart was pounding hard, and the normal anxiety I had managed to control came racing back. I placed my hands on his chest to push him away, or maybe keep him from coming any closer. He was doing something weird to my head. The crippling fear was twisting into something else that I wasn't sure I liked any better. I felt the hard muscle under his T-shirt and suddenly wanted to run my fingers all over his body. This wasn't right for so many reasons. Avro was at the top of that list.

Jace looked down at my hands, which had yet to push him away, and smirked as his eyes found mine. He made a noise between a groan and a growl that did all sorts of wrong to my body.

Jace released the shelf on one side, and I immediately looked at my escape route, only to have him grip my chin in his fingers. He tilted my head up, forcing me to look into his eyes.

"I do like a challenge," he said, and I was tempted to pull a Dennis Copland on his ass. "Fuck, you're hot." He lowered his head to the side of my neck, and I was sure he could see my pulse pounding out of control under my skin. "I would eat you up if you let me."

I felt paralyzed, unsure of what to do next as my mind swam from all the new endorphins. My stomach twisted into a pile of knots. For a moment, I contemplated following through on my knee-to-the-crotch idea, but ending up on the front page of every paper and media outlet as the girl that made Jace Everly unable to have children was not the headline I ever wanted to make. I never wanted to be on any front page for anything, especially not for something like that. If I thought I was an outcast before, that certainly would take it to all new heights.

"Is that so? Well, I'll be more than just a challenge. I'm not interested. Can you please step back now?" I asked, trying hard to sound in control even when I felt like I was spinning out.

Jace inched closer to my lips, and I pushed myself back into the shelving unit until the sharp bite of the shelf pressed into my spine and forced me to stop moving.

"Raine...I like how that sounds, but you need a nickname. Something sweet and feisty, just like you. Don't you think?" His lips were a breath away from mine.

"How do you know my name?" We hadn't spoken since he arrived. Jace just smiled.

"Yo, Raine, you down here? They're about to open the doors," Avro called out, and I'd never been more relieved to hear his voice.

I could hear the soft sigh leave Jace's mouth as he pulled back and released me from the cage he'd made with his arms.

"Back here," I managed to call out. "I'm going to need that back." I pointed up to the box Jace had set up high, and his lips curled up like he found me amusing.

He grabbed the box, and I gave him the best *fuck you* look I could muster. "You can bring that, since you've put me behind schedule."

I left him standing in the aisle like he was no more than an employee and spotted Avro picking up the box at the bottom of the stairs. I grabbed a couple of whiskey bottles on the way past to give my hands something to do and didn't even care that I didn't write it down.

Avro looked up as he picked up the box, and his mouth dropped open, but nothing came out.

"Nothing was going on," I answered before he could ask the question. "Jace here had a question about his setup and was nice enough to offer to carry the box." I glared over my shoulder at the guy who I would be happy if I never saw again. "Isn't that right, Jace?"

"Oh, I definitely had a question about the setup, all right," he said, his voice dripping with sarcasm. It felt like he meant something else, and I narrowed my eyes, but he was no longer looking at me and was staring at Avro instead.

I couldn't deal with this or them right now. I needed to get back to work. Maybe I was excreting extra pheromones or something. First Avro all day, then Dennis, and now Jace. It made me worry. What the hell did the rest of the evening have in store for me?

I did not just put that out to the universe. I did not put that out to the universe.

I looked up at the ceiling as I stepped out of the cellar. "I take it back. I never thought that or said anything," I whispered under my breath, but already, it felt like I'd just sealed my fate with something a whole lot worse.

Snake

Chapter 9

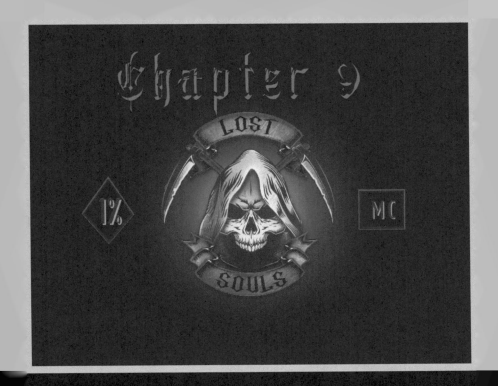

K aivan

Roach marched right up to the bouncer, past the long line of people, and whispered in his ear. I saw him hand over a large roll of cash. There was a couple of grand in that, easy.

Either he was in love with Lane, or Hollywood gave the best blow jobs that I knew nothing about because that was a shit ton of money to get into a club. Roach was many things but loose with his money was not one of them. He made my lack of spending look frivolous.

The bouncer nodded and pushed open the door. The loud music from the band on stage assaulted my ears as we stepped inside. The place smelled like fucking sweet candy and flowery perfume. Then again, a sea of mostly screaming women would do that to a place.

Roach pointed to a group that had gotten close to the stage

"Great," I said with no enthusiasm.

I followed in Roach's wake and felt like I had somehow ended up in teeny-bopper hell. Had I not spent enough time being tortured by going to jail? Now I needed to be surrounded by a mass of screaming girls as they swooned over the dude singing on stage, ignoring me like I didn't exist. Maybe I really had died, and this was my hell.

The lead singer knelt near the front as he drew out a long note, and it was clear that someone fainted as he reached out and touched their hand. Really? I needed a drink, but the main bar was on the other side of the club, and that meant wading through the throngs of hysterical females to get there. That felt a little like I was taking my life in my hands. I nudged Roach's shoulder.

"I'll keep an eye on your girl, but you're going to get me a drink for being dragged into this," I yelled into his ear.

"She's not my girl." He glared at me.

"Don't give a fuck. I want a drink." He nodded, and I watched as he was swallowed up by the sea of people.

Leaning against the wall out of the way, I kept one eye on Lane and the other on the stage. I could admit that the music wasn't terrible. It wasn't what I usually listened to, but it didn't make my ears bleed. The guy looked around my age, maybe a little younger, but it was his atti-tude that grated me the wrong way. He reminded me too much of the guy I was before I went to prison. Full of cockiness, potential, and dreams. This guy was the walking epitome of what I could've been.

Lane and the other sorority girls she came with jumped up and down, clapping as the singer made his way to their end of the stage. I snorted as he grabbed Lane's hand and kissed her knuckles. If Roach saw that, this guy was going to lose his cock later.

The song wrapped up with a bang, and the lead singer bowed and blew kisses to the crowd. "Next up, we have the Eclipse chal-lenge," he said, and the crowd went bananas.

I covered my ears as a swarm of screaming people turned toward the bar. What the hell was wrong with this place?

"Time is on the clock," the singer said and pointed to the massive clock, showing three minutes, on a countdown clock at the opposite end of the room. Beside it was a massive projector screen as big as any movie theatre. I was drawn in like the rest of the crowd, waiting to see what would happen.

"The contestants are ready!"

The camera panned to the bar and showed a guy looking like he'd just stepped out of a gothic vampire porno. My eyebrow raised at not only the outfit but the man himself. Some dudes had it all, and it seriously wasn't fair. He looked like he could either be on the cover of goth weekly as the next hot thing or strip it off and go full Magic Mike. You shouldn't be allowed to have both types of hot. What was left for the rest of us?

"In our first corner, we have Avro, who is tall, dark, and sexyyy." If this guy decided he didn't want to sing anymore, he could make it as an emcee, cause he had the flare down. "Avro is coming in at six foot three and has a fetish for making you melt with his moves on the bar," the singer said, and his voice dipped suggestively, which caused another round of cheers. Of course, this guy would confirm that the bartender Avro could dance on the bar. If not, why not? Come on, seven circles of hell.

"In our other corner, we have Raine, who comes in at five-four and is the spicy underdog. Raine takes no shit, and boys, don't let that hot little body fool you. She has moooves," he said and bit his lip.

My eyes snapped away from the stage to the screen, and my world narrowed on the face that was smiling and waving to the crowd. Those big blue eyes were the same, the thick full lips hadn't changed, and that smile could still stop a car in its tracks. Her cheeks were pink with the same look of embarrassment she always got when called out. It made her look ripe for eating.

My heart stopped as the world stood still. Leaning harder into the wall to keep myself from falling over from the shock, I watched every little move she made. From the flick of her pinky to the wink she gave the other bartender.

She was still stunning, still made me jittery, and now hard as a rock. The old bitterness and anger kicked open the door and marched to the surface until I was grinding my teeth, and my knuckles cracked as my fist clenched. Fate was a bitch, and she had a sick fucking sense of humor.

"And go!"

The clock on the wall began to count down, and as it did, Raine poured drinks like the devil himself was chasing her. She had two bottles per hand, and she would move on every few seconds, filling the massive lineup of shot glasses spread across the length of the massive bar. She smiled and looked over at the second bartender coming from the other direction, and a growl rippled from my throat as he gave her a flirty look.

The crowd cheered louder and louder as they neared the center of the large, curved bar, and by only a glass, the guy finished filling his first, raising his shot in the air before knocking it back. Everyone got quiet as the bartender held a finger over his mouth. Even the music stopped playing, and I could almost feel the heartbeat of the crowd as they waited to see what would happen next.

"As my prize tonight," he called out and then paused, as if making sure that he had everyone's attention. "I want a kiss from..." He held up his finger, and all the girls squealed and began jumping around, waving their hands in the air as they begged to be chosen. "Her," he said, and his finger pointed at Raine.

My nostrils flared, and my arms fell from where they'd been crossed over my chest. As the camera flicked back to Raine, she looked genuinely shocked as her mouth hung open, and her face went from soft pink to bright red. Then again, this girl was a liar. She could've been fucking this guy ten minutes before the place opened and probably still pulled off the act. She had certainly gotten away with a much harder performance.

"Kiss, kiss, kiss, kiss!" The chant went up around me as the bar began cheering the two on.

The bartender wrapped his arm around Raine's waist, and as he did, her face paled like she might faint. With a show of dipping her over, he said something against her lips that the mic couldn't make out before he kissed her. It was not a little peck on the lips. The guy made a show of it for the screaming audience as her jaw relaxed and her hand went to his cheek. The seconds ticked on, and rage rolled through my system like a desert storm.

I could feel her throat under my hand and the look on her face as she gasped for air and scratched at my arm. I was breathing hard as I seethed, glaring at the screen, at Raine all happy with her lips on another man. My cock ached as I pictured taking from her what she'd accused me of doing. Pushing her face down onto the bed and fucking her hard, making her scream my name.

"Yo, Snake! What the fuck is up?"

I glared at Roach, and he stepped back from me, holding up the drinks like a shield.

"Damn, man, what the hell happened? You look like you're ready to kill everyone in the room."

I glanced back up at the screen once more, showing the lead singer on stage as he fanned himself like the kiss had been hot. The music started back up, and within moments, all the girls shrieked again.

"I'm going to kill her," I mumbled, and Roach looked around.

"Who?"

"Raine, I'm going to fucking kill that bitch." My eyes found Roach again. "She's going to regret the day she ever crossed me."

Raine

"What the hell was that, Avro?" I paced the office and pointed toward the bar, which was still just as loud.

"What do you mean?" he asked, making me want to strangle him. He fucking knew what I meant.

I paused in my pacing to glare at him. "Don't give me that. You know exactly what I'm talking about. The kiss. You freaking made me kiss you. Out there. In front of all those people. And...what was with the sweet, *I've wanted to do this for so long*, statement?"

He leaned against the wall, his lip slightly curled up like he was amused with himself. "Made? That's a bit harsh. And what I said was true. I have wanted to kiss you for a long time. Was it terrible? Did you not want me to kiss you?"

"That's not the point," I said and rubbed my eyes.

My stomach was all fluttery, and it was like the kiss had ripped off the final bit of blinders which had allowed me to keep the friend line firmly in place. It didn't help that the kiss was exactly as I imagined it would be. Hot and yet somehow sweet, just like the man himself.

"It is the point," Avro said and walked across the room until he could sit on the edge of my desk.

I'd only been the manager for six months, but I had to say that having my own office made me feel pretty badass as I ranted. I went to walk past him, and he snaked an arm around my waist, forcing me to stop.

"Raine, look at me." Avro ran his hands down my arms until he could hold my hands, and even that little touch made me nervous and agitated, like I had too much adrenaline running through my veins. "Did you like the kiss? It's a simple question with a simple answer. Yes or no?"

I swallowed hard and wished I had superpowers to disappear as I stared into his eyes. "Of course I liked it. How could I not? But that's not the point."

"Why isn't it the point?" he asked.

My mouth fell open, and my brain went blank as I fumbled through all the reasons and excuses in my mind, but I couldn't find one that made sense right now. I'm sure there was at least one reason, but staring into his eyes made my brain mush.

"Because we're friends," I finally managed to get out. "And this is our place of work." I licked my lips. "And what if this ruins..."

Avro stood, and whatever argument I had died on my tongue. Avro didn't hesitate and dropped his lips to mine. Just like the first time, a warmth burned bright in my gut as our lips moved in sync. He made me feel like I was floating in warm water while eating a rich chocolate cake.

"Come over tonight. We won't do anything you don't want to," he said, breaking the kiss.

My head was light, and my lips tingled.

"I...I...I don't know," I said, moaning as he softly kissed the side of my neck, spiking my pulse.

"Spend more time with me. You know me, Raine, and at some point, you need to stop being terrified that everything will turn into whatever horror movie you have playing in your mind. I'd never hurt you, and I'd never let anyone else hurt you." I shivered and grabbed hold of the statement that hit too close to home. "But I'm done pretending that all I want is to be friends," he whispered, and I shivered. "I've wanted to be more than friends for a very long time."

"Who said I think everyone is a horror movie waiting to happen?" My eyes fluttered closed as he trailed his lips along the side of my neck.

"Because right now, it's written all over your face. And because, at one time, you would move away from me if you felt I was too close. You kept your eyes on me no matter what we were doing and refused to have me at your back. You always carried a box cutter, even when we had no boxes to open. Every move I made, you reacted as if I was going to beat you," Avro said softly.

I hated that he saw that part of me. I thought I did a good job hiding it from the world. In my mind, I was still that scared version of myself, screaming wildly and saying no. Every man was potentially one of my attackers, and any moment alone with a guy, no matter who it was or where it was, had a hidden agenda. It was the part of my brain I was trying to learn to control rather than have it control me.

"Okay, I'll come over."

I could feel his grin against my neck. "Oh, you naughty boss you, pulling me into your office to proposition me," he teased as he stood up straight.

The door opened just then, and the office filled with Jace's voice and cheering people as he sang another song.

"Sorry, am I interrupting?" Mr. Allen Lawrence, Jace's agent, asked. I rolled my eyes up at Avro before plastering a smile on my face. I stepped around Avro as we turned to face the man I wanted to choke.

"May I speak to you alone, Ms. Eastman? I have a few things I'd like to go over," Allen said.

"Of course, Mr. Lawrence, come on in," I said, happy that I could pull off the professional attitude. I held up my finger as he stepped forward. "But next time, wait until I say you can enter before opening my door. Just a professional courtesy, I'm sure you understand."

Avro lifted an eyebrow that only I could see, but I knew he was impressed. So was I.

"I'll go help with the bar again," Avro said, giving me a wink that was both sexy and calming.

Had I been blind to his affection all this time? He was always funny and flirtatious, but he'd dated so many people that I lost count after ten. Was he trying to make me another one of his numbers? I kicked myself mentally and shoved away the nagging doubt that no one would want me unless it were to hurt me. That was the kind of mentality that had made me scared to leave the house, and I was never going back to that person ever again.

"All right, Mr. Lawrence, what can I help you with?"

Chapter 10

Kaivan

The ride back to the clubhouse was quiet. No matter what Roach asked, I didn't dare speak, or I might've leaped across the console and killed him simply for being there. We pulled into the Lost Souls parking lot, where I kept my bikes even when I was at home. I didn't even wait for the truck to come to a full stop before I hopped out and stomped to my bike. Roach didn't try to stop me. He knew me well enough to know that someone was going to die, and he didn't want to end up on my list.

I was going back to that bar and waiting as long as it took to see Raine and follow her home.

The image of my hands on Raine and her screaming as she fought me was so vivid that my step faltered mid-stride. Oh, the evil she conjured in my mind. The old darkness that filled me and kept me going night after night in the pen was once more taking over.

Mannix used to say I looked possessed when I got this angry, and he wasn't far off the mark. It felt like that, too. Like the world was narrowing in, and all I saw was red. He also told me that I needed to harness it, or I would end up back behind bars before I was even released. He hadn't been wrong about that, either. For the most part, I was able to, but there were just some times in life when you tossed all that control aside and simply did what felt right.

"Hey!" a voice called as I reached my bike. I was so consumed that I hadn't noticed that anyone else was out here with me. "Over here," the gravelly voice came again, and I looked over to see Wilder's version of the swamp monster hanging onto the chain-link fence. He blended with the chaotic background so well that I would never have noticed him.

He was always dressed up in the strangest outfits. This time he was coated in mud, a blanket of grass and water dripping from his body. Had he been lying in the water with the gators? If he was, the guy was crazier than I thought, or one hell of an animal whisperer.

I didn't have time for whatever he wanted, but considering Wilder rarely spoke—and he could probably sneak down my chimney or find a way inside my walls—it was better that I played along rather than ignore him. There was no telling what the hell this guy would do.

I walked over to the fence and stuffed my hands in my pockets. "Hey, man," I said. "What's up?"

"You need help killing whoever you're going after? I have skills that are itching to be used," Wilder said.

"I'm sure you do, but no, not this time." I stared at the long pieces of seaweed tied to the getup. "Can I ask why you're dressed like the swamp monster?"

"'Cause you can never be too careful," he said and nodded, so I nodded along with him.

"Okay. Did you want me for something?" My own hands were itching to get on Raine's fair skin.

"Oh, yeah. You fuck a lot of girls, right?"

Of all the questions that Wilder could've asked me, this was one I wasn't prepared for. I had no idea the guy knew what a girl was. He rarely spoke, and when he did, it was about guns, bombs, or how someone was after him. I didn't know if that last part was true, but regardless, women was not where I thought this conversation was headed.

"Um...yeah, I do alright, I guess. If you consider a couple of girls a week a lot, then yes." This conversation felt fucking weird, but now that I was into it, it was like quicksand, and I had no idea how to back the fuck out.

"Is it normal for a girl to cry after getting fucked?"

My brow furrowed as I thought about how to answer this landmine of a question from Wilder.

"Are we talking like that was the best fuck of my life crying, or are we leaning more toward crying for real?"

He looked confused.

"I mean, is she like, *oh my god, what just happened* type of crying? Or is she trying to get away from you?" I figured it was best to clarify the issue.

"Hmmm, difficult to say. She can't get away," he said, and my mouth fell open. Did he just admit to keeping someone hostage? "Tell me, what's the difference? Does the crying sound different? I mean, tears are tears, right?"

"Well, yes, but there is a difference," I said as I tiptoed around the image of Wilder attempting to have sex with someone in a cell or maybe chained to a wall. Not that I didn't think the guy could get his dick hard, but the idea of him having sex and not with a farm animal was a different story.

Wilder sighed like I was being difficult, so I tried to explain. "Let's try this. If the girl is crying after being fucked, but she's all like, *oh, Wilder, that was amazing. Yes, give me more. I want to take your cock down my throat. Do it again. I can't get enough.* Then that is good, and she liked it, so I would lean toward normal."

"Would her voice go that high pitched?" he asked, and I had to hold back from smacking myself on the forehead.

"Maybe, I don't know. Look, if she's screaming at you to get away from her and says she never wants you near her again while the tears are falling, then I'm going to say that falls under the not normal column." Lifting my shoulders, I let them fall. "Does that make sense?"

He rubbed his cheek, leaving behind a dirty streak. "Huh, okay. I think I need to go back to the drawing board," Wilder said, then bent low as he ran across the property.

I watched him until I couldn't see him any longer, then shook my head and stomped back to my bike. There was some shit you just couldn't explain, and that conversation was one of them. I feared for any girl who caught his eye.

Jumping on my bike, I revved her and flew out the open gates. I didn't bother to stop even though a car was coming, and the sound of the horn had me flipping the guy off. One year, three months, and two days ago, I was released, and I would go back to that hellhole just for the satisfaction of seeing Raine die by my hand.

There were still cars in the customer parking lot, so chances were that Raine was still inside. It didn't matter now that I knew where she worked. How fucking close she was this entire time. I was willing to sit outside this place every single night. Grabbing the smokes from my jacket, I parked the bike down a side street and sat there with the engine off, my eyes on the door as I waited. I held the cigarette between my lips and remembered the first time I tried one.

I'd stolen a couple of smokes from Mr. Collins's pack and snuck out back. It was late, and no one was awake. I sat down to lean against the tree. It had been a strange six weeks, and I wasn't sure what I thought about all that had happened. It was six weeks to the day that I'd taken the garbage out to the garage, and Mrs. Collins followed me. It took me all of ten seconds to know what she was after. It wasn't hard to guess after the whole movie situation that this was coming. When she grabbed my cock through my track pants, I almost came on the spot. No one other than myself had ever touched me like that.

In a garage, up against the chest freezer, was not how I thought I would lose my virginity, and the fact that she acted like it wouldn't be a onetime thing kinda wigged me out. I mean, it was a shit ton better than my hand, but it felt...weird. She was my foster mother.

Did that make me a man now? At least I didn't have to go to college a virgin. So why was it that I felt guilty? I didn't care about Mr. Collins. The guy was never home, and when he was, he was a jerk or ignored us, but I did care about Raine.

Fuck, I shouldn't feel bad. She was practically still a kid, and I would be gone in a couple months, but there was a definite nagging sensation in my gut.

I pulled out the first smoke and the little book of matches and stared at them. My father liked to smoke. I remembered it clearly. The red and white pack he kept rolled up in the sleeve of his T-shirt. I'd always thought it was so cool how he sat on his motorcycle with one hanging out of his mouth and my mother sitting on his lap. The faint scent of smoke that clung to his clothes. At least I thought it was cool until I got a little older, and I realized that he was a fucking asshole, and my mother was miserable.

"Hey, can I sit?"

I jumped at the soft sound of Raine's voice as she stepped around the tree and sat down before I answered.

"By all means, join me," I said sarcastically.

The sweet, shy smile on Raine's face fell. She looked down at her hands, blonde hair hanging around her face, and I kicked myself for snipping at her. What had been happening between me and Mrs. Collins wasn't her fault, and neither was my feelings for her that I wasn't supposed to have. Every time I was near her was a conflict and battle of wills.

"I can go. I didn't mean to bug you," she said, and I sighed.

"No, I'm fine. Just in a mood, guy stuff, before you go asking. Here, you want one?" I held out a cigarette for her to take, and she shook her head.

"That's what gave me my asthma. At least that's what the doctor says."

I pulled the little match across the flint, and the flame rushed to life. I did what I'd seen a thousand times and sucked back hard on the smoke as I lit the end. Immediately, I began to cough and gag at the terrible taste and burning sensation sticking to the back of my throat. I had asthma as a kid, but I'd grown out of it and wanted to see why everyone liked these things. So far, I was not impressed.

"You okay?" Raine asked and got up on her knees to rub my back.

I winced away from her touch as my dick stirred in my pants. See, this was exactly why I couldn't be around her anymore, and I definitely didn't need her trying to make me feel better. That was not how this situation was supposed to work. She crossed her arms in a huff.

"Fine, choke to death, see if I care," she grumbled. "I don't even know why I bother hanging out with you anymore. It's obvious you don't want me around. I don't know what I did to piss you off, but if you don't want to be my friend, just say so." Her eyes filled with tears, but I didn't know what to say.

She didn't piss me off. Of course, I wanted her around. I wanted her around too much. I wanted to hold her hand and kiss her and all the shit you would do if you were dating someone, but she was my foster sister and two years, two weeks, and two days younger.

Raine stood, and I grabbed her hand and tugged, though I wasn't sure why. "Don't go." She had the prettiest eyes I'd ever seen, and how she looked at me now with her very Raine attitude made me smile. "Please?"

I added in a little pout for good measure, and she laughed. "Fine."

"I still want to be your friend. I've just got a lot going on, and I've been off. Nothing to do with you," I lied. It had a lot to do with her, but none of it I could share.

She sat back down beside me, and it felt good to have her nearby. She laid her head on my shoulder, and for a few minutes, everything felt right.

Raine had already been here when I arrived, and she was the same now as that day. Sassy, a straight shooter who preferred her jeans and hoodies over anything else. She thought she was awkward, while I thought she was adorable. Of course, now that I was a few weeks from eighteen and she was only fifteen, I felt like I was a creep.

"You gonna keep doing those fights?" she asked, and I lifted her much smaller hand into mine, staring at it. Hers looked so sweet and innocent next to my much larger, newly tattooed one.

"Yeah, the money is good. I need to pay for college somehow." I shrugged. "They're not bad. The key is knowing who you should fight and who to stay away from."

"I guess so," she said, and I knew she wanted to complain more. She already had, and I told her more than once that she had to stop worrying so much.

"You know what you want for your birthday yet?" I asked, and she shrugged. "That's not an answer."

"What I want is impossible." She looked back at the house and then at me. "Ever just want to run away and go somewhere else?"

"Not really. Where would I go?" I linked our fingers together. This was dangerous territory. I should tell her I was too old to be her best friend while I walked away. Yet I couldn't make myself do it.

"I don't know. Just somewhere different. Somewhere that has snow at Christmas and mountains to hike, someplace that doesn't have so many mean people, and no one would bother us," she said, and I raised an eyebrow at that.

"Us?"

"Yeah, you're my best friend. Of course, I want you to come with me. I mean, only if you wanted to," she quickly added.

Hooking the long hair behind her ear, all I could think about was kissing her. "We better go in before they realize we're missing. Don't want anyone to get the wrong idea."

"Yeah, that would be terrible," she said and let go of my hand.

The way she said it bothered me. It was like she wanted more too, or maybe I was projecting. I'd learned in school that was a thing. Mind you, they weren't talking about what I had going on, but was pretty sure it didn't matter the emotions.

As she turned to walk away, I grabbed her arm and pulled her back. I wrapped her up in my arms and held onto her, not saying a word. I expected her to protest or at the very least ask what I was doing, but instead her arms slowly wrapped around my waist. I never wanted to let her go, she was the first and only good thing in my life.

Tossing the finished butt on the ground, I leaned back on the bike and watched for my prey. There was a lot of shit in this life that I could get over and move on from, but not this, never this. Her reprieve was over. Fate had stood up and pointed me in the direction I needed to go. Raine Eastman was going to pay for what she did. If it was the last thing I did, she would know the mistake she made the day she named me as the man who assaulted her.

Raine

Chapter 11

Raine

What the hell was I doing? Leaving the bar for someone else to clean was not helping my trepidation about the situation. I was practically shaking as I walked out with Avro. It must have shown on my face, because Avro spoke up as we reached his car.

"Raine, look at me," Avro said, leaning on the passenger door. "It's me. Tell me honestly, do you really think I would hurt you or let anything bad happen?"

I didn't, but then again, I hadn't with Kai either, and I still couldn't think about that night.

"No, I don't," I said.

"Okay, then this is a perfect moment to take a few more steps."

he smiled. The look on his face warmed me as I remembered his lips on mine. Either this was the bravest or stupidest thing I'd ever done.

Pulling open the door, I took a moment and looked around as a chill swept up my back. It was still dark, and my eyes searched all the corners and bushes, but I didn't see anything out of the ordinary. I would've sworn that someone was staring at me, but then again, I'd spent so much time looking over my shoulder that it was hard to tell anymore.

"What's going on?" Avro asked as he leaned over and glanced around outside.

"Nothing, I just thought...it's nothing," I said, slipping into the car. "Where is your place?" I felt stupid that I didn't know. What kind of friend didn't bother to find out where he'd moved?

"Not far, I was leaving it as a surprise, but I managed to get a three-story near the beach. I finally took possession a few months ago. The tips have been great lately, and I put a huge deposit down to buy the place."

"Avro, that's amazing," I said.

He smiled wide, his real smile, not the one he gave to the crowd at the bar. It was sexier than the fake one he presented to the customers. I glanced out the window to the world passing by and watched the glistening water shimmering in the moonlight. Everything was so quiet and peaceful. Not so very long ago, I saw that beach at this time of night in the same light as I saw everything else...a place to be attacked. Avro turned the radio on, and "Old Town Road" played, making us laugh.

"That routine is still my favorite," he said.

"I have no idea how you talked me into getting up on the bar and pretending you were a horse." I shook my head and laughed at the memory.

"It was pretty epic. We still get requests for that routine," Avro said as we pulled into a pretty area.

His place was nestled in a great location where all the homes looked out toward the beach. The parking was at the back of the house, and I was shocked to see Avro had enough room to park six cars with space. That was rare. Getting out, I looked down the long alley. It seemed like a quiet spot.

"Are you kidding me? I'm never getting up on that bar again. It is one of my top three most embarrassing moments. I was so happy when we switched to a different routine. Although, tonight may have topped it," I said as Avro looked over his shoulder at me.

"Never say never," Avro teased.

"It's a really quiet area you found here." Only two other places had cars or lights.

"Most spots are rented to those coming in for spring break or Christmas. The rest of the time, it's like I have no neighbors at all."

I was startled when a loud motorcycle drove by. Why was I so jumpy? It had been months since I felt this way. I guess some shit was harder to shake. Avro opened the door, turning on lights as he went. Stepping up to the threshold, I stopped.

Avro happily talked as he walked through the house. Mentally berating myself, I stepped through the door and closed it behind me. Maybe it wasn't being alone with Avro or in his space that made me edgy. Perhaps it was because I knew he wanted to be more than friends, and I didn't know how to handle that. I wasn't sure how to navigate the feelings that felt like a mass of scrambled wires inside me.

"I mean, look at that view," Avro said as I entered the large room that was a cross between a living room and a games room. There was an almost ceiling-height speaker in the corner, an air hockey table, and a pair of dart boards. A massive television was mounted on the far wall, and three couches made a horseshoe shape for viewing. He even had a small bar with an assortment of bottles almost as extensive as at work lining the shelf.

This room said party, while my home said spinster. All I needed was a bunch of cats to complete the look.

"Well?" I looked at Avro and realized I didn't know what he'd been saying. I guess my blank, blinking stare told him I didn't have a clue. "What do you think so far?"

"I think this is pretty incredible." I walked over to stand near the tall bay windows and stared out at the water.

"Come on. I'll give you the rest of the tour."

From one room to the next, I followed him, amazed by his style and ability to maximize the space given. There wasn't a single thing out of place. I was a total slob and always had been. Tossing my jacket and bag wherever and living out of a laundry basket was normal.

We made our way upstairs, and the wooden steps and glass railing were as impressive as everything else. There were very few images on the walls, and the ones Avro did have were either nature shots or photos of himself at different performances before his accident. They'd been blown up to poster size and framed.

I paused at a small image at the top of the stairs. It was a newspaper clipping announcing his acceptance as a headliner in the newest Las Vegas Cirque performance. The date on it was six years ago before he damaged his knee doing a difficult trick. It was so bad that he ended up backing out of the show. He had multiple surgeries to stabilize his knee, and the doctors told him he couldn't go back to the extreme dancing and performances he'd been doing.

"You coming or what? This is the best room in the house," Avro said as he stuck his head out of a door. My heart ached for what he'd lost. To work that hard, to dream that big, then to have it all ripped away in a blink was heartbreaking.

"Coming," I said and tore myself away from the clipping. I was starting to realize just how cut off I'd been. Knowing it and understanding it were two different things.

I knew Avro had given up his dream, which was how he ended up at Eclipse. He would've found that transition difficult, but did I understand what he went through? The pain and rehabilitation of each surgery just so he could walk again, let alone do what he did four nights a week at the bar? Was he sore? Did the knee ever ache? Did he come home and stare at the wall of what could have been? I wanted to wrap him up in a hug and tell him I was sorry for never asking, and not being the kind of friend he deserved.

I walked up to the door Avro had disappeared into, and my mouth dropped open as I looked around the bedroom. It was massive, like he'd taken all the bedrooms on this side of the house and made himself one large space with a wall of glass facing the water. The bed was gigantic and took up almost half the room. He also fit a sitting area with a coffee machine right there for when you rolled out of bed. The balcony looked brand new, stretching the entire length of the bedroom, complete with tables and chairs.

"Avro, this is wow...just wow," I said, stepping into the room.

I hadn't been in a guy's bedroom since Kai. I'd sat on his floor or spun around on his desk chair, but as an adult, this was new. I wasn't a virgin—that had been stolen from me—but there'd been no one since.

Avro leaned against one of the supports for the windows, staring outside, and all my earlier fear returned. I felt like a child. At twenty-six, I'd only ever been kissed twice. Once when I was fifteen, and tonight. My pulse pounded in time with my hammering heart.

Avro was one of those people that made you do a double take on the street to make sure your eyes weren't playing tricks on you. I glanced at my reflection and wondered what the hell he saw in me. Of all the elegant and beautiful people out there, why me? I was suspicious. What could Avro really want? Did I doubt he was my friend? No, but today was different. Sure, I'd fantasized about being with him. Kissing him and running my hands over his body, but I'd never let my mind travel off the trail of fantasy. Today at the beach confirmed that I wanted someone in my life, but I wasn't even in the same league as Avro, let alone the same game. Fuck, I wasn't even in the same sport.

"This is my favorite spot. I love this room and the view. I'll be happier when it is officially all mine," he said, breaking me out of my thoughts. "I know the guy that owns the place next door wants to sell and I'm thinking of making an offer and rent it out until I can afford to attach the two places together."

"You should be proud of yourself," I said, and I meant it from the bottom of my heart.

I'd done nothing useful with my life and hated who I'd been for so long. Seeing what Avro made of a bad situation only gave me more determination to make better choices. What did I want to do with my life? Did I want to be a bar manager forever? Did I want to own my spot one day?

Avro turned to stare at me.

"I didn't get a chance to tell you, but Grimhead Crews's agent decided to have them do a second performance tomorrow night. Well, I guess that is later tonight now. Anyway, Allen said that social media is going crazy, which has given him a few more ideas for PR."

I rubbed my face, not sure how much more I wanted to be forced to hang around Jace Everly and his intense silver eyes that made my stomach toss and turn.

"Don't get me wrong, we made a killing off having him there, but he's just so full of himself, and...." I struggled to get out the right word.

"So, um...yeah, about Jace...." Avro started and then stopped when his doorbell rang. "Well, that was terrible or perfect timing," he grumbled. "I may have invited Jace over, too," he said, walking out of the room. My mouth fell to the floor.

"What? Why? What's going on?" I followed him down the stairs as the bell rang again.

Avro looked out the peephole and swore under his breath before putting his hand on the door. "I'm so sorry, it was only supposed to be Jace," he said, and opened the door.

Are you fucking kidding me?

There had to be at least twenty people outside. Members of the Grimhead Crew band walked in first, each with a pair of girls on their arms. DJ Club Chaos and his entire entourage were next, but the man at the back of the group had my earlier nerves bouncing around inside of me like a million hummingbirds. He seriously invited Jace Everly over? When? How? Why?

Jace stepped through the door like he owned the place, and it suddenly felt a whole lot smaller. Surprisingly, he didn't have a girl on each arm. Why that made me more nervous instead of less was a mystery. As the door closed, Jace pushed the hood of his sweatshirt off his head and there he was in all his sexy, arrogant glory.

"Party area is that way." Avro pointed toward the living room. "Feel free to wander and use any room except my bedroom. If I catch you in there, I'll toss you out," he said.

The group all seemed in agreement. At least they did now, but who knew what would happen once they had some drinks?

Jace stared at me as he walked by, and our eyes locked. My stomach flipped inside out at the memory of him in the storage room with me and the irrational feelings he caused. Unable to help myself, I rubbed my hands on my jeans like that would remove the feel of his chest from my memory.

There was something about Jace that sucked you in. My insides were a jittery mess, but I forced myself not to show any emotion. I lifted my brow in question as he continued to stare, silently asking what the fuck he wanted. Jace smirked and looked away. I was pretty sure I knew what he was doing, and it bothered the shit out of me.

As everyone fell into a comfortable groove talking or pouring drinks, I recognized the character flaw in myself. Socializing was something I rarely did, and I preferred it that way. Despite how much I loved my job, when the show was done and people were gone, I was happy to be alone. I couldn't remember if, as a child, I felt comfortable plunking myself down in the middle of a group and talking. It didn't matter what the topic was. I always felt uncomfortable in a group. The bar was easy. Something separated me from the crowd, and I knew what they wanted: alcohol. I didn't have to make conversation. I could just pretend to be someone else.

Avro pulled a release on the wall, and everyone cheered as the bookcase pulled out to show off a secret compartment. It reminded me of those fold-up beds, except this was full of DJ equipment. In seconds, the quiet house had turned into a loud party.

Staying just outside the living room, I quickly turned toward the kitchen. I needed a drink, and I wasn't walking in front of all those people to get to the alcohol.

I opened the fridge and stared at the perfectly arranged containers of food. They were labeled with the contents and the date it went into the container. Was Avro for real? This level of organization was intense. I mean, he kept his side of the bar looking immaculate, but I didn't realize his obsession stretched over everything until now. The entire house was the same way, and I was secretly envious. I could only imagine what he thought when he walked into my tiny bird house of a home. Would he faint when he saw my bedroom and my clothes hanging off every available space?

Other than two large bottles of champagne, there wasn't any alcohol in the fridge—just homemade fruit or vegetable juices. Closing the door, I stared at the stainless-steel appliance and wondered if I should stay or go. I wanted to spend time with Avro—the chemistry between us was there—but I was still waiting for him to jump up and yell, just joking. Like he would realize I was a walking mess and wouldn't want anything to do with me.

"Here, I made you this," Avro said, startling me as he stepped into the doorway. He looked sheepish as he rubbed the back of his neck. "Sorry, I should've given you a heads up about Jace, but I didn't want you to back out, and I didn't know about everyone else...shit, there's no excuse. I should've told you he was coming."

He'd removed the cat-eye contacts, yet I could still picture him purring as he begged forgiveness. I almost smirked as the CATS musical began to play in my mind.

"I may not have made the best decision, but you're here now, and I want to spend time with you. We don't have to go in there." He smiled wide, and I couldn't stay annoyed with him. "Forgive me?" he said and bit his lip. Was it hot in here?

"When did you and Jace become so close that you invited him over?" I took the drink, sniffing at what he'd made.

"Well, that's the other thing I need to tell you." He rubbed the back of his neck. "I actually know him really well."

"Come again?"

"We grew up together," he said, and other than the music in the other room, neither of us moved or made a sound.

"Did you know he was coming to the bar?" I was annoyed and hurt that he hadn't told me this sooner. I'd bitched about the man all day.

"Minutes before you did." He held up his hands. "I swear."

Did it really matter now? Maybe, no, yes, no. "I don't like secrets, Avro," I said.

"And yet we all keep the darkest and saddest parts of us hidden until we're ready, including you," he said, and I swallowed hard.

"Touché," I smirked. "It smells like peaches," I commented and took a sip. I closed my eyes as I tried to pick out what else was in the drink. This was a game we played when making new concoctions for the customers. "With a hint of banana and spiced rum."

"Not bad. Can you do that with every drink?" Jace's smooth-yet-annoying voice was loud, and I opened my eyes.

He was just behind Avro and seeing them standing so close to one another was picture worthy. I had the urge to whip out my cell-phone and have a fangirl moment, but that was so not happening.

Avro seemed totally at ease with a rock star in his home, which seemed odd regardless of their knowing one another. Who was this calm with a celebrity? Again, just another reason why Avro and I were on different levels. I should've set the drink down and said goodnight before I ended up hoping for something that was never going to be possible. All I could think was, why the hell was I here?

My eyes roamed over the two walking gifts to eyeballs every-where. They were pretty close in height and build, and the sensuality oozing off of them made me squirm. It was so hot all of a sudden that I had to grip the glass harder to stop myself from whipping off my hoodie to try and cool off.

"Most drinks. Avro has tripped me up a time or two, but I always get it right when I taste it," I said. Even though Jace hadn't said anything or given me the once-over that most guys did, it still felt like he was touching me.

"Would you prefer to sit in here?" Avro pointed to the table.

"Sure," I answered.

"You not into the party scene?"

I didn't want to answer Jace. In fact, I hoped he would turn around and walk away, but instead, he followed us to the table and sat down across from me.

Avro took the chair beside me and casually draped his arm on the back of mine. His presence was comforting, despite my attraction. He had a calm aura and a way of setting me at ease when I felt like I should be spinning out.

"I prefer the quiet after a long night of loud music," I said, sipping the drink that was a punch of flavor to my tastebuds I licked my lips and stared at the glass in wonder. "Wow," I said. "That is really good."

"I had the same thought," Jace said. I looked up to see him staring at my lips.

Avro's fingers touched my shoulder and squeezed like he was trying to comfort me, but I couldn't stop the jump from the light contact. "Don't push so hard, Jace. This was just supposed to be a get-to-know-us. She's not ready for all that," Avro said.

I was instantly transported back in time. I'd heard those words before when I was only fifteen. They pissed me off then and pissed me off now. No matter how long I'd known Avro, he didn't get to make those decisions for me. Wasn't ready for what? I was a grown-ass woman. If I wanted to jump out of a plane, I could. If I wanted to go partying at a sex club, I could. If I wanted to buy a gold car that cost more than I made in fifty years, I could. Not that I would do any of those things, but it wasn't the point.

"Don't give me that look," Avro said before I opened my mouth. "Getting you here without bolting down the street was tough enough, and don't deny it. I've been asking you to come over at least twice a week for months," he said, lifting a brow that made me squirm.

"So," I said, my back bristling.

"Fine, tell me honestly; do you really think you're up for what-ever Jace has planned?"

He tilted his head and stared at me, waiting for an answer. I would never know what came over me at that moment, but the second I opened my mouth, I knew I was fucked. Not only had I painted myself into a corner, there was a very good chance that Avro had prepped and pampered the pillow under my ass in my honor. I could see him in my mind holding out my favorite drink and patting the seat beside him while a little smile played on his lips that screamed, got ya.

"I don't know. Maybe I am." Easily top three of the stupidest things I'd ever said to date.

Avro's lips curled up exactly like they had in my mind, and I swallowed hard. His eyes were more intense without the cat-eye contacts in. They were naturally amber, and I loved the unique shade. Why he chose to hide them behind fake spring green and vampire red was beyond me.

My eyes flicked between the two men, and I knew I'd bitten off more than I could chew. Maybe it was an overreaction, but now that I'd opened my mouth, I wasn't backing down.

"Don't just say that because you think you need to," Avro said softly against my ear so only I could hear.

I sucked in a sharp breath, my body lighting up with him so close, and I squirmed in my seat. He smelled so good. He always did, but I wasn't normally close enough to pick up on the scent of a cool sea breeze and fresh citrus that made me want to bury my face in his neck and breathe deeply.

"I think she's lying, Avro," Jace said.

My eyes lifted to his, and it wasn't what he said or even how he said it. It was the look in his eyes. It was the same look I'd gotten from Kai many times.

"I am not." I clenched my teeth together.

"Oh yeah? Then prove it," Jace whispered, and the hairs on the back of my neck stood up. His eyes locked with mine, and I felt like I was trapped in a snare.

Avro glared at Jace. "Raine, you don't need to do this," he said softly, his fingertips brushing against my neck and making me shiver.

Jace leaned back in the chair and crossed his arms as he stared me down.

"Yeah, I do," I said. "It's time I stop running."

I had no fucking clue what I was signing up for, and maybe I should've asked, but all I saw was another guy telling me I couldn't do something, and I wasn't having it.

Jace smiled, the look sexy and terrifying at the same time as my pulse jumped. He slowly stood and looked down at Avro and me.

"Are you two coming?"

Oh fuck.

AVRO

Chapter 12

Avro

I held out my hand and didn't expect Raine to take it. It had taken me months to get her into my home or to spend more than a couple of hours after work relaxing. Today was a revelation, from the beach to the kiss and to now.

From the moment we met, I felt a tug in my chest. It wasn't just that she was beautiful, although she was. Raine had the best sense of humor and looked out for every employee who came through the door. She was patient and kind, and I'd seen her change so much over the last year as she worked at tearing down the walls holding her back. If asked, I knew Raine would say she was the ugly duckling. She had no idea how amazing she truly was. It had been painful to pretend for so long that I was only interested in her as a friend. I knew I couldn't push until now. I wasn't sure she was aware of the shift in her lately. I understood her even though she never said a word. I saw the same scars in her eyes that lined my soul.

My eyes didn't waver as I stared into hers. I could tell she was on edge. She'd put herself out there, pushing herself, but I hoped it was for the right reasons. I hadn't even had a chance to explain the relationship that Jace and I shared or how I wanted her to be part of our lives long term. Jace was doing what Jace did best, he pushed, but I worried that it would backfire.

Raine lifted the glass I'd given her and gulped it all down. I couldn't help but smile as she sat the glass down and placed her hand in mine. My pulse spiked with her touch. The hope I'd kept tempered bloomed in my chest as she stood.

"Coming?" I said, my eyes meeting Jace's.

"Better believe it," he said.

"Whoa, I'm...ah...you mean both of you, right now? But..." Raine started, but I wasn't letting her get this far and not at least shed one more layer to the protective walls she'd wrapped around herself.

Cupping Raine's face, I dropped my lips to hers and tenderly kissed her lips. I was met with tension and nervousness that I could taste on my tongue as she opened her mouth. Fuck, I wanted her so bad.

I wanted to sit her on the counter and fuck her until she was spent and passed out in my arms. As our lips moved together, I felt her take a shuddering breath, and her body relaxed against mine. I groaned as she opened her mouth, and I explored, tasting the sweet peach flavor that lingered. I was greedy and wanted it all. I wanted her to melt into my body, but that required trust, and I already knew that would take more time.

A hand grabbed my ass a second before Jace's lips found the side of my neck, and the feel of the two of them pressed up against me had my heart pounding like a trapped animal. This was my fantasy.

Before Jace was the big shot star, we were each other's person.

We still were. Best friends didn't come close to what we shared. Most didn't know that Jace grew up an hour from here. We lived on the same street, met in pre-school, and had been close since Jace punched a kid in the face for picking on me. Jace was also the first guy I was interested in other than girls. He was my first tentative kiss as I explored who I was and realized that my interest in him stretched beyond simple curiosity.

The real confusion came when I still found girls hot and dated them as easily as guys. Of course, my girlfriends I brought home; the guys were kept a secret except for Jace. My parents had no idea for years that we were anything more than best friends who played video games, rode bikes, and were on the basketball team together.

"Fuck, I've missed you," Jace whispered in my ear as he pressed his body harder into my back, pushing me harder into Raine. Our relationship had changed multiple times over the years, but one thing remained the same. We realized that no matter what, we couldn't live without each other.

Was it possible to be in love with two people at the same time? I hadn't known for sure until now, but my feelings for Jace had never diminished, no matter what part of the world he traveled to or how long he was gone.

Raine started as a fascination, this beautiful woman who dressed in the worst outfits, as if she were purposely trying to hide and never be noticed. But I noticed. I noticed everything about Raine. How her smile lit up the room, and her blue eyes sucked you into their pretty depths and made your heart beat fast. I also noticed that she had a big heart and found a way to help anyone who needed it. She was tough with a quick wit and was beyond talented, especially behind the bar. She was dedicated to anything she put her mind to, and she made me feel better, no matter the shit I had going on.

By my third month, I was more than fascinated, and by the end of the first year, she was the reason I never left Eclipse. Jobs came and went, but the people that made you feel whole, you hung onto them with both hands.

I needed Jace to want Raine, and Raine to want Jace. I wouldn't hide my relationship with Jace from her and try to sneak him in later. That wasn't right, and it wasn't who we were. It was both of us, or I had to choose, and fuck, I didn't want to have to make that choice.

Jace and I always had the same tastes, so with nervous anticipation, I hoped he found Raine as irresistible as I did. Then I had to pray that Raine wouldn't decide she'd rather punch Jace in the face, because he really loved to push those lines. It was his thing.

Jace coming back to town forced me to press things with Raine faster than I wanted. I hoped to lay out the entire situation and do dinner with them, but I should've known that would never happen. Jace had a style all his own, and he'd never been one to conform. I'd been talking about Raine for the last year, when Jace asked if I was in love with her. Of course, I told him yes, and he hadn't taken no for an answer about meeting her. Now apparently, he was going to see how far he could push her and there was nothing I could say or do to stop him other than throw him out of the house.

Raine didn't consider herself brave, but that was because she didn't see herself the way I did. Breaking the kiss with Raine, I admired her swollen lips and glassy eyes before turning my head to capture Jace's mouth. He was far more demanding, and his tongue immediately invaded my mouth as his hands roamed over my body. His kisses were always desperate. It felt like he was trying to devour every second we had together, a meal that would have to sustain him until the next time he passed through.

This wasn't the life I imagined for us. It certainly wasn't what I would've chosen, but it was the situation we were in currently. He was worried, or maybe jealous. I didn't know exactly, not that he ever had anything to worry about, but Jace talked his agent into letting the band do the show at the bar so that he could meet her. The show being a hit was just an added bonus.

His hand snaked around my waist, and Raine jumped as he slid it between our bodies. I broke the kiss and locked eyes with Raine once more. She was staring at the spot where Jace drew lines up my neck with his tongue as he teased me.

Raine's eyes held the desire I longed to see, but she was guarded.

"You still interested?" I lifted my brow. This was it, the moment of truth.

"I'm not sure. I thought the next logical step would be dinner or something. This is very lightning paced," she said. It might seem that way to her, but for me, it had been years of coaxing.

"We've eaten dinner at the bar after work almost every night for four years. We drank coffee and talked until all hours of the day and night as we discussed everything from a new routine to our dreams. Recently we streamed new movie releases on the screen in the bar when it was closed."

She smiled, the blush creeping across her cheeks. "You brought the popcorn," she said softly. Raine lifted her eyes from my chest. "You've been planning this a long time, haven't you?"

"Almost from the first day we met," I said, and her face deepened to a rose color. "I just didn't know how or when to tell you about my feelings or Jace, but I can promise that we won't make you do anything you don't want to do. If you want to stay in your clothes and just be upstairs with us, then that's fine. You want to touch us, but we don't touch you. That's also fine. You want to have a shower and pass out, then do it. All I'm asking is that you stay. Rip off a layer of the protective coating and take the leap."

I didn't want to give her the way out. I wanted to grab her hand, drag her upstairs, and make her scream as we fucked her senseless, and she begged to stay forever. We had a third in our relationship on a few occasions, but this felt different. I didn't want her to be a few nights of fun. I was desperate for Raine and Jace to get along. Adding her to our mix meant everything to me.

"Unless you're too scared," Jace said, lifting his mouth from where he was making a hickey I would have to cover later. I glared at him, but he completely ignored me. "You're sexy as fuck, Peaches, but you definitely don't seem like the type that can handle two men. Especially us. I think Avro was right. You're not ready for us. You may never be." He lifted his shoulder and let it drop. "No shame if you wanna go home."

Raine's eyes flared, and she narrowed her eyes at Jace. "Oh, really?"

I could feel her bristling, and the competitive edge she always had in spades at the bar was firing on all cylinders in her eyes.

Jace broke contact with my body, and I instantly missed his presence. There'd always been something about Jace that called to me, that had me on my knees begging.

He opened the fridge and smiled. "I do love your organization. I miss that on the road."

Reaching in, he pulled out the two bottles of champagne and the plate of chocolate-dipped fruit. Whenever Jace was in town, we made it a celebration. Those sexy-as-fuck eyes met mine first, then went to Raine. "Well, I don't see you moving to prove me wrong. Are you all talk?"

"Jace," I growled at him, but he just smirked.

Jace disappeared out of the room, and I knew that by the time we got upstairs, there was a good chance he would be fully naked.

I looked back at Raine. "I really want you to be part of this. Ignore Jace. Whatever you're good with is fine. He likes to run his mouth, but he'd never force you into something."

She bit her lip, and I could see the gears turning as those big blue eyes found mine.

"Alright, but no promises on how far I'll go, at least tonight. And,

Avro...." She paused, and her eyes grew serious. "I need you to know it's only because it's you that I'm willing to try this."

Nothing could've wiped off the smile that spread across my face. Her trust in me was intoxicating. Dropping my head, I gave her a quick kiss.

"Thank you, and whatever you want is totally fair. I did kind of press fast forward on us."

Stepping away, I took her hand and led Raine through the house, past the crowd well on their way to turning my sitting area into an orgy. I didn't mind Jace's band mates. Allen held auditions and hired them after Jace was signed, so I never got the chance to know them well. They rarely came over when Jace was in town, and I didn't ask if that was their choice or by Jace's design. All I knew was that I was gonna need to sanitize the shit out of my room, but that was tomorrow's problem.

"Can I ask a question?" Raine said as we walked up the stairs. "What do you call this that you have with Jace? I mean, after the beach and the kiss, I thought you wanted to date me, but I can't quite figure this out. Am I an add-on to a fun night for you two?"

I stopped walking as I realized just how oblivious she was. Had I really done that good of a job hiding my feelings, or had Raine not picked up on any of my flirting, teasing, and suggestive ideas?

"Raine, I wasn't joking. I've wanted you since practically the first day we met. Jace has been in my life for as long as I can remember, but if you're willing, I want to bring you into our relationship. It would be our relationship, as in the three of us."

Her eyebrows shot up. "Like on a regular basis?"

"Like permanently. As in, it would be the three of us from now on," I said. "When Jace is away touring, you'll have to settle for just me." I smirked at her. "But when he's in town, it would be the three of us."

"So no one else is involved? You're not going to come home with someone from the bar, and Jace isn't in another relationship on the road?"

I swallowed hard, and my heart pounded in my chest. "No, just us three from now on," I said.

Jace was going to kill me for suggesting that. We'd agreed on an open relationship until he was done touring. He could have those one-night stands, and I could date whoever as long as there was no permanent attachment of any kind. My prepping for this moment hadn't just been to make sure Raine wouldn't run for the hills, but that Jace would be okay with closing off the open portion of our relationship.

The only thing was, I hadn't mentioned it to him yet. He had no idea I wanted to make us exclusive. He was gonna be pissed—I knew he would be pissed—but I opened my mouth, and the words tumbled out.

He was gone for months at a time, with women and men throwing themselves at him constantly. I didn't doubt that he loved me, but I understood the temptation when isolated and alone, which was why we'd agreed to this type of relationship.

"Permanent...oh, wow. That's...that's definitely a jump from friends."

"Is that really how you see me? Nothing more than a friend?" My gut ached at the idea that the feelings I'd had for so long weren't reciprocated, and I'd built this entire moment up in my head to be more than what it was.

"Well...." She went a bright scarlet, her fair skin showing the blush spreading to the tips of her ears. She looked away from my eyes, sighing, and I stood like a statue, waiting for her to respond. "I have thought about us as more than friends, but Avro, can we please be real for a moment? You are not someone who dates someone like me. Other than admitting to myself that a girl can dream, the train stopped there."

"Girl, I am tired of hearing you put yourself down. Rule number one if we are going to be together." I held up my finger to make sure I had her whole focus. "You will no longer be allowed to talk shit about yourself. You're amazing, understand? Come on," I said, not giving her the chance to respond.

I tugged at Raine's hand, and she didn't resist as we wandered into my bedroom, and I closed the door. Jace wasn't completely naked, which was shocking, but he was only in the black, silky boxers I'd given him, sprawled out on the bed like he didn't have a care in the world. The shiny material did nothing to hide how hard he already was.

My eyes trailed over his body. I never got sick of the sight of him. Hard abs that made my mouth water and long, muscled legs with tattoos running down his thighs. He had his arm behind his head, which only accentuated his chest. Never mind the face. He was currently holding a chocolate-dipped strawberry above his mouth, tracing the bottom with the tip of his tongue. My cock jumped and was instantly hard.

I smirked as I glanced down at Raine, her mouth hanging open at the sight of Jace. I always had the same reaction to him, and it was comforting to see that it wasn't just me he affected.

"Keep drooling, Raine. I like it when girls make a mess of my cock," Jace drawled, his eyes intense with the same challenge as downstairs.

Raine's mouth snapped shut, and I quickly intervened. "Fuck, Jace," I growled, my eyes pleading with him to rein it in. "Why don't you go shower," I suggested.

"Huh?" Raine looked up at me as I pulled my T-shirt off and tossed it aside. Her eyes roamed over my body, and she bit her lip. All the pent-up energy I tried to control went straight to my cock, begging to be touched behind the fly of my jeans.

Instead of repeating myself, I guided her to the bathroom and pulled a couple of massive fuzzy towels off the stand, handing them over. "Have a shower and try to relax. We're not going anywhere, and I won't barge in on you," I said.

"Are you sure about this? I mean...." I laid my finger on Raine's lips to stop the litany of reasons she came up with to stop this from happening. I was sure she already had a thousand and would come up with a thousand more if I let her. Some may even be legitimate concerns, but I didn't want to hear about them right now. Whatever they were, they could all be worked out later.

"You're safe. This is a safe space. Now go shower," I said and closed the door as I walked out.

Jace and I already shared a secret shower together at the club. There was a changing area that was never used upstairs, and while everyone else was cleaning, he'd talked me into taking the edge off. Honestly, he could talk me into doing it anywhere. That was one of his superpowers.

Magazines everywhere would've killed for a photo of Jace Everly lying like this, mostly naked, with a bottle of champagne in one hand and a strawberry in the other. Tattooed sleeves lined his arms and looked dark against the creamy-colored sheets. The barely contained bulge had my mouth watering, but he just couldn't resist and took it an extra step. I watched as he tipped the bottle of champagne to his chest. The liquid looked like gold as it dribbled out and left a trail down his abs before it was caught by the black silk material. I groaned at the sight.

No matter how many times we'd been together, my reaction was always the same. How did I end up being the chosen one? Was this even real? When was the dream bubble going to pop?

"Oops, I'm making a mess. You better lick it off," he teased, eyes shining with mirth. There were two things Jace never lacked: arrogance and a sarcastic sense of humor. He used both very well to hide the softness of the man underneath.

"Asshole," I muttered as I kicked off the flip-flops I'd worn home.

"Maybe," he said, as his hand slid down to the front of the boxers to grip his cock. He groaned, and the sound called to me like I was on the end of a rope and he was pulling me in.

My feet moved of their own accord, and I barely remembered moving as my eyes remained locked on him.

I knelt on the bed, and my mind registered that the shower had turned on, which was good. It meant Raine was fighting her fears, and that made me very happy for her.

"Well?" Jace asked as he dribbled more of the champagne on his skin. I licked at his body, not wanting to miss a single drop, and smirked when a new line of goodness traveled down and into my mouth.

"Don't think I forgot you cornering Raine in the storage area," I said, then drew a wet line up his chest with my tongue.

"I don't expect you to. I wanted to see how she'd respond. You know me."

That I did all too well. He loved pushing all the boundaries, every single one of them. Drawing gasps and moans from Jace, I moved up and down his body until I was satisfied I'd gotten all the champagne. Swirling my tongue, I finally reached his lips, and this time I was the aggressor and made sure he remembered why he missed me. Why he didn't want to board the plane and fly off. We were both breathless before I finally broke the kiss.

"I missed you too," I said. "Tell me, do you like her?" I held my breath for the answer. Jace's eyes went to the bathroom door and then back up to mine.

"I think she's smart and sexy as hell. I also think she is exactly what we've always wanted, but I have my reservations." He glanced at the door for a second time. "She's terrified, Avro. The bravado is covering something terrible. You must see it."

"Yeah, I know, she...she reminds me of me," I said quietly, and Jace searched my face.

"That may be difficult to unpack," he said, his fingers trailing down my arm. "You ready for that? I'm not here to help you."

"Were you ready to help me when I needed you?"

He licked his lips. "Fine, if this is what you want, I'm willing to give her a shot. Something about her gets under my skin," he said.

Dropping my lips to his nipple, I licked at the droplet of champagne I'd somehow missed.

"Fuck yes," Jace groaned, his hand gripping my hair.

Jace would give Raine a shot. Now all I needed was to get Raine to see that this was what she wanted too. Easier said than done with all the fear she had bubbling under the surface.

Raine

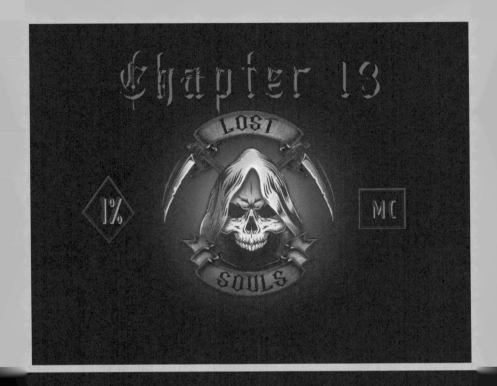

Chapter 13

Raine

The shower felt incredible. I was so caught up in the wide assortment of shampoos, conditioners, soaps, and all the other goodies that I almost forgot why I was in this shower in the first place. Almost.

My nerves were still happily jumping around and making me edgy. I had too many reasons now, and I couldn't seem to focus on which one was the most important. Laying my hands against the tile, I let the hot water seep into my back and run down my body.

Closing my eyes, all I could see were amber eyes and an equally sexy pair of silver. That was a fucking hot combination. Never mind the kiss that had me blushing and would've set anyone's underwear on fire. I may have lived in fear for a long time, but I wasn't oblivious

Hell, the way Avro kissed me was enough to have me begging for more. I could only imagine what his touch would do. Then there was Jace. I wasn't sure about him. He made every hackle bristle with his smart mouth and penetrating stare that challenged me all on its own. I trusted Avro. He made me feel safe and accepted. I didn't feel like I was some alien or freak when he was near me, so if he trusted Jace, I needed to try and trust him.

I was so curious about how they'd begun their relationship. I suddenly wanted to know everything. How did they meet? How long had they been dating? And most importantly, how the hell did you keep something like that secret? I'd never once seen Avro in a magazine, tabloid, or newspaper. He was the full-time love interest of the guy who'd just hit the cover of Sexiest Man Alive, and no one freaking knew but me and maybe his bandmates? Was that possible?

Stepping out of the shower, I quickly dried off and realized I had no spare clothes. Fuck, I didn't even have my regular clothes. I glared at the door as I realized Avro had snuck in and taken them, but at least he left a large black robe in their place. It served me right for not locking the door. I looked at the handle and realized there was no lock, then paused.

I hadn't locked the door. I hadn't even tried. I'd stripped naked, got in the shower, and wasn't worried about locking the door. I covered my mouth as a well of emotion burst inside my chest. That was massive for me. It needed an award. I felt like I'd just climbed Everest and reached the peak.

I made my way over to the massive, intimidating mirror, stared at my shocked, smiling face, and took a moment to think.

This was a big step for anyone. This could be a whole new chapter in my life that I hadn't even dreamed of, or it could be a disaster. Avro was my best friend. Shit, he was my only friend, and if this went wrong, I'd be losing the one person in my life that I'd learned to trust and even lean on.

On the other hand, here I was in my twenties with all of one experience to my name, and I knew it was time for me to try to move past it. I needed to make strides to find out who I was and what I wanted for myself within a relationship dynamic. Was that both of them? I couldn't answer that. I didn't even fully understand it yet, but I knew I wanted to be with Avro, and that meant I wanted to try.

My heart fluttered, and my skin got hot as I pictured them out there on the bed together.

"Seriously, what the fuck is up with this?" I clutched the counter hard and leaned over as I tried to steady my breathing. The thoughts of them made me lightheaded.

The voice in the back of my mind was screaming that they only wanted to use and embarrass me. I was nothing more than a joke. The logical part of my brain told me that Avro was a great guy, and I felt in my gut that he was the same decent person I'd always known. Hell, he'd practically dated me without me even realizing it and had never made me feel uncomfortable. That took skill and patience.

The kiss at the bar and stealing my clothes aside, he'd never pushed or asked for anything that I hadn't been ready for, and somewhere along the line, I'd begun to see him as more than a friend. Hell, I tried to convince myself daily that we were only friends, but the pangs of jealousy would stand up and call me a liar every time. I couldn't even remember when I first fantasized about him, watched him work, and wondered, *what if?* I'd needed to drink extra water and had been tempted to stand in the walk-in freezer to cool off after watching him dance.

So why now? Why was he suddenly whisking me off to the beach and kissing me in front of a packed house? There had to be a reason for the rush and showing me all this now and all at once. I looked up, and the answer hit me. Jace. Fuck, this was wildly complicated.

It was like elementary school, and I was the item for show and tell. At least that was how it felt, even if Avro didn't mean it that way.

The moment we knew Jace was coming to town, he'd been different. A little bolder and then he'd asked me out and kissed me in front of him. He was proving a point or showing me off, maybe. I wasn't sure, but I knew he was doing this because of Jace, whether Jace asked for it or not.

"Okay, enough thinking. You can do this," I said to myself, like I was giving someone a pep talk. "You're going to go out there and act like an adult, badass woman and fuck two men," I said, and I swear I watched my reflection take off out the door. "Who am I trying to kid? I'm not ready for that. I'll be lucky to get past kissing without having a coronary." I shook my shoulders and did a ridiculous little jog on the spot, like I was getting ready for the hundred-meter dash.

"Thank God they can't see this," I mumbled, then looked around the bathroom for a camera. "Okay, stop being crazy. Just walk out there. You've got this."

Grabbing the thick robe that was huge on me, I wrapped it tight around myself and tied it into place. Gripping the door handle, I took a final deep breath and opened the door. I froze as a very naked Avro kneeled on the bed, giving Jace the hottest blowjob I'd ever seen. Nothing could've prepared me for the stunning sight of these two men together.

My hands dropped to my sides, and my mouth fell open as Avro looked up, but his mouth never stopped working. I blew out a breath, trembling as a roaring heat spread throughout my body. My eyes followed his movements as his lips traveled up and down the long cock. I could feel my pulse in my throat, and my heart hammered inside my chest as the spark of passion flared into a raging inferno. I was shocked by my own wanton desire.

Jace was lying in the same position as when I'd left the room, but now he was fully naked, and Avro knelt beside him, facing me. Avro's eyes never strayed from mine, and I knew my face was bright red by now. I was so hot and turned on watching him.

"Fuck, that feels good," Jace groaned and leaned on his elbows so that I could see both of their faces clearly.

Jace's eyes met mine, and there was a smoldering heat so intense that it miraculously forced the temperature in my body higher. The house coat felt like too much clothing as I practically cooked inside the fuzzy material. Jace gripped the back of Avro's head and pushed down, forcing himself deeper into his mouth. Avro made a choking sound, and suddenly, the entire cock disappeared.

My hand instinctively went to my throat, and the earlier trembling became full-on body tremors. I couldn't decide if I was more excited by what I was watching or horrified that they wanted to do this with me.

"Fuck yes. Fuck, Avro," Jace's face darkened a moment before his head fell back, and he yelled Avro's name like there was no one for miles. His body jerked up, and I knew he was cumming. There was no denying it, as I rubbed my legs together, that watching the show made me wet.

Avro slowly lifted his head, his tongue drawing lines along Jace's shaft, and then licked the tip like Jace was a delicious treat. Those amber eyes turned to meet mine, and all the earlier courage I'd managed to muster took a swan dive out the window. Backing into the bathroom, I flicked the door closed and turned to lean against it. My hand clutched the fuzzy coat tight to my chest as I tried to calm the wild fluttering of my heart.

"Raine," Avro said a moment later, with a soft rap on the door.

I jumped like he'd pounded on it and gripped the material tighter as I stumbled away to sit down on the edge of the bathtub. I couldn't draw a breath and felt a panic attack coming on. I knew that if I kept it up, I was going to faint, and yet that didn't matter. My mind was screaming hysterically. It was like someone screaming, *Run! They're going to get you!* in my ear. What was it about panic attacks that left you spinning out of control? The harder you tried to stop them, the worse they became.

I didn't hear the door, but Avro was suddenly in front of me. His hands were on my knees, and his eyes locked with mine, but I couldn't understand a single word that came out of his mouth. It was all white noise, like someone had left a fan on, way too loud inside my brain.

Warm hands cupped my face, forcing me to stare into eyes that held so much warmth and compassion that they felt like a tender hug all on their own. He was exaggerating a breath in. I copied his action, and then he slowly blew out. I couldn't say how many times he made me do that before I could see without the spinning or hearing the loud hum.

"That's it. You're okay, Raine. I've got you. Just breathe," Avro said softly, and the sound of his voice brought tears to my eyes.

"I'm so sorry I'm ruining your night. I should go. I'm a mess, and I..."

"Shh, Raine. I said just breathe." He laid his finger on my lips, and I felt like such a fool. I couldn't believe that I'd had a panic attack over hot sex. I was completely insane. Anyone else would've run across the room and done a swan dive between them; yet here I was crying.

"I see your mind is still racing. Just focus on me and push all of that extra chatter aside." He cupped my chin, and even though I didn't want to, he forced me to keep staring into his eyes. "I said I've got you, and I meant it."

"But...."

"There is no but. I knew this would be hard for you and that you may not be able to follow through, but this is a huge step, Raine. You went from a few months ago not getting in a car with me to being in my home, showering, and sitting here in nothing but a bathrobe. From where I'm standing, those are massive strides."

I didn't say anything. All those things seemed so small and normal. They shouldn't be celebrated.

Avro smiled wide. "You kissed me in front of hundreds of people and went to the beach with me all alone. You came up here completely blind to what might happen. Raine, stop beating yourself up."

I shook my head. "Why do you even care? I've never told you what happened. I don't understand why you care this much."

"You don't understand because you refuse to see your worth. That needs to change. Second, I see in you the same emotional scars I carry around and battle every day. Even now, they creep up on me, but I've learned to control them, and you'll get there too," he said, and took one of my hands and placed it over his heart. "I was attacked and raped by someone that I thought I could trust. I see the same fear in you. You don't need to tell me now what happened, but I hope one day you will."

"Avro, I'm so sorry." I'd never have known if he hadn't said anything. He hid it so well. Something about the quiet admission made me feel more at ease. He truly understood and saw me. They weren't just words to placate me or calm me down.

"Don't be sorry," he smiled. "Here, I brought you this," Avro said. I looked to see what he picked up, and I laughed as I took in the fuzzy Minion pants and plain white T-shirt. "I knew you'd want your clothes clean for the morning, so I put them in the wash. Come on, stand up. I'll help you put this on."

He held my hand and helped me to my feet, and I couldn't explain it, but this felt like a monumental moment for me. Like I was finally finding my way off the roundabout I'd been stuck in. My heart swelled with Avro's nearness, and I was seeing him for the first time through eyes no longer tainted with crippling paranoia.

He helped slide the T-shirt over my head, and of course, it was way too large on me. As soon as it was in position, I let the towel fall.

Hanging onto his shoulders, I stepped into the sleep pants he held open for me and watched his hands as he tied the strings into a perfect bow.

"I bet you didn't think you would need to dress me tonight," I teased, my voice coming out as a whisper.

These last few hours had been the most intense I'd ever seen Avro, and when he laid his hands on my shoulders, I felt the weight of that gaze. "I would dress you a million times over again if it would keep you looking at me just like that."

My mouth curled up in a smile, and I couldn't stop blushing. Avro had that effect on me. I brushed it off at work, but here in this quiet moment, he wasn't performing for anyone. This was all him, the real him.

He ran his hands over my short hair. I'd kept it short since my attack. I could clearly remember the feel of the first guy's hand wrapping in the long length I'd been so proud of and pulling me back as I tried to run. I shuddered and pushed the image aside.

"I love your hair like this," he said, leaning down, his lips brushing against mine. "Will you lie with us to sleep?"

"Won't I just be ruining the little time you and Jace have together?"

"Do you mind if we play with one another?"

My mind drew a blank at that question. I'd never slept beside anyone other than Kai, and that was by accident while watching a movie or when I had a scary dream and would end up in his room on the floor. Kai would always be so angry when I did that and said that I was going to get him into trouble, but I just wanted to be close to him. He made me feel safe. Rather, he *had* made me feel safe.

To sleep in the same bed and then have them possibly have sex beside me sounded hot and all sorts of naughty at the same time. Surprisingly, I wasn't nervous about the idea.

"Is this normal?"

"You mean with three people?"

I nodded, and Avro cocked his head as he thought. "It's different for everyone." He rolled his shoulders. "Jace and I are very comfortable together and want you to feel the same. This shouldn't be a scary situation, Raine, or one where you are okay with me but scared of him." I nibbled on my lip as I thought about the teasers I'd already witnessed and knew I wanted to see more. "What does that mean exactly? That's open for discussion, but I can tell you that it means you can be with me or him or us together, and the same goes for us. There can't be any jealousy between us. That is the steadfast, hard, cut-and-dry rule. We have nothing if we don't have trust and are jealous of each other's individual time together."

My mind was reeling. This was a lot to toss at someone when they had a ton of experience, let alone me, who had none. What I did know was that I wanted to try. His confidence in me made me want to try.

"Okay," I said, and the smile that spread across Avro's face made it feel like everything in the world was rainbows and cotton candy. It was a lie, though; the world was far from that, but that was how he made me feel.

Avro linked our fingers together as we walked out of the bathroom. Jace was under the covers with his arm casually tossed over his head while the other lay on his abs, which always seemed to be flexed.

"Raine has agreed to sleep with us, but that's all for tonight," Avro announced, and even though I knew it wasn't his intention, it sounded like I was a kid coming over for a sleepover. I groaned as Jace's lip curled up like he was thinking the same thing.

Those inquisitive silver eyes found mine. "Alright, but if I want to fuck Avro, I'm going to," he said, and the image of Jace doing just that flashed before my eyes.

Damn, that image was hot. Maybe I was being corrupted, but I was already along for the ride. Unlike Avro, who asked if that would be okay, Jace just proclaimed he would do what he wanted. My eyes flicked between them, understanding their personality types and getting a glimpse of their dynamic. I nodded, not trusting my voice.

I thought for a moment that Avro would put me between them, but he lay down in the middle as we got on the bed. He held the covers up, pulling me into his body as I climbed in. He was so warm to the touch. I always bundled up when I went to bed with flannel pants and thick socks, sometimes a sweatshirt, but with the thin cotton material, the heat from his body soaked into mine. I sighed, and my muscles relaxed as I let myself be snuggled for the first time.

So this was what it felt like to be the little spoon. I flinched as an extra hand touched my stomach. I knew it was Jace, his hand was warmer, and his fingers were firmer. I couldn't see him or his hand, yet it felt like he'd just commanded us to stay put. Biting my lip, I was so tempted to lift the blanket and look at the two hands holding me.

"How do you feel?" Avro whispered, his breath fanning my ear.

It took a moment to assess myself because I didn't understand the subtle sensation that had taken over. I was never entirely calm; it always felt like I was looking around for a threat when there wasn't one, but right now, there was none of that.

"I feel...relaxed, actually. This is the safest and most peaceful I've felt in years." As I said the words, I let the truth and weight of them into my soul. It was as if one of the scars smoothed out and became whole once more.

"Good." Avro kissed my neck and found a way to cuddle closer. I was dwarfed by his tall frame, and I loved it.

For so long, the touch of another human had been terrifying, and a single tear trickled from my eye with the realization that there was hope for me yet.

Chapter 14

Kaivan

I didn't know who I was going to kill first. The rage at seeing Raine go home with that bartender was bad enough, but then the fucking rock star and his friends showed up. From my hiding spot, I'd glimpsed the three of them going up the stairs together. No one else did.

I'd stayed all night, wide awake and ready for any sign of movement. The first to leave as the sun came up was the larger group of people who had stayed somewhere on the lower level. I didn't give two flying fucks about them. My stomach complained that I hadn't eaten anything in twenty-eight hours and thirty-two minutes, but my stomach could go fuck itself as well. We'd gone longer in prison. It could handle a day now.

The black car, with blacked-out windows, left at 4:17 p.m., and watched it head down the street toward the bar. I waited until it was far enough ahead and with vehicles in between to pull out. I was seriously considering investing in a small nondescript car. I did enough stalking that it would certainly be helpful and a shit ton less noticeable than either of my bikes.

I followed them into a lower-income area with small homes that reminded me of birdhouses. Each one was painted a different color but hadn't been kept up. The lawns were cut, but most of the grass was yellow or just dirt, and the house the car pulled up to was not much better.

My eyes tracked Raine as she got out and jogged up the steps and into the house alone. I could kill the guy in the car. Just walk up and shoot him now. No, that was my irrational anger talking, and besides, the fucker did me a favor. I now knew where Raine lived, and as soon as the car left, I could sneak in and teach her a proper lesson.

That fucking car never left. Nope, it stayed there until she came back out. She had changed into a new outfit and carried a bag. A bag big enough to hold multiple nights' worth of clothing. My jaw cracked as I ground my teeth together.

She got back into the car, and I swore as it started back my way. I parked in a driveway with a truck and stayed on the bike with my jacket collar pulled up until the vehicle was long gone.

Not wanting to be seen later, I circled the area, learning all the potential hiding spots I could use to access the home, and then went past the bar. Sure enough, the sedan was in the parking lot, and my anger took on a life of its own.

Then Mannix called, and now here I was, as angry as a bear woken up during hibernation.

"Are you fucking joking?" I seethed.

My hand cracked down hard in the middle of the guy's face. Blood coated my fist and sprayed me with each new blow.

"Man, take it easy. The guy is dead already," Roach said. "We have a couple others you can spend this energy on instead."

My fist stopped mid-air, and I stared down at the mangled face. "Fine, lead the way," I growled, pushing myself to my feet. I wasn't even close to being tired. In fact, I was just getting warmed up.

"You know you're just making this a harder clean-up job, right?" Roach said as I reached where he was leaning against the wall, watching the show.

"Don't fucking care. You either get me fresh meat, or I go back to what I was doing," I said, eyeing Roach. He held his hands up like he was surrendering.

"Geez-us man, don't look at me like that. You freak me the fuck out." Roach pushed away from the wall of the beachfront property and led me down the hallway toward the bedrooms near the back. He pushed open the door, and two more guys were sitting on the floor, with their hands and feet tied up as they sat back-to-back with wide silver tape covering their mouths.

They started to beg for their lives, the sounds muffled through the tape, but I could understand them. They stopped when their eyes traveled from Roach's face to my bloodied shitkickers, and up to my face. In cartoon fashion, their eyes went wide at the same time. That's right, fuckers. Death has found you tonight.

"Gentlemen, let me introduce you to Snake. He's our enforcer, and he's just a little pissed off," Roach said and signed dramatically. "He really doesn't like it when people hurt those in our club." He lowered his voice to a whisper. "He scares me." Roach shivered, and the guys looked like they were going to faint.

"I found one more hiding in the carport. Stupid idiot tried to run out in the open, but he didn't get far," Mannix called out, but I was barely paying attention. "What the fuck? Did we use a sledge-hammer on this guy's face?"

"Naw, just Snake's fist on a rampage," Roach answered and casually chewed on the end of a toothpick.

"Can I do whatever I want to them?"

I stepped farther into the room, and a moment later, Mannix pushed a third man through the door. As soon as he saw me, he tried to turn and run. My name and reputation held weight in more than just the MC circles. I'd done jobs for the Mafia, casino owners, and politicians who didn't want to get their hands dirty. I went after those who disrespected or hurt family members of the MC, but I was more than an enforcer. I'd graduated to gun-for-hire for the right price and the right favors.

"No, no, no, please," the guy said, who was trying to find a way out the door that was now filled with a wall of muscle as Mannix and Roach blocked the way. "Please, I didn't do it. I swear to God that I didn't touch Kitten," the guy begged.

I had no idea why we were here to begin with, and it honestly didn't matter. Mannix said he needed my help and to meet him here. Teach these guys what it meant to mess with Lost Souls' property. He wanted an example made out of them, which was like ringing a dinner bell in front of my face.

I yanked the one guy off the floor. He tried to scream through the tape and writhed around like that would make me let go.

"Yes, you can do whatever you want, Snake, but we need to be out of here in two hours and not a minute more. That guy Chase calls the Dragon is coming to make sure this property is..." Mannix looked around and shrugged. "Burnt to a crisp."

"That crazy psycho?"

Mannix and Roach lifted their brows at me. Probably not the best choice of words as I stood holding a knife to a man's throat and looking like I was auditioning for the lead in *Carrie*.

"Well, now, that doesn't leave me much time, but it will have to do." I ran the knife I was holding across the man's throat. He began to choke as he collapsed to the ground.

The man sitting on the floor dropped to his side and tried to roll away as I reached for him. That was the funniest shit I'd seen in a long time. He turned onto his stomach and used his face and body to inchworm toward the door.

Where the fuck did he think he was going?

"Please let me go, please. I'm telling you the truth, I never touched Kitten," the last man to join the party begged—sniveling sap.

"Which one is Kitten's father?" Mannix asked, and the guy pointed to the man trying to make his grand escape one inch at a time.

"Are you lying to me?" Mannix asked as he stared down at the guy begging for his life. Mannix always looked big, but today he looked like a giant beside the scrawny man.

I slammed my boot down in the middle of the inchworm's back as he reached the door. It was humorous for the first few seconds, but now I was just annoyed. I kept him pinned there while Mannix questioned the captive that didn't have tape on his mouth.

"No, no, I'm not lying. I never touched his daughter. He was the only sick fuck who did that," the man said, throwing the other one under the bus and letting us drive over him.

"But you are Steve, right?" Mannix asked, pulling a picture out of his pocket. He tapped the image and I couldn't see the photo well, but I knew the answer was yes just by the way he hesitated. He looked at the photo and then up into Mannix's eyes as if weighing what would be the wise answer.

"Um...well, yeah," he finally said.

"So you helped assault Kitten's underage friend, just not her? In a way, you still hurt one of the Lost Souls family," Mannix drawled, and I knew he was playing with the guy. He was never getting out of here, even if he said that he was the next coming of Christ.

"Um...I...I didn't know her friend was underage." Steve pointed to the man on the floor. "He said she was legal when I started fucking her," he blurted out, and Mannix's nose flared, his steely eyes turning hard as stone.

He leaned down closer to Steve, who wisely took a step back. "I didn't even know that part. She was too embarrassed to tell us exactly what happened, but thank you for the confirmation." Mannix was quick with his long knife. He stabbed Steve three times before the guy even registered that something was wrong.

In prison, you learned to work fast and kill faster. There was no hanging around or making it fun and drawn out like this. You killed your target, and you moved on.

Steve stumbled back and stared down at the red seeping into the front of his crisp white dress shirt. I would've killed these fuckers simply for what they did for a living. Fucking rich assholes always thought they could get away with anything. It was highly possible that if I'd been born into a wealthy family or had a rich lawyer, I wouldn't have ended up behind bars wasting the ten best years of my life.

I watched Steve fall to his knees, then sighed and looked at Mannix. "You just fucking killed my fun."

"You still have one. Besides, we don't have time for you to kill two," Mannix said, his voice calm. "You tend to dally." He wandered over to Steve, who was sadly still breathing, his mouth gaping open in shock.

"Dally? Like, as in dilly dally? What the fuck? Are you suddenly eighty?" Roach snorted as Mannix glared.

Mannix kicked out, and his massive shitkicker found the underside of Steve's chin. The sheer power sent him flying but also

knocked him out cold. Now the asshole would die peacefully on top
of it being quick.

"There, now you can focus on the one." He flicked his fingers at
me like he was shooing a child. "Go on, get going. Take out whatever
the fuck this is that's crawled up your ass on someone other than us,
you ornery bastard."

"Fine, but for the record, you're no fun."

Putting my knife away, I bent down and lifted Kitten's father,
who had tried to inch his way to freedom. With a heave, I tossed the
pencil neck over my shoulder and marched out the back door. One
nice thing about rich people, they liked space. I guess that was one
thing we did have in common. I tossed the guy down on the beach.
He made an oomph sound as he hit the sand. Taking a moment to
arrange him so that he was facing the water, I yanked up hard on his
arms tied behind his back, and the muffled scream was like a sweet
lullaby as his shoulders dislocated with a loud pop.

Tears welled up in the man's eyes as I looped the rope holding his
bound wrists over the fence post, and he hung there looking like a
pathetic scarecrow. I worked quickly, cutting off the dress shirt,
pants, and boxers. Taking a step back, I had to wonder what made
someone hurt their own kid. He looked like a typical middle-aged
dude.

There was nothing nefarious about him. There was no sign
hanging around his neck that said, 'I like to rape little girls.' Had I
looked like the type who would? Was that why they locked me up
and tossed away the key? Was it because I'd been in and out of
homes in the foster care system until I landed at the Collins' with
Raine? Was it because I'd gotten into fights at school, was born into
an MC family, had tattoos by the time I was seventeen, or had a
father already in prison? Was it just expected I'd be the same? The
joke was on them, because I wasn't until they locked me up.

Was that what they'd seen in me over this plain, nondescript guy? I couldn't help wondering what would've happened if it had been this douche with his crisp white shirt and polished shoes.

Didn't matter now. My justice would be so much worse than anything that ever would've happened on the inside. Yeah, he may have been laid over a table or two, but other than that, he would've survived. They liked to keep weak asswipes like this around so that they could have some easy fun or pawn off chores.

"Pwease, pwease don' 'ill me," he mumbled through the tape.

"And why exactly shouldn't I kill you?"

He mumbled apologies. From the little I'd been heard inside, this guy assaulted his own daughter, and they said I was an asshole. Kitten was Kickstand's house mouse. His family had taken her in a bit ago, but it was only recently that she'd confessed to them what had happened to her. We took hurting our members seriously, and that included everyone.

I gripped his chin in my hand. "Don't worry. The devil looks after his own. I'm sure you'll have a perfectly toasty seat to perch upon in hell." I smirked, the humor never reaching my eyes, as I stepped back and thought about what cut I wanted to make first.

The screaming began as the first cut was made. I glared into his eyes as I slowly sawed back and forth through the flaccid cock hanging between his legs, then held up my prize like I'd caught the biggest fish of the day.

"You weren't packing very much, were you? How did Kitten even feel this little thing?" I stretched it out like I was playing the accordion in front of the man to see.

I knew he vomited in his mouth, but it had nowhere to go, and I watched his face go green as he tried to swallow it back down.

"I hope you didn't eat too much," I said. "Would be a shame if you had a lot of seafood. Lobster and scallops coming back up would be nasty with its half-digested stench that fills your mouth and nose like it was already rotting." I already knew they'd been dining on a fancy lobster dinner by the remnants left in the kitchen.

Right on cue, he puked again, and I stepped back as bile was forced out his nose.

"This seems like a fascinating way to drown," I said, and laid the cock down on a rock so that I could continue my work.

By the time I was done, I was thoroughly impressed with what I'd accomplished in a short period of time. Mannix and Roach were walking along the path to where I displayed my pièce de résistance.

"What the fuck, man? I swear you get more sadistic with every passing day," Roach said as he screwed up his face at my work. "And I'm very fucking happy you like me."

"You just have no appreciation for a dramatic flare," I countered.

"That is certainly dramatic," Mannix drawled, his eyebrow cocking in my direction.

I looked back down at the man I'd decapitated, gutted, and set his head between his legs with a cock sticking out like his tongue.

"In all fairness, you said earlier that this man should be forced to suck his own cock, so really, it's your fault," I said and shrugged.

Mannix rolled his eyes at me. "Is whatever brewing in you settled down now, at least?"

"No," I growled out and clenched my knife harder.

"Wanna share?" Roach asked, crossing his arms.

"No."

"Are you safe to travel with?" Mannix asked, and it was my turn to stare at him like he was crazy.

"I'm pissed off. I don't have rabies."

"Are you sure about that? I've wondered for a long time if one of those rats in prison got to you," Mannix said and smirked.

I picked up the butt I'd smoked and smoothed the sand around the asshole's body. The guys took the hint and stepped onto the hard path as I made sure no print was left behind. I'd been very careful and was even nice enough to sanitize the cock before I shoved it in his mouth. Probably more than the girls, he decided to rape got.

Mannix handed me a towel and wet wipes to clean my face like we'd just eaten chicken wings and not killed four men. Putting everything in a bag, we marched around to the front of the house just as a nondescript white van pulled into the driveway. My hand instinctively reached behind my back for my gun when Mannix shook his head at me.

The guy that stepped out of the driver's side was a little taller than me and was almost as ripped as Mannix. His unusual lagoon-colored eyes found mine from under the shadow of the black hoodie, and I knew without asking this was Derek West. Chase started referring to him as the Dragon after Ava had called him that. I hadn't taken her seriously. I mean, it was hard to take anything that girl said seriously, but as it turned out, she wasn't far off the mark.

Fire followed this man like blood did me. We were one and the same in many ways, and true to our natures, neither of us spoke a word.

"We're done, and don't worry about the body in the back. He's kind of a message," Mannix said. "Feel free to cook all around him in case we missed anything, and here, can you destroy this as well?" Mannix held out the bag.

There was only a subtle nod from Derek as he took the bag and marched for the front door. I didn't see any tools and couldn't help wondering what he would use to start the fire. You would think it took longer to engulf an entire house in flames, but for this guy, it was only as long as it took for us to make our way the quarter mile down the beach to where our bikes were stashed.

Looking back over my shoulder, I saw the smoke rising steadily into the air in long black torrents while the glow of flames flickered through the trees like a fiery beast. The plain white van passed us before we got our bikes pulled from the shadowed corner of the life-guard tower. We all paused to watch the Dragon drive away.

I didn't know where he came from or how Chase had met him, but he was one motherfucker I didn't plan on messing with. I'd seen what he did to the Reaper's hideouts. In one night, he killed more of their members than we had in a couple months. Even Chase's rampage couldn't compare to the fatalities. Derek West was more demon than human. That was high praise from me.

"Don't expect me back tonight. I have things I need to take care of." I left them staring after me as I rode back to where Raine worked.

She wasn't getting out from under my wrath that easily. I had a score to settle, and I was just getting warmed up.

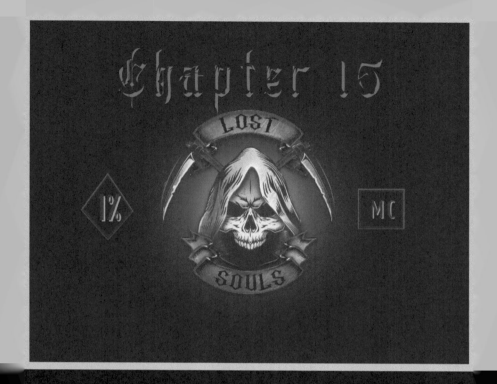

Chapter 15

Avro

I gripped Jace's hip with one hand and reached around to stroke his cock while I had him bent over. I stopped to play with the ring in his tip, making him shudder with just a touch. I loved that reaction. The sounds he made had my own body ready to explode. We were too pent up to head back to my place like this. We both needed this release after cuddling all night with Raine and not taking things any further.

Jace hadn't tried anything, even with me. That told me he was trying to respect Raine's boundaries and issues, but I also knew it wouldn't last long. He wasn't a patient guy, and if I didn't help him take the edge off, he'd bend me over the bed all night to prove a point.

I groaned as my cock surged and swelled at the thought of him taking me again. I'd already sucked Jace off, but as soon as he came, he ordered me to fuck him hard. Who's going to say no to that invitation?

"Shh," I said, as Jace's moans grew louder in the small shower. "The walls aren't that thick."

"Feels so fucking good," he mumbled between my thrusts.

"You want it harder?"

"Yes, I'm so fucking close again," Jace said, and I smirked.

"Do you cum like this for everyone?" I slammed home hard, the sound echoing.

"No," he groaned.

"You sure about that? You didn't sound certain. If you can get it better elsewhere...." I smirked as Jace glared over his shoulder at me. I took that moment to pick up the pace, and his eyes rolled back, his mouth hanging open. "You didn't answer. Should I stop?"

"Don't you dare fucking stop. You know you're the only one I want."

I smiled wide and looked down to where my cock disappeared inside his ass. He felt incredible. That was the only word for how Jace made me feel with every touch. He always had. Closing my eyes, I let myself go, and there was no holding back.

"Holy fuck, yes," Jace yelled, and I was too lost in my own pleasure to care that everyone downstairs may have just heard me fucking Jace Everly. Trying to keep our relationship secret was a full-time job.

Where anyone else would wear it as a badge of honor and try to get themselves in a tabloid, I wanted nothing to do with that. The stardom, screaming fans, the red carpet, and fancy afterparties were his thing. What we had was ours alone. It was our private time to be who we really were and love one another without putting on a show.

Whenever he came to town, he always took different ways to get to our place. He never got caught up in any drama, so the paparazzi never chased him around waiting for their next big photo. Anything they did for publicity was always staged, and his manager would invite all the photographers. It didn't matter that it was fake. The pictures sold, which was all they cared about, so they left Jace alone the rest of the time.

Draping myself over his body, I clapped a hand over his mouth as he got louder. He groaned behind my hand, and his body shuddered a moment before he came. I couldn't hold back any longer and released his cock for him to finish off and gripped his hips with both hands.

My head fell back, staring up at the ceiling as my body pushed past that glorious peak. I opened my mouth, silently screaming, as my body went rigid with the powerful release that gripped me in its clutches. Legs weak and wobbly, I stumbled back and leaned against the tiled wall, trying to catch my breath.

Jace recovered first, turning to face me. I couldn't get over that this man was mine, and I was terrified that I would ruin it with the next thing I asked of him.

He molded himself to my body until no part remained untouched and bit my bottom lip.

"Fuck, I love you," he said.

There was a sadness in his eyes that I understood all too well. We only had a few more stolen hours, and then he was gone again. I hated it. Every damn second he was gone, I yearned for the next stolen day or night, but I would never ask him to give up doing what he loved. Music had been a lifeline for him during a very dark time, and he was amazing. His talent needed to be shared.

Cupping his face, I kissed him hard and tried to convey every last bit of emotion I felt into the kiss. "I love you too."

Our eyes locked, and neither of us moved, trying desperately to stop time, just for a little longer. Swallowing down the fear lodged in my throat, I held Jace tighter like that would help convince him to say yes.

"What is it? Something is wrong. I can tell by the way you're looking at me," Jace said, his muscles tensing. "Are you breaking up with me?"

My mouth fell open. "Are you crazy? No, of course not. I've told you before that you're stuck with me until I die or you get sick of me, whichever comes first."

His lip pulled up, and his teasing eyes shimmered. "Okay, then, what's wrong? I know you well enough to know when you're holding something back that you don't want to say."

"I can never hide anything from you." Grabbing the soap off the shower stand, I squirted more than I needed in my hand and began cleaning Jace's body.

Jace gripped my chin, his eyes commanding the answer.

"I'm scared to ask this of you," I said honestly.

"Scared? What the hell would you have to be scared of?" His brow furrowed with confusion.

"That you'll say we're over. You'll say I'm breaking one of our rules and decide that life with me is no longer what you want."

Jace stepped back but placed both palms on the wall by my head. His muscles flexed, and he looked exactly like the dominating ass he could be. I'd seen this look more than once, especially when he thought I was being stupid about something.

If there was one thing Jace was not known for, it was tact. He had none, not even a tiny bit. If he thought you were an asshole, he told you to your face, just like that. If something tasted bad, sounded horrible, or in this case, was stupid, he told you. He would never make it as a politician, so it was a good thing he preferred singing.

"Did you get hit in the head?" I smirked and snorted. "Seriously, Avro. I've been in love with you since we were ten. Do you really think I'm just going to walk away now because you asked for a favor?"

"You haven't heard the favor," I countered.

"All right, what is it? What is so terrible that you think I would want to end us?" He crossed his arms over his chest and leaned back. I licked my lips. Damn, he was sexier every time I saw him.

I took a deep breath and jumped off the proverbial diving board into the deep end. "I want us to go exclusive with Raine," I blurted out. "And I may have already told her that you'd be exclusive with us," I finished in a rush and then waited for the explosion.

"I'm sorry, you want what?"

Sighing, I rolled out my shoulders and stood up straight. "Jace, I'm tired of the different partners coming in and out of our lives. I'm tired of seeing you all over the world with people other than me or someone of our choosing on your arm at parties. I'm simply tired of seeing you a grand total of twenty-five days a year."

I ran my hand through my hair. "I love you. I love you with every-thing I have, but I want more, and I'm lonely all the time without you. I know that I promised we wouldn't have this discussion until you were done with tour commitment, but...." I held out my arms. "It's how I feel, and I don't know what to do. I wasn't searching for Raine, but she's everything we ever wanted, and I fell in love with her."

Jace held up his finger, his eyes hard as he stared at me, which did nothing to comfort me. "Let me get this straight. You not only want to add a permanent third person—someone you decided on before speaking with me or letting me meet her any of the other times I was in town, to our relationship—but now you want me to travel the world alone without any form of physical interaction with anyone at all."

"Jace...."

"No, I'm not done. While I'm doing that, which you already

know is supposed to be for another two years, you are back here playing house with Raine, and I get zoom calls. To make this worse, you already promised her, someone not even in our relationship, before speaking to me. You do see what an asshole move this is?"

When he said it, it sounded like I was being a selfish jerk. In my head, it hadn't sounded the same way at all. Leaning back against the tile, I crossed my arms and stared down at his thigh, tattooed with our names in the intricate artwork.

"Fuck, I screwed up. I'm sorry." I shook my head. "I don't know what to do. I don't know if I can last another two years like this. It feels like getting stabbed every time you have to leave."

"Is that what this whole thing with Raine is? If so, then just come with me. You don't have to be in the spotlight, but we can spend every night together," he said, reaching out and placing his hands on my shoulders.

"No, my feelings for Raine are real." Taking a chance, I gripped his waist, and that fact he didn't immediately jerk away from my touch gave me hope.

"You know I've dated, done the one-night stands, and all the other hollow, empty things we said we would do to experience life. I may sound like I'm being a selfish asshole, but I've never lied to you, and I'm not going to start now."

Jace looked away, and panic pierced my heart. "I don't know if I can do what you're asking, and it really burns my ass that you made all these plans, like my opinion no longer matters to you. Like I don't matter to you." His voice broke like he might cry, and the sound gripped my heart. I never meant for him to feel like he didn't matter.

"It wasn't like that. I swear, Jace. I love you more now than I ever have, and of course, your opinion matters." I took a deep breath. "I just sort of blurted it out when I was talking to her last night, and I couldn't take it back. Now that I said it, I don't know if I want to." Placing my hand on his cheek, I forced him to look at me. "I shouldn't have excluded you from any of these decisions. For that, I'm so, so sorry."

"But you want things to change, right?"

I bit my lip and nodded.

"Fuck, Avro. I don't want to promise you something I don't know if I can keep," Jace said, backing up to the other side of the shower stall. The water was cooling off and mirrored the chill running through my body.

"Are you saying I'm not worth it? You don't want to be with just me or me and Raine?"

His eyes narrowed as his anger flared, and I felt it coming before Jace opened his mouth.

"Don't you dare turn this around on me. You know I have no problem being exclusive. We've been exclusive before, and if you remember, we chose to have this open relationship together when I signed the contract to go on tour. Do you remember that conversation? The one where I spoke to you before making a decision," he growled as he narrowed his eyes and clenched his teeth like he was chewing on glass.

He put his hands on his hips, and I knew what was coming. I'd set myself up for this. "In fact, I'm pretty fucking sure it was your idea to have an open relationship. You even set our timeline to settle down and find a third person after my contract ended. Is any of this ringing a bell?"

"Yeah," I said.

There was nothing else to say. He was right. I was the one going back on the carefully thought-out rules and plans we had put in place so that we didn't end up in an argument just like this.

But that was before Raine came into my life, back when I was supposed to travel just as much as he was. I talked to Jace as much as possible, but he was still only here two days a month. What the hell was that? It was nothing, a speck of time. I stayed in bed, staring at the ceiling, dreaming about his touch, and holding a pillow, wishing he was with me. It wasn't his fault I'd found our third, but I hadn't planned any of this. I didn't know if you could plan when to fall in love with someone. Raine and my feelings for her had snuck up on me.

"Fuck." Jace grabbed the soap bottle and scrubbed down like he was as pissed with the soap as he was with me.

I could only watch him. I knew if I tried to touch him while he was this angry, it would only escalate the situation. We'd been there before.

"Fuck." He rinsed off and stepped out of the shower, pulling a towel from the pile. "Fuck!"

I lifted my eyes to look at him as he whirled around to face me. "I guess...see if Raine will come over again tonight, but Avro, what you're asking is a fucking piece of shit move. I need to think." He yanked on his clothes and left, the door slamming behind him. I slowly sank down against the wall.

Had I just ruined us for good? For nearly seventeen years, we'd been together in some form of relationship, and suddenly it felt like I couldn't breathe. I loved Raine, and I loved Jace. What the hell have I done?

Chapter 16

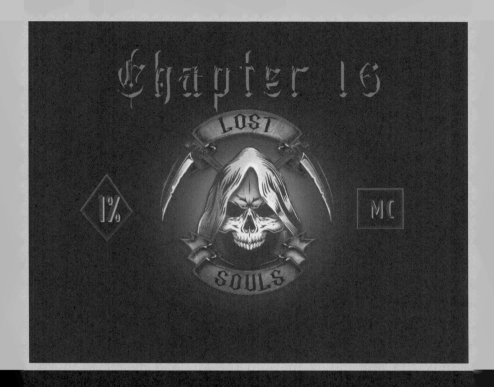

K aivan

    If I thought I was angry before, then I didn't under-stand what real fury was until I watched Raine once more get into the black sedan after work and head in the opposite direc-tion of her home.

    I knew where they were going this time, and I wasn't sitting around seething and doing nothing. Nope, this time, I was going to use this infuriating inconvenience. Pulling my bike out onto the street, I drove toward her small home. It was exactly three-thirty-three in the morning when I pulled onto the walking path that led to the park across from her house. The witching hour and I planned on doing a little dark magic myself.

    Pushing the bike behind the overgrown shrubbery, I took the keys and chained the wheel to the fence. There were shady people around, and you could never be too safe. I smirked at my own joke. As long as someone wasn't trolling with bolt cutters at this hour, my baby was as safe as she was going to get.

Pulling on my black hoodie, I stuffed my hands in my pockets and wandered up the street. I was just like everyone else around this spot, up to no good, but I didn't want any trouble. Blending in was something I excelled at in prison. Once I learned the art of not being seen, it was game on. Every opportunity I got to prove that I could've escaped, killed someone, or even stole items without being seen, I did. I wanted to hone my skills and make sure that I could put them to good use when I got out.

That was the thing about prison. It didn't really help to set anyone on the right path. It simply gave us more skills and contacts. By the time we got out, we were pissed off enough that we didn't care if we ended up back inside. Besides, who the hell is hiring a guy fresh out of prison for rape? Not many, which is why meeting Mannix and him induct me into the MC had meant so much. I wouldn't have had a pot to piss in if not for him.

Glancing around to make sure that no one was peeking through a drape or walking down the street, I turned to follow the path to Raine's backyard. I had no idea if she lived alone, but the house was dark, so it was worth the risk.

The backyard was similar to the front. Overgrown with weeds, but not a blade of grass could be found in the dirt. A single chair was on the cracked and weathered patio, but aside from that, there was absolutely nothing. I pulled my small bag of tricks from my pocket and turned on the miniature flashlight. Holding it between my teeth, I worked at the lock. It was surprisingly sturdy for a shitty little house.

It took a lot more time than I anticipated, but I finally got the door unlocked. I hadn't met a lock yet that I couldn't pick. Reaching out with my gloved hand, I slowly opened the door and looked around for an alarm system. I didn't think she had one. No little sticker in the window acting as a ward or any extra wires, cameras, or lights, but it was always best to be safe.

Moving to the front door, I also checked there for a security panel before relaxing. It felt strange to be inside Raine's personal space again. The last time was when I kissed her, setting off a chain of events I never saw coming.

I knocked on Raine's door, and she looked up from the book she was reading. Fuck, she was pretty. I hated that I thought my best friend, who was off-limits, was hot. It was a blessing and curse that we lived in the same house.

My birthday was yesterday, and it was bittersweet. I was now an adult, and I would be heading out into the world to forge my own path, as the lame-ass Mr. Wright would say. But it meant I was leaving Raine, and she was still considered a teen for two-years, two-weeks, and one day. So it was a good thing I was going to be moving out, because every day was a temptation. She was who I dreamed about at night. Raine was also the star of my dirty fantasies, and I knew I'd break if I stayed. I would end up doing something that would get us both in deep shit.

"Hey, Tink, can I come in?" I held out the last piece of my cake and two forks. "I bring a halfway decent cake with way-too-sweet icing but a surprisingly decent jam filling."

Raine laughed, and it made me smile. No matter what, she could always make me smile. "That was a heck of a sales pitch. Not sure you're going to make it as a used car salesman, but I'm sold on the okay-but-not-so-great cake."

Walking in, I paused to close the door most of the way. I didn't dare close it fully, just in case we were found in here alone. My unusual meetings with Mrs. Collins had become more frequent the last month, and she insisted I see her at midnight. I had to refuse because of my fight later. She looked pissed at me, and I wanted to stop, but I felt trapped between a bad spot and a fucking worse one.

If I told someone what was happening, there was a good chance they would think I was just some horny teen who took advantage of Mrs. Collins. If she told her husband, I was a dead man. My best option was to move out, go to school, and never look back.

"You okay?"

I lifted my head from the heavy thoughts and winked at Raine. "Yeah, of course. Why wouldn't I be?"

One adorable shoulder lifted and fell. "I don't know, but you haven't seemed very happy lately. I miss my teasing Kai, who would make fun of the fact I have my hair in pigtails and call me his Tink."

I laughed. "They do look dorky," I teased. "Just a lot on my mind, I guess," I lied. I hated lying to Raine, but I couldn't tell her what was really going on in my head. I stuffed a forkful of the cake in my mouth and chewed, not really tasting it.

I couldn't help staring at her. She was lying on her stomach, feet swaying back and forth in the air. Raine was small for her age, which made her look younger than she was. She was obsessed with pink. I hated the color, but of course, it looked amazing on her. Today she had on a cotton candy-colored tank top and shorts, showing way more skin than I should notice.

"You going to eat any more?" Raine asked, breaking me out of my thoughts.

"Naw, you go ahead. I have a fight later. That much sugar will make me feel sick," I said.

"I don't think you should go," Raine said softly before polishing off the last of the cake.

She pushed herself up and maneuvered so she was sitting beside me but facing the opposite direction. Wrapping her arms around her knees, she nudged me, and my heart jumped around in my chest as she stared into my eyes.

"Tell me you won't go, at least this once. I didn't mean to, but I saw your side earlier when you were changing." Her eyes flicked down, and her cheeks pinked. "You had your door open. I wasn't spying or anything, but I saw the bruises."

Her eyes lifted to mine, and I don't know what came over me, but I leaned in and kissed her softly. Raine's eyes went wide, but she didn't pull away, and before I knew it, I was cupping her face and kissing her hard. God, she tasted so sweet, so perfect, exactly how I imagined.

A strange desperation had taken hold of me, and I didn't want to let her go. I didn't want to leave her here in this house while I went off to school. She was the only thing that made me feel like I wasn't just the kid who watched his mother die or had his father carted off to prison for murder. When I was with her, I wasn't the asshole that got into fights at school, and I wasn't the guy everyone thought wouldn't go anywhere. She made me want to be better just by being her.

"Stop, stop," Raine said.

Hands hit my chest, and my eyes snapped open. I stared down into Raine's eyes in confusion, trying to remember when I pushed her down onto her back or how I ended up lying on top of her while we kissed.

"Shit," I swore and pushed myself onto my knees.

As soon as I did, Raine jumped up, tears in her eyes. "I'm sorry, I'm not ready."

She bolted out of the room and down the stairs so fast that I didn't even have time to form a sentence.

"Son of a bitch," I growled out and punched the floor as hard as I could. What the fuck had I just done?

My hands touched every surface. From the top of the television to the soft grey pillows on the couch. I looked at the small framed pictures she had, but there were none of Mr. and Mrs. Collins or anyone I recognized. I pulled the frame off the wall and opened the back to find nothing but the original image that it came with from the store. I looked at the photo of the fake smiling family, and my brow furrowed.

I couldn't say why this bothered me, but it didn't feel like the Raine I'd known. The girl who had made art out of rice and pop-top tabs and it still looked fantastic. She had posters on every wall and kept the most ridiculous pictures of us that I wanted to throw away. She kept everything and loved life. I looked around, and the room seemed empty and void of all emotion.

Putting the image back exactly how I found it, I went up the stairs. My heavy boots creaked on every step like I was in a haunted house. Well, if anyone else were home, they sure as fuck knew I was here now. The place was as tiny upstairs as it was down. There was a linen closet that looked like it could hold all of one set of sheets. A bathroom you could barely walk into and turn around without hitting your elbow on the shower stall, and two bedrooms, if you could call them that. I wasn't one for expensive things, but even I felt claustrophobic in this place. The roof was old, low, and angled, so I could only walk three-quarters of the way into the room before ducking or hitting my head.

Taking my time, I opened her nightstand drawers, but there wasn't much, other than a couple of magazines and a book. I was closing the drawer when I recognized the cover of the book. It was *Flowers in the Attic*, the same book that Raine had been reading the day that I kissed her. Lifting it from the drawer, I opened to the first page. I wasn't sure why, but I kept flipping pages, then turned the book to fan the pages toward the floor. A picture fluttered to the ground.

Dropping the book back into the drawer, I leaned down and picked up the photo. I didn't need the little flashlight to know what I was staring at, but I shined the light on it, anyway. There we were, two happy, smiling kids. This was Raine's fifteenth birthday, and I had taken her to the movies as her gift. Her arm was wrapped around my waist while mine was draped on her shoulder. I remember how it felt to have her pressed up against me. She smiled up at me, and my hands shook with the torrent of emotions the image dragged to the surface.

I sat on the bed and couldn't peel my eyes away. I ran my thumb over her face and remembered how excited she'd been when I grabbed a large popcorn and drink for us to share. It hadn't been a super scary movie, but Raine had always jumped at the tense spots, and more than once, she'd grabbed my hand until I linked our fingers together for the rest of the show.

Turning the picture over, I read the writing that simply said, Kai and me on my fifteenth, and there was a little heart drawn. How did we go from this to one kiss and one year later, Raine accusing me of rape?

I gripped the picture, ready to tear it in two, but my fingers trembled. I couldn't do it. It felt like I would be tearing apart the only good memories I did have. That thought hurt as much as her accusation. Instead, I put it into my pocket and stood from the bed.

Making my way over to her dresser, I opened every drawer, not sure what I was looking for, but I kept looking anyway. The next one I opened had a wide variety of black underwear. Picking up a pair, I held them up and groaned at the thought of seeing her in these.

Fuck, stop that shit.

I dropped it into the drawer and slammed it shut. Finished with the drawers, I moved on to the closet and still came up with nothing. She had like ten outfits to her name. I had more clothes in my closet.

"What the fuck, Tink?" I mumbled. "You have to be making coin at that place. What are you doing with it all?" My fingers played over the cheap metal hangers, bare except for a few sweatshirts and T-shirts.

Leaning over, I sniffed the black hoodie closest to me, and I could still smell the lingering scent of her body wash through the clothes detergent. I turned in a circle and spotted a backpack stuffed in the back corner of the closet. Pulling it out, I looked inside and whistled low. It was filled with money and rolled clothes. I knew a go bag when I saw one. Why the hell did she have this?

Putting it back, I marched out of the room and jogged down the stairs. There was only a single closet, two-piece bathroom, and a living room. The kitchen wasn't much bigger than those Easy-Bake oven things she used as a kid. Raine was always trying to talk me into sitting with her while she baked a cake. It was oddly sweet, and I could clearly remember her squeezing frosting out and swirling it around like a professional before she'd shake on sprinkles. I quickly wiped that memory from my mind, but they were never gone for good. She was always there in the back of my mind, the memories quick to surface.

Hiding the flashlight, I slipped out the backdoor and relocked it. I didn't know what I expected to find, but the sparse and impersonal home I'd just walked through was not it. It seemed like she was ready to pick up and run at any moment, and maybe she was. Maybe she only stayed in one spot so long before moving on to the next.

It wasn't a terrible way to live. I could picture having a big RV, cruising the countryside, and picking the next stop by closing our eyes and placing a finger on a map. I had no idea why I was getting all nostalgic about Raine, and that could've, should've, would've been crap.

At the end of the day, the past was what it was, and she did what she did, and I was now who I was. The guy she tossed into jail was dead. I was what had emerged from the cage, and I was a whole lot meaner, and a whole lot pissed off.

Raine

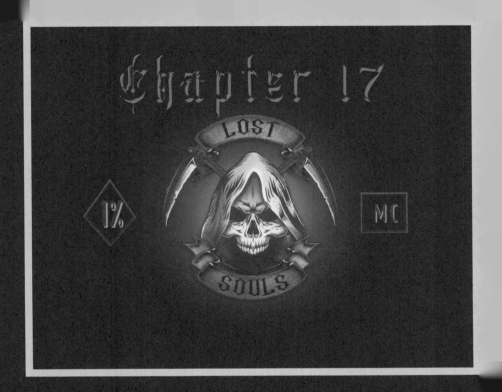

Chapter 17

Raine

To say that things were tense tonight was like saying the ocean had water. Jace and Avro barely spoke during dinner and kept staring at one another like they were communicating with only their eyes. It was a totally different vibe from the relaxed breakfast we'd shared, filled with waffles, mimosas, and laughter. I'd even teased them both and asked questions to learn more about how they'd started dating and how Jace liked touring.

But now, it was like they body swapped with two different people. I'd agreed to come over again and see if I felt any more comfortable, but I was beginning to wonder if I should've just gone home. I picked at the rice I was eating and finally couldn't take it

"Can someone please tell me what's wrong? I can cut the tension between you two with a knife," I said.

Both men glanced my way and then went back to eating. Fed up, I stood, prepared to call an UBER to go home. I had no interest in staying around this all night long.

"Where are you going?" Avro asked as I went to the door to get my shoes.

"I'm going home. Whatever you two have going on isn't going to be solved with me here tonight," I said.

Avro met me at the door and held my hands to keep me from putting my shoes on.

"What do you think you're doing, Avro?"

"I'm sorry, and we don't mean to make you feel like you're stuck in the middle. We had a disagreement earlier, and..." He sighed. "We need to figure out the details, but we want you to stay. I'll put the argument aside if Jace is willing to do the same."

I looked between Avro and Jace, who lifted his head from staring at his equally barely touched food.

"Yeah, that's fine." Jace's eyes swung to mine. "I'm sorry," he said, but I couldn't tell how he actually felt.

Nodding, I dropped the shoes and walked back to the table to sit down. Avro seemed more like his normal self, but it was hard to tell with Jace. I didn't know him well enough.

"I found a new song for a new routine if you want to hear it," I asked Avro.

"Why don't you use one of mine?" Jace interjected before I could finish.

"We usually use something that is...." I started and looked to Avro for help.

"Silly, I guess, is the best word." Avro shrugged as he popped a strawberry in his mouth from the plate in the middle of the table.

"Yeah, silly. That's a good word. I mean, we can use one, but I didn't think you would want one of your songs turned into a drinking game," I said.

Jace shrugged. "That's fine, whatever. It was just a suggestion," he said in that same monotone voice. He seemed dejected and maybe hurt. I stared at him as he pushed his rice around. That was enough of whatever was going on.

"Okay, that's it. Tell me what the fight was about," I said.

Avro started to answer, but I stopped him with a hand on his arm. "No, I want to hear it from Jace."

Jace leaned back in his seat and crossed his arms. "You really want to know?"

"Jace, please," Avro pleaded, and I could tell he just wanted this whole topic to disappear, but we were past that, or at least I was.

"Let him speak, Avro, please."

Sighing, Avro stood and walked to the sink. Jace's eyes followed him with every stride. "Fine, you want to know, here it is. We're arguing over what gaming console to get."

"I'm sorry, what?" I asked, not sure if this was the truth but pretty sure it wasn't. I was positive it had something to do with me, and I had no intention of coming between them if that was the case, but a game console?

"Yeah, I want a PlayStation, but he wants an Xbox. You see, we play when I'm on the road, but we've only ever had one type, and now he wants to change it. I prefer to keep the same type for a couple more years, so I don't have to relearn all new games. Anyway, what do you think?"

I couldn't tell if this was some veiled argument, but the look on Jace's face was serious as he leaned on the table and stared at me.

"I'm not sure I'm qualified to answer this. I've never had either, but if the fight makes you this angry, then..." I glanced over at Avro, who was now leaning against the counter. "Maybe don't change," I said tentatively.

"Ha, don't change. Love that response," Jace said, and Avro rolled his eyes.

"Yes, but the old system sucks when you're on the road," Avro argued.

"Only for you," Jace countered.

"It's been three years of bad connection and terrible service. It's time to try something new," Avro argued.

"Wow, three years? Okay, I might have to agree with Avro. That's a long time to put up with a horrible system," I offered and then wondered why I'd asked in the first place. This was the strangest argument ever. Was this a guy thing?

"But I like my old system. It works well for me, for now," Jace said, leaning back in his chair. "I'm more than happy to learn any system you want once I'm home more."

"Maybe, but it feels like it is slowly killing me. Nothing ever feels right, and I'm always panicked for the few moments that there is...a stable connection," Avro said.

Jace groaned and pushed himself up from the table to pace the room. This all seemed very dramatic for a gaming system. I knew people got into it and chose sides and their favorites, but this was more intense than I'd ever pictured.

"Okay, new idea, hear me out," I said, and they looked at me. "Maybe it's time to try something completely new and go with a Nintendo Switch." I smiled. "You know, get some of those interactive games, and it would be new for both of you."

Avro and Jace looked at one another and laughed. Just like that, the tension evaporated.

It was the first laugh I'd heard from either of them all night. Avro walked over and held out his hand. "Who knows, maybe you're right, but I'm not sure arguing over it anymore tonight will make a positive decision."

Slipping my hand into Avro's, I stared at him and then looked over at Jace before standing. "For whatever it's worth, I don't think you two should argue over this."

My heart skipped a beat as Avro slid his arm around my waist. "Oh yeah, and why is that?"

"I haven't spent much time with the two of you together, but it's easy to see the love you have between you. One console or the other, it doesn't matter as long as you get to be with one another. Isn't that what's most important?"

"And you," Avro said.

"Me?"

"Yeah, I told you I want you to be with us long term, so the console decision includes you, too."

I lifted a shoulder in a shrug. "I can't make that decision. I've never played with any console."

Jace snickered and walked over to where we were standing, a smile pulling at the corner of his mouth.

"Well, that's going to change very soon," he said, his voice sounding like a soft growl and just as suggestive.

My heart went from sputtering to full-on freakout mode as Jace held out his hand for me to take as well.

"Come on. It's time for you to step out of your comfort zone." He tugged on my hand, and my feet felt like lead weights. Jace cocked one of those sexy eyebrows at me, and I shivered as he ran his thumb over my bottom lip. "I didn't take you for someone who backs down and gives in to her fears. Was I wrong?"

I swallowed around the throbbing worry in my chest. Stubbornly, I straightened my spine and rolled out my shoulders. "No, I'm not. At least not anymore. Lead the way."

Jace smiled, and Avro squeezed my hand. His pace was quick as he practically dragged me out of the room and up the stairs. With each step, my courage wavered, but I refused to give in to the anxiety that had repressed me for years. We barely made it over the threshold of the door to Avro's bedroom when Jace whirled around, and in a move that I hadn't been expecting, he gripped the back of my neck and dropped his lips to mine.

I sucked in a shuddering breath as the butterflies in my stomach exploded into fireworks. Everything with Avro was easy and calm. Even his kisses, which left me breathless and made me feel safe and warm. There was nothing safe about Jace. He demanded the kiss from me, taking over all my senses like they had forgotten how to function.

I realized I must have let go of his hand, as he was now cupping my face, and I was pushed backward. With a thud, I came into contact with the wall, and my adrenaline spiked, but instead of wanting to run, I moaned and allowed him to deepen the kiss. I felt something touch my tongue and realized that he had a stud in his that was textured with little rough spikes. It wasn't painful. If anything, it was turning me on more as my mind quickly imagined that tongue in other places.

Was I really kissing Jace Everly? *The* Jace Everly. Where had I made the wild left turn to get to this moment?

Jace released my face but didn't let up on the kiss igniting a fire within me. I jumped when his hands found my waist, and he pressed his body into mine, trapping me against the wall. The adrenaline coursing through my veins made me shake and want to run for the door or, hell, maybe run to the bed, but my decision was made when my body chose for me.

Wrapping my arms around his neck, I hung on through the storm he had created. His hands slid around my body to cup my ass, and with a small yelp, I was lifted up, and my legs wrapped around Jace's waist. I opened my eyes and didn't see Avro anywhere until Jace laid us down on the bed, and I realized he was already there waiting for us.

Jace released me from the intense kiss that had stolen my breath and left me speechless like my brain had completely misfired. Turning my head, I found Avro's heated stare, but Jace touched my cheek and forced me to look back into his silver eyes.

"You only look at me right now," Jace ordered.

I swallowed and nodded. He moved, and my body finally realized I was under his weight. He must have seen the spark of real fear within me. Jace waggled his finger back and forth in front of my face.

"There is no room for fear in here with us. It doesn't belong, and I won't tolerate it."

I arched an eyebrow at him.

"You won't tolerate it?"

"No, I won't. I wouldn't allow it with Avro, and I won't with you."

If there were ever a pair of eyes that could command you into agreeing, it was Jace's. I was tempted to quip back, and I didn't understand why, but the challenge in his eyes made me want to push back and agree at the same time. Dropping his lips to mine, he sucked my lower lip into his mouth, and the sassy comment on the tip of my tongue was lost to the taste of his mouth.

I moaned, gripping his shoulders as he writhed back and forth against me. Taking my hands in his, he moved them so they were above my head. The old vulnerable feeling was there, but it felt different this time. I was still standing on the edge of a cliff and could fall either way, but the choking sensation didn't take over. It felt more like I was riding a wave as he pressed his hips into me, and the friction hit all the right places.

"Do you know what I'm going to do to you?" Jace asked, his lips barely touching mine but still holding the same commanding air.

I shook my head. Words were lost to me. Jace smiled, and that only made me swallow harder. It did nothing to ease the tension.

"How about this? I'll tell you what I'm not going to do," he said, smirking, his lips flirting upward. "I'm not going to fuck you. Neither of us will fuck you, but you will watch us."

I licked my lips, and the sensation of wanting more and hating being told what to do pushed to the front of my mind.

"You're not going to fuck me, even if I wanted you to?"

"Not even if you begged on your knees with my cock in your mouth," Jace said. His voice was casual, and holy fuck, that was the hottest thing I'd ever heard. My breathing skyrocketed through the roof, making my nipples rub against Jace's chest.

"Are you sure you could hold off?" I asked, with the blooming urge to defy and push him.

Jace laughed, and I bit back the moan that wanted to escape with the movement of his body. "Peaches, I like your fire, but you don't have the skill to make me cave...yet."

It was a slap in the face, and worse because he was right. I was out of my league and treading water, my arms flailing about, but not really knowing how to swim. I was relying on water wings or maybe one of those floaty boards, but I definitely had no idea what the hell I was doing.

He dropped his lips to my ear and made a sound caught between a groan and a growl. "But that doesn't mean we don't plan to teach you, because I crave seeing that happen."

Shifting, Jace lay beside me, and like a dance that needed no words, Avro moved in close to my other side. My body came alive between one heartbeat to the next as both their hands touched me. Avro snaked his hand under my T-shirt, his fingers rolling my nipple between them and making me gasp.

His lips found mine when I turned my head. He was like taking a deep breath of fresh air after holding it for so long. I felt the flick of a button and heard the pull of my zipper. I broke the kiss with Avro, only to arch my back and whimper. Jace was quick to slip his hand down the front of my jeans and swirl his fingers against my clit.

Avro gripped my chin, and once more, I was kissing him. I so badly wanted to touch him, but Jace firmly held my hands above my head with his one hand.

"Oh fuck, you're wet," Jace whispered in my ear. "Are you hot for two hard cocks?" I'd never had anyone talk like this to me before. "You want to touch us, don't you? Your hands are itching to feel our skin, explore our bodies, and taste our cocks in your mouth. Am I wrong?"

His fingers were like magic as he moved my panties aside and slipped his finger inside my pussy as he nipped at my ear.

"Oh my god," I cried, my body demanding more now that they'd stirred something deep inside me.

"Answer me. Do you want to touch our hard cocks, Peaches?" He groaned as his finger pushed deeper. I was quickly coming undone at the seams. "You want to hold them in your hands, stroking us, making us cum all over you?"

Avro had somehow got my shirt up, and I opened my mouth to answer Jace when Avro's mouth found my nipple. The hot sucking with his unrelenting tongue sent another wave of ecstasy racing through my body. A pleasure that I'd never understood and had been too terrified to explore.

Gasping for air with all the sensations, I could feel my body rushing for orgasm. Then suddenly they stopped. They didn't just stop. Jace stood from the bed, released my hands, and Avro rolled off the other side.

I had no idea what they were up to now, but I rubbed my legs together, trying to relieve the ache throbbing between my thighs.

Jace's eyes found mine as Avro stepped up to him. They looked like a painting.

"And now you get to watch, Peaches, because naughty girls who don't answer my questions don't get to cum," Jace said, his eyes filling with a dark, erotic edge that made me shiver.

All I could think was, *oh my.*

AVRO

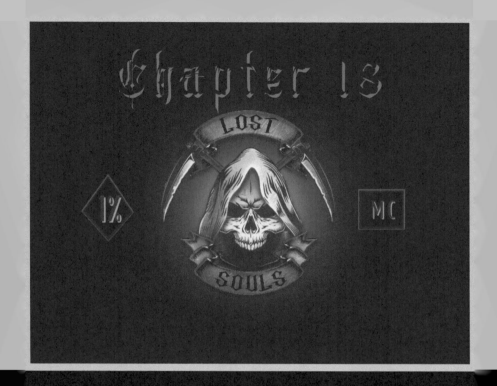

Chapter 18

Avro

Jace may not have said that he was all in on my idea but the way he looked at and spoke to Raine were all cues that he was giving it serious consideration. Jace didn't waste time he didn't have on people who didn't interest him. The world knew an entirely different Jace. On tour, he became the man that took what was needed to satisfy his hunger, then showed them the door.

Raine stared up at us, her big expressive eyes showing how much she wanted to see the show. Jace had a way with people. I could've said the same thing, the same way, and it wouldn't have had the same effect. I whipped my T-shirt off over my head and cheekily tossed it at Raine. She smiled as she grabbed it out of the air and

She looked like she was caught between being the naughtiest girl in the classroom and the girl in the front row offering the teacher an apple. Scratch that. She was the naughty one who gave the teacher the apple before corrupting them. She had no idea the power she wielded in those eyes. Jace wouldn't try unless she interested him, and the mischievous glimmer on his face as he copied me and pulled his shirt off to fling at Raine said he was very interested.

I was still looking at Raine when Jace grabbed me and pushed me up against the wall. I loved it when he took control like this. He was always commanding, but when he went the extra step and stripped me of all control, it made me melt. I craved it from him. At one time, it scared me just like Raine, but now I couldn't imagine him any other way.

"Oh fuck." I groaned as his kiss went from hot to I'm-going-to-burn-you-up in the blink of an eye. My body was on fire, and as his hand cupped my cock through my jeans, I almost dropped to my knees.

Jace broke the kiss and stepped back, undoing my jeans before he grabbed for the button on his. It gave me enough time to lean over and use my tongue to play with the bar pierced through his nipple. I loved playing with his piercings and loved even more when he shuddered under my touch. There was nothing about him that I didn't love.

He'd started as my friend, then became my best friend, which slid into crush, then dating, and finally, what we were today. There were bumps and issues along the road as we navigated who we were and what we wanted, but we'd been inseparable for years. Jace knew all my secrets and deepest fears, and I knew his. I wanted more than anything to get to know Raine the same way, for her to look at us with the same love that I felt for her.

Abandoning the button on his jeans, he ran his fingers through my hair and gripped it between his fingers. I groaned and sucked harder, drawing an aggressive sound from Jace that rumbled in his chest.

The room swam as Jace's hand found my cock through my open zipper and stroked along the hard length. Lifting my head from my teasing, I glanced at Raine, still as a statue on the bed, but her eyes were pure desire. Jace quickly finished undoing his jeans and kicked them off, leaving him deliciously naked.

My eyes roamed over him like I was seeing his naked body for the very first time. Broad shoulders cut with muscle but not too bulky, chest and abs that were equally tight. His legs could've been used for any men's magazine, and finally, his cock, which was standing straight out from his body.

The artwork that spread out along his legs and arms stood out on his fair skin, but it was the glint of metal in his pierced cock that had me getting on my knees in front of him. A droplet of pre-cum sat on the tip of his cock, and with a quick swirl of my tongue, I licked him clean, taking my time to play with the piercing. Jace groaned as the tip of my tongue moved the ring back and forth slowly before sucking just his head into my mouth. I did it again and again, knowing that it drove him insane. It always did. This was his favorite tease. Feeling him shudder under my touch spread molten lava in my veins. Everything about him made me want to beg for more.

"Take your shirt off," Jace ordered, and I looked up at him, confused. His eyes were focused on Raine, and I slipped the tip of his cock back into my mouth. I could see Raine out of the corner of my eye, and she was slow to move. "Did you not hear me?" Jace asked, and I sucked him a little harder to keep him from leaping onto the bed. "I said take your shirt off."

His hand found the back of my head, but he didn't press, at least not yet. Raine moved on the bed, and I could see her hands shaking as she slowly pulled her T-shirt off over her head and set it aside.

"Good. Now the bra," Jace said.

It was such a fucking turn-on to hear him barking out orders like that. I rubbed his balls and then licked down his shaft until I could take one of them in my mouth, making Jace gasp.

"Oh fuck, that's good." He groaned and spread his legs wider for me.

"Come over here," I heard him say and knew it wasn't me he was talking to this time. I continued sucking on my prize before switching to the other one. "Don't look at me like that. I know how fucking wet you are and how much you want to touch me. So get over here, now."

Fuck, he was hot. This was what I was missing by not bringing Raine in sooner. Maybe she wouldn't have been ready, or maybe she would've been our third a long time ago, but the missing link was Jace. He pushed. He wasn't mean, but he wouldn't put up with not being listened to, and I was better at soothing.

"That's it. Good girl, Peaches," he said, his voice dripping with praise.

His fingers dug into my hair before he wrapped his hand around my neck to pull me closer. I closed my eyes and sucked harder on the sensitive area. Jace groaned and shivered, and the sound went straight to my aching cock.

I started to stroke my cock, but Jace snapped, "Avro, don't touch yourself. I didn't say you could."

My hand froze mid-stoke, and I ached so badly to be touched that it was a battle to force each finger to let go.

Raine gasped and then moaned. I couldn't see what was going on from this angle, so I quickly switched positions so I could watch the two of them as well. Licking Jace like he was my favorite treat, I watched the two of them kiss while his hands tweaked her nipples and cupped her tits in his large hands.

Breaking the kiss, Jace looked down at me. "Keep sucking. I didn't say you could stop."

My cock twitched, but I kept my hands on his thighs, so I wasn't tempted to disobey. Not that a punishment from Jace was ever a bad thing, but that was a game for another night. I moved my attention back to the tight balls and sensitive area right behind that I knew he loved to have licked.

"Touch me," Jace said, and my eyes flicked up. I smirked at the expression on Raine's face. She timidly reached out and placed her hands on his shoulders, and I snickered as Jace stared at her hands. "No, touch my cock," he said, and her face flamed a bright red.

"Oh...I...um...."

"What do you think it's going to bite you?"

"No, it's just that...."

"That what?" He waited for her to answer, but no words came out as she looked between the two of us. "You're touching me. I'm not touching you. You're the one in control. Now touch me." Raine licked her lips. "Do you want to leave?"

"No, I...."

"Then touch me," he said again, less aggressive this time but somehow sounding just as in control.

I held my breath as I waited to see what Raine would do, but just like every other time Jace challenged her, she met the challenge head-on. Reaching out, her hand wrapped around his shaft. I moved out of the way and slowly stood.

For someone who obviously didn't have much experience, she stroked Jace like she knew exactly what he liked.

"Fuck, that's good," he groaned. "Now him as well," Jace said, and I turned to make it easier for her. Before Jace could bother scolding me for helping, I kissed him hard and stole the complaint from his mouth.

I shivered as her small, cool hand touched my cock, which felt like it was on fire in comparison. Her stroke was soft at first, and I gripped her hand and applied more pressure, so she knew how much I liked.

"Holy hell, you two are hot," Raine said. We broke apart and stared down at her. Her hands stilled, and she swallowed hard.

"You think that's hot?" Jace stepped away from Raine and guided me to the bed. "You haven't seen anything yet."

Raine

I couldn't decide what was sexier, watching Avro work Jace over or watching the two of them kiss. They were perfect and better than anything I could've imagined. No amount of understanding or watching late-night movies for my own pleasure could ever prepare you for these two in person. I didn't know if all guys together were like this, but it was like watching a dance of dominance. The ebb and flow between them was so smooth and in sync that I felt like an outsider staring in on a private show.

Yet, the way Jace included me and how Avro looked at me made me feel that I could have this, too, if I wanted it. The only question was, did I want this? The only answer that came to mind was yes—a million times, yes.

The feel of their cocks in my hands was completely new, but I couldn't deny I loved the feeling. The look of pleasure on their faces was a drug, and I would never tire of the silky-smooth texture and the way they pulsed in my hands.

I licked my lips, dying to try them, to lick that pre-cum off their tips and play with the ring in the end of Jace's cock. I couldn't stop staring at it, and my tongue tingled with the need to lick and play with it and see what reaction I got from him when I sucked him hard.

"Holy hell, you two are hot." It was all my brain came up with, and I couldn't keep it to myself any longer. Had I ever seen myself as a two-man kind of girl? Hell no! I was scared to be with one, let alone two, but fuck, I would call anyone a liar if they said this was not fucking incredible.

"You think that's hot?" Jace stepped away from me and guided Avro to the bed. "You haven't seen anything yet."

I shivered, wanting to be close to them, and missed the heat, even if it was just in my hands.

"Come over here and get comfortable in the middle of the bed." Jace pointed to where he wanted me to go. I crawled onto the bed—which wouldn't even fit in my entire house—and lay down on my back. "Good, now take off your underwear."

I just stared at the thin lace material, and logic told me it offered zero protection. If they wanted to hurt me, then no little triangular piece of lace would stop them. Yet, my hands trembled, and my thumbs stayed firmly curled around the elastic top, not moving any further.

"Raine, look at me," Avro said, and I searched out his calm expression. "You can do this. Jace already said we're not having sex with you. We're not going to pressure you into it. Do you believe him?" I glanced between them and nodded. A smile played along his lips. "Then you need to trust us, and I know you don't know Jace as well as you do me, but I think I've done all I can to earn that trust from you."

He was right. Irritation burned inside of me. This anxiety I'd never been able to shake had controlled me long enough. I wasn't letting that one night over eleven years ago define me anymore. I was done having it taint all my actions and relationships.

Taking a deep breath, I lifted my hips, pushed the panties down, and tossed them aside, but Jace caught them out of the air. The dark look he gave me as he dangled them between his fingers made me flush hotter than if I'd stepped inside a burning building.

His eyes never wavered as he commanded my stare, and my mouth ran dry as he brought them to his nose. "Do you taste as sweet as you smell Peaches?"

There were some moments you could never prepare for, and this was one of them. Jace lowered the panties and licked his lips before running the small swath of material along the length of his cock. Jace growled as his amused gaze turned to Avro.

"I get your ass tonight, but she's all yours," Jace said, and I sat up a little straighter. Had they lied?

"Don't worry, it's not what it sounds like," Avro said as he slowly crawled onto the bed. It took a second for me to realize what Avro meant as he gripped my thighs and gently pried my knees apart. I could hardly breathe past the pounding of my pulse as he moved between my legs. "Do you trust me?"

Avro's voice was scarcely a whisper, but I heard him loud and clear and found myself nodding despite the old demons in my mind screaming for me to run away. He smiled when I yelped as he slid his hands under my ass, but any fear was swept to the far reaches of my mind as his tongue swirled around my clit.

I gasped as he did it again, and with a coy smile, he dropped his head completely. The pleasure could not be explained, and my back arched as he sucked hard like I'd just become dessert.

"Oh my god," I cried, grabbing his hair. The pleasure was so intense I couldn't decide whether to push him away or pull him deeper.

"That's it, Peaches. Let go and let Avro make you cum in his mouth. He's dying to taste you," Jace said, then groaned. I looked over and couldn't pry my eyes away from his hand, stroking his hard shaft.

Avro's tongue dipped deeper into my pussy, and I moaned, my body and mind finally coming together for the first time in my life. I pulled him harder into me. "Holy shit, don't stop."

Avro groaned, and as if that sound alone was the key to all my desires, I crested the peak of my orgasm. "Avro, oh fuck, yes."

"Now that was fucking hot," Jace said from where he was standing beside the bed. Avro lifted his head but continued to draw long wet lines along my pussy, making me shudder.

"Yeah, it really was," Avro answered, but he never stopped what he was doing.

Jace flicked open a bottle of clear liquid and poured it all over his cock before rubbing it in, and even in my passion-induced haze, I wanted to be his hand. He tossed the bottle onto the bed, and my head lolled to the side to read the words peach flavored. I smirked.

"I'm going to destroy this ass tonight, and you know you deserve it," Jace growled like he was part animal, as his hand cracked down hard on Avro's ass. "Lift this ass for me."

Avro shifted position enough to get his knees underneath him. "Oh, fuck me," he groaned into my pussy as Jace pushed forward.

I couldn't take my eyes off them. His muscles flexed, and all the cut lines became more defined. They froze in position, both breathing hard. Jace had his head back and his eyes closed. If I didn't know better, I would say he was in pain. He was so intense, and that look made me wiggle, wanting more.

"You ready?" Jace asked, but I had a feeling it wouldn't matter what Avro said. He would do what he wanted if Avro was ready or not. Avro nodded and then yelled as Jace slammed into him with no abandon. I watched Avro's face, those amber eyes hooded with pleasure from what Jace was doing.

I was so caught up in the show that Avro took me by surprise as his head dropped to my pussy once more and attacked it the same way that Jace was his ass. My knees fell open wider, and I gripped the blanket hard as his relentless tongue worked in and out of me. The last orgasm left me hyper-sensitive. I'd thought it was almost too much before, but now even my fingertips tingled, and my back arched as I yelled. Avro only sucked harder and swirled his tongue around my clit.

"Oh, fuck, that's it," Jace said through gritted teeth as he slammed into Avro harder, which pushed his face deeper.

I cried out as the second climax hit, and I couldn't help wondering if this was real or a dream that my mind had conjured. There was no way that the body could endure this over and over, and yet as the guys continued to fuck, their moans and groans getting louder and more desperate, I reached that sweet bliss for a second time and flopped back on the bed.

"Avro, yes, yes, fuck, I'm cumming," Jace grunted and drove into Avro hard. His body jerked the whole bed with a powerful thrust.

Avro suddenly rose to his knees, a hand wrapped around his throat and another on his cock as Jace pumped him hard and fast.

"Jace, I'm so close. Please, just like that," he groaned, but his yell was swallowed by Jace, who covered Avro's mouth with his own. Something hot hit my stomach, and I looked down as more of Avro's release landed on me.

It took a second to register what exactly had happened with my brain still doing the backstroke in endorphins. Swiping my finger through the cum on my stomach, I stared at it and then stuck my finger in my mouth.

"Oh fuck me, do that again," Avro said as he stared at my finger, his amber eyes dark with passion.

I drew another line through the cum and exaggeratedly sucked it off my finger. Both men groaned that time, and the sound made me shiver and want to puff out my chest with pride.

It was hot and salty—saltier than I'd been expecting—and I suddenly had the urge to do a tequila shot.

"You like that?" Jace asked as he stared at my fingers in my mouth.

"Would taste great with tequila and a lemon," I said, and both Jace and Avro burst out laughing.

The guys slowly stood and held out their hands to help me up. "Don't worry. We'll work up to you taking it all down the throat." Jace winked. "I have a feeling you're going to be a natural, but for now, we're going to shower."

"All together?"

"Peaches," Jace said, and cocked one of those arrogant brows. "On the bed, in a shower, on the floor, hell, outside in the backyard. Naked is naked. I won't randomly stuff my cock in you if you bend over in front of me. We do have control, you know?"

My cheeks burned with embarrassment for the completely irrational thought that Jace picked up on. Stepping close, he bent over, so his breath feathered my neck as he spoke. Goosebumps rose all over my body.

"Unless, of course, you ask me to," he growled softly, and my knees shook.

Jace stood up straight, and when he held out his hand, I felt confident in my decision for the first time. I'd never been one to fangirl over someone, but I understood what people saw in him. Maybe they only saw a small part, but I wanted more. Whatever it was that his aura held, it was addictive.

A couple of hours later, I was lying between them this time, and even though I was relaxed and content, I couldn't fall asleep. Avro's arm was wrapped snuggly around my waist as he cuddled me to his body. I felt his even breaths against my back, and his body twitched as he fell soundly asleep.

I was startled when Jace spoke, his voice soft in the dark room.

"I know you're still awake. Are you okay, Peaches?"

"Yeah, I'm great," I whispered back.

He shuffled down a little closer so we could stare into each other's eyes. "Can I ask you something?"

"Sure," he said.

"Were you really arguing about a game console?"

Even in the darkened room, I could see the smile pull up at the corner of Jace's mouth. "No, not really, but it was a good metaphor."

"It was about me, wasn't it? You don't really want me involved with you guys," I said, my heart sinking at the thought. A couple of days ago, I would've said that being disappointed to be left out of a threesome was ludicrous, but here I was, worried about his next words.

"Yes and no. Not you exactly, just the entire situation," Jace said as he ran his thumb over my cheek. It was nice to see this softer side of him. I'd seen him give Avro loving looks and soft touches, but he only had a firm hand with me so far. I wondered if that was by design. He understood I needed the push.

"What do you mean?"

"When I was offered a five-year contract to go on tour, we decided to have an open relationship, but only with people who didn't matter, and we would never get emotionally involved. We'd discussed and decided that, at some point, we would add a permanent third person to our relationship, but it had to be someone we both chose."

I sighed and looked away from his eyes. "And Avro wants me, who you'd never met, and he wants you to be exclusive," I whispered as all the pieces began fitting into place in my mind.

"Yes."

"And you don't want either."

"Don't go putting words in my mouth. I didn't say that. I'm not happy with how he thrust this on me. It's unfair, and I wouldn't have done it to him, but…I knew it would likely happen." I lifted my eyes to Jace's again. "This is not the first time we've tried the open relationship. Shared partners have never been an issue, but Avro has a huge jealous streak that he hides well. Most of the time." Jace smirked, but there was warmth in his eyes like he actually liked the jealousy.

"So what are you going to do? I guess I should ask if you'd like me to leave. I don't want to come between you two, and I'd never tell him why I'm not interested."

As the words came out, I knew I never wanted to go back to the girl who sat home alone with her pillow and the television.

"Are you interested?" Removing his hand from my cheek, Jace linked our hands together, and my heart soared. I felt like parts of the old me were learning to breathe again. They made me feel alive, and I didn't want this to end.

"Yes, I am. I didn't think I would be, but the answer is yes," I said. Even in the dark, his silver eyes seemed to penetrate my mind.

"Good. Then we will find a way to make it work." Leaning forward, Jace kissed me softly. The temptation to deepen the kiss was too much, and I licked at his bottom lip.

"Mmm, my sweet little Peaches, you're getting an appetite," he teased, but he wasn't off the mark. My body was already gearing up for another round. Jace opened his mouth and let me explore his as he shifted closer to my body. "Careful, or you may bite off more than you can handle," he whispered, breaking the kiss. "That's not a challenge, just a fact," he said, like he needed to make sure I understood the difference.

I'd gained a lot of courage, but he was right. I was playing with fire, and Jace was the type that was nice for only so long before he took what he wanted. I'd seen it in his eyes, and it made me hot, but it was also terrifying.

"Then again, what's one more time?" Jace said, and I shuddered as his fingers slipped between my thighs. "I want to feel you cum on my fingers, Peaches," he said, his voice deep and gravelly.

My entire being felt full. The shell I had been was cast aside and replaced with someone who wanted it all out of life and this potential relationship. I didn't even know what that meant, but I wanted it all the same. My heart was learning to beat all over again.

Snake

Chapter 19

Kaivan

Leaning back in my chair, I crossed my arms and gazed around at the images on the wall. Most were old posters from a much earlier time for the club. There were a few framed cuts and patches, but everything in here honored the Lost Souls. Where they came from and all our leaders right up until today and our Grand Fucknut Mathers.

Usually, the church meetings didn't bother me. It was all just what you expected when you joined a motorcycle club, but that was when I wasn't in the middle of stalking Raine Eastman. We'd only had a dozen of these since my release. Most were to plan an attack or figure out a cleanup after the attack. So I was curious why one was called today, or I was until I realized Beast was just trying to keep the unrest at bay as Chase remained in Canada despite giving us no details other than he went to help his cousin.

I didn't want to hear any more of this garbage, so I hurried the meeting up. "Yo, Beast. Cut to it already. When are Mathers and the rest of them coming back?"

All thirty-one of the remaining members' heads turned in my direction. Thirty-two, if you counted the stray orange cat that decided this band of burly assholes was better than living on the streets. That said a lot about this part of the city if we were the preferred choice.

"I was getting to that," Beast barked, his voice rippling with annoyance.

"Not fast enough. I have things to do today, and listening to you kiss Mather's ass even when he's not here is getting old. Either cut to the meat of the matter, or I'm out of here."

The room went dead silent. You could've heard a pin drop as the guys sitting around me held their breath. Beast slowly stood from his chair. He looked like a giant bear up on the small platform, but he didn't bother me.

None of them did except Mannix and, some of the time, Roach. If they came at me, I might pause, but if anyone else did, I would slit their throat and feed them to the gators. They all knew it too, which was also why they tended to keep their distance.

We had our honeymoon phase when I first got out. I mean, anyone would be happy to be out of prison. I was the first to grab a gun and yell, 'point me in the right direction.' Like any relationship, the longer you were there, the more you saw the bullshit people wanted to hide.

I'd only been on the outside one year, three months, twelve days, and eleven hours. That was enough time to realize that Chase never wanted to be our leader. I'd never spoken to the man before we went to Ashen Springs. As shocked as I was to learn that the leader I never knew existed was alive, I wanted to prove myself and fought as hard as any other member.

Once we got back, I spoke to Chase a handful of times about meaningless crap before he took off on a drinking and drug binge that left a trail of dead in his wake worse than Jack the Ripper. Now he was gone again, had been for weeks with no end in sight. Worse yet, he took two hundred and fifty of our men. We had no one left, and his parting words to me were, 'keep them safe.' Were you fucking kidding me? Me and what army was keeping the club safe from all the assholes that wanted our territory?

"If you walk out that door, then—"

"Then what?" I pulled a smoke from inside my jacket, lit it, and put it in my mouth to dangle between my lips. I rose to my feet as the two of us squared off.

"You're already down the majority of your men. You gonna cut your enforcer loose, too? Doesn't seem like a smart decision with three other gangs nipping at our heels 'cause they all fucking know that Chase is off gallivanting across Canada where they can't help us."

"He's up there helping family. That is what we do for family," Beast argued.

I snorted. "Aren't we his family?" I looked around at the down-turned heads and defeated looks. "Are you blind to what he is doing to this club? We can't sustain protecting our doors or turf for very long with ninety percent of our members gone with no return date." A few braver guards had been taking extra shifts and had been shot at more than once already.

"Tell me, Beast, why didn't Mathers leave us with an ally to have our back? Oh, that's right, he has none. He's either pissed them off or lost their respect. Why isn't he here earning the respect of the current members he claims he now wants to take care of?" I held out my arms. "That's right. His cousin called and said he needed help. A motorcycle club that isn't ours in a territory that isn't ours. He'll be lucky if he doesn't come back to find the Desert Vipers in his chair."

"He can't control how long it takes, and helping his cousin will give us an ally," Beast said.

Taking a puff of my smoke, I stuffed my hands into the pockets of my jeans.

"Great, so we could all be dead, but when they get back, they'll have earned an ally for some time in the future. Only three things are keeping the other gangs at bay. The first is the fence and the gators. It makes us harder to hit." I walked around to the back of my chair and leaned on the old leather. "The second is the amusement park next door that everyone is convinced is haunted. People go in and never come out."

If they only knew the reason they didn't come out. To the best of my knowledge, only a small handful, including Chase and me knew Wilder even existed.

I glared daggers at Beast. I had no problem with him, really. What I hated was his devotion to a man who had yet to prove he had the stones to be our leader and not a knock-off of his father's legacy.

As the story goes, Mathers senior handed the club's reins to Chase. Chase's brother got pissed and killed his family, but instead of exacting revenge and taking down the Reapers then, he pretended to be dead and hid for ten years while Beast and Mannix tried to hold the club together from constant attacks. In the meantime, Chase didn't care that his members were killed by his brother and only came out of hiding when he needed us—some leader.

"Lastly, but certainly not least, is me." I placed my hands on my chest, knowing that I was being a dramatic asshole. "All those fuckers out there know that if my bell is rung to go and kill them, they better be prepared, or it will be their souls that are lost." I gripped the chair. "So go ahead and kick me out. What the fuck do I care at this point? But don't expect me to cry or be held responsible for other clubs spitting on our sign and pissing on your corpses when they come knocking."

I looked around the room.

"Orrrr, you could shut the fuck up about Chase and his lack of accomplishments and tell us when they'll be back. That's really all we give a fuck about. They may not be asshole enough to say it, but we're all wondering. How long do we need to try and keep this place safe from the hundreds of men who want it?"

Beast looked like he was gearing up to charge across the room and toss me out, and I was almost hoping he would. I wasn't just angry at Raine. I realized that I was angry at the world. I was so fucking pissed off with the hand that I'd been dealt and the never-ending run on a treadmill that pointed up.

Was it really too much to ask to have a couple of things go right in this life? Or was it set in stone the day we were born that some people would get it all while the rest of us poor saps got the scraps? I was already neck-deep in the shit that had been sent my way, and if any more was added, I might as well let myself drown because I was sick of treading this disgusting water.

Mannix stood from his seat but didn't say anything. He didn't need to. He was silently telling Beast to back off and me to calm down. He showed no sign of aggression, and I knew he wouldn't. Mannix was the eye of the storm.

From where I stood, I could tell Beast was grinding his teeth as the muscles strained in his neck with the effort of holding himself back.

"Fine, they're running behind, and I don't know," Beast said.

I sneered and shook my head in disgust. "So I have to ask, does Mathers actually plan on coming back, or is he searching for another hole to rot in and expects us to do his work for him?" I shrugged. "I mean, it's a fair question. He's up in the fucking Great White North, doing what? We don't know, and now what? Are they planning on taking a scenic tour on the way back? Maybe stop in Frontenac and get a steamy as they lick their wounds."

Beast's eyes narrowed as he squared his shoulders. "You have no idea what it's like to go through what he's had to. We all process loss differently, and you need to give him a break and show some respect."

A snort left my mouth. Sighing, I pulled the smoke from my mouth and butted it on the bottom of my boot.

"Beast, we all have our crosses to bear. Do you think Mathers and I should sit down and compare notes? Maybe sip some tea and talk about how we overcame the pain of our woes, scars, and evil deeds?" I asked, my voice laced with sarcasm. I crossed my arms over my chest.

"Not going to fucking happen. Yeah, his family died horribly, and it sucks. I get that. But who in here hasn't lost someone they love? Or have no family at all? Or had their entire fucking lives destroyed for no good reason? Fuck, the whole reason your old lady is dead is that Chase couldn't kill his brother, or am I wrong about that too?"

Beast's face morphed from anger to pain, and I knew that the blow of my words was low and hitting hard with the loss of Jaz. It was a jerk thing to say, but I was sick of the rose-colored glasses routine. I'd liked Jaz. She'd treated me decent and hadn't deserved to die, and she wouldn't have if Chase had done his job. Just another soul lost in his wake.

"The point I'm trying to make is that you're still here working, I'm still here working, everyone is still here working but...Chase Mathers is the one person who is supposed to be making the decisions and taking care of the duties of this place. But no, it's more important to help his 'blood' family. Shows how much he gives a fuck about us. How many years have you given up to cover his ass?" I growled. "I won't do it, and I won't follow him blindly. If he doesn't come back soon and prove to be a worthwhile leader, you won't have to worry about kicking me out, Beast, 'cause I'll already be gone."

"Are you suggesting we get rid of our leader?" Beast asked.

Pushing away from the chair, all the guys looked at the floor like I'd just beaten them all with a stick, and I shook my head.

"No. I would have no problem with the guy if he did his job and looked out for us the same way we've been covering his ass. That's really not too much to ask. It shocks me every day that out of all of us, you, who had to take over and man up to run this club, is still the one who paints him as a fucking messiah." I tossed my hands up when no one said anything. "I'm done. You want to kick me out for being the only one brave enough to speak up, then go for it, but I have important things on my list, and I'm going to go take care of them."

I marched for the door and flung it open, leaving it that way in my wake. If they all wanted to show undying loyalty to Chase, then they could. I was more of the show me with actions to prove it type because words were fucking cheap, and so far, all I'd seen was a bunch of lip service.

"Snake," Mannix's voice stopped in my tracks.

I slowly turned around to see him coming out the door and closing it behind him. Internally groaning, I remained where I was until he reached me.

"Follow me," Mannix said, and I followed along the hall to the far end, away from the church door. "Look, I know you have many very valid reasons as to why you're angry with Chase," he said.

"If you're going to tell me that I need to show him respect..."

Mannix shook his head. "No, I won't say that. In fact, I think you're right, and Chase would tell you that same thing. He doesn't deny fucking up and knows he needs to make amends."

"Then why isn't he here?" I countered. "Why is he in another country fighting for an MC that has nothing to do with us?"

"It's complicated. The thing is, you're not wrong with anything you said in there, but I'm going to ask you to tone it down. The aggression, although justified, isn't helping, and it has nothing to do with Chase's ego. We can't afford to lose anyone else. We already had one member pack their shit and leave in the night. The club can't sustain any more losses, and as angry as you are right now, I know you don't want to see this place fall apart."

I sucked in a deep breath. "Fine, that's a fair point. Do you need me to kill whoever left?"

Mannix laughed. His mouth turned into a lopsided smile. "Best enforcer ever. No, it's all good. I made sure he won't cross us."

"So, is that it?"

"Naw, man, I'm going to ask you to lay off until Chase is back and proves one way or the other that he's a leader, and I'm asking this as a favor to me."

"Fuck," I swore under my breath. He knew I would never say no to a personal favor. This was a sneaky tactic, but I wouldn't be alive without Mannix, and I respected the fuck out of him. "Fine, but know this. I will follow you wherever you need me to go, but if Chase gets back and it continues to be this dog and pony show, I'm done. You can beat the shit out of me and break both my legs. I don't give a fuck. I refuse to follow someone as spineless as my father was."

Mannix nodded, and I turned and stomped down the hall, so absorbed with my thoughts that it took a moment to register the yelling. The shrill sound out in the main club room nearly had me turning around and going the other way.

Almost anything was better than dealing with Naomi. Now that she was pregnant, she was more annoying than ever. At least before, her rants were just irritating. Now they ended in tears and her rubbing her belly as she demanded things like cocoa butter. It was 'cringe worthy', as she would say.

All the sweetbutts were gathered like they'd been herded, and Naomi screamed at the top of her lungs as she pointed at them.

"What the fuck is going on here? You sound like you've been possessed by Satan." I stared at her red face and messy blonde hair, which was normally neat and perfect. "You kinda look it, too. Are you sure it was Chase that knocked you up?"

A few of the girls appreciated my sense of humor and smirked or laughed, earning a glare that could've shattered glass from Naomi.

"And what fucking part of no drama by the old ladies do you not understand? Do you need it read slower to you?"

Her face turned a fiery shade of red. "I'm not an old lady!" she wailed, and I cringed. "I'm in my prime. I'm too young for this," Naomi said and looked like she was about to burst into tears when her face shifted as fast as a transformer, and she stomped in my direction.

"You, it was probably you," Naomi said, and just like that, the finger swung in my direction.

"Be careful where you point that thing. Something may bite it off," I growled and stepped farther into the room.

I had zero intention of hurting her shrieking ass. As far as I was concerned, old ladies, even ones causing drama, were the responsibility of their man. Chase wasn't here, but if Beast were reporting back, he knew what was going on, including any of the shit Naomi pulled.

She tried to give Chase's office a freshening-up paint job a week ago with a color called wheat fairy. She said the simple, grey walls were depressing and looked dirty. I left when Beast finally called Chase to talk her down.

But I also didn't have to put up with her antics. She wasn't my old lady. We had one sexual interaction when she gave me a blowjob to piss off Chase, and I honestly have had better from my bike.

Three things kept her breathing and acting like a raving lunatic.

The first was that she was shacking up with Chase. I may not be happy with his leadership qualities, but to kill his old lady, fuck no.

The second was that she was pregnant. Only a real piece of shit killed a woman while pregnant. I was a grade-A asshole and had killed a long list of women on missions for the club, but only a man with no morals would do that crap.

The last was that as much as I didn't like her ninety-nine percent of the time, the one percent was mad respect. I'd watched her step off a boat onto a dock and do the thing that Chase needed to do and couldn't. Killed his brother. Point blank range, she walked up and pulled the trigger like she was swiping her credit card at Versace. That right there earned her a free pass for life unless she came at me for some reason. Any bitch who could do that was a bitch worth keeping.

She looked at her finger and then up into my face. "Whatever," she said but put her arm down. "Just tell me where she is."

My brow furrowed. "Who the hell are you talking about?"

"Don't play stupid with me. I know you know where she is." She crossed her arms over her chest and glared at her blood-red nails. Had the pregnancy hormones gone to her head? A voice in my mind warned me to keep that thought to myself unless I wanted her to go all banshee again.

"The only girls I know of are in this room and Raine," I said.

"Who's Raine?"

"My point exactly." I mirrored her pose and even added the foot tap she had going on just so she knew how ridiculous she looked.

Naomi looked me up and down and huffed out a sound that sounded more like a rabid squirrel, but I was sure it was her version of annoyance. "I'm talking about Bailey. She's missing, and I know one of you assholes took her."

I held my hands out. "Who the fuck is Bailey? And why the hell would we want her?"

Naomi chewed on her lower lip. "Bailey is my roommate."

"The blonde? I thought her name was Ava," I said and wondered if I'd been calling that girl the wrong name all this time.

"No, not her. My other roommate."

I shook my head and stomped toward the exit. "I have no idea who the hell you're talking about, but maybe you should visit the amusement park next door."

"What? Why?" Naomi gasped, her face horrified.

"I don't know, but maybe your crazy ass will get lost in the house of mirrors, and we won't have to listen to you wail in here." I paused at the top of the stairs and looked back at her. "At least if you're over there, people are already used to the haunting shrieks of insanity coming from inside."

"Funny, Snake. Ha, ha," I heard her yell as I jogged down the stairs. The others could try to pry her crazy ass out of here. I wasn't spending another second more than I had to. There were some things that even I, as the enforcer, refused to do.

Heading to my bike, I paused and looked over at the amusement park as an idea came to me. I walked over to the fence and tried to spot Wilder among the piles of broken things. He was always out here somewhere. It amazed me that the other guys hadn't seen the man lurking on the property. Then again, maybe they had but were too drunk to register that the walking pile of garbage was more than the booze talking.

"Wilder, man, you out here?" I called out and heard a hushed, "Shhh, this way."

I looked around for the source of the voice and spotted a pile of mangled rides near the fence. A head slowly rose from inside one of the rollercoaster cars. *This guy is fucking crazy. What are you doing?* Walking along the edge of the fence, I ran my fingers along the chain link, making little thudding noises as I went.

"Hey, man," I said once I reached the spot I'd seen Wilder appear.

I stared inside the car that was at eye level, searching for the man himself.

"Shhhh, I'm down here. I don't want them to know where I am."

My eyes dropped, and there he was, lying on the ground, staring up at me from under the massive pile. Wilder had painted himself today, the same mishmash of colors as the cars. *How the hell had he done that?* Nope, wasn't asking.

"Do you want me to look somewhere else?" I asked.

"Naw, man, no need to be paranoid. What's up?"

I let that comment sink in and couldn't help wondering if he saw the irony in that statement. In the last ten minutes, I'd dealt with three levels of insanity, but Wilder and his ridiculous behavior were at least humorous.

"How easy would it be to get a tracker?" I asked.

"That's all you want?" He scoffed like I was the one being ridiculous and then shuffled back under the pile. I heard him inside, rooting around like a massive rat. Then again, the only difference separating him from a rat at this point was that Wilder could talk.

A moment later, I heard an "ah ha," and the man reappeared, but this time from inside the car. What the hell? Did he have an entire fucking system of tunnels? Wilder reached out and stuck his fingers through the links, and I took the small black square from his fingers.

"You just happen to have a tracker in here with you?"

"Yeah, of course. You never know when you're going to need one."

I licked my lips and swallowed as I wondered how many of us had trackers on us already. Did he watch us all day? Nope, not going there either. If he did, he did. I didn't want to know about it.

"So, how does it work?"

"Turn it on, sync it to your phone, and put it on the person you want to track. Easy," Wilder said, moving back into the center of the blue and yellow car. "Can I ask you a question?" he asked before I could make my escape.

"Sure," I said, not really sure I wanted to know after the last question.

"Chase told me that girls like flowers, but it doesn't seem to be working," he said, and my eyebrow rose. When the hell had Wilder talked to Chase? And why about flowers?

"Well, that was your first mistake. Chase ended up with Naomi. Does that seem like the right person to ask?" It was a low blow, but it made me feel better.

Wilder stared at me as if contemplating the joke as a real moment of understanding. "No, it does not. Good point, no flowers."

"Okay," I said, not sure what else to say at this point.

"I need another idea," he said. "I'm unskilled in the ways of creating affection."

I wanted to yell *shocking* but kept it to myself. "Do you know what her interests are? Does she like sailing or biking or books? Maybe she likes art or animals."

"No, why would I need to know that?" he asked, and my brain started to fry.

I could only handle so much insanity in a day before my meter was completely full, and it was getting pretty fucking close to full now.

"Alright, forget knowing her interests. Girls love it when you spend time with them. Take her out, make her a part of your day, and show her that you care about her interests. They also like a good meal," I said, hoping that I didn't just sentence some random girl to death.

"Fuck, you're good. I'm coming to you from now on," Wilder said.

"Oh, that's great," I mumbled under my breath.

"Thanks, man." Wilder dropped down into his maze, and a

second later, he sprinted across the open lot to the center of his chaos.

"I should've just used the black market," I grumbled and stomped toward my bike. This was turning out to be a weird fucking day, and I didn't see it getting any better from here.

Chapter 20

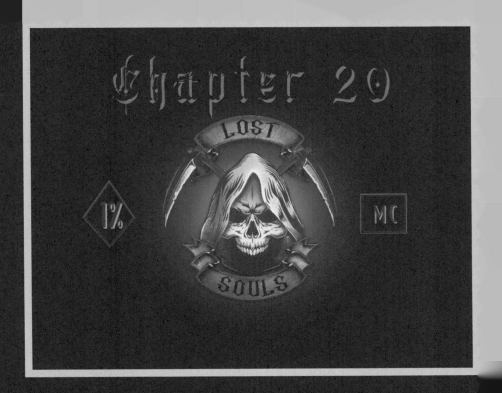

Raine

"Are you sure you don't want me to stay?" Avro asked a[s] we pulled up to the employee entrance of the bar, o[r] maybe it was more of a club now. It was tough to decide.

Mondays were my paper and general catch-up day at work. We weren't open Monday to Wednesday, so the place was blissfully quiet. Why I thought running everything for Chris would be fun wa[s] beyond me. He was off spending more time with his other busi-nesses, and I was left holding the reins. The pay increase was nice though.

"No, it's fine. I like the quiet to get the paperwork done, and [I] have a feeling you'll just be a distraction. In the best way possible, o[f] course," I teased. Getting out of the car before I did something stupid [l]ike say yes, I walked around and leaned into his driver-side window.

"Me, a distraction? I take offense that I resemble that statement," he quipped, and kissed me.

It was more difficult pulling myself from the bed with Avro and Jace than I ever thought it would be. The warmth of their arms soaked into my body, and it felt like they were warming my bones and healing parts of my mind. Avro was a cuddler, and the few times I wiggled away to try to cool off, I was quickly pulled back into his arms. It was totally adorable, and I was so not used to it. There was something to be said for being able to sleep in a starfish position when you wanted.

"Try not to have too much fun going to the airport," I said, hitching my backpack higher.

"The drive there won't be much fun, but once we get there, I plan on molesting Jace one more time before he gets on the plane."

I couldn't tell if he was joking, but knowing Avro, he fully intended to take his fill of Jace Everly. Jace still made me as nervous as a cat on a hot tin roof, and I found myself talking too much or stumbling over my answers when he looked in my direction. He was amused, and I was not.

"I'm sure you will." I smiled, and he smiled back. The expression lit up the whole car. "I'll talk to you later," I said and waved as I flicked through my keys to find the one that opened the back door. Avro waited until the door was open, and I gave him the thumbs up before he drove off.

Jace's regular driver was sick, so everyone from the band was finding their own way to the private airfield. The drive took a couple of hours, and his flight didn't take off until eight, so long as the weather held out. They'd both offered to stay and keep me company until they needed to leave, but that was all sorts of a bad idea, and I needed time to unpack everything floating around in my head.

Grabbing the remote, I turned on the television as soon as I walked into the office. I loved that the place was quiet, but sometimes it really freaked me out. Every shadowy corner felt like someone was hiding. I was starting to realize that the thought was very conceited. The very idea that every guy was looking at me, hiding to attack me or whatever else my brain conjured, was irrational.

The channel was on the local news station, and I watched as the reporter pointed to the large screens showing the coming storm. By the look of it, there was a good chance that Jace's flight wouldn't get off the ground.

Sitting down, I booted up the computer and laid my hands on the desk. My emotions swirled as much as the colorful clouds on the news screen as I tried to digest the last two days. Closing my eyes, I played over the conversation from last night and the feel of their touch. But all that did was make me wiggle in my seat.

"Okay, you came here to work. You can wonder about your rapidly changing personal life later." I looked at the 'In' basket on my desk and groaned.

"Darryl," I grumbled, not seeing the final inventory boards from the alcohol storage. That was the one spot I hated to go, even when people were in the building. When the bar was empty, I avoided it like it held the plague.

"Shit, shit, shit!" I was tempted to go home and get Avro to go down with me tomorrow. "That is the most chicken-shit thing you've considered doing yet," I scolded myself as I pushed to my feet. "You're trying to be braver, remember?"

Squaring my shoulders, I stomped out the door and down the hallway that led to the storage area, like the stomping would somehow make the images of ghosts in my mind go away. I whipped open the door and swallowed hard as I stared at the black hole. It was only six stairs down, and technically it was still above ground, and yet it felt like a bottomless pit that disappeared into a cavernous void.

"You got this. You now have a wicked right hook," I encouraged myself, reaching for the light switch. Why were these storage areas so scary? Was it because from the time we were children, there were a million movies with things sneaking in or crawling out of these things? Or was it because we intuitively realized this was the closest we came to being in a windowless coffin while still alive? I paused with my foot hovering over the first stair. Unless, of course, you were buried alive in a coffin.

Okay, enough of that.

I trotted down the wooden stairs and decided to start at the farthest spot and make my way forward. That seemed logical, and then each aisle I completed was a reward, getting a little closer to the exit.

Walking down the last row, I swallowed hard and picked up the clipboard. I suddenly wished I'd turned on some music. At least then, it wouldn't be so quiet. I jotted down the remaining wine on the chart and grabbed the paper. When I stepped out of the row to move to the next, I heard a scraping sound. I froze as my eyes searched the rows of bottles and boxes, but with the product on the shelves, I could only partially see to the end.

My heart pounded hard as my fear spiked, and every muscle shook as I put one foot in front of the other. I moved toward the spot where I'd heard the sound. It seemed way too loud to be a mouse. Gripping the pen like a weapon, I glanced down each row I passed. I looked up the stairs as I stepped in front of them and once more contemplated saying fuck it and getting the hell out of here, but I was determined to stare fear in the face and defeat it. Too many years, too many ghosts, too many demons of my own making, and I was done.

Everything seemed to be heightened, the smell of the cardboard, the faint scent of mildew from the dampness that permeated everything, and the stale aroma of old alcohol from broken or spilled bottles. The scraping sound was louder now that I was closer, and one of the boxes moved slightly. My nostrils flared, eyes wide, and pen at the ready as I counted down each remaining row. As I reached the last row, a rumble of thunder echoed down the stairs, and the lights shut off, plunging the room into complete darkness.

Terror gripped my throat, and I slammed against the wall as the memory I tried so hard to forget stormed to the front of my mind.

"Shit," I mumbled as I jogged down the street.

It was late, and this was a terrible part of town, but I had to speak to Kai. I just couldn't leave things the way that I had. I couldn't believe he kissed me, and instead of hanging on forever, I freaked out. It was my first kiss, my first real kiss, from the guy I always wanted it to be, and I pushed him off me and ran from the room like a loser.

I'd paced the school yard until dark, and when I got home, Kai was already gone. Crawling into bed, I tried to sleep and told myself that I would catch him in the morning, but with each minute that ticked on the clock, my anxiety grew until I wanted to throw up. I wanted to see him— no, I had to see him. He was my friend, but I'd been secretly crushing on Kai from the moment he showed up at the Collins house.

I'd seen too many dead people in my short time alive. I'd stared into my parents' unseeing eyes and known they were dead. I didn't really know what to call it other than with the angels. Were there really angels, though? I didn't know anymore. I certainly didn't think so.

I'd also watched a man choke on his own puke and another suffocate to death while others convulsed on the floor. It was confusing at the age of six. I was unsure what was going on, but scared out of my mind. I didn't want to get anyone in trouble, but maybe if I hadn't cared about that, my parents or even one of their friends would still be alive today. I couldn't be expected to save them, yet their deaths weighed on my mind.

I glanced at the scar on my hand, the white line across my palm where

I'd cut myself on glass that night. It was a constant reminder that my parents didn't give a fuck about me. The police came to the shitty little apartment, and I was hauled away.

I'd stared out the window for days, hoping that it was all dream and my parents would come for me. Like a television show where they showed up at the house, and we would run to one another and hug. The television lied, books lied, and people lied.

All but one. Kai told me the truth, no matter what I asked. He'd never treated me like a kid, and it seemed like, overnight, I couldn't help thinking about what would happen if I snuck into his room. Would he hold me all night? Would we talk and laugh as we tried not to get caught? I snuck in once and claimed that I had a terrible dream, but Kai said we couldn't stay in his room, and we ended up sitting outside. It was still nice, and he hadn't yelled or told me to fuck off, but I realized he didn't see me as anything more than a friend and foster sister.

At least, that was what I thought until earlier tonight. That kiss had been made for books. I could still feel the warmth against my lips and the sweet taste of the icing on my tongue from Kai's cake. The way his hand touched my cheek and the scent of his body wash had made me light-headed. My heart had jumped around inside my chest like an animal looking to escape, and the feelings that came over me had me bolting for the door.

I pulled my hood down lower and stuffed my hands in my pockets to make myself look intimidating. That was not easy to do. At five feet four inches, I wasn't tall and was slim in all the wrong places. My pants drooped on my hips, and I had very little in the way of boobs. At fifteen, I looked more like a boy, except for my long hair.

Some guys stumbled past and laughed as they talked about the fight where they'd just won money. The strong scent of beer and cigarettes made my nose curl. I had to be close. Daring to lift my head from watching my sneakers, I looked around for anything that would give away where the street fights were. Across the road was another large group of people standing around outside a building. They were smoking and talking on phones or with each other, but not one of them looked like anyone I would want to ask for information.

Slipping into the alley, I watched the group and peeked up and down the street. The glass doors behind them opened, and loud shouting caught my attention. I watched as three men came out, pissed off. I had no idea what they were screaming about, but they were yelling at the massive guys dressed all in black blocking their way.

"They must be guards. That's got to be the spot," I mumbled.

My eyes traced up the front of the building, and a smile tugged at the corner of my mouth as I spotted the large eye with an 'O' and other fonts surrounding it. The paint job was faded, but it was definitely an eye, and Kai was always talking to the other guys who fought about the place being called the Oracle. While the argument continued and everyone was distracted, I ran across the street and slipped down the alley beside the building. I pulled on each door I came to, but they were all locked.

Walking around to the back of the building, I spotted one more door but only took a couple of steps when the door opened, and I darted behind the stacks of boxes and garbage cans.

"Fuck off, Joe. I'm tellin' ya, and I'm not lying. I have the perfect match for your guy. Big money fight. The spectators will go crazy for the match-up. Yeah, I know. The kid's name is Snake."

Daring to peek, I lifted my eyes above the garbage, but the guy had walked in the other direction as he spoke. They were definitely talking about Kai. That was the name he made everyone but me call him. He tried to get me to call him that stupid name, but I wasn't hearing it. I wasn't calling him a reptile just because he thought it was cool.

Light shone out the crack in the door, and I realized this guy had left the door open a little. Taking the risk, I moved like a cat on a tightrope and ran to the stairs, then tiptoed up to the door as quickly as possible without giving myself away.

The door was open just enough that someone tiny like me could slip in.

I ended up in a stairwell with two options...up or down. It wasn't that loud in this back hallway, but I could feel the vibration from loud music through my feet and decided that I'd go down and quickly sprinted down the stairs, taking two at a time.

With my small size, blond hair, and always being light on my feet, Kai dubbed me Tink. I hated that he saw me as this cute little thing, but I would take him calling me that over never speaking to me again.

Reaching the bottom floor, I stared at the black door with the dents like someone had punched it hard a thousand times. Licking my lips, I slowly reached for the handle and pulled it open, only to be abused by the loud cheering and even louder rock music. I kept my hood firmly in place but stood up straight and tossed a bit of swagger into my walk, just like I saw the guys on my street do. It annoyed me how they would walk like they owned the road, but watching them strut around like a bunch of birds in a mating dance helped me now.

I moved through the crowd until I was positioned close enough to see who was fighting, and my heart soared and then sank when I realized it wasn't Kai. I didn't want him to fight, but did this mean he'd already fought, or was he next?

A hard bump from the guy beside me had me stepping sideways, and I glared at him out of the corner of my eye, but he didn't notice me. My foot slipped a little, and when I looked down, I spotted a program under my foot. I picked it up and stared at the list of names that were supposed to fight tonight. There were no times.

Dammit.

My eyes lifted to the cage when the crowd erupted in loud applause. One guy was pressed up against the chain link cage while the other guy repeatedly punched him. I didn't like watching this, and I couldn't believe that Kai subjected himself to this just so he could pay for school. There had to be a better way.

A buzzer went off like a fire alarm, and the guy left standing in the cage threw his hands up and cheered. I guess he was the winner.

"Winner, The Void!" the man acting as the announcer called into the microphone he was holding, and I glanced down at the form to see that they were the second last fight, which meant that Kai was next. I was jostled to the side again as more people pushed into the already packed room.

Bang

I ducked at the sound. It took an extra second for everyone else to register the sound of the gun. In a blink, everyone turned to run away from the cage area. I was dragged along, and my chest hurt as the crowd pushed and shoved hard. A hand hit the side of my head, and the hood I'd kept in place slipped down, but I couldn't worry about it as I tried to stay on my feet so that I wasn't trampled.

Bang

The group that was practically carrying me with them was diverted, and we ended up running back the way we came. Slipping through the small cracks that the stinking, sweating bodies left, I managed to get to the wall and pressed myself against it as hard as I could. My heart was pounding so hard that I thought I might pass out, and my lip hurt. Touching my mouth, I realized that it was bleeding.

Bang, Bang

A light smashed, sending little shards flying, and I covered my head as the pieces rained down. Some of the guys dressed in black pushed their way through the throngs of people still shoving their way out of the exits. They held up guns, and at that moment, the fear that had remained dormant due to shock took hold. Pushing away from the wall, I slipped under arms and dodged around the next group of people. Spotting the door I came through, which wasn't marked with a big red Exit sign, I peeled away from the group and ran for it.

When I pulled it open, and the light from the stairwell poured in, I could see people turn my way and break away from the group.

Where the hell was Kai in all this? Was he okay? Did he already get out? Please don't let him be one of the people being shot at.

I pushed away from the door and darted up the stairs, breathing hard as I took them two at a time. A hand landed on the rail beside me, and my heart leaped as I stared at the same tattoo Kai had gotten just a few weeks ago. Looking back, I stared up at the tall figure wearing a black hoodie. I couldn't see his face, and there was no time. It could wait until we were outside.

The door slammed open as I hit it, and as soon as we were outside, I turned to speak to Kai, but he was running along the back of the buildings away from Oracle.

"Kai!" I yelled and ran after him. "Kai, it's me. Wait up." I could hear sirens in the distance and pushed my tired legs harder.

Rounding the corner to the dark shadows where I'd seen Kai turn, I called out again. "Kai, stop! It's me."

I hadn't gone very far when someone in a hood stepped out of the shadows. I tried to stop, but it did no good as I ran straight into them. Bouncing back, I landed hard on my ass and stared up at the person I'd hit. I tried to see inside the dark hood, but the thumb hooked into the pocket showed off the back of his hand, and there was the tattoo.

"Kai, thank God. It's me," I said, looking around as two more people stepped into the alley. I couldn't tell what they looked like with the only light at their backs. I swallowed hard as I stared up at the three men. None of them spoke.

"Get her up," a gruff voice barked out.

"No, don't touch me." I tried to jerk away from the vise grip that wrapped around my biceps. "Ow! Let go," I yelled and tugged on my arm.

"Shut her up."

A hard hit to my stomach came out of nowhere, and I doubled over. Tears sprang to my eyes, and my knees buckled as I tried to breathe past the sharp pain.

"Better than nothing. Actually, this may work out even better." The same man sneered. He stepped in close and bent low to my side, but I still couldn't see his face in the dark. I caught the strong stench of alcohol and

cigarettes. My foster dad smoked all the time, and it reminded me of that scent. "Bag her."

Black material was placed over my head by the second guy who had stepped into the alley, and everything in me screamed that I needed to fight or I was going to die. I had no idea why Kai was doing this and listening to this jerk, but how he'd said it "may work out better" sent a cold dread racing down my back. Kicking out hard, I didn't care what I hit as long as they let me go. I opened my mouth to scream at the top of my lungs when something hard hit my face. Then all I saw was black and little dots behind my eyelids.

The lights came back on, and as they did, my mind was pulled back to the present. I screamed and jumped back as a cat darted toward me and hit the stack of boxes at the end of the row. The boxes swayed dangerously.

I watched the grey cat disappear up the stairs and slumped against the wall, laying a hand over my eyes.

"Fuck," I swore and pulled at my shirt as my heart fluttered so hard that I thought I would pass out. "You know what? Screw this. Inventory can wait until tomorrow," I mumbled, every part of my body shaking with the adrenaline and lingering fear that always accompanied the memory.

I raced up the stairs and closed the door, so my furry little intruder couldn't run back down. I needed to finish up a few odds and ends, and then I was getting the hell out of here. Rome wasn't built in a day, and my fear wasn't going to disappear overnight.

I rarely asked for anything, but I would happily trade my tattered soul to be rid of the memory of Kai and his friends.

Raine

Chapter 21

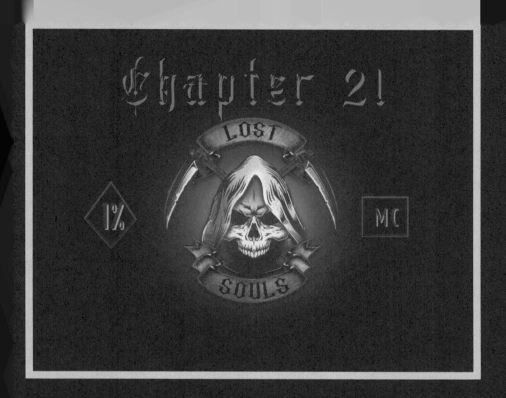

Raine

Damn this storm. I tried waiting it out, but instead of getting better, it only got worse. Digging around in my wallet, I pulled out the money to give to the nice lady who had risked life and limb to drive in the torrential downpour to bring me home.

"Thanks again. Here, take this for your trouble," I said, handing over double the Uber fee.

"You don't have to do that," she said, smiling, but still took the money and stuffed it into her pocket.

I'd been very frugal over the years and had money put away in case I needed it, for what, I had no idea. It wasn't like I spent money on lavish items, clothes, or even had a car, but you just never knew what was around the next corner.

Grabbing my bag, I jumped out of the Uber and sprinted for the front door. I was used to Avro driving me home and waiting till I got inside, but not this woman. She was gone before I reached the bottom step.

"I should've just taken today off," I mumbled as I tried to get my key into the door, but it wouldn't go in. "Why the hell is it so dark?"

Reaching over, I tapped my outside light, but it wouldn't turn on. Great, just great. Digging my phone out of my pocket, I tucked myself close to the door to keep it from getting wet and hit the flashlight option. Of course, I'd been trying the wrong key. It really had been one of those days. I got the stray cat out of the club, but in the process, it knocked over five hundred dollars' worth of bottles in the main bar, and I had to clean all that up. Then once I managed to get a hold of him, my arm got scratched up for my effort. I made it to the hospital to have it cleaned and wrapped and get a tetanus shot. All in all, it had been a day I wished I'd just stayed in bed.

Picking out the right key, I slipped it into the lock and pushed open the door as the thunder rumbled outside. I'd lived here my whole life and had never gotten used to the way the storms hit, and even though it wasn't a hurricane, it still felt like one.

I was soaked to the bone and shivering, as if the water had seeped right into my marrow. Locking the door behind me, I dropped my bag and hit the light switch, but it didn't want to turn on either. Glancing out the window, I saw the house across the street had light peeking through the closed drapes. It must be the breaker.

"Of course, why would anything want to go right?"

I stomped down the hallway toward the kitchen to grab a flashlight, so I didn't get my phone all wet. I glanced back at the wet prints and trail of water I'd left and groaned. I would clean that up after. The stupid fuse box was outside, and if my night hadn't been bad enough, I wouldn't be surprised to come face-to-face with a gator in my backyard.

"Fucking shit luck today. My stars must be out of alignment," I mumbled, holding up the phone as my guide. The lightning flashed outside, making me shudder a moment before the thunder boomed so loudly that I jumped and then ducked, covering my head. It sounded like it was right above my house as the walls shook. I didn't see myself getting any sleep tonight.

My luck, the house would catch fire. Seriously, could anything else go wrong?

Another shiver ran up my spine when I marched past the closet. My foot faulted as the little light on my phone reflected off the glass of the kitchen window. It wasn't my reflection that made me pause, my mind slowing to a crawl. It was the closet door opening silently behind me. As if I were dumped into the middle of a horror movie, I was suddenly staring at the monster I'd been hiding from all these years. I blinked, not sure this was real or if I was conjuring it in my terror-riddled mind. Goosebumps rose on my body, and my pulse tripled as my adrenaline soared through the roof.

Run.

My feet didn't listen to what my mind screamed to do. They seemed to be rooted to the spot.

Run.

Something large stepped out of the closet and turned in my direction. It was a man. My breath caught in my throat as the shock transformed into dread.

Thump, thump, thump. My heart pounded viciously behind my ribcage.

Run.

I couldn't breathe as the lightning flashed again and illuminated a pair of blue eyes I would never forget. Those eyes were burned into the deepest recesses of my brain like they'd been branded. Forever marked.

"Hey there, Tink," Kai said. His voice was much deeper and rough, but everything that I remembered. The same shot of excitement punched me in the stomach that I always had whenever I saw him. But this time, the thrill was quickly followed by terror.

My feet finally listened to the warning, and I lunged toward the kitchen. I barely made it a stride before I screamed. Hands much larger than I remembered grabbed me by the back of my neck and my sopping-wet sweatshirt. It didn't even register that I'd been jerked off my feet until I sailed through the air and crashed into the coffee table.

The sharp pain was instant as my elbow and shoulder slammed into the hard edge, before sliding across the top and landing on my shoulder hard. My phone was knocked from my hand and slid under the recliner.

"No, no, no," I whispered.

Fear roared through my body. I thought I knew what it was to be scared, but I was wrong. I clawed at the ground, trying to get my feet under me, but my wet sneakers slipped on the laminate floor. A massive boot slammed down in the center of the coffee table. I cried out with the loud crack that mirrored the echo of thunder, announcing that the table had snapped in two. I was being pursued by a monster and not a man.

"Kai, no," I cried out and scrambled to get away and reach my phone. Glancing over my shoulder, I couldn't see him clearly in the dark, but I felt his eyes boring into me with so much hate and anger. I knew he would come. I had always known he would come for me.

This was the nightmare that played on a loop in my mind.

Gripping the arm of the chair, I stuck my hand under to try to grab my phone, which softly glowed like my only beacon for help. My fingers grazed the edge when those strong hands yanked me back by my hoodie and choked off my air supply. A scream ripped from my throat as he picked me up like I weighed nothing, and once more, I was thrown through the air.

"Ah!" I cried out, my ribs taking the impact as I hit the partially open closet door and slammed it closed. "Get off me," I yelled as he grabbed me again.

Words I'd said so many times before and it hadn't worked then. I don't know why I thought they might work now. Tears burned my eyes as I battled my panic to think straight.

The fight was slowly returning to my brain. If I didn't fight, he was going to kill me. *Fight, damn you, fight.*

When he pulled me to my feet, I used all my strength and brought my elbow up like I was trying to perform a finishing move in a video game. The blow wasn't true and glanced off the side of his chin, but it was enough that he swore and stepped back.

Only a tiny bit of space separated us, but I let my right fist fly and caught him squarely across the cheek. The crack of my knuckles told me I definitely made good contact, but I'd hit him all wrong, and I cried out with the pain in my wrist. His head snapped to the side, a small cut opening up on his cheek from the little silver band on my middle finger. Ironically, it was the ring he'd given me the night before he attacked me. I didn't know why I kept it, why I couldn't throw it away, or why I wore it, but it never left my finger.

My victory was short-lived as his head slowly turned toward me. Blue eyes burning with malice glared into my soul, and I shuddered in his hold.

Not wasting a second, I grabbed the front of the leather jacket he was wearing in my fists and pulled in while I brought my knee up, but I only hit his hands. He shoved me hard, and I winced as the back of my head cracked off the hollow wooden door with a thud.

"Kai, stop, please," I cried out as he reached for me again, but he didn't stop.

His fist curled around the front of my sweatshirt, and I struck out with my left hand, smacking him as hard as I could from the awkward angle. The sting in my hand burned like it was on fire, but he didn't even flinch. My mind was unraveling, and instead of precise movements with strategic hits, I began lashing out like I was feral. I knew what I needed to do. I knew I couldn't act like I had last time, but I realized now the pathetic amount of training I'd done was nothing more than a mental bandage.

Kai was far stronger than I remembered, and it was like he was made of stone and didn't feel anything as my fists, feet, and knees struck out at him. I was nothing more than a tiny kitten in the jaws of a giant predator. I was the tiny Tink he called me.

Tears spilled over and trailed down my cheeks. Nothing moved him. Nothing lessened his strong grip or wavered that unnerving stare. I tried to claw at his face, aiming for his eyes, but he kept himself just out of my reach.

His lip pulled up at the corner in a smirk that was once so sexy but now only sent cold dread racing along my spine.

"You having fun, Tink?"

He yanked me towards him and spun my body around. I cried out as I was smashed into the door, my cheek and already sore ribs taking most of the blow. Pinning me against the wood like an insect on a board, Kai got close to my ear, and all I felt was the heat radiating off his body.

I closed my eyes, and my body shook uncontrollably in his hold. Kai ran his nose up the side of my neck.

"You smell so good, Tink. You smell exactly how I imagined you would."

"Get off of me, you asshole," I growled and kicked backward, trying to find any soft spot or even a knee, but he must have been expecting that, and I didn't hit anything.

"Keep it up, Tink. I like hearing your screams."

"Oh, I know you do." Gathering all my strength, I pushed with all my might against the door and swung backward as hard as I could with my elbow.

"Fucking bitch," Kai yelled as my elbow made contact. I felt his grip loosen on my sweatshirt and spun around. I broke his hold and bolted for the front door.

The house that had always seemed so small now felt like a marathon run to the door. My legs pumped hard, my lungs burned, and my head felt light with my erratic breaths. I knew I might pass out with this much adrenaline pumping, but I couldn't stop it, no more than I could stop the hand from grabbing hold of the hood on my sweatshirt. The cool touch of the door handle grazed the tips of my fingers, and just like that, I was wrenched off my feet and crashed to the floor.

Everything went numb. The air was forced out of my lungs, my fingers and toes tingled, while my head spun.

I cried out but could only wheeze as a heavy weight pressed into the middle of my chest. The lightning flashed, and the thunder rumbled like the sky was as angry as the man that held me. Kai's knee was on my chest, but the hand wrapped around my throat, and the fingers that steadily pressed in until I couldn't breathe told me that I was going to die.

I grabbed at Kai's arm, begging with my eyes to let go. I locked eyes with him, and there wasn't anything left of the boy I remembered. The boy I'd fallen in love with, the boy who broke my heart, stole my virginity, and now was going to take my life.

How I wished I'd just gone to the airport.

He raised his fist, and I glanced at those large knuckles and then back up into his eyes.

"P...l...ease," I pushed past my constricted windpipe. "Kai..."

His arm shook as the fist hovered, but it didn't matter now. Black dots exploded behind my eyes, and I tried but couldn't get a breath into my burning lungs. Hot tears slid down my cheeks and were the last thing I felt before the world went dark.

Snake

Chapter 22

Kaivan

"Fuck," I roared and released Raine's neck.

I dropped to my ass beside her limp body and watched as her head lolled to the side. She looked like she was peacefully sleeping, eyes closed, and her long lashes wet from tears.

The rage still flowed like lava through my veins, and yet I... couldn't kill her. I could've easily crushed her windpipe and ended it. So many nights, I'd lain awake and stared at my small cell, picturing exactly how I wanted her to die after she finally paid for what she did to me. The lies she spread put me in the one place I promised I would never end up.

Ultimately, I didn't care as long as she was no longer breathing. Walking through her house, I'd envisioned all the possibilities, but now that the moment was here, I couldn't fucking do it.

How many people had I killed without a second thought, but the one who'd caused me more pain than anyone else...she broke me. My mind and body revolted when my hand closed around her throat. I stared into her big blue eyes that looked the same except filled with terror. My hand wouldn't listen, and my mind screamed that I didn't want to do this.

Those blue eyes haunted my mind like a viperous spirit ready to strike, and tonight they had. They'd snatched my retribution. I should be ripping them out of her head, not admiring how beautiful they still are.

"Fuck my life!"

She made me no better than my old man, and now, after everything I'd done...I was worse.

"Fuck you, Raine! Fuck you!"

Memories of her smiling and laughing as she wore her little pink outfits raced through my mind. The feel of her touch lingered as she hugged me and told me she would miss me when I left for college. Her lips on mine as I kissed her, and for those few brief seconds, my life had been perfect.

Why? I needed to know why.

Fuck this. She would pay another way.

My body shook with anger so potent I could taste it as I pushed to my feet. I bent down, picked her up, and held her in my arms as she draped across them like a doll. Her breathing was subtle, but it was there, her chest slowly rising and falling. I was thankful I hadn't killed her, which just confused me more.

Stomping up the stairs, I shouldered her bedroom door open with a bang and laid Raine out on the bed. My eyes raked over her face and then slowly trailed down her body. I pulled my knife out of my pocket and flicked it open. The front of her wet, black sweatshirt split in two with a quick slice. She was wearing a plain black tank top, and that was next to go. I groaned as the damp material pulled away, leaving her braless tits exposed to my hungry stare.

She shuddered as the cool air hit her damp skin, and her nipples formed hard little peaks. My cock twitched and came to life. Raine was still just as beautiful as I remembered, more so now that she'd lost that teenage softness. The only difference was the pixie-cut hairdo, which didn't detract from her beauty. She just looked different. I couldn't help wondering why she cut it off when she'd made such a big deal about growing it to her waist.

"Avro," she murmured, and the rage that had quieted to a simmer flared again. Oh no, she didn't just say some other guy's name.

Grabbing the front of her jeans, I cut off the decorative belt just as her eyes snapped open, and her fist flew at my face. I shifted and blocked the second shot, swatting her hand away.

"Really? We gonna do this again, Tink? It is entertaining, but I thought you might have had enough," I sneered, and spun the blade in my hand.

"Fuck you," she snarled.

She was quick, I gave her that, and she still had all the fight I'd see burning in her eyes as a teen. Rolling off the bed, she ran for the bathroom, the door slamming behind her. Sighing, I closed the switchblade and stuffed it into my pocket before shrugging off my leather jacket. Tossing it on her dresser, I walked over to the bathroom door. There wasn't even a moment of hesitation as I hauled off and kicked the door as hard as I could. My shitkicker hit dead center and broke that cheap door right off the hinges as it crashed inward.

Raine screamed and covered her head from her perch on the toilet.

"You know, Tink, I'm having way too much fun chasing you around the house. I wish it were bigger. It would make this game so much more thrilling."

I reached into the bathroom, and she yelled again. The sound went straight between my legs as she tried to kick at me and hold her ripped top closed over her tits. Damn, she looked sexy all fired up like that, and fuck, she smelled even better. All the anger and hurt I'd been carrying was suddenly channeled into something far more carnal.

Getting a hold of her flailing legs, I yanked her hard, and to her credit, she flipped over as she fell and gripped the toilet seat. Any other time, I may have laughed at the ridiculous sight we made, but right now, there was only one thing on my mind. Taking what I was owed.

There was a squeaking sound when her hands slid off the seat, and she wiggled and fought as I dragged her back into her room. I bent over and pushed her legs aside—they were more of an annoyance than an actual threat—and tossed her on the bed. Raine bounced and tried to scoot off the other side like a little rabbit, but she wasn't quick enough.

Using her legs as leverage, I yanked her back onto the bed and pinned her on her back with my larger frame. My hand wrapped around her delicate neck once more, and those big blue eyes filled with the same fear as downstairs, but something else burned underneath. It was just a flicker, but I saw it. There was lust in her eyes.

"Get off of me, Kai," she yelled, and tried to push my arm away from her neck. I was so fucking hard as she wiggled under me that I groaned, and she paused in her struggle. "This is what you want? To rape me again?" she snarled, her eyes snapping at me as fiercely as her tongue.

"I didn't fucking rape you!" I roared, and my free fist punched right through the cheap drywall, leaving a huge hole behind. "Stop fucking saying that."

Raine shook under me. Her eyes closed tight. I stared down at her terrified face and loved it and hated it at the same time. The wild and toxic mix of emotions was quickly becoming addictive. I wanted to taste that fear. I wanted to fuck her hard until she admitted it hadn't been me.

"Just go away, Kai. Please, just leave me alone," she said, her eyes fluttering open to stare at me. Tears trailed down her cheeks, but I couldn't just go. "Why do you want to torture me like this?"

A growl rumbled in my chest, and my hand tightened a little more. Her nails clawed at my bare forearm, and every red line formed made my cock harder. I pulled my knife from my back pocket and hit the release. The sharp blade glinted in the flashes of lightning from outside.

Raine sucked in a sharp breath and froze as she stared at my hand. I felt her pulse spike under my fingers, and I groaned again.

"Hands above your head, now."

She swallowed hard, the trembling in her body getting worse as she slowly let go of my arm and laid her arms on her pillow. Pressing the blade against her delicate skin, I lowered my head, drew my tongue along her cheek, and licked up every one of her tears.

"These are mine, Tink. They're my payment for your deceitful tongue." She pressed her lips together like she was going to say something, and I arched my brow at her. "You got something to say?" Her nostrils flared, and there was again the flash of something more than fear in her eyes.

My lip curled up. "Undo your jeans."

"No."

"Do it, Tink."

"I'm not helping you. You want it, then take it," Raine said, her voice laced with anger, but it was her eyes that intrigued me. They told another story than the one spilling from her lips.

"You want me, don't you, Tink? You want me to fuck you."

She narrowed her eyes. "You're insane."

"Admit it," I growled.

"Fuck. You."

I shook my head slowly back and forth at her. "Fine, you want to play it that way? I can play."

Raine watched my hand as I slammed my knife down hard into the nightstand, so it stood up straight.

"Just remember, this could've been better for you. What happens next is all on you."

Raine opened her mouth, but before she could get a single word out, I flipped her body over and yanked her arms hard so I could kneel on them and keep her from being a pain in my ass.

"Kai! No, get off me!" she wailed and thrashed, but all she did was rub her ass against my cock.

"Yeah, rub against me just like that."

Raine froze, and I smiled. I grabbed my knife off the nightstand, yanked up hard on the back of her jeans, and stabbed into the material, stripping them down to expose her ass. "Unless you want a knife in your back, I would remain still."

She turned her head and glared over her shoulder at me as I slit the sexy little thong she was wearing and ripped it away. Locking the knife, I put it back in my pocket, just in case she managed to free her hands. She was pesky enough that I could see her going for it.

Fuck, that was hot.

I hadn't been this hard since I was seventeen and wanted to fuck anything with a hole. Not a single piece of clothing or a shower was safe in those later teenage years. Raine made me lose my mind, and I was so into this.

Reluctantly, I lifted myself away from her ass, and with one hand on her back, I quickly undid my leather belt. Raine jerked at the jingle my belt made as it dropped.

"Please, Kai...fuck, please don't do this ag—" She stopped before she said the word, but I knew she was going to say, *again.*

"I'm really sick of hearing you say that. If you're smart, you'll keep those words out of your mouth. Don't tempt me to cut out your tongue," I snarled.

Raine whimpered as I grabbed her hands in one of mine and pinned them behind her back. Unzipping my jeans, I slipped my hand inside and released my cock.

"Goddammit," I groaned, stroking my shaft, and watched as a clear drop of pre-cum dripped from the tip and landed on her sexy little ass. I shivered at the sight, and I pictured getting inside of her. With a hard crack, my hand landed on her ass, and Raine cried out. Her body jerked, and she began to fight all over again.

"Oh, you don't like that? Or do you, and you don't want to admit it?" I smacked that tight little ass again.

"Go screw yourself," Raine bit back as she tried to twist herself enough to look at me.

One eye glittered in the lightning flashing through the clouds outside. It lit up the room like a strobe light in a club. The snarl that pulled up her lip was as much of a turn-on as anything else. I smacked her again and again, her screams getting louder until my hand stung and Raine was reduced to sobbing. Her whole body shook as the tears fell in a steady stream.

"Let's see, shall we?" I mocked and slid my hand between her legs. She tried hard to close her legs to keep me from invading her pussy, but she couldn't with me kneeling between them.

We were long past that. Every cell in my body screamed to fuck her. My finger slipped between her folds, and a jolt flowed throughout my body as I came into contact with her wet little cunt.

"Fuck, Tink. You are kinky. Do you feel that? Feel how wet you are?" I stroked her soft pussy lips and let them slide between my fingers. She didn't answer me, but her rapid breathing told me she was fighting off her enjoyment. "You're a sick little fuck, Tink. You accused me of assaulting you, and now you're wet for me. Not just wet, you're dripping down the inside of your legs wet." I continued to bait her and was mildly impressed when she managed to keep quiet.

On my next downward pass, I slipped my finger into her. Fuck, I was gonna cum all over her ass without getting inside of her. My cock kicked and jerked, the head throbbing for the release that I had neglected for days now. I was too busy between Souls work and stalking Raine to fuck anyone, and my balls were begging for it now.

I stroked my finger in and out of her pussy. Raine turned her head into the pillow and tried to hide her face, but the muscles squeezing around my finger said it all.

Rubbing the wet from my finger all over my cock head, I couldn't wait any longer. My body weight pressed down on Raine as I took her arms and forced them over her head. She struggled but only helped my cock slip off her ass where it had been trapped to nudge her wet pussy entrance.

"I'm going to take from you what you made me pay for," I growled in her ear. Raine sucked in a gasp, her words reduced to an incoherent mumble as she begged me to stop. "You told the world I raped you and then tossed my ass in jail for a decade. This is what you get. I might as well do the crime, right, Tink?"

Grabbing my cock, I slipped the head between her pussy lips and groaned as I thrust balls deep inside her. Her screams and tears only made me want her more.

"Oh, fuck me." I clenched my teeth as her tight walls squeezed around the intrusion. She wiggled from side to side like she was trying to dislodge me as a high-pitched squeal escaped her mouth, but all that did was push me deeper into her body. "Fuck, you feel incredible. So tight, hot, and wet."

"Get. Off. Of. Me," she said, but each word was a pant and ended in a moan.

"You can't fool me, Tink. You're enjoying yourself too much to lie to me," I growled.

Keeping my hands firmly on hers, I bit hard into the soft area at the base of her neck and let loose. Raine screamed and bucked up hard. It was useless to fight me, but I loved that she tried. She pressed her ass up into me and twisted her body. I smirked at her wild horse routine.

"Not happening, Tink. You're not getting away from what you did to me."

Each stroke felt better than the one before. The only thing louder than the slapping of skin as my cock slammed home was her begging me to stop.

Both drove me crazy. The intense pleasure was amplified when I felt her body quake and shudder around my cock. She moaned and buried her face in the pillow. I smirked and let go of her neck, bruised from where I bit her.

"You come for me, you dirty slut? You're so fucking nasty, Tink. There is no way to deny the wetness flooding my cock." I slowed my pace just enough to emphasize my point as I slid almost all the way out and then slipped back into her pussy that, despite the orgasm, was still tight, as if this was her first time. "Mmm," I moaned in her ear. "You make me so hard, Tink. I could get used to fucking your tight hole."

Raine moaned softly, so low that I almost didn't catch it. I knew I could make her cum again. Forcing her to cum for the man she charged with rape seemed like fucking great payback. I closed my eyes and fucked her as hard as I could, with the bed banging into the wall rhythmically.

"I'm never cumming for you again," Raine yelled, but her breathy voice contradicted her words.

I stared at the side of her face as she sucked her lower lip into her mouth. I wanted to taste her but figured that might be too dangerous to attempt. At least right now.

"We'll see about that." I smiled, knowing that she was going to cum again.

I slid my free hand under her body, and she yelped, but I ignored her and found her clit. Picking up my rhythm, I rubbed that little bundle of nerves, and Raine made a noise that had me chuckling as she fought to keep from having the second orgasm.

"Oh, that's it," I said and fucked her in time to my rubbing fingers, and sure enough, her walls quivered around my cock as it slid in and out of her wet heat. "You smell like spring rain and tequila. That's fucking hot, Tink. Were you day drinking at work?"

"Come on," I cooed in her ear as she trembled under me. "Cum again. Show me how much you hate my cock inside of you. How much you hate my big cock filling you up."

"I hate you," she growled.

"You may, but trust me, Tink, when you cum for me again, you're going to hate yourself more than you ever could hate me."

She was right on the edge, and I felt her breath quicken as her walls did their little clenching thing. Raine yelled as she came this time, harder than before, and she arched against my hold as the pleasure gripped her body. I relished how much she would hate herself with each passing second.

"Yeah, that's it. Give it all to me. I want you to remember that no matter what, I can make you cum all over my cock. Doesn't matter that you hate me. I can still make you cum, because you're mine. You always have been." I breathed in her scent, and a shiver raced down my spine.

Picking up my pace, I grunted as her body relaxed and became soft in my hold. Her breathing was heavy, and her face was the picture-perfect snapshot of pure, quenched desire. I pulled out, slid my cock between her ass cheeks, and humped her as my load sprayed from my cock with an intense force that stole my breath. I growled as the first stream landed on her back.

"Ah, fuck," I shouted when the second one found its mark, but I managed to keep myself from letting my entire release spill.

Dipping my cock back into her pussy to get it good and wet, I slipped out and quickly lined up with her ass.

"No! Kai! No!" Raine's panicked yell only made me more determined to fuck her tight little ass.

My cock begged for the rest of its release, like a dog begging for a treat. She was my treat, this ass, her screams. They were all her fucking penance. She wiggled hard, but I pressed into the tight rosebud and moaned as the sensitive head of my cock slowly slipped into her ass.

She wailed, her body tense, as one slow inch at a time, I pushed deeper into her body. She was so fucking tight that I could hardly move, and by the time my pelvis touched her ass, I was sweating. I held still, or I would only get a single thrust in before I exploded.

Raine was crying fresh tears, her body trembling with quiet sobs.

"Holy fuck me, Tink. You have the sweetest ass." I groaned and took a steadying breath, but my cool didn't last. "What were you thinking? That I'd settle for just a single shot at your pussy. No, no, no," I tsked. "That isn't punishment enough for what you did. The pain you caused me, the fear, the betrayal of your words. My life was stripped from me all because of you."

Releasing her hands, I gripped her hips and pulled Raine up until she had her ass in the air at the perfect angle. She cried out as I moved her, but I'd been kind up until now, and I was taking what I wanted. I thrust into her ass hard and shivered with every scream. My cock swelled as I hammered her hard as I could and quickly pulled out.

"Fuck! Yes!" I yelled as my hand slid up and down my cock at a blinding pace. The rest of my climax I'd held off thundered up from my balls, and I came with the same ferocity as the storm that raged outside. Every last drop was squeezed out of my cock before I grabbed her tear-stained cheeks and forced her to look at me.

She whimpered something and then began sobbing hard.

"What did you just say?" I asked, holding her face firm as she tried to pull her chin away. "Say it again," I growled.

"It wasn't you," she cried.

"I fucking know that," I said, stuffing my cock back in my jeans. "I. Fucking. Know. That."

Raine

Chapter 23

Raine

I blinked, not sure what had happened, but realized that the nightmare was real. Panic gripped me as I heard the rumble of men's voices, but I couldn't make out a single word or who the guys were.

Why had they taken me? Why was Kai letting them take me?

This was how girls ended up sold and overseas as sex slaves. I'd learned about it from the crime shows I liked to watch and, until tonight, had been so careful not to end up in a dangerous position.

Even though the bag was still over my head, I could see through it, but everything was blurry and shadowed, even with the bright lights. Where were we? I tried to move, but my body screamed as the pain of the hits I'd taken registered. My jaw ached, and my side felt like something was broken. The pain was sharp and made it hard to breathe. I was lying on something soft, but it stank like it was old and dusty. My nose wiggled as I held back a sneeze.

Pushing myself up with my arms, I tried to get the stupid material off my head, but it was tied too tight at the back. I could breathe okay, but the fear and the tug around my neck made it feel impossible. Holding my hands close to my face, I saw that my wrists had those awful white zip ties. They were cutting into my wrists and hurt every time I moved. Looking around, I tried to figure out where I was, but nothing seemed even familiar, and everything was shadow blobs through the stupid thing on my head.

The muffled voices were getting louder. "I don't fucking care! Someone needs to pay, and you need to learn to take control. You're a sap, a doormat, and it's time you were a man."

That was the man with the disgusting breath. Jerking upright, I didn't care if I could see well or not. I tried to run but screamed as I stepped and realized my legs were tied together. I landed hard on the floor. It was hard and cold and looked all grey, like a factory floor.

"Did you hear that?"

Oh shit! They heard me. I rolled over and sat up, hoping to get back onto what I now realized was a couch, but the door slammed open with a bang.

"Think you're going somewhere?" the man said as he stepped into the room. I couldn't see his features, but the shadow of him with the light at his back told me he was a large man.

Two more men stepped into the room, but they were both wearing black and maybe animal masks. It was hard to tell between the material on my face and the terror trying to take control. What the hell did they want from me?

"Let me go, and I won't tell anyone. I just want to go home," I said, and the man in front of me laughed. "I mean it, I promise."

"Oh, the word of a teenage girl, such a reliable source. How old are you? Fifteen, maybe sixteen? What are you doing in this area, anyway?"

"I came to see Kai fight." I looked at the other two hooded figures and couldn't tell if either was him, but the chances were good. *"Kai, tell them we're friends,"* I said, still hoping he would step in and stop whatever the hell was going on.

The man in the middle bent over, and I could partially see his features. He had a long beard and dark eyes. He smiled, and I shivered. "Oh, that is very good news for me and very bad news for you."

My forehead crinkled in confusion, but it didn't last long as he stepped forward and ordered the other two men to grab me.

"Get off of me! Don't fucking touch me," I yelled, trying to yank my arms and feet away. *"Kai, why are you doing this?"*

I lifted my eyes to the man stuffing his arms into a leather jacket, and the sobs that overcame me wracked my body. What he just did was... I couldn't even comprehend how I felt about it yet. It was the knowledge that it hadn't been him. I'd sent him to prison, and it hadn't been him.

The men who did this to me were free all this time. I knew two weren't caught, but I never understood why Kai wouldn't name his accomplices. Now I knew. He had no names to give.

Grabbing my pillow, I gripped it to my chest and rocked as I cried. They were the soul-shattering tears that only accompanied having your heart ripped out. I'd cried like this only once before, and it was the day my foster mother told me Kai had taken the deal and was going to prison. It had been the final confirmation that it was him. He didn't try to fight it, didn't say it wasn't him, and didn't want to look me in the eye. I thought he was guilty and too ashamed.

"Why?" I managed to get past my closed-off throat.

"Why what?" His face was hard as he looked at me. Those light blue eyes had always been cool with his bad-boy demeanor, but now they were ice. Nothing of the guy I remembered stared back at me.

"Why did you take the deal? Why didn't you fight the charges? Why didn't you force me to go to court and make this go away?"

Kai stomped toward me, and I instinctively backed up until I hit the wall and had nowhere else to go. I clung to the pillow like a shield, my fingers digging into the softness.

"Why? You want to know why?" he barked out, stopping at the side of the bed, his hands going to his hips.

He looked so different. Even in the poor light, the sweetness was all gone. Tattoos covered his neck, and even more were on his face. He was muscled and looked like he could snap my neck with a flick of his wrist. Yet, I still found myself cataloging every feature. He was still just as sexy, and even though it was crazy after what he'd just done to me, my heart fluttered with him here. I'd never stopped loving him. It was insanity and a loop of self-loathing mixed with the sense of loss and love that had my emotions trapped in a vortex of fucked up.

"Fuck, Tink. I had no money, a stupid public defender who could barely stay awake any time we spoke and who acted like I was lucky not to get life, and then on top of that, the Collinses abandoned me. Me and what army was going up against you in court?" He held his hands out to the side as the thunder rumbled again. The weather seemed to mirror the storm that had just gone through here.

"I could picture it playing out. You on the stand crying about how I molested you in your room, and you ran off to get away, only to have me attack you later and take what I wanted. Are you fucking kidding me? The judge or jury or whoever the fuck was listening was never going to believe me. I was the asshole that came from a bad family. My father was already doing time. I got into fights at school and fought illegally. I had no backup, no support, and no decent character witnesses. You were the only real thing in my life, the only one I trusted, and it was you I would've been fighting."

He leaned against the nightstand and crossed his arms. "The guy representing me told me that you pointed me out dead to rights in a lineup, and I could get twice as long if I didn't take the deal."

I covered my mouth, remembering the day he was talking about so clearly. He'd walked into the room with the two-way glass. I was in a wheelchair and didn't want to but pointed at Kai. He looked confused and scared, like he didn't know why he was there, yet I never saw that as a clue that it wasn't him. All I remembered was the feel of him forcing me face down on that couch as he stole my soul, and all I saw was his tattooed hand holding mine in place. Inches from my eyes, it was burned into my memory. I stared at that bird and cried. The tears made my vision blurry, but I could see it clearly in my mind.

"Why did you lie? Why did you say it was me?" he growled, and I felt the anger building inside of him again. He filled the room with his presence. He always had, but now he didn't just turn heads. I was sure people jumped out of the way when they saw him coming.

"I didn't lie," I said.

He moved so quickly I barely registered it until he had me by the jaw, his fingers once more digging into the sensitive skin. My heart rate tripled in time as he stared me in the eyes.

"It. Was. A. Lie," he growled. "I never fucking touched you, and I will cut your fucking tongue out if you say it one more time."

I swallowed hard as I tried to choose my words. "I didn't think it was a lie." His fingers softened. "I was raped, Kai. That wasn't a lie."

His brow knit together, and his hand dropped away from my jaw. With shaking hands, I moved the pillow and slowly opened the front of my ruined jeans. I pointed to the scars on my stomach and looked away to compose myself as more emotion bubbled to the surface.

"What the fuck?" Kai said.

I jumped like he'd electrocuted me when his finger touched my skin and traced the six distinct lines and the scar from surgery that would never fade. I was stuck with them as a reminder for the rest of my life. A warning that you were never safe and couldn't trust anyone.

I couldn't look at him as I spoke, or I would break down all over again, but I needed to get this out. "I went to the fights to see you. I was upset that I ran out after you kissed me. I had all this shit in my head, stupid teenage crap, but mostly I was upset that I realized you might like me, and I'd ruined it. I thought you only saw me as your foster sister, a kid." I wiped the tears off my face. "I thought you were happy to go off to college and be rid of me. So I had to talk to you. Why it couldn't wait till morning, I don't know. I just needed to see you."

I licked my lips and closed my eyes, hating having to relive this. "When I got there, I snuck in the back, and I'd only been there a few minutes when the shooting started, and everyone was running. I was crushed between bodies; there were so many people, but I managed to get to the stairs that led out. The man behind me had your tattoo. The flower with the bird."

Kai finished tracing the last scar, and I couldn't sit still. Rolling from the bed, I marched over to my closet, peeled off what was left of my clothes, and tossed them aside. Pulling on track pants and a sweatshirt, I knew that no amount of clothes would stop him, but at least I felt better. I needed a shower, but I had to finish this first.

Kai stared at me from the other side of the bed, but I couldn't read the expression on his face. It was too dark, but it felt like his stare penetrated my soul.

Crossing my arms, I tentatively stepped out of the closet, but he said nothing. In fact, he was eerily quiet.

"When I got outside, I saw the man I thought was you running away from all the commotion. He had on a simple black hoodie like you always wore and was around your height, but it was dark, and I was alone and scared. All I could think about was getting to you, my safe person, so I chased after him. He turned down an alley, and when I went down it..." I stopped and pulled the thick sweatshirt tighter like that would keep all the terrible things that had already happened from happening again.

"There were three of them. They all wore hooded sweatshirts, so I never saw their faces clearly, but he had your tattoo and was where you said you would be. I...I'm sorry," I said and covered my mouth, stifling the sob.

"What happened?" he asked, his voice as cold as his eyes. I looked at the bed.

"They put a black bag on my head, one of those ones you see in movies. I could sort of see, but not well, and they hit me until I passed out. I regained consciousness in some office. I don't know where. I hurt everywhere, and my hands and ankles were tied. They...um...they took turns with me until..." I cleared my throat. "Until they couldn't get it up anymore." My body trembled, and I wanted to yell and scream and tell myself to stop it. Instead, I paced across my small bedroom.

"The one I thought was you held his hands in front of my face when he was holding me." I stopped pacing to demonstrate what I meant. "My face was pressed down, and the only thing I could see the entire time was his right hand. When they were through, the leader did this." I pointed to my stomach. "They had to do two surgeries to fix the damage. The doctor said he didn't know how I survived and made it clear I probably should've bled out." My eyes flicked up to his. "I didn't want to live, though. He kept saying I was lucky. I didn't feel lucky. I felt anything but lucky." My eyes pleaded with him for forgiveness.

"Kai, I thought my best friend, the one person in this world I loved with my whole heart, did the unthinkable and left me for dead." I gave up on trying to hold back the tears. It was impossible as they traveled in streams down my cheeks.

His face seemed just as fierce as I walked around the bed, but I didn't feel the same explosive anger. Like a balloon letting out air, it had simply floated away. Reaching out, I took his hands and stared down at the tattoos that now lined them.

"If all this happened, why are you so certain it wasn't me?"

I looked into his eyes and silently begged for forgiveness.

"Wrong hand," I said, looking down at the back of his left hand and the tattoo. I tapped the bird and flower image that I'd never forget. "Wrong hand," I said again and choked back a sob. "Wrong fucking hand," I yelled and dropped to the floor. I screamed like I was possessed as I slammed my fist down on the old floorboards.

Looking up at Kai, I didn't know what I expected to see, but that eyebrow lift and the contempt in his eyes was not it. My heart was breaking in two, and he seemed completely unaffected.

"So what you're telling me is that you put me away for ten years based on a tattoo," Kai said.

My mouth fell open, and I searched for the words to defend myself, but my mind was stuck in neutral and spinning its wheels.

"Kai I...."

He squatted down so he could stare me in the eye. I felt like we'd traveled back in time. The way he looked at me right now was the same look he gave me when I said something he considered stupid. I tried to turn away from that intense stare.

"Don't you dare look away from me," he said calmly, but it felt like he was screaming in my ear. "Five years. I'd known you for five years. In all that time, did I strike you as a rapist?" I opened my mouth, but he held up a finger. "That was a fucking rhetorical question. No, I know I didn't. I also don't remember ever hurting you. In fact, I always stuck up for you and beat the shit out of bullies for you. I remember bringing you cake, taking you to the movies, and making you smile when you got a bad grade. I held you when you cried or had a bad dream. I played board games with you, and we made plans to see the world." He paused, and the look he gave me lanced my heart with more precision than any weapon.

"What I know is that you were my best friend, and you didn't stop for even a moment to consider that it wasn't me. I would've thought you, out of anyone, knew me." He stood, and my eyes followed him, unable to look away.

"I guess I was wrong," he said softly and veered around me to march out the door.

I heard the heavy thump of his boots on my stairs and then the slamming of the front door. I didn't think that I could hurt any more than I already did. I didn't know there was another level to the torture that attacked me all these years and made my body tremble, but I was wrong. Something far more powerful now gripped me in its clutches as it tried to rip out my soul.

I now understood guilt.

Snake

Chapter 24

Kaivan

My bike roared to life, and I sat there, letting the unrelenting rain crash down on me as if it would somehow wash away or roll back time. Pulling onto the road, I flew through the rising water that no one else would be stupid enough to drive a motorcycle in. It didn't matter that I could hardly see where I was going. As if I was on autopilot, I found myself pulling into the Lost Souls parking lot.

My hands gripped the handles so hard that they shook, and my knuckles cracked. I stared at the chain-link fence, water running into my eyes, and I felt nothing and everything. My life was one big game of fucked. There wasn't a single thing that I could remember that hadn't been painted with a toxic brush.

A terrifying rage was consuming my body and spreading at

rapid pace. The temptation to get drunk, pull my gun, and go on a rampage was erotic and enticing to my battered heart. I would never admit this out loud, but for the first time, I understood Chase Mathers and his streak of destruction.

It was only as I stared into Raine's heartbroken eyes that I realized I'd been living with no real emotion in my soul. My heart had blackened with my time in prison until I was numb, and nothing bothered me. My only real emotion had been anger, but now...now I was fucking feeling them all, and all at once. Shock, sadness, loss, betrayal, love...fuck, I still loved her.

I fucking hated to look into her face, knowing that she didn't have enough faith in me to at least speak to me before she accused me of a crime I didn't commit. But the thought of her being assaulted like that and left for dead enraged me even more. The terror in her eyes when she stared at my knife was real. The image of someone stabbing her six times made my blood run cold, and it had nothing to do with the cold water soaking me.

There was only so much you could take before you snapped, and tonight Raine filled my cup until it spilled over the edge. She'd inadvertently opened all the floodgates in my soul, and I didn't like any of the emotions pouring out.

"Hey, man, what are you doing?"

I jumped and almost fell off my bike as Wilder spoke from right beside me. "Geez-us fucking shit balls, man."

I glared at the guy as my heart restarted. What the hell was he wearing? Wilder looked ready to go deep-sea diving to attack a submarine. He was wearing a solid black outfit that was molded to every part of his body. There was more of Wilder's cock outlined than I'd ever wanted to see. He had weapons strapped to every inch of his body and was sporting night vision goggles on his face. He looked ridiculous and terrifying at the same time.

"Do you think you could give a guy a little warning instead of sneaking up on him in the dark when it's pouring rain?" I growled.

He tilted his head as if he were thinking about the concept before lifting a shoulder in a casual shrug. "But then you'd know I was coming."

"Kind of the point," I mumbled. "Is there a reason for you coming over here and giving me a heart attack?" I looked around the lot and then back to Wilder. "How did you get over here?"

"Oh, I just jumped the fence. I do it all the time," he said like that was the most normal thing in the world.

I turned to look up at the tall ass fence with the barbwire on top and shook my head. I suddenly had the urge to put this guy in a max security prison just to see how long it took before he was sitting on their front lawn doing yoga.

"I was wanting to know if you had any other tips to woo a girl?"

My brow rose. To woo a girl? Did he really just ask me that? At the moment, I was the worst person in the world to ask. He could pick the homeless guy on the street and get a better response than I could muster.

"I'm afraid to ask this, but what do you mean by woo?"

The rain suddenly stopped as if God or whoever was up there decided to flip the switch. I wiped my face off and wasn't sure if being able to see Wilder better was a good idea.

"I would prefer for the female of my interest not to scream and cry hysterically in my presence."

I bit my lip as I wondered what the fuck he was doing to some poor girl and then decided I really didn't want to know. Not my circus or, in this case, not my amusement park.

"I suggested that we watch television, but she didn't seem interested in watching anything."

"What did you put on for the two of you to watch?" I asked.

"Her friends," he said, and the corner of his mouth tugged up. That was as much of a smile as I'd ever seen on his face.

"Okay, well..." My brain screeched to a halt. "Did you just say watch her friends? Do you mean the show *Friends*?"

"No, her actual friends. You know, the ones from the sorority." I stared at him, not saying anything as I tried to piece together what code he was speaking. "See," Wilder said.

He pulled his phone out of somewhere extremely too close to his cock, which was disturbingly long as it traveled down his leg. Shit, man, wrap that around your leg or something.

Reluctantly, I took the phone from his hand and almost dropped it. One of the girls on the many little screens stripped and shook her tits for one of the other girls as they laughed and then started to make out.

"What the fuck?" I whispered, looking over all the small images of people. I found Naomi in her sorority room and held back a laugh, watching her. She was sitting cross-legged on the floor with a bag of potato chips in one hand, a jar of pickles in the other, and a massive container of peanut butter between her legs. The food was odd enough, but the bawling, like she was horrified by what she was eating, was classic.

Her friend Ava chatted enthusiastically and laughed like she was oblivious to Naomi's troubles, which made my night just a little bit better.

"Why do you have surveillance on the girls at the sorority," I asked, spotting the blonde, Lane, that Roach was obsessing over. She was brushing out her long hair as she sat on her bed with nothing more than a sports bra, flowy shorts, and bunny slippers on.

Oh fuck. Roach would be stealing Wilder's phone and jerking off to her every five seconds if he knew about this. My lip curled up. I so wasn't telling him. Fucking with the guy was going to be so much sweeter.

"I'm not really supposed to say, but I like you, Snake. You're my only friend," he said.

I was oddly torn between yelling what the fuck, driving away, and never returning or wanting to say aw. Yup, I'd definitely been hanging around the insanity too long, and here I thought prison was bad.

"Chase asked me to keep an eye on them and make sure that they were safe from Jax," he whispered, and looked around at the empty parking lot. Of course, I had to look as well, just to be sure.

"But Jax is dead. He has been for months," I said.

"I have not been told to cease my surveillance, so I will continue until told otherwise. It is my duty as a soldier."

So he really was a soldier. I mean, I figured, but that was the first time he'd said it out loud. I shook my head in wonder and tried to imagine what it was like inside Wilder's mind. Was it all just him? Was it PTSD? Was it both?

"Do you have anyone else you're watching?" I asked, wishing I could see his eyes instead of staring at the large goggles on his face that made him look like an alien.

"No."

I nodded.

"Well...no, unless you consider tracking people watching."

Reaching over, he touched the screen, and the next thing to appear was a bunch of little dots in an array of colors. Some were labeled as important buildings and landmarks, but it was the little floating bubbles with names in them that made me want to laugh. It was terrifying that I'd already wondered if he was keeping an eye on us.

All the Lost Souls members were red. There was a pin for Roach, Beast, Mannix, Tanner, and Chase. There was a pin for almost all the Lost Souls members, but there were others. A half dozen people that I didn't know were labeled in different colors.

Chase was definitely still in Canada, so we weren't going to see the fucker for a while. At least he hadn't lied to Beast. I had my doubts and couldn't bring myself to trust him.

"I don't see a pin for me," I commented, and he smiled.

"I removed your tracker. We're friends, and I don't track friends."

I decided to get the conversation back on the rails. "So other than her friends, what else did you show your love interest to watch?" Wilder screwed up his face. "Love?" he scoffed. "I do not love. She is merely interesting, and I enjoy observing her. Much how one enjoys watching animals at the zoo."

I bit my lip. Such a way with words he had. No wonder this poor girl was screaming. "I have a number of mission videos, but she didn't seem to like those, and the only other thing I have is a snuff video. That also didn't make her smile."

I needed a fucking Academy Award for being able to keep my face straight. I really wanted to know why he had a snuff film. The question was on the tip of my tongue, but I swallowed it down. That seemed like a very dangerous question.

I cleared my throat. "Well, it has been my experience that it's best to ask her what she would enjoy watching. She may like romantic comedies or action films, or straight-up horror. I also suggest offering her favorite snack and drink while you watch the movie." He opened his mouth, and I just knew what he was going to ask and cut him off. "Just ask her. She will tell you what she likes, and if she doesn't, you can grab snacks for her, like popcorn or chocolate-covered peanuts," I clarified. I could suddenly picture him offering her army rations or something.

Wilder rubbed his chin. "Once again, you have offered me good advice. I enjoy these chats." Wilder reached out and grabbed my shoulder, and I stared at his hand, trying to decide whether this newfound friendship was a good thing or not. "I'm learning so many new things from you."

Wilder turned toward the fence, and before he could do whatever acrobatics he planned to scale back over, I called out to him.

"Hey, Wilder?"

He looked over his shoulder. "What happened to all your other friends?"

"Oh, they died."

"Well, if that wasn't the most comforting thought," I mumbled as Wilder leaped onto an old crate and flipped over the top of the fence, landing without a sound. He stood and sprinted off into the dark. Great, I lived beside Batman.

I needed a new fucking life.

I'se The B'y that builds the boat and
I'se The B'y that sails her and
I'se The B'y that catches the fish and
Brings 'em home to Liza

I belted at the top of my lungs and held the round of...whatever in the air. Some liquid sloshed out and soaked my hand, but caring about shit like that was beyond me. Getting shit-faced was the most logical thing to do in my predicament.

Hip-yer-partner Sally Tibbo
Hip-yer-partner Sally Brown
Fogo, Twillingate, Morton's Harbour,
All around the circle

What else does one do when one found out that you spent ten years in prison for no good reason? I mean, I always knew that I'd been in prison for no reason. It wasn't like my cock had jumped off my body and fucked Raine before reattaching itself. The thing was, when I thought she was being vindictive and hateful like we'd been at war, I could accept that. Two enemies were facing off, but the reality was worse. Raine sent me to jail based on a tattoo—a tattoo on a board on the wall of my foster father's friend's tattoo parlor.

Sods and rinds to cover your flake,
Cake and tea for supper
Cod fish in the spring of the year,
Fried in maggoty butter

I looked down at my hand and the bird and flower tattoo and thought about cutting my hand off. Would it help? No, but maybe I could burn the thing off or slice it off. Glancing out at the room of bikers keeping their distance from me, I smiled and then yelled.

"Come on fuckers! Sing with me." I managed to pull myself up onto the bar, and the bartender ran for cover as I continued to sing and kick the glasses off the top.

Hip-yer-partner Sally Tibbo
Hip-yer-partner Sally Brown

Crash. The first glass hit the wall and shattered into a million little pieces. Why was it that everyone else could let loose and party and act like an asshole, but when I did, they stared at me like I'd sprouted horns on my head? Then again, maybe I had. I turned to look in the large mirror behind the bar, and the image was fuzzy, but there were no horns.

Fogo, Twillingate, Morton's Harbour,
All around the circle
I don't want your maggoty fish
They're no good for winter

Crash. Another glass shattered, and two guys standing around dove away from the airborne projectile. Laughing hard, I raised my glass, toasting those in the room, and then took a big swig and decided to chug the rest of it down. It burned on the way down like it was trying to burn the sin right out of me, but there was no hope of that.

I'd been born and bathed in the blood of sin. I was created by assholes, fucked over by assholes, and now I was the biggest asshole of the bunch.

Well, I can buy as good as that,
Way down in Bonavista!

I paused in my rendition of the song as the rest of the lyrics were lost to my fuzzy brain, so I just started over. Pulling my gun, I held it over the tattoo on my hand, and everyone scattered.

I'se The B'y that builds the boat and
I'se The B'y that sails her and
I'se The B'y that catches the fish and
Brings 'em home to Liza

"Whoa, there, Snake!" I stared down at Roach. His eyes were wide, his hands up in the air like he was surrendering.

"Where be da po po?" I asked and struck what I thought was a damn good gun slinger pose with my legs spread and the gun out in front of me.

"Get him off of there," one of the guys yelled.

"Fuck off, man, can't you see I'm singing here?" I yelled and turned in his direction.

"Shut up, Sparky, unless you want a hole in the head," Roach yelled.

"Yeah, a fuckin' hole in the head. What he said." I looked back to where Roach had been standing, and he was gone. "Where did he go?" I asked, amazed that Roach had leaned to disappear.

"I'm right here, bud," Roach said from my other side. He was now on the bar with me. I looked between him and the place he'd just been.

"How'd you do that?" I smiled. "Teach me. I'd like to learn how to disappear."

"Sure, once you give me the gun, and we get down." Roach held out his hand, and I stared at it with wide eyes as it went in and out of focus.

"Dude, ya need to stop moving it first," I grumbled.

"For fuck's sake." Roach touched my arm and slid his hand all the way down until he reached my hand.

"You just wanted to feel my muscles, perv," I said to Roach.

"Yup, that is definitely what I was doing," he agreed as he took the gun from my hand. "All right, let's get down."

"But I was singing for the audience. They loved my song," I said. "I was just about to dance. Wanna see me do the moon?"

"Okay, you're cut off. We don't need to see your ass. Come on down, and we can dance all the way to your house." Roach jumped to the ground, which seemed really far away.

"What does my ass have to do with a moon?" I asked, confused. "Look, I'll show ya." I went to walk backward like Michael Jackson, but Roach grabbed my leg.

"Down! Right the fuck now," he ordered.

"Guess I found the po po," I mumbled and decided to sit down before making the final daredevil leap off the bar. "Rawr!" I yelled as I landed and lifted my arms like I was going to attack him.

"What the fuck was that?" Roach asked.

"I'm a monster," I said. "Isn't it obvious?" I turned to the sitting area of the clubhouse. "Fuck, man, why are all you fuckers running in circ..."

Chapter 25

Avro

I tapped my finger on the table and stared at my phone like that would somehow magically make it ring. I was being the over-possessive worrier, and I knew it. My eyes flicked up to Jace arguing with his manager on the phone. Jace would say I was too needy and should back off and give Raine some space to breathe and process. He was right, of course, but there was this knot in my stomach that wouldn't go away.

I chugged down the rest of my coffee and put my phone in my pocket before signaling to Jace that I was going to the bathroom. He nodded, and I slipped away. Stepping into the men's room, I pulled out my phone and hit Raine's number. It rang four times and went to voicemail.

"Shit." I called her again and tried to keep the worry from

creeping into my pores. If that happened, then I would be in full-on panic mode.

Hi, this is Raine. You know what to do.
Beep

"Hey girl, it's me. Um, nothing wrong, but if you could give me a call when you get a second. I'm still at the airport with Jace. Talk later."

My thumb hovered over the delete message button as the door opened, and I spun around to see Jace leaning against the door frame. He smirked and shook his head.

"You just couldn't resist, could you?"

I opened my mouth and looked at the phone, my brain scrambling to find some excuse that wouldn't make me sound like a total loser.

"Don't bother lying. I know you tried calling her. The stench of guilt is wafting off you."

"Shit, I just...fuck, I have a bad feeling. I can't explain it," I said as Jace walked toward me.

"How is it that someone so fucking sexy is so insecure?" My face heated with the compliment that also happened to be an insult. Jace wrapped his arm around my shoulder and forced me to turn and look into the mirror. "Look at yourself. You're lickable."

I smiled and shook my head. "You're also crazy. I'm not worried about her not wanting to be with us." Jace lifted his eyebrows. "Okay, I may be a little worried about that, but I don't know...I just have a bad feeling. Like one of those nervous, I can't explain it, feelings."

Jace didn't say anything as he walked over to the urinal, relieved himself, and washed his hands with the overly orange-smelling soap. I knew he was thinking. He got all introverted when he was deep in thought.

"Could it be the storm," Jace finally said. He tossed the paper towel into the air and made a little swooshing sound as it sank into the garbage. "Still got it." His eyes turned back to mine, and I shrugged.

"I don't know. Maybe, I guess."

"Avro, at some point, you'll have to find a way to stop letting your uncle control you. The man is dead, and he's not coming back from the grave to attack you. If he does, I'll be fucking running right beside you. That's straight-up *Walking Dead* territory."

I rolled my eyes at Jace. "I don't think he's springing from the grave. I just still get edgy about storms." I crossed my arms. "Besides, trauma is different for everyone, Jace. I don't choose to be like this."

Those silver eyes met mine, and I knew the rant was coming. "Avro, are you really wanting to start the laundry list argument? I may not have had a shitty uncle, but I fucking know pain and fear."

"Oh my god. You are so different from me. You're pedal to the floor, no looking back, take on the world, nothing bothers you for long," I said and then looked at the door as someone opened it.

The orderly with his bucket and mop stopped and stared between us, looking like we were ready to come to blows. Without a word, he backed out, and the door closed behind him.

"The point is, I'm not like you. I'm never going to be like you, and as much as I would love for storms not to bother me, they may always bother me. Are you going to call me out on it for the next fifty years?"

Jace took a deep breath, and the sound seemed so loud in the quiet bathroom. "I'm like that because I have to be." He paced away from me.

"What are you saying, Jace?" He didn't say anything as he stared at the door. "Jace?"

Jace whipped around, and his eyes narrowed in anger. "I'm like this because I'm always the rock. I have been since we were eight years old, and except for...well, you know the shit, I've always had your back and taken on the world for both of us." His words were a punch to the gut, and I took a step back. "Now, I know that I chose to be, just how I chose to be there when shit went sideways at school or home or with your uncle or afterward and then every night since."

"So you're saying I'm a burden?" My anger dangerously mixed like a cocktail in my system.

"No, never a burden, but Avro, let's be real for a moment. From the day we met until today, when have you been the rock in our relationship? Forget my family shit." He held up his hands. "Aside from those few months where I will admit that you and my music were the only things that got me through. Aside from that, when? Did you comfort me when we did what we did with your uncle? Have you spent any time since wondering how that night affected me?"

I hated that he was calling me out like this. Our life had felt perfect for so long, a fairy tale that others never got to live. Now Jace was poking at that image in my mind. Water was leaking out, and it was supposed to be my fault? It was true that I'd never spoken of that night again or asked him how he was, but we'd promised not to mention it. I thought I'd been there for him as much as he was for me, like we balanced one another out.

"Fine, don't say anything. I'm going to go sleep on the plane." Jace had the door open and was gone before I even got my stubborn lips to move.

I followed him out into the small area before the glass doors and the private jet sitting in the hangar. I could see Jace marching for the plane, but I needed a moment. Sitting at the table, I stared at the phone that refused to ring and ease my worry. As the rumble of thunder outside grew louder, the memories of that night came back to me.

. . .

"Mom, you know I hate camping. Why are you forcing me to go?" I asked, dragging my back duffel behind me like a ball and chain.

Camping felt like a death sentence. It had been the same way my entire life, yet every year my mom made the same plans with the same people to do the same things I hated. It took us forever to get there, and everyone wanted to sing and play games that made me want to cry. I was thirteen. Singing "Ninety-Nine Bottles of Beer on the Wall" or playing Eye Spy was no longer fun.

I just wasn't the type who liked to be out in the wilderness with bugs, snakes, and whatever else. I hated that there was no good way to charge my phone unless my Uncle Martin and Aunt Tilly let me use their truck. I hated that the only way to bathe for the entire week was in the little springs. Most of all, I hated leaving Jace behind, but my mom insisted that this was strictly family time.

"Alex, you're going to be going off to college in a few years, and you will have these memories with your family for the rest of your life," Mom said, her face glowing as she smiled.

As I suspected, it was seventeen hours of hell before we reached the campsite.

"Alex, help your cousin set up her tent," Mom said, but Courtney glared at me. You couldn't find two more opposite people, and for reasons I'd never figured out, Courtney hated me.

Doing as I was asked, I wandered over to Courtney. "Hey, did you want help with your tent?"

"If I wanted help, I would ask for it," she bit back.

I went to turn away but stopped and instead took a step closer. My voice lowered so only she could hear. "What the hell is your problem with me? I rarely see you, and I've never done anything to you, so why the fuck are you like this?"

Courtney looked around, making sure that the adults were engrossed *in their own conversation. "I may only see you three times a year, but I can't get out from under your shadow. When we were little, all my parents talked about was you and how much they wished they had a boy, a boy just like Alex. Then it was how academically smart you are and how you'll get a full scholarship to whatever school you want. You couldn't stop there, though. Nope, the one thing I had was soccer, and I was amazing, but the moment you picked up a basketball and made the senior team, I lost that too." Courtney took a step closer. "How many games do you think my dad made after that? None. Why? 'Cause he was too busy going to your games to support you."*

She put her hands on her hips and glared at me, her eyes narrowed into slits. "All I hear is how amazing you are and how they wished I could be more like you. If he weren't my dad, I'd say he fucking likes you."

"First, how is any of that my fault? Second, that's fucking disgusting, like I'd want to fuck your dad, and lastly, all it says is your parents are jerks," I said and realized that it was louder than I intended. I looked over my shoulder, and four sets of eyes stared at us. Shit.

"Huh, looks like you might have just dropped down a peg there, Alex. Thanks," Courtney whispered and walked away.

The rest of the week was awkward. It was obvious that everyone had heard, and yet in our family, you didn't 'air your grievances,' as my mother would say. My aunt and uncle took turns glaring at me, but Courtney was miraculously much nicer. Fuck, I hated camping.

Thankfully, we'd reached the last day, and because it was storming so hard, it gave me the perfect excuse to remain in my tent while the others took turns hanging out. The storm was getting nasty, and my tent blew around me like a tarp. The rain that drowned out everything continued without any end in sight. We would've floated away by now if we'd still been back home.

J: You back tomorrow?

A: Yeah, thank god.

J: You wanna hang out when you get back?

A: *Not sure what time I'll be back, but I'll text you.*

J: *Cool. Check ya later.*

A: *Night.*

I turned off the phone and placed it in my bag for safekeeping and realized just how dark it had gotten. I didn't know what time it was when I was woken up. It was still dark outside, and the thunder rumbled with the driving rain.

I hadn't heard my tent flap opening or registered the blanket disappearing until hands gripped my sleeping pants and tugged them down. My half-asleep, muddled mind made me think it was Jace until a hand gripped the back of my neck.

All the sleepy fuzz dissipated, and my eyes snapped open, but I couldn't see who had me.

"Get off me," I said and tried to push myself up off the ground.

A heavy weight pressed down on my back, and hot breath fanned my ear. I was fit for my age, but as hard as I tried, I couldn't move. My heart was racing wildly, and I wanted to yell for help, but something was stuffed into my mouth when I opened it to scream.

"You're a disrespectful little prick." I froze at the sound of my uncle's voice. This wasn't some stranger that had wandered into our campsite. This was someone I knew.

"I'm sorry," I mumbled, but he didn't listen. "Courtney made me angry. I didn't mean to..."

"Shut the fuck up, and before you go squealing to your parents, they'll never believe you. They'll throw you out of the house, disown you for making trouble, and make sure that all your friends and family know exactly what you are...a cock lover."

I gulped down the panic of what his words meant, and my body trembled with the spike of adrenaline. He held me down harder, my face painfully pressing into the pillow so that I could feel the rough ground beneath the thin tarp bottom. I struggled to breathe and kicked out, thrashing around, trying to break free of his grip. At six-five, he was a big *man, but I'd never seen my uncle as a threat until this moment. As he forced my legs apart, all I could see was his glare from earlier in the day.*

How had I missed the malice in his eyes?

I whimpered as his naked cock pressed down on my ass. I knew what was coming. My brain had revolted against the idea that this could happen, but it was hard to deny when you felt the reality against your skin.

The reality was that someone I loved and trusted could do this to me. That someone I thought was family would hurt me like this. But as he took what he wanted, and the tears fell, I didn't know if I could ever trust anyone again.

Thunder crashed and made me jump from my seat. I looked down at my shaking hands and then toward the plane as the lights flashed. There was only one person I learned to trust with my whole being after that day. Well, now two, but only one of them was here.

Marching across the small terminal, I pushed open the doors to the private jet and jogged up the stairs. I expected Jace to be asleep, but he was lying in bed writing in his songbook.

As soon as he looked over, I knew that he was right. I'd leaned on him from the moment I got back from that camping trip and never stopped.

"I'm sorry." Jace lowered the book. "You're right. I never asked you if you were okay. I figured you'd tell me if you weren't, and it was selfish of me to think that just because you were the rock I needed, you weren't suffering."

"Pfft, he got what he deserved," Jace said, pointing to the other side of the bed. I smirked.

"True, but still." I sat down and kicked off my sneakers before stretching out.

"You're not the only one that needs to apologize. I don't do the sharing thing well, and I find it easier to let you lean on me than share, but I can't get mad when you did exactly what I expected you to do."

We stared at the ceiling as I tried to picture living like this all the time, traveling the world and sleeping in the jet with him. The moment I thought about it, Raine's face floated into my mind, and my chest ached. No, I didn't want to leave her, but I didn't want Jace to go without me, either. I felt like I was in a trap of my own making.

"What were you writing?" I asked.

"New ballad. Was kinda thinking of doing a love song about being torn between two people," Jace said, turning his head to look at me.

"Is the song for me or about me?" I smiled, feeling like he'd hit way too close to the mark.

"I guess we will have to see once it's done," Jace said.

I pushed myself up and stared down into his eyes. "You know I love you, right? Don't ever think that has changed."

"What happens if I say I have my doubts?" Jace ran his tongue along his lip, and that one little act had my blood heating and my cock twitching.

"You may need to be reassured that I do still love you. I wouldn't want you flying off and having any reservations," I said, laying my hand on his stomach. His abs flexed under my touch.

"Is that so?" Jace wrapped his hand around the back of my neck. "Then I think I have many, many doubts."

I leaned down, and our lips met, as potent as the first time we kissed. I really did love make-up sex.

Chapter 26

Kaivan

"Fuck, my head," I groaned as the man with the ice pick stabbed me in the eye.

I grabbed my forehead and sucked in a breath as I tried to push myself up. I didn't remember much of what happened, but it definitely involved large amounts of alcohol. Had I been singing? I had a warped memory of "Ninety-Nine Bottles of Beer on the Wall" from earlier in the night.

The pain throbbed and gripped my brain as my stomach flipped. *Not good.* Jumping up, I ran to the bathroom and looked like I was doing a fancy dance move as I dropped to my knees and slid the last couple of feet to the toilet. I made it just in time. Gripping the sides of the bowl, I emptied my stomach and then wanted to throw up

"Fuck," I mumbled, flushing the toilet and leaning my head against the wall.

"Well, isn't this a pathetic fucking sight?" Roach yelled.

I cringed with every word, like he was screaming right beside my ear.

"Shh," I managed to get out and turned my head enough to see his arrogant and way too happy expression as he leaned against the doorjamb. *Prick.*

"Oh no, no. Not after what you pulled last night. I'm going to make your life a living hell, and I'm starting with this. *I'se The B'y that builds the boat and I'se The B'y that sails her,*" he roared at the top of his lungs.

I groaned and cowered away from the noise, praying that the wall would swallow me.

"I'm going to kill you when I can stand," I said, slowly pushing myself to my feet.

Roach laughed. He turned on the water faucet, and like a homing beacon, I followed the noise and braced my hands against the counter as I let my stomach settle.

"How much did I drink? Feels like I tried to chug everything in the clubhouse," I said, splashing my face with some water and rinsing my mouth out before that felt like too much exercise.

"You drank more than I've ever seen you drink, and there was no sipping. You started the night drinking from a bottle of whiskey, and things didn't improve from there," Roach said as he slipped an arm around my waist and helped me back out of the bathroom.

I would never tell the guy this, but I'd always appreciated Roach's friendship. He could be as annoying as the bug he was nick-named after, but I always knew he had my back, and in this world, that went a long way. He helped me sit, and I realized it was my living room couch. I had no memory of making it home and hated that sensation. I'd lost control of so many things in my life that I refused to put myself in a position where I had to rely on others. I did that last night—just another thing I could blame on Raine.

"Here," Roach said and held out a bag and coffee. I peered into the greasy bag, and my stomach rolled as if telling me to go fuck myself. "Eat one. You need something to sop up the shit in your stomach."

Even though I didn't want to, I pulled one of the breakfast burritos out of the bag and slowly unwrapped it. I stared at it, and it stared back. I think we were officially in a standoff.

"All right, spill." Roach flopped down on my powder blue recliner. He looked ridiculous, and I wondered if I looked just as strange when I sat there. As if reading my mind, Roach stared down at the chair. "Huh, surprisingly comfortable."

"You want to analyze anything else while you're in here? How about the position of the television, perhaps?" I took a bite of the burrito and swallowed, and when it didn't hit an immediate ejection button, I kept eating.

"Nope. All I want to know is why you've been an asshole for days. What, or should I say, who has got you acting like an asshole dipped in something sour and rolled in shit? You've been practically hostile, so I'm not leaving until you talk." He crossed his arms, and I wanted to punch his annoying face.

"I'm fine," I said. Stubbornly, I tried to push myself to my feet, but that wasn't happening. The room spun, and the band began to play in my brain again.

"Oh yeah, you look real fine." Roach leaned forward and hit me with a hard stare. "Talk, or I'm going to sing the Barney song at the top of my lungs, over and over." His lips curled up.

"That is the stupidest and most horrifying threat I've ever heard," I said, and we both smirked.

The coffee was from the shop I liked. I popped the lid off and took a huge gulp before meeting Roach's gaze.

"You're not going to leave, are you?"

"Not a fucking chance. I've given you space to deal with your shit, but instead of getting over whatever crawled up your ass, you're getting worse." He dug around in his pocket and pulled out his phone. I heard my voice and cringed before I took the phone from his hands. I watched myself standing on a bar waving a gun and singing a song I didn't even know I knew.

Hitting stop, then delete, I tossed the phone back.

"Asshole, don't fuck with my video. I'm pulling that out of the trash. It's my blackmail." Roach smiled and spun the phone in his fingers. "Now talk."

"You remember how I ended up in prison?" Roach lifted a brow and stared at me like I was a fucking idiot. "Okay, fine, you remember. The point is, I found her."

"Damn, no way." A smile broke out on Roach's face as he leaned forward. "Where's the bitch's body, and do I need to cover anything up?"

A flare of anger ignited in my chest. "Don't fucking call her that." I knew it was a mistake to say anything as soon as the words were out of my mouth.

Roach smacked a hand off his knee and began to laugh. "You still like her!" He laughed as I glared. His face sobered. "Oh shit, you really do," he said, his voice losing all the humor. "Fuck, I was only joking. How the hell is that possible?" he yelled.

His annoyingly loud enthusiasm was splitting my head in two.

"Shh, man. Fuck." I groaned and rubbed at my forehead.

"All right, tell me everything. I need to know how you can still like her after everything."

"I'm not your personal soap opera," I said. "Fine, whatever," I grumbled when he just stared. "She didn't send me to prison out of spite. She actually thought it was me."

Roach screwed up his face. "But I thought you didn't do it?"

"I didn't."

"Okay, then why the hell would she pick you, of all people? I mean, weren't the two of you friends or some shit?"

I sighed as I thought over what all Raine had told me. If I hadn't been so furious, I might have asked a couple more questions, but last night I needed to get as far away from her as possible. I yanked another breakfast burrito out of the bag and tore into it.

"She went down to the fights where I was supposed to be—don't ask me why, but I wasn't there. I was too banged up to go but didn't want to be around the house. Anyway, she was attacked by three men, and one of them had the same tattoo as this." I held up my hand and pointed to it.

"That still doesn't make sense. How did she not see his face? Are you sure she's telling you the truth and not something to keep you from hurting her?"

"Too late for that. I messed her up and may have done what I was in jail for," I said. My cock twitched at the thought of being inside her. Feeling her come all over me. The smell of her skin.

Fuck! Enough of that.

"Damn, and people call me the asshole." Roach held out his hand. "Gimmie one of those."

I tossed a burrito at him and chugged the rest of my coffee before continuing. I hated to admit it, but my stomach seemed pleased with the addition of solid food, and my head hurt less.

"Point is, I don't know what to do with this. She should've at least spoken to me before she named me as her attacker, but she was fifteen, terrified, stabbed, and left for dead. So...there's that. Before you ask, I don't know why I only got ten years. I'm thinking Raine had something to do with that, but I was too pissed to ask last night."

We ate in silence, and I stared out the window. The sun shone like mother nature hadn't just tried to kill us yesterday.

"Don't get pissed with me for asking this..." He shrugged. "But do you still have a thing for her? Like not of the obsessive hate variety?"

I laid my head back on the couch. My first instinct was to yell no and tell him to fuck off, but the reality was, I didn't know. No, that wasn't true. The ache in my chest and the pounding of my heart at the thought of her told me I was trying to lie to myself.

"I think so," I admitted. "But the hate for what she did to me, regardless of why, is as strong as any other emotion."

"Oh, I love hate-sex. I'm in."

I lifted my head to glare at Roach.

"I didn't mean with her. I just meant that it's one of the best ball-boiling, euphoric experiences," Roach said, his lip curling up.

"That's a mighty big word to be coming out of you," I teased.

"Shut the fuck up," Roach said and then looked out the window. The sound of a vehicle had him standing and pulling his gun as he did. "You know anyone with a little red car?"

"Nope."

I managed to get to my feet and hobbled over to the window. Fuck, my head didn't like that, and I had to grab at the wall.

"Damn, she's hot. Who the fuck is that? Someone looking for directions, or is she lost? I would give her directions right into my bedroom," Roach said, sticking his gun in the back of his jeans.

I reached the window and saw Raine bent over, talking to the driver. A moment later, the car backed out and disappeared. My heart stumbled in my chest at the sight of her. The sunshine bathed her like a little fairy in my yard.

"Fuck, that girl is fine. I'll be right back," Roach said, and I snatched his arm.

"That's Raine. You go anywhere near her with your cock, and I'll kill you," I growled.

"That's her? No wonder you have it bad. How the hell did she find you?" Roach asked as a soft knock echoed through the house.

"I don't know," I mumbled, releasing Roach's arm. Roach walked to the front door. "Where the hell do you think you're going?"

"Oh, I'm not staying here for this. I need plausible deniability." He smirked as he whipped open the door dramatically. I saw Raine jump back like she'd just been hit. I couldn't blame her.

"Um, hi. I was told Kai is here," she said, and my traitorous cock stood at the sound of her voice. I couldn't get my head to stop spinning, but my cock worked fine. Figures.

Roach stepped onto the porch, and Raine's eyes swung from him to me.

"Hunt me down when you're done. I have an errand I need you for," Roach said as he looked over his shoulder at me. His look said it all. He would fuck her if I gave him even a sniff of an opportunity.

His eyes were filled with mischief as he stood beside Raine, and I realized just how small she was. The anger that started last night over her attack flared in my gut. In a flash, I pictured her at fifteen, lucky to weigh eighty pounds soaking wet, trying to fight off three grown men. My teeth ground together until my jaw cracked.

"Don't have too much fun," Roach said, smiling as he jogged down the stairs.

Prick.

I pushed the pain in my skull aside and stepped up to the door, and as I looked into her big blue eyes, I knew it didn't matter why she was here. My fucking heart was in trouble.

She had her hands stuffed inside her sweatshirt pocket, but her back was straight as she stared at me.

"What are you doing here?" I looked around outside. "And how the hell did you find me?" It was a little annoying that she'd found me in less than twenty-four hours.

"I noticed your patch last night." She lifted a shoulder and let it drop. "A girl that worked at my club used to hook up with one of the members. She used to talk about this place and where it was." Raine pointed to the fence and the guards keeping watch. "I asked for you, and they pointed me here."

I was going to have to have a chat with those fuckers. I didn't care who it was. They shouldn't tell anyone where the fuck I am.

"Fine. Why are you here?"

Pulling her hands out of the pocket, she played with the cuffs of her hoodie, a nervous habit she had even back when I met her. She'd ruined more sweatshirts than I could count when the threads would finally give up and the cuff would fall off. I always loved to see her in mine when she stole them, but I would scold her for trying to ruin them.

"May I come in? I promise I won't stay too long. I just need to speak to you." She met my stare, and I cocked a brow at her as I ignored the steadily growing interest in my jeans that very much wanted her to come inside.

"You trust coming in here and being alone with me after last night?"

She crossed her arms and looked away.

"You proved that you will find me and take what you want anyway, so what does it really matter if I'm here or somewhere else?" she asked, and my back bristled. She wasn't wrong, but I still didn't like being called out like I was the bad guy.

"Whatever."

I stepped out of the way, letting her walk past me, and closed the door. She jumped but tried to hide it. Once again, I was conflicted by her presence. I loved that she jumped, and my cock stirred more with her reaction, but the reason she was so scared bothered me. A psychiatrist wouldn't even be able to wade through the confusing shit floating around in my head.

"Alright then, speak," I said and went to sit on the couch.

Raine looked like a cat, wary of its surroundings, as she slipped across the living room and sat in the chair Roach had occupied not long before. I watched her carefully and took in every bit of her body language. Raine rubbed her hands on her legs and then sat on her hands. Again, something she'd always done.

"I came to say I'm sorry." She paused and looked at me, and I shrugged.

"That's it? That's all you got?"

Her eyes narrowed before she took a deep breath. "All night, I thought about what you said, and you're right. I should've talked to you before I gave the police your name." She turned her head to look out the window, and I could see the stress in her eyes. I had the urge to wrap her in a hug like I would've done before all this shit went down, but now I stayed put.

"What is this? Do you feel guilty or some shit now? Little too late for that, don't you think?" I leaned forward, and her heated glare met my own. "Look at me. You ruined my life. Your guilt is not my problem. That's a you problem."

Her eyes filled with tears, but her jaw tightened, and I could see her fighting not to let them fall.

"You're right. It's not your problem." She bolted to her feet. "Forget it, Kai. I just wanted you to know that I'm going to speak to a lawyer about the steps to retract my statement and have the charges removed from your record. I'll pay for it, of course."

"What fucking good is that going to do? I already did ten years."

"Well, at least this way, you won't have to worry about police seeing that you're a parolee or have a record for rape. I'll have it all removed, and I'm going to have it sealed. I'll probably need you to sign paperwork, but it's the only thing I can think of to apologize for what I did."

A wiped record? I actually liked the idea, but instead of saying that, I stood and stared down at her. I liked that she stood tall and held my gaze.

"It will never make up for what I went through."

"Maybe, maybe not, but I haven't learned how to build a time machine, so it's all I've got," she snipped back, and my lips curled up. Fuck, she was hot when she was scared and sexy as fuck, riled up. My eyes went to the bruise, peeking through the makeup on her neck before I stared her down.

"Okay. Thanks."

Nodding, she turned to walk away, and I called out to her, unsure why I asked.

"Tink, before you go. Tell me something. Who found you, and why did Dave and Irene never come to see me?"

She turned to look at me, and her face was twisted in confusion. "I don't know."

"What do you mean?"

"I mean, I was in an old industrial building and didn't make it to a phone." She held up her wrists and walked close enough that I could see the scars I hadn't been able to see in the dark last night. "My wrists and ankles were bound with zip ties. As for the Collins-es..." She shrugged. "I don't know. As soon as I mentioned the tattoo to the officer, Dave ranted about how he always knew that under all of the trying to get good grades, you were a fuck up. Then Irene chimed in and said you'd propositioned her. She started crying and said she could've prevented this from happening."

"She said what?" I barked out, and Raine took a step back. Her eyes went to my hands, clenched into fists.

"That you asked her to have sex with you. She said that you pushed her up against the freezer and said that you could fuck her better than her husband. She said it wasn't the first time you'd gotten aggressive with her, and she'd feared for her life but was too embarrassed to say anything."

"Son of a bitch," I growled and marched away. I spun around and faced Raine. "Let me guess, you heard that, and on top of the tattoo, all you could picture was me attacking you?" Her eyes flicked away, but she didn't need to say it. I saw it in her eyes. "You know what the irony is?" She shook her head. "I was fucking Irene." Raine's mouth dropped open, and her hands fell to her sides. "The bitch hit on me watching a movie and then cornered me in the garage and threatened to have me kicked out if I didn't fuck her. Don't get me wrong. I was seventeen and horny. The idea of sex with anyone interested me, but I didn't force her. Not even once."

Raine put her hands on her hips. "Let me get this straight. We were hanging out all the time, and you kissed me, but you were fucking our foster mother?"

I ran my hand through my hair. "As I said, she threatened to toss me out. Besides, I was young, dumb, and horny, and you were off limits, anyway."

Raine tilted her head to the side as she scrutinized me with her stare. "Doesn't look like much has changed in the dumb and horny department."

I growled and was on the move before I realized I was even walking. Raine squealed as I grabbed her and pushed her up against the wall.

"You're pretty mouthy for being inside my home," I said as she glared at me. I was tempted to kiss her. She licked her lips, and it was all I could think about, but I pushed away from her instead.

"Get out. I don't want to see you again."

"I need to ask you something," she said as I marched away from her and went to the kitchen to make another coffee.

"Yeah, well, I'm done talking to you," I snarled as she followed me.

"This is important," she said and leaned against the doorjamb. She looked way too sexy and adorable. I wanted to crush her and eat her up all at the same time.

"Will it get you out of my house if I answer?" I asked and busied my hands, making the pot of coffee.

"Yes. I just need to know if you're clean," she said, and my hand stilled as I was about to dump the little grounds into the filter.

"What the fuck did you just ask me?" I turned my head and stared at her.

"Don't do that, Kai. Don't act like I don't have a right to know," she said, her voice inching up a few octaves with her anger. "You attacked me last night, and I haven't seen you in over eleven years. Most of that was spent in prison, and I have no idea what you've done since you got out. You could've screwed your way around the world and back again for all I know."

My teeth ground together, and I wanted to tell her to fuck off and take her chances. Just looking at her brought up the memories of last night and what it felt like being inside her. I needed to calm the fuck down, or I was going to take her right there against my wall. I might've contemplated it longer if my hangover didn't choose that moment to bite like it was trying to rip out my brain.

"You okay?" Raine asked as I squinted and sucked in a breath. She took a step toward me, and I hated that she still acted the exact fucking same. Worrying, checking up on me, and showing affection when I didn't deserve it.

"Stay away from me, Tink, unless you want more of last night." She froze, her eyes going wide. Fuck, that was hot. "Haven't you learned your lesson by now? Don't put your arm inside the dangerous animal's cage." Raine swallowed and backed up to the doorway again.

Stomping over to the black organizer in the corner by the old landline, I thumbed through the paperwork until I found my last test results. I tested all the time. I wasn't unsafe, but I wasn't exactly celibate, and prison can make you a little paranoid. Yanking the sheet out, I walked over to Raine and tossed the paper at her.

"In case you're wondering, I only got tapped once in prison. Luckily, the guy was clean, but he had an unfortunate accident a few days later." Raine's mouth dropped open. If she only knew the body count, I had in my wake. "And other than you, your royal highness, I have always used protection and get tested every six months. So yeah, I'm fucking clean."

I turned back to the counter as Raine unfolded the page and began to read. "Maybe I should be asking for one. Who knows where your pussy has been?" I growled.

"Fuck you, Kai." Tossing the paper on the floor, she turned and marched for the door.

My body shook as I held myself in place and didn't chase her swaying ass down. Fuck, she made me hard and hot, and I wanted to put my fist through another wall and fuck her until she was screaming my name.

"Show yourself out," I yelled. She didn't say a word or look back, which pissed me off even more.

I leaned against the counter and slumped at the sound of the front door slamming. Fuck, why didn't that feel right? I should never want to see her or her big blue eyes again, but...

"Fuck!" I slammed my fist on the counter. She was making me crazy all over again.

Raine

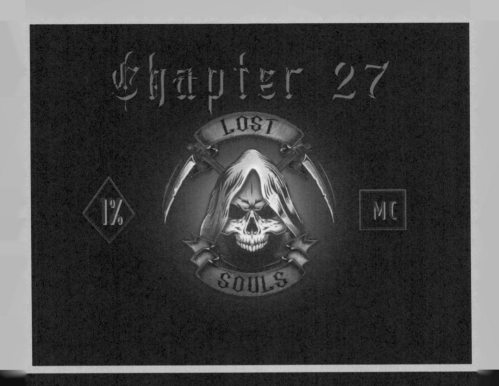

Chapter 27

LOST SOULS
1% MC

Raine

I wandered down the sidewalk toward my house, my head a swirling mass of confusion, as I tried to ignore my aching muscles. Even if I could, my body wouldn't let me forget what happened last night.

No matter what Kai said, he wasn't blameless. I understood his anger. I was angry at myself for not giving him a shot to explain that it wasn't him, but last night happened. He attacked me in my home and there wasn't a doubt in my mind that he had planned to kill me until he decided to do what he did instead. What was worse was that I'd started to enjoy it, and I hated myself so much for that. Why? That was the burning question with no answer.

I hoped that what I offered him as an olive branch was enough for him to leave me alone. It was his clean slate.

If Kai wanted to remain a gang member, he could. If he wanted to move away and start a business without his past hanging over him, he could do that too. Heck, he could go back to school if it was what he wanted. At least the choice would be his again. I couldn't erase the past, but I could at least make sure that people didn't judge him for something he'd never done.

My mind was busy making notes of everything I needed to get done today, including a new screen for my phone since mine cracked in the fight last night. I was so engrossed that I didn't notice the black car and the man leaning against it until it was too late to turn around.

A warmth spread throughout my body at the sight of Avro, and I suddenly wished I wore a turtleneck even though it was eighty-five outside. I hadn't even begun to contemplate how to explain Kai or the attack to Avro and Jace, or if I should just keep my mouth shut. Shit...

"Hey, what are you doing here?" I smiled as I turned, so the bruised side of my neck was away from him.

Avro didn't answer. He just reached out and grabbed me, pulling me into a hug. Why I wanted to cry suddenly was beyond me, but as I wrapped my arms around him and took in the sweet comfort he offered, I could feel the tears prick at the back of my eyes.

He kissed the top of my head and didn't say anything for a long time. "Why didn't you answer my calls last night? I was worried when I couldn't reach you," he said.

"Yesterday was very strange, and I don't want to talk about it right now." I forced the words past my constricted airway. I could feel where Kai choked me as if he was still gripping my throat. "Did Jace get away okay?"

"No, he's here for a couple more days. Not that I'm complaining. The next two concerts couldn't be rescheduled, so the rest of the band left for San Francisco. He didn't have to leave yet and opted to stay and spend more time with us."

I held him a little tighter. Avro was like bathing in a warm, sensual bath of muscle. I opened my mouth to tell him about last night, but I just couldn't. The words wouldn't form. How did you say, 'I was raped again, but it was okay this time because I felt like I deserved it?'

The next issue was that I didn't know how to hide the bruises all over my body or spend time with them and not stay the night. My life had suddenly gotten much more complicated in the blink of an eye.

"That's great," I said, unsure what else to say.

"You heading into work?" Avro asked. "I noticed that the inventory isn't done. I stopped there on my way here to find you."

Stepping back, I rubbed at my face. "Yeah, I'll have to go in. I spent most of yesterday chasing a stray cat all around the bar. It broke a bunch of full bottles, and I got scratched and had to go to the hospital. It was a really weird ass day."

"Okay, let's go. I'll help you. Jace is busy working out the melody to the new song he wrote, and when he's in that headspace, you don't go near him. Not unless you want your head bit off." Avro winked. "I still like to entice him from time to time, just to make sure my ability to corrupt is still aces."

"I'm pretty sure he always has a hard time saying no to you." I smiled back and vividly remembered how sexy the two men were together.

"Let's just say it is one challenge I thoroughly enjoy winning, and I have a feeling that you will find it just as entertaining." The sexy look that lifted the corners of his mouth made me blush.

I cleared my throat. "I'm sure you're right. I guess we better go. Too much to do and not enough hours."

I wasn't sure this was a great idea, but I couldn't think of a single excuse he would actually believe. I got in the passenger seat, and while he walked around the car, I bunched my hood a little more around my neck.

Avro slipped into the driver's seat and looked over at me. "You sure you're okay? You seem...distant. Not your normal self."

"I'm fine."

"Which is code for you're really not. Did you decide that Jace and I aren't what you want? If you're not interested, then please tell me." He looked down at our hands as I linked our fingers together.

"No, it's nothing like that. I'm more committed than ever to a relationship with you both. I didn't sleep well. I never have during storms," I said, and he squeezed my hand before lifting it to look at my knuckles.

"How did you bruise all of your knuckles? And your hand seems a swollen."

I swallowed hard. Why did he have to be so observant? "The cat. I tripped and fell, then cracked my hand off the bar multiple times while trying to catch him. The power flickered at one point, and I walked into a wall," I said. It wasn't a complete lie. Those things sorta happened but didn't cause the marks on my body.

Holy shit, how many other lies would I have to tell to cover up what happened? This felt so familiar. The night of my attack, I started making excuses for why I was in that dangerous area. I said I was meeting a friend, but the lies quickly unraveled the more I was questioned. The problem was, I didn't even know what the hell the truth was anymore. Kai asked a question I'd never analyzed too much, but now I couldn't stop thinking about it. Who found me? How long was it before the ambulance arrived? I had snippets after I was stabbed, but not much. It was mostly a blur or nothing at all.

Had some homeless person wandered in because the door was

open? Had the door been left open? I briefly remembered keys. Had one of my attackers worked there? My heart began to pound hard as little things that had never occurred to me before as significant were suddenly a lot more important. All this time, the three men who'd attacked me were still out there and never got punished. I hated to think about what they were doing out there, what they could've done to someone else. Maybe I'd passed them in the grocery store and never knew.

I shivered and cuddled into my sweatshirt as if it would help. Now more than ever, I couldn't help wondering why me? Was I a random choice, or had they set out for someone else, and I'd run into their trap? Was my attack meant for another girl? If so, then who?

As Avro drove, I watched everyone we passed and felt so detached, like I no longer belonged in this world. A woman jogged with her dog by her side and pushed one of those running strollers. People played frisbee on the beach while others drove by wearing suits in fancy sports cars. So many lives and variations, and not one of them worried about a girl left for dead in a building years ago. Not one of them cared that I was driving by now, watching them, and wondering if they were the person who'd attacked me. None of them knew that I sat here wishing I could've had a normal childhood, but when you watched your parents die, nothing is normal after that. It was an omen that followed me with its taint ever since.

"I watched my parents die," I blurted out into the silent car. I didn't look at Avro, but I could feel his eyes on my face.

"What?"

"My parents died when I was six. I shouldn't be able to remember it so clearly. I mean... I was six. Who remembers what happened to them at that age?" I asked, not expecting a response.

"What happened?" Avro asked, his voice full of concern.

"They were addicts. As far as I know, my mom got clean long

enough to have me but couldn't stay off them once I was born. I remember going to the hospital once, not long before they died. She'd been locked up in this special wing that made me uncomfortable." I stopped and licked my lips as I gathered myself.

"I was terrified of being there, but didn't know how to say it, so my dad held me in his arms, and I just hid my face in his neck."

I put my hands in my lap and looked down at them as I played with Kai's ring. Even after last night, I still haven't taken it off.

"It wasn't until years later that I understood she'd tried to get clean again. It was some sort of a rehab facility, but I'm pretty sure she left before it was finished." I shook my head. "I wish I'd been old enough to help her. It may not have worked, but I would've tried."

"So where did she pass away?" Avro asked.

"At home. It was like any other Friday. I was picked up from the babysitter's house, and we ate dinner like a normal family. We even played a few hands of Go Fish. It was bedtime when their friends started to arrive. I recognized the other faces. They'd been over before, but just like all the other nights, I never spoke to them."

I took a deep breath as I remembered my mom and dad tucking me in and kissing me goodnight, saying I needed to stay in bed. It was far too late for little girls to be awake. I bit my lower lip as the images of that night flashed before my eyes as clearly as if it had just happened.

"I'd fallen asleep, but I woke up and needed to pee and get a drink. When I called out, no one came. I could hear music playing and crawled out of my bed with my blue bear tucked under my arm."

I lifted my head and realized Avro was parked at work, and I hadn't even noticed we'd stopped moving. "The party was them all getting high. All six of them were lying on the furniture and the floor and were very still. I remember thinking how strange that was. My parents were near a large chair I used to sit in to watch cartoons, and

I tip-toed closer. I didn't want to wake anyone else, but I didn't have to worry about that."

"They all died?"

I nodded. "Tainted drugs. All six of them were gone or in the process of dying. I don't really know. I reached out and nudged my mom's arm, but she wouldn't wake up, so I went into the kitchen and got myself a glass of water." I licked my parched lips. "Being brave, I decided to use an adult glass, but once I filled it with water, it was too heavy and slipped through my hands and smashed on the floor." The glass had seemed to fall in slow motion, and when it hit, little pieces went everywhere. "I thought for sure that my mom or dad were going to wake up and come storming in, but they didn't."

"Holy shit, Raine. I'm so sorry. So then, what happened?"

I shrugged. "I tried to clean up the mess but cut myself on my hands and feet, and I was crying. I went to my parents again, and they still wouldn't wake up." As I recalled that night, I put a hand over my mouth, feeling a small pang of emotion for the first time. "I was bleeding and scared, so I took my mom's phone, and I remember fumbling, trying to get it to work, but finally I got it open, and I called my babysitter. I was crying so hard that she could barely understand me and said she was on her way over."

I leaned on the door and stared up at the club. "I don't know why, but I've never felt anything until now. It was all just this blank void in my heart. I've rarely even thought about it. Does that make me a bad person?"

"No, Raine, you're not a bad person. Do you mean you don't feel bad that they died?"

I locked eyes with Avro. "Sorta. I just don't really feel anything. Don't get me wrong, I understand now that they were addicts, but they were both good to me when they weren't getting high. I can't say they were terrible people and mistreated me or left me places." I sighed, trying to collect my thoughts.

"The thing is, when I think of them, I see their dead faces looking so peaceful, their heads touching like they'd fallen asleep resting on one another. I feel like they died doing the one thing they loved more than anything. Loved more than me. Is that the whole truth of the situation? Maybe not, but it's still how I feel." I lifted my shoulders and let them drop.

Avro reached out and grabbed my hand again. This time, he brought my cut knuckles to his lips and kissed each one.

"I worry, Avro. I worry that I'm always going to be damaged and broken. Something is wrong with me inside, and I can't put my finger on how to explain it to anyone." I turned my head to look him in the eyes. "I'm terrified that I will always feel hollow, and nothing will ever fix it. I've spent my entire life expecting the worst to happen, and I can feel it coming for me like I'm running along tracks and a train is barreling down on me. I've become desensitized to everything other than the crippling fear."

Reaching out, I touched his cheek. "You are the first person in a very long time to make me feel anything, but that scares the fuck out of me. I don't even know what to do with the emotions or how to navigate the new waters."

Avro didn't say anything as I stared into his amber eyes. I wanted to feel everything with him. I wanted to feel sad and disappointed. Laugh at his jokes and keep a tight grip on the butterflies I felt with him and Jace the other night. I wanted to know what it was like to love and be intimate without the touch of fear clouding every waking moment. Fuck, I wanted to try skydiving and scale a mountain. I wanted to run a marathon and travel to a different country. I'd never been outside of Florida, and my view of the world was on my phone and television.

"I feel so little, Avro." I sniffed and closed my eyes as the tears formed and slowly dripped down my cheeks. "I feel like this tiny shell of a person waiting to be crushed. I know it and know I need to fix it, but I don't know how. Most days, I'm filled with terror and an ache of loneliness that never wants to leave."

"Raine, you're so far from empty inside. Yes, you're struggling. I can see it, but you just said you felt something with me, right? And you felt something with Jace and me the other night?"

"I do and did, but how can I trust my feelings? What if all those emotions, hope, excitement, and passion all disappear once the hollow feeling catches back up? It always catches up with me. I feel like Artreyu, trapped in that desolate place with the sphinx in the movie *Neverending Story*. You know the part where he thinks he's getting somewhere, but then his heart betrays him, and the sphinx fires, and he narrowly escapes being killed?" Avro smiled at me. "Okay, maybe not the best analogy."

"Actually, it works perfectly, but remember that he made it through that test and the ones after that. That was the point. He kept pushing on and proving to himself that he could do it, and so will you. Every day you wake up, brush your teeth, and look in the mirror, you are staring the world and all the terrible shit in the face and saying that you won't quit. You will run the gauntlet of terror, and no matter how scared you are, you still do, and each day is a day to heal."

I wiped at the tears sliding down my cheek. "How did you get to be so smart?"

"Blame Jace. He's the insightful one, believe it or not." He smiled, and we both laughed. Avro sobered and wrapped my hand up in both of his. "We'll get through this together. The three of us will figure out how to make sure that each day is a step forward."

"What if some days there are steps back?"

"Well, we'll remind you that you're stronger for going through the pain rather than avoiding it."

I'd certainly gone through the pain last night. It was sad, or maybe pathetic, but I knew I would never get Kai out of my head.

The feel of his rough touch and his glowing eyes were forever tattooed on my brain. How do I get over the boy I loved and lost and now the man that I realized a part of me still loved?

The heart was one map I couldn't figure out, but I wished I could. I really wished that I could.

Chapter 28

Kaivan

I pulled into the gas station beside Roach and wanted to kill him more than usual. The rumble of my bike cut off and I fought the urge to grab my head as more of the little men with ice picks went to town on my brain. There was a reason I didn't drink too much, and today was a good fucking reminder.

After Raine left, I watched her pathetically from the window as she walked down the street. Then I ran to the bathroom and threw up all the burritos and coffee like my stomach was trying to turn itself inside out. I probably had alcohol poisoning, but you wouldn't see me in a hospital unless I was heavily sedated and dragged there.

"I think I may kill you," I mumbled, dismounting my bike.

"Why?" Roach asked, leaning on his bike with a big old smile.

"You said that you had important business and that I needed to help you with. You call this your urgent business?" I stuck my thumb out in the direction of the front door.

"Naw, man. This is just a pit stop. I need smokes, fuel, and snacks." Roach took off before I could decide if it was worth the pain in my head to tackle him to the ground.

Grumbling under my breath, I followed behind Roach. We reached the doors just as they opened, and two girls walked out. They stopped and smiled as they giggled. The logo splashed across their crop-top sweatshirts proudly announced they went to the university. They were nowhere near campus, the dorms, or the beach, which meant they were in this shit part of the city looking for trouble—drugs, sex, maybe both.

Any other time, I would tap that. Ride them hard and fast and boot them out the door just as quickly, but at the moment, no part of me wanted anything to do with them.

"Hi," the girl with dark hair said.

Roach opened his mouth to answer, and I cut in. Grabbing the door, I leaned in close to the girls. "I'd fucking break you," I growled low enough that only they could hear. The smiles slipped from their faces. "And if you were lucky, I'd bury your bodies deep enough that the animals didn't dig you back up." Standing up straight, I glared down at them through my dark glasses. "Get the fuck out of here."

Removing my arm, the girls dashed away, and Roach glared at me. "What the fuck? I could've had some fun. Why are you such a dick?"

"We are supposed to be on a super important mission. I was just doing you a favor." I smirked. "Wouldn't want you to get distracted or anything. Besides, what if they are Lane's friends and tell her you fucked them?"

"Once upon a time, I thought we were friends. Fucker," Roach mumbled under his breath as he stomped into the store ahead of me. "I need to take a piss."

Wandering the store portion, I was very aware of the guy at the counter staring at me like I was gonna run at him with a gun. Not that I blamed him. That had happened more than once in this area. Yanking open the fridge, I grabbed a large container of chocolate milk and the biggest energy drink I could find. It wasn't exactly the healthiest hangover drink, but it fucking worked.

The bell on the door chimed as I was staring at the chips, and I froze when I heard a familiar voice.

"Well, fuck me. Is that you, Kaivan?" Turning my head, I stared into the piggish eyes of Dave Collins. "As I live and fucking breathe. I thought you were dead or rotted away in prison," he said, smiling. Another guy walked around the corner with him, and neither of the men looked to be having the best of days.

I gave Dave the once over and took in the man who used to be my foster father. He looked like he'd just crawled out of a dumpster. His shirt was stained and untucked over his beer belly. He was wearing grey sweatpants that he should never have wiggled his ass into and had on running shoes that were on their last go around. He was sporting a beard now but was bald except for a thin ring of hair.

"I'd say it was good to see you again, but I'd be lying," I drawled. "You look like you've seen better days yourself. Did the old bitch finally toss your useless ass out on the street?"

His eyes narrowed into thin slits, adding to the pig look he had going on.

"Still have that smart mouth on you. That didn't get solved while you were locked up," Dave said. He stepped closer, and I smelled the alcohol wafting off his body like a bad cologne.

"Naw, it didn't. No thanks to you or Irene. I really appreciated all the support the two of you showed me by not showing up for...well, anything."

Dave took another step, the fake-ass smile completely slipping from his face.

"Dave, don't do it," Dave's buddy said.

"I'd listen to your friend Dave. He gives sound advice." I looked at my nails, flashing the fist full of rings that would knock his ass out if he tried anything.

"You got what you deserved—manipulating my wife and raping poor sweet Raine the way you did. You should've gotten life," he growled. "And you better watch out, or I'll send you back there," he threatened.

"Oh really? And on what charge would you have me go to prison for this time?" I asked as Roach reappeared from the bathroom. He gave me a look over the top of the two guys, and I gave him a subtle nod that I was okay.

"That fancy crest you have on your back. I'm pretty sure your parole officer would love to know that you've been hanging out with a motorcycle gang." He thought he was invincible. That much was clear as he took another step forward. "I'm pretty sure they would send you back to where you belong, with the rest of the animals."

"Ironic coming from you," I said, and purposely stared at what was most likely a cheese stick imprint on his shirt. Before Dave could say anything else, I smiled and continued. "I guess you're not in the family loop anymore. Did poor, sweet Raine not tell you? I'm shocked you weren't the first call she made," I drawled and leaned against the freezer door.

I suddenly wondered what Raine's relationship was with the Collinses. Did she still speak to them, or had she left them behind and never looked back?

"What the hell are you spouting off about?"

"Raine went and had my name cleared. She remembered a lot more pieces from the night of her attack and realized it wasn't me." Dave stepped back like I slapped him, and I watched him carefully. He was actually shocked, which meant that Raine made the decision and either didn't call them or didn't speak to the Collinses at all.

Then again, maybe she planned on sharing the news when Christmas came around. There was something else under the shock, though...fear...maybe, it was hard to tell.

"You're lying," Dave growled, his hands balling into fists. At one point in my life, if he'd done that, I would have immediately gotten up in his face, but I was older and wiser now. I also had no idea how long it took for charges to be cleared, but I doubted it was the same day. It wasn't like a fast-food drive-thru, so it was best to mind my P's and Q's.

"Not at all." I opened my cell phone to show Raine's name on my contacts list. Courtesy of my stalking, but again, Dave was on a need-to-know basis. "Did you want to talk to her and ask her yourself?"

I could see Roach milling about on the other side of the store, making sure that the guy at the counter didn't get too antsy or Dave didn't try anything stupid.

"I don't need to talk to her. I fucking know you did those things. I just wonder what you did to her to make her recant her story." Dave pointed a finger at me.

His buddy must have seen the look on my face as I wondered about cutting it off Dave's body here in the store. His friend didn't look as smug as Dave and grabbed his shoulder. Probably a smart move. It had been a few days since I killed anyone, and I felt the weight of my blade strapped to my back.

A grin pulled up the corner of my mouth. "Oh, come now, Dave. I didn't say anything about Irene. In fact, I don't deny fucking your wife. She did have a fine wet hole."

Dave's face turned a violent shade of red that made him look like a cartoon character, and his friend took a firmer hold.

"But manipulating Irene into it, that's a no. She was quite the needy cougar," I said, unable to help myself.

Roach slowly moved closer until I could feel him standing behind me. Dave may have been oblivious to the danger he was in, but his buddy looked like he was going to shit his pants.

"The truth is, Dave, she threatened to kick me out if I didn't 'service her,'" I said, making little air quotes with my fingers. "Apparently, your limp dick didn't stack up to a hard eighteen-year-old cock. That's pretty sad, man, but at least now you know your wife is a cheating whore and wasn't pressured into anything. Better to know late than not at all, I guess. Now Raine, on the other hand... naw, I never touched her, and now she knows it, too." I rubbed at my chin. "In fact, she says she has a few theories on who the three attackers were," I lied, but it made me look like I knew a lot more than I did. I also didn't think Dave was on the up and up. There was something about the uneasy look in his eyes that said he knew something.

I could see the muscle twitching in his jaw as he ground his teeth together. I sighed and shook my head. "You should be more concerned that Raine's attackers were never found. That's disturbing, isn't it?" I asked, and the weight of that statement firmly planted itself in my brain as the scars she showed me danced behind my eyes.

I sucked in a steadying breath as I pushed my shoulder away from the freezer. "Well, Dave, this has been a wonderful reunion. I can't wait for the next one. I hope the two of you have a pleasant day. I know I will."

Smiling wide as much for his benefit as the store cameras, I stepped around Roach and let him have the final stare-down as I made my way to the register. The guy behind the counter looked relieved when I pulled out my wallet. The bell rang, announcing that Dave and his friend had decided to move along.

"I'll also pre-pay forty on each of the two bikes out there," I nodded outside.

"That was intense," Roach commented, dropping some chip bags and candy on the counter.

"Yeah, but there was something weird about it." I pulled out two hundred in cash and dropped it on the counter as the guy put our stuff in bags. "Keep the change," I said, grabbing my stuff.

"How so?" Roach asked as we made our way outside.

"Did you see how he reacted to hearing that Raine had dropped the charges? I mean, he seemed shocked, but not about that. I don't know. The whole thing is strange as fuck. My gut is saying he knows something."

"Are you sure that's not just your hangover talking?"

I glared at Roach as I straddled my bike. I twisted the milk lid off and drank enough to pour the energy drink inside.

"Dude, you are fucking disgusting," Roach said as he stared at my concoction.

"Says the guy eating onion rings with sour candies. That's fucking weird, and I'm concerned you're pregnant."

I rested on my seat, staring at nothing, and let the conversation with Dave replay. The fact that the three men who hurt Raine were walking around scot-free while I went away for ten years pissed me the fuck off. I tried hard to ignore the anger that had nothing to do with prison and everything to do with Raine being hurt.

I'd loved her then. I loved her now, and they almost took her from me forever. If she'd died...I shook my head to rid the thought. No matter what words I said to Raine, she was mine. She always had been, and I was going to find the fuckers and give them the justice they deserved. It wouldn't be in a six-by-six with three square meals a day. No, that was too good for them.

Their blood was already running red in my mind.

AVRO

Chapter 29

Avro

After four hours, I was convinced that Raine was hiding something. She was quiet, and even though she made jokes, they came out forced, like she was trying too hard. She also kept standing with her left side to me. I'd glimpsed some bruising on her neck, but she refused to stand still long enough for me to check if it was what I thought it was. That was the other odd thing. We'd been doing physical labor all afternoon, and she had yet to remove her hoodie. I could see the beads of sweat from here, but she never even moved to take it off.

Being a jerk, I turned off the air about an hour ago, and it was getting even hotter in here. Raine's eyes were focused on her task, but it was a cover. I was sure of it. She was burying herself in work to avoid something, and at the moment, that something was me. The question was why.

More had to have happened last night. I could feel it. Jace hated it when I said that. He was also creeped out that I was always right. She was rearranging chairs for the third time, and the more I watched, the more certain I became that my hunch was right. Her movements were short and quick and reminded me of a worker bee as she dashed from one side of the room to the other. She would also wince, then cover it quickly.

"Would you like a water?" I asked.

"Sure, that would be great," she said, never turning to look at me.

Pushing away from the bar, I grabbed two bottles and called out, tossing one her way. "Thanks."

"I'll be right back," I said, wandering down the hallway to the offices and bathrooms.

I slipped into her office after checking that she wasn't following or watching me. Luckily, the computer was still on, and I quickly clicked on the security footage and pulled up yesterday. I fast-forwarded to when Raine arrived, and I watched her walk to the storage room door. I knew she hated going down there. Watching her now, I half expected the eerie horror movie sounds to start playing.

About thirty minutes later, a cat did run out the door, and Raine wasn't far behind, closing the door behind her. I clicked on another camera and held back a laugh as I watched Raine dash around the bar. The cat made a huge mess as she chased it. She stopped in the middle of the dance floor and walked toward the patio, opening the doors wide. It was storming hard enough that the rain was driving in. The cat seemed distracted by the wind, rain, and the blowing blackout blinds, then Raine made her move and captured it. I watched as she took the cat outside, then stomped back in, looking like a drowned rat, as she closed and locked the doors.

Everything was as she said, except for the falling or running into walls. I'd been fed a half-truth—a cover story for what really happened.

"What are you doing?" Raine asked from the doorway.

I turned and leaned against her desk to stare at her. "I wanted to check your story," I said.

Her eyes narrowed into slits. "So what, you're going to be one of those overly controlling boyfriends now? Or whatever you want to call us," Raine bit out, her tone laced with the same venom that was in her eyes.

"Nope, I'm nothing like that," I said. "But I also know when I'm being lied to." It was subtle, but her face shifted just enough that I knew I was right. "You see, Raine, I know you. I know you so well that I have your routine memorized and how you like to do things. I also know that you would've tossed that hoodie off two hours ago, and you would've let me kiss you when I reached for you earlier." I lifted my fingers as I counted off all the oddities in her story.

"You've been tense, which could've been from our conversation on the way here, but you would normally put that behind you to work. You also aren't listening to your favorite soundtrack. You haven't put on any music at all. Lastly, your eyes are cagey, like you want to tell me something, but you're fucking avoiding the topic."

"Oh my god! You should be a damn detective," she fumed and marched into the room but still didn't come near me. Instead, she paced the floor, her hands pulled inside the long sleeves of the hoodie like she wanted to go full turtle and disappear.

"You want to know what else I know now?" I asked, keeping my voice even.

"I'm scared to ask. You may tell me what I ate for breakfast or how often I've used the bathroom today."

"See, that right there. That was also not you, but what really sealed the deal was looking at the footage from yesterday. You know what it showed me?"

Raine stopped pacing and looked at the door like she wanted to bolt. To prevent that, I walked over, closed the office door, and leaned against it. I was getting answers.

"Avro, please."

"Please, what? Don't tell you I saw your cat, but you never fell. Or, how about I don't tell you that you never ran into the bar or smacked into it or any wall? You know what that tells me?"

She swallowed and bit her lip. "Please stop."

"No, Raine, I won't let you cover for someone hurting you. I know that was what happened, and if it wasn't here, it happened during your ride to or from the hospital or at your house. So which is it? And more importantly, why don't you want to tell me?"

When she didn't say anything but stood in the middle of the room looking more defeated than I'd ever seen, I couldn't stop myself from going to her. Raine tilted her head up when I stopped in front of her, and her eyes glistened with tears.

Gripping her chin, I forced her to turn her head to the side, and using my thumb, I wiped at the makeup hiding long purple finger-prints. Fingerprints that belonged to a man or woman in the WNBA, but whoever it was, intended to hurt her. Maybe kill her. My blood ran like ice in my veins at the thought.

"Raine, what the hell happened?" I asked, my stomach dropping. I'd never hoped so much in my life that I was wrong about something.

"I can't tell you," she said.

I lifted my head and stared into her eyes. "Why?"

"Because it's a long and very complicated story, and if I tell you, then I know what you will want to do, and I can't go to the police. Not with this, not this time."

Moving my hands to Raine's shoulders, I tried to understand

what she was saying, but it sounded like a riddle. "Tell me what happened."

"Avro, I can't. I want to. I do, but...I should just go home. I'm sorry," she said and tried to pull away, but I wasn't letting her take off like that.

"No," I said and held her in place. "Look at me. You can't cover or hide whatever this is. Whoever left those marks at the very least wanted to hurt you badly, or worse, they wanted to kill you. What if they come back?"

"They won't," she said.

"How are you so certain?" I pushed.

Raine jerked away from my touch, and my heart raced with panic. "I said just leave it alone."

I turned and went to stand in front of the door, then locked it. "You want to beat the shit out of me to get me to move, then so be it. I'll take whatever punch or kick you want to dish out, but I'm not moving until you tell me what the hell happened to you." I held out my hands as I pleaded with her. "I know you're getting used to the idea of us together, but to me, you're already part of my life in every way and have been for years. That means if someone hurts you, they hurt me. If they make you smile, they make me smile. You see how that works?"

She resumed pacing but didn't attack or tell me she never wanted to see me again, so it was a win.

"Tell me, Raine. Tell me, or I'll call the cops right now and say you were attacked. Even if you say nothing, they will have to drive out here and will want to interview you. Is that what you want?"

"Avro!" she yelled. "Fuck, why can't you just leave this alone?"

"Because I love you!" I yelled back and then snapped my mouth shut. Shit, this was not how that was supposed to go.

Raine stilled, her eyes finding mine as her arms dropped to her sides. "You love me?"

"Worst way for it to come out, but yes. I love you. I've been in love with you for so long, and not saying something has been one of the hardest things I've ever done. I can't tell you how many times I've almost slipped up while dropping you off or saying goodnight."

She looked shell-shocked, and I was terrified for a whole new reason.

"I'm not looking for you to say it back, but you asked why. That's why. I love you. That means I'm not letting you leave this room until you come clean. The whole story and why you don't want me to say anything. Please, Raine."

Raine walked toward me, and I could tell she was searching my face, but for what, I didn't know. "All this time, you've loved me?"

I reached out and ran my thumbs over her cheeks, then cupped her face.

"Yes. All this time."

"What about Jace?"

"What about him? He knows how I feel. We don't hide anything from each other. He loves me, and I love him too, and I hope that with time you two will fall in love as well," I said, tracing her bottom lip.

"I don't understand this, but it feels...."

"Right," we said at the same time and smiled.

My fingers trailed down her shoulders and arms until I could hold her hands. I looked at the marks from her punching something or someone. I wanted to pull her into my arms and protect her forever from whoever this was.

"Please tell me," I said softly.

"I will, but not yet."

My brows drew together, and confusion must have shown in my eyes because Raine touched a finger to my lips. Taking the hint, I kept my mouth closed while she stepped back and pulled the hoodie off. The tank top was next, and my mouth dropped as I stared at not only how beautiful she was but the marks and bruises all over her body.

"Don't stare at the bruises, just tell me...would you make love to me?"

My eyes snapped to hers. "What?" My mouth was suddenly parched.

Reaching behind her back, she undid the clasp for her bra and let it fall to the ground, and all I could do was groan as my cock came alive.

"You heard me. You say you love me. Will you make love to me before I tell you?" she asked, her big blue eyes pleading with me.

"Why do you want me to make love to you first?"

Raine licked her lips, and I followed the movement.

"Because when I tell you the entire story, you may never want to see me again, and I want to know your touch. I want this moment to hang on to if you decide to leave and never look back."

"Raine, nothing you could say would ever make me want to leave," I said, and my heart broke that she thought that.

"Then this should be an easy deal. I promise to tell you the whole sordid tale, but this is what I want first." She pushed the yoga pants down and stepped out, leaving her in only a sexy black thong.

I wrapped her in my arms and dropped my lips to hers. This wasn't how I saw our first time happening, but I would show her how much I loved her. Then I was getting the answers I was after and killing the man who did this to her.

Raine

Chapter 30

Raine

I kept waiting for the fear to rush up like it always did when someone touched me, but it stayed dormant. If anything, my body and mind were calm. I thought about calling this feeling The Avro Effect because he was the only one who made me feel like this.

Lips moving together, Avro picked me up, and I wrapped my legs around his waist.

A gasp escaped my mouth as his fingers gently explored my body like I might break in his arms. They traced soft lines, and as they did, goosebumps broke out all over my skin, making me shiver.

"Hey, don't look at the bruises. Pretend they aren't there. I don't

His eyes searched mine, and I didn't know if he believed me, but he nodded.

Avro smiled against my lips. "I like it when you shiver," he said and ran fingers down the middle of my back.

I arched with the sensation that lit up all my nerve endings. His hands gripped my ass and squeezed, making me moan.

Everything about him was sensual and fluid. Nothing was rushed or overdone. Avro seemed to know exactly what my body wanted, and it didn't take long before I was a panting mess. I wiggled in his hold, and he broke off the kiss with a smirk.

"Lean back and close your eyes. Don't worry. I've got you," he said. I tentatively unlocked my fingers from around his neck. He smiled. "You do remember what I was training to do? I can hold my entire body sideways on a pole. Holding you is a breeze," he said, and I knew it was the truth. I'd seen him do it, and it always amazed me.

I did as he asked but yelped and jerked up straight again. I would've sworn I was falling and about to crack my head off the floor.

"Stop worrying. Let me take care of you." I licked my lips. "Close your eyes and trust."

Closing my eyes, I tried again and leaned back until I felt the firm press of his fingers holding my lower back.

"Oh," I moaned as the tip of his tongue ran little trails along my skin.

Warmth spread as I leaned more into his hold, and his finger pressed into my skin. I felt secure in his arms. Avro had always made me feel safe, and I could be myself.

His wandering tongue drew circles around my nipple before moving on to the next. With my eyes closed, the world was dark, yet I saw more than ever before. The tenderness in how he touched me and the whispers he placed on my skin were all I needed between us. Every caress made my heart pound harder, and the passion I'd been hiding from came alive and coursed through my system.

"God, Avro, please."

"Please, what?" he asked, his voice filled with a deviousness that I'd always known he had, but this was new.

He wasn't holding back or hinting at the mischievousness that lived inside of him. His teeth grazed along my ribs, and I fought the urge to open my eyes and watch as I shuddered in his hold. I let my arms drape back over my head, and it felt so freeing to be like this, trusting him a hundred percent to hold me and not let me fall.

"More," I managed to say, my mind nothing but a muddled mess.

"More of this?" Avro asked.

Warm hands slid up my back and forced me to sit up a little, and I sucked in a shuddering breath as he sucked my nipple into his mouth. There was no swirling or teasing this time, and the sensation of his insistent mouth had me gripping his hair and pulling him closer.

"Yes, more, please," I mumbled between the ragged breathing.

Releasing my nipple, Avro kissed me again, and I wanted everything he had to give right this second. I wanted the release. I wanted to feel him inside of me. I wanted to push away what happened to me years ago, and a part of me wanted to forget last night—not all of me but a part. I wanted to start clean, with a fresh slate, and fill my mind with new and better memories. Memories that would make me wet and crave the touch of another. Memories that would make me feel like I'm a woman to be desired, not damaged and broken inside.

I hadn't noticed us walking until Avro sat down, and my knees touched the cool leather surface of the couch. The shock had my eyes fluttering open, and I was greeted by the warmth of Avro's amber eyes. I had to take a moment to stare into them and make sure he was real.

"I love you looking at me like that," he said, nipping at my bottom lip.

"Oh yeah, and how is it that I'm looking at you?" I smiled and settled into his lap.

"Like I hung the moon for you. Whether I did or not doesn't matter. That's what it feels like when I look into your eyes."

My face heated, and I wanted to fan myself. "Have you always been this romantic, and I'm just now seeing it? Have I really been that oblivious?"

"I may have been hiding it, just a little." He smirked as he slowly leaned us over until my back touched the couch. I hissed. "Too cold?"

"No, just need a second," I said.

Avro pulled away and stood up. I shivered as I frowned at him, hating to lose the feel of his body. He laughed and peeled his T-shirt off before tossing it at me. I snatched it out of the air and felt like Jace from the other night as I brought it to my nose to breathe in his scent. He always smelled so damn good.

His hands went to undo the button on his jeans, and my body jerked like we were connected. With each agonizingly slow click of the zipper, my body temperature rose until it felt like I was melting as his cock came into view.

"Do you want me to use protection?"

Avro slid his jeans down his legs and stepped out of them. Licking my lips, I tried to form words as he stood tall before me. Avro snickered, but it sounded sexy. He turned and walked over to the large shelf that held the refilled jars of condoms that we placed around the bar for patrons.

"How about I do until you tell me not to? Deal?"

I nodded, still no sensible words coming to mind as I feasted on the sight of his muscled back and tight ass. I could just make out the scars, a lighter shade than his tanned skin, on the outside of his knee.

Avro turned around and held up a condom as he walked closer.

"I got peach," he said, his lip curling up. "I find that very fitting." He held out the shiny little packet to me, and my hands shook as I took it from him. "I want you to put it on." Bending over, he placed his fingers under my chin and lifted my head, so I had to stare into his eyes as he spoke. "You're in control here, Raine. I'm yours to do with as you wish." His lips brushed mine, the slight contact sending a charge through my system that spiked the scorching desire to a whole new level.

Avro stood straight, and I was left staring at the long cock directly before me. A tiny glistening droplet of pre-cum formed, then dripped down the head, and I suddenly wanted to taste him. Leaning in, I tentatively traced my tongue along the line the little droplet had traveled. Avro groaned, and it felt like that sound was directly connected to my own desires. I felt myself getting wetter, and the ache building between my legs had me wiggling on the leather.

"Fuck yes," Avro groaned.

Wrapping my hand around him, I did what I'd always fantasized about and slipped his cock into my mouth.

"Damn, Raine, you have a hot mouth."

I was quickly learning that I liked the praise. It wasn't something I'd ever thought about, but every word, groan, or touch of encouragement increased my desire. Closing my eyes, I let go and allowed myself to be in the moment and enjoy this time with Avro, letting the weight of his hand resting on my head and the noises he made fuel me.

"Fuck, I need you to stop." Blinking, I looked up at Avro. His eyes seemed darker, with his black hair falling forward, shadowing his eyes. I really loved this color on him.

"I want you now," Avro said, and I shivered with anticipation.

I struggled to open the packaging, and as soon as I did, I smiled at the scent of peach hitting me in the face.

"This is really going to be my nickname forever," I asked, pulling the condom out.

"Yeah, good luck getting Jace to change it, and the more you don't like it, the more he will purposely use it." Avro smirked.

"Good to know." I stared at the condom and realized that I probably should've practiced this at some point. I wasn't even sure which way it went.

Seeing my dilemma, Avro gently plucked it from my fingers. Turning it the right way, he sat it on the tip of his cock the proper way and I placed my hand in his. There was something incredibly erotic about doing this with him. Our hands worked the latex into place, and his eyes never left mine. As bold as I had been the last few minutes, it became clear that I was in control.

Avro had given me power, and this was my consent. It felt strange, like an out-of-body experience, as I lay back on the couch, and Avro gripped my panties, skimming them down my legs. An old nagging memory tried to form, but I crushed it as I pictured stepping on it in my mind and kicking it away. Nothing was ruining this moment for me.

I couldn't take my eyes off his as he moved over me, and his weight blanketed me in warmth. I wrapped my arms around his body, soaking in the feel of him and savoring this quiet moment between us. No walls. No boundaries. No fear.

"Is this what you want?" He baited me as he wiggled his body back and forth. The tip of his cock brushed against me.

"Yes."

He kissed me again, still just as controlled, while I felt frantic for him to continue. My body was singing with need and screaming with sensitivity at the same time.

"Then put me in," he said against my lips. The command was soft, but it was clear that Avro wasn't giving it to me unless I took what I wanted.

I slid my hand down, and he lifted his hips, so I could wrap my hand around his cock, doing as he told me. I took control. I rubbed him all over my clit and moaned from the teasing before lining him up. I was so wet, and the throbbing in my pussy was almost painful.

"You ready?" Avro whispered in my ear, and all I managed was a nod. My mouth was dry, and my brain was misfiring.

"You sure?" he said again, urging me to use my words.

"Yes, please," I panted.

I sucked in a deep breath with the feel of his body flexing and his cock easing inside me. My back arched off the couch as he pressed forward until I was sure he couldn't all fit.

"Wrap your legs around my waist," Avro said, and as soon as I did, he sank deeper. I yelled out with pleasure that was verging on pain as he bottomed out. "Oh fuck, Raine. I want to be gentle with you, but I'm already so close. I need to calm down," Avro groaned.

I didn't want him to be calm. I wanted him to feel as insanely wild as I felt. I clenched my thighs around him, and he shuddered in my hold. Gripping his shoulders, I bucked up into him and cried out with the delicious sensation.

"Fuck, Raine, you need to stop that, or...." He sucked in a ragged breath, his large body shuddering as my hips became more insistent. "Fuck it," he growled out and rose on his arms.

I hated to lose his heat but didn't care about anything as he pulled out and thrust in so hard that my mouth was forced open in a scream of pure pleasure. My nails ran down his muscled arms as he picked up the pace, and I could feel the climax coming.

"Touch yourself," Avro said, and I opened my eyes, confused by the order. "Rub yourself, Raine. Cum all over me," he said through clenched teeth.

I had a brief moment of insecurity as I slid my hand between our bodies and felt his hard abs brushing the back of my hand, but it dissolved, and he thrust into me faster until I was a moaning mess.

My fingers rubbed my clit tentatively at first, but the sensation was too delicious, and I picked up the pace. Avro groaned loudly, and even though he didn't say it, I just knew he was close. His eyes were clenched shut, and every muscle was flexed. I slipped my fingers down lower and marveled at the feel of him disappearing inside of me and wanted to see what he looked like so badly. I wished I had a mirror so I could watch.

"Come on, Raine, do it. Slip over the edge. Cum on me and just let go," Avro said, his voice strained.

I rubbed my wet fingers over my clit and let go of the tightly wound stress that felt like it was sitting on my chest.

"Yeah, that's it, right there." Avro encouraged me as I moaned and pushed up to meet his powerful thrusts.

"Fuck me. Take what you need," he growled.

My climax hit, and I cried out as waves of pleasure washed over my body. I dug my nails into Avro's shoulders, and his unrelenting pounding became frantic.

"Yes! Oh fuck. You feel incredible," he said, the sound of our bodies coming together loud in the quiet room.

"Avro, yes, please don't stop," I yelled and begged as my orgasm kept going.

My arm muscles were tired from the workout, yet the continuous wave was building toward a second orgasm, and I could feel myself tumbling toward it. I never wanted this feeling to end.

"Oh god, yes!" I screamed as I reached the peak, and the wild noises he was making only added to the moment. "Fuck, Avro," I cried as the second climax hit me. I froze like it had physically gripped me and held me arched off the couch as the pleasure slammed into my body and flowed out to the tips of my fingers and toes.

"Oh fuck, Raine." Avro's movements were desperate and choppy as he slammed into me and stilled. His muscles bulged as his cock kicked and twitched inside of me with his release.

What would it be like to feel that release deep in my body as he came? I shuddered, thinking about Avro fucking me without protection.

Avro slumped on top of me, both of us panting hard.

"You all good?" Avro asked softly against my neck, and I shivered as he swirled his tongue in little circles and nipped at my ear.

"Yeah, I'm better than all right," I said, and a tear trickled down my cheek. Not because I was sad or scared but because I wasn't. I'd had sex for the first time and felt only pleasure. Smiling, I realized I wanted to do it again, but I wanted to ride him this time. "How long until you can go another round?"

Avro chuckled and slowly pushed himself up to stare down at me. "Give me five," he said and then narrowed his eyes. "This isn't getting us out of our talk."

"I know." I clenched hard around his still-firm cock, and he groaned. I loved that reaction. "I just really want to ride you first."

His lip curled up. "Who am I to deny you that?" he said, kissing me soft and sweet before pulling out of my body.

My mind filled with images of having him and Jace together, and my fingers slipped between my legs. What had changed inside of me, I couldn't say, but I was different. I felt the shift, and hiding underneath was an appetite for more. Much more.

Snake

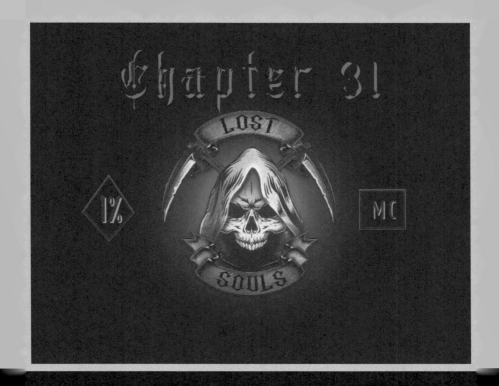

Chapter 31

Kaivan

After Roach dragged my ass around town all day on a mission of doing nothing but annoying the fuck out of me, I drove home and collapsed on the couch, staring at the ceiling. Images of Raine were stuck in my head on a loop, and nothing I tried got her out.

Then I realized my sneaky hand had slipped inside my unzipped jeans. Instead of pushing her out of my mind like I should've, I only wanted another taste. Her screaming my name played like a broken record, and I could feel her pussy cumming all over my cock.

I sat up in a rush. "Fuck," I growled.

I stared down at my cock, which had a damn mind of its own lately. I'd even invited one of the sweetbutts over, and I've never been so fucking annoyed as when the thing twitched, got a semi, but that was it. I had no interest. I even pulled all her blonde hair back into my hand so she'd look similar and still nothing as she dutifully bobbed her head. I sent her on her way when it became obvious it was a fruitless effort. Yet here I was with a steel rod and only one person to blame.

There was a lot of shit I was piling on the Raine train, and each time I tossed another layer on top, I should've wanted her less, but nope, I wanted her more.

I swore a blue streak as I stood and marched toward the bathroom, pulling my cell out of my jeans. I hit Roach's number as I pushed them down.

"What the fuck?" Roach answered the phone on the fourth ring.

"You asleep?"

"It's four in the morning. What the fuck do you think?" Roach barked back.

"It's three-fifty-seven, to be precise," I mumbled, reaching into the shower to turn on the water.

"Whatever, close enough. Hang on." I could hear sheets moving, and a rustling sound before Roach came back on the line. "Okay, I'm back."

"You're getting a blowjob, aren't you?" I asked and wished my cock was nice and let me have one earlier.

"Of course I am. You wake me up, and I'm hard. What do you think is going to happen?"

I shook my head. "I don't know. Maybe wait till I'm off the phone. Just a thought."

Roach groaned, and the phone was muffled as he covered it again, but I could still clearly hear him giving directions.

"Yo, can you knock it off so I can get this out?" I yelled.

"Fuck, no need to yell, man. I'm not deaf."

Before I reached through the phone and killed him, I took a deep breath.

"I need you here at eight," I said.

"Like tonight, right?"

I stared at my phone, tempted to call him an idiot.

"Why the hell would I call you at three-fifty-now-nine in the morning and wake you up if I didn't need you until tonight?" I asked, my voice thick with sarcasm.

"Dude, we are night owls. I'm not sure if you understand the term, but it means my ass doesn't roll out of bed until eleven in the morning if you're lucky," he bitched and then groaned.

"Just fucking be here at eight, bring your truck, and stop getting sucked off in my ear," I yelled. Roach laughed as he hung up.

I finished stripping and got into the warm water, letting it beat down on me. The water didn't do anything to cool the churning rage in my gut that, for whatever screwed-up reason, was making me so hard my balls ached.

"I give up. It's not like anyone is in here," I mumbled.

It was just me, myself, and my mind calling me out on my feelings. Pushing the annoying voice aside, I grabbed the soap and lathered up my cock. A deep groan rumbled from my mouth as I stroked my shaft. Closing my eyes, I shuddered as blue eyes danced with pleasure and fear in front of my face, and I let myself remember exactly how Raine felt.

I squeezed my cock a little tighter as I let the memories flick from one image to the next like an old projector. I could picture her riding me, her tits bouncing as I sucked on them. I vividly remembered how tight and wet her pussy was and how she tried to deny that her body wanted me, yet she came all over my cock.

"Fuck," I murmured and pressed my free hand on the tile for support. I could hear her yelling my name. The sound echoed around in my mind like a ping-pong ball with nowhere to go.

My hand moved faster along my aching cock. I wanted to taste her for real. No little peck as teens, but an all-consuming kiss that would steal the air from her lungs. Then run my tongue in a line down her body, making her squirm under my touch until I reached that sweet little pussy and ate my fill of her.

I wanted to sit her on my lap in the clubhouse and let all those fuckers see her body bounce as she rode my cock in front of them. They would be hands-off, or I'd cut theirs off, but fuck that image. They'd all want her, but none would dare touch her because she was mine.

"Oh, fuck me," I said, my teeth clenching as my jaw snapped tight. The sound of the soap and my hand helped me visualize my cock slamming into her body. "Shit!" I yelled and came hard. I watched the shot hit the wall, closely followed by more than I'd ever cum before.

Draining the rest of my release, I swore a streak that would impress a sailor. The girl was fucking with my head. Not just my damn emotions. No, she had to go for the gusto and take it all. My mind, my heart, my cock...the next thing she would be after is my soul.

I quickly finished my shower and hated and loved the euphoric feeling that imagining Raine gave me.

"What the fuck?" I yelled as I whipped open the curtain and found Wilder sitting on the counter by my sink. Grabbing my towel, I tied it around my waist as I glared at the guy trying to give me another fucking heart attack.

"Wilder, what the hell, man?"

"What?" he asked and then sucked on a purple slushie.

"How long have you been in here?" I wasn't shy about whacking off or having sex in front of others, but it was usually something I chose to do, and a lot of alcohol was involved.

"A while. I didn't want to interrupt you jerking off. I figured that was rude."

He figured that was rude. I couldn't stop staring at him.

"You really should get a clear shower curtain. It would make it harder for people to come in without you knowing, if that's what's upsetting you." He shrugged. "It would upset me. Anyone coming into my bathroom would be there to kill me. You're lucky it was just me."

"Have you ever heard of boundaries, Wilder? This scenario, for example, didn't strike you as an inappropriate moment to visit with me. Especially since you didn't plan on killing me."

Wilder twisted his head like he was thinking. Why I found that particular look as creepy as I did, I couldn't say, but the guy genuinely made me wonder what the fuck they were feeding the soldiers overseas.

"So tell me then...." He pulled a small black book and pen from inside his black jacket. "When would be a good time to drop in?"

"Gee, I don't know. Maybe when I'm taking a shit." I lifted my eyebrow as he jotted that down.

"And when exactly would those times be?" Wilder asked.

Was he serious? Did he actually think I scheduled my shits? And was he planning on dropping in for them? Maybe he would hide up in my fan next, a single eye peering down at me.

"Um...it was a joke."

"You shouldn't joke about bowel movements. You need to keep a tight rein on them, so you never need to use the bathroom unexpectedly. That works unless you have water that you shouldn't. Very unfortunate things happen when you jump out of an armored vehicle to use the bathroom. Don't shit on a landmine. It doesn't end well."

I couldn't tell if he was joking or not. With Wilder, anything was possible.

"Riiiight," I drawled out as I waited for the punchline.

Gathering my clothes, I walked out of the bathroom, not surprised to find him hot on my heels. Once more, my creep factor rose as I looked over my shoulder to see him slinking from one spot to the next, as if he'd memorized all the boards that made any noise. Who was I fucking kidding? That was exactly what he did.

"Okay, I'm going to go with the obvious question here. Why the hell are you in my home at—" I looked at my phone. "Four-thirty-one in the morning?"

I tossed my phone on the dresser and let the towel fall to the floor. I figured Wilder had already gotten a close-up view. What the hell did it matter now? Images of having sex in my bed and Wilder slinking out from underneath to ask a question suddenly popped into my head. I felt him staring at me while he took notes in his little black book. I needed to fucking move. That was the only answer, and even then, I didn't think the other side of the world would be far enough for this level of insanity.

"I wanted to let you know that the male fucking your girl has a very unusual past."

My hand clenched as Wilder mentioned the guy I'd seen leaving the bar with Raine. Why was Wilder following him around? That was the question that led to more questions. Was he really following me around, so he was technically following them around? Was I being stalked while stalking? Fuck, my head hurt.

"Why are you following Raine and the bartender around?" I asked, praying he didn't say he was following me. I pulled on a pair of black sleep pants. I still had the goal of getting a few hours of sleep tonight if I could get Wilder out of my house.

"I can't tell you that. It is on a need-to-know basis, and you are not yet needing to know," Wilder said.

I pulled on a T-shirt and turned to face him. Wilder had made himself comfortable. He was sprawled out on my bed, with his arms behind his head, like it was his bed, not mine. Why the fuck not? At this rate, I should just let him fuck me. He'd invaded every other part of my life. Why not my ass?

"Fine. What can you tell me?" I leaned against the dresser and tried hard to be interested in what he was saying. I expected him to say something like the guy used to run with squirrels and dance in a circus.

"I can tell you that he has a checkered past and one that should be looked into. There are some questions that should be answered."

"How very cryptic of you," I drawled.

"Thank you." He smiled as if I meant it as a compliment.

I'd learned over the last few months that common sense and sarcasm were lost on Wilder. He took everything as a literal fact that couldn't be changed. If I said I loved toast for breakfast, he questioned why I switched from toast to cereal one morning. Then wouldn't understand why I wanted variety. He reminded me a little of Sheldon Cooper from *The Big Bang Theory*.

"Why exactly don't you have him under surveillance?" Wilder asked.

I shrugged. "Why would I? Raine isn't my girl, and she's free to fuck whoever she wants," I said, but I wasn't fooling myself. The thought of her not being mine was equivalent to tossing gasoline on the flames of fury in my gut. The earlier rage that had died down was waiting to re-ignite.

"But you like her, yes?"

"I feel something," I said, not wanting to admit that I may still like her. Fuck, I couldn't even think that without calling myself a liar. I fucking loved her.

I had zero interest in sharing that piece of information with Wilder, though. We'd be here the next two days as I tried to explain emotions I didn't fully understand.

"I know this sensation. I feel something too for the object of my interest." He tapped the pen off his lower lip. "Sometimes I like to watch her, sometimes I want to kill her, and many times I like to fuck her. That is proving to be fun when she stops screaming. Well, I better get going. I need to get some rest."

Oh fuck, he really did have someone he was torturing. I pressed my lips together and beat back the urge to ask who the lucky girl was.

"Such a novel fucking idea," I said instead.

He jumped from the bed and was already marching out the bedroom door. He was still as light as a cat, and I reached the bedroom door just in time to see him make the last few strategic steps to the top of the stairs.

"I'll follow you down and lock the door." I stepped into the hallway to follow Wilder, but he held up his hand.

"No need, I have my key," he said and smiled. "I find that easier than breaking in all the time."

I opened my mouth to ask, 'why the fuck are you breaking into my house all the time?' and, more importantly, 'where the fuck did you get a key?' Then I realized it didn't matter. I had visions of the guy going all *Mission Impossible* on my ass. I actually pictured waking up in the night to find him hanging over me like a giant spider on a string as he waited to ask his next ridiculous question.

Crawling into my bed, I set the alarm, knowing I would feel like a bag of smashed assholes with so little sleep. But I was after answers, and I knew exactly where to start.

Snake

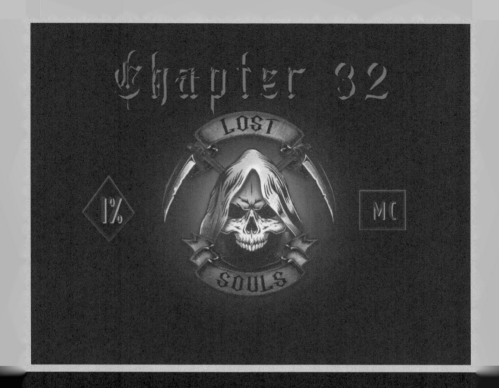

Chapter 32

Kaivan

Roach's munching made me want to pull a gun and splatter his brains all over the window. I watched as another large and overly crunchy triangle was plucked from the bag and went into his gob of a mouth. Unable to take it anymore, I put my window down before snatching the bag from his hands.

"Hey, that's my breakfast," he complained, but I only smiled as I stuck my arm out the window and dumped the rest of the bag on the ground.

"It was either that or I shoot you. Since I actually like you, I decided this was better," I said, tossing the empty bag on the floor of the truck as Roach glared.

"Dude, you dragged my ass out of bed at the ass crack of dawn and we've been sitting here staring at this stupid shop for over a hour. Other than a coffee, I haven't had anything to eat. You need to find new friends to hang out with that can put up with your sour attitude." Roach crossed his arms like he was a sulking child.

"Oh, really? And you've never yanked me out of bed, ordered me to get dressed, and forced me to stalk a certain girl with you?" I tapped my chin. "Now that I fucking think about it. This is all your fault, so you have no one to blame but yourself."

"How the hell do you figure that?"

"Well, you befriended me in prison. That was your first mistake. Then, when your ass was getting out early, you agreed to look out for Hollywood's sister. Now you've taken stalker to all new levels, and lastly, if you'd never taken my ass to that bar, Eclipse, I still would've been completely oblivious about where Raine was." I shrugged. "See, this is all your fault."

"If only I could go back in time," Roach mumbled, but he didn't know how true that statement was. There were a shit ton of things in my life that I would've done differently if I could go back. "So what do you want to do? It doesn't look like this shithole is planning on opening up."

"Well, the car registered to his name is around back, so he's got to be in there," I said.

"You do know this is the Mamba's territory? If they think we are down here working, they won't be too happy," Roach said, his eyes following every car that drove past.

"It's not for work. This is personal."

"Yes, I'm sure that will look wonderful etched into our tombstones." He shook his head. "Might as well pay the guy a visit."

Roach hopped out, and I followed. I hadn't planned on this stakeout becoming any more than a watch-and-learn, but Roach was right. The fastest way to get what I wanted was to kick some doors down.

We casually walked across the road and stepped into the shade of the alley. It felt like the temp dropped ten degrees, not that it helped the wet and sticky feel from the humidity.

Roach was already pulling his lock-picking kit from his pocket as we rounded the backside of the building.

"Not exactly the Ritz," Roach said as something furry scurried into the large pile of garbage.

It could've been a cat, rat or maybe a possum, but whatever it was, it was butt-ass ugly and moved fast. This entire neighborhood was one of those that should be burned to the ground so a developer could start over. I was sure that Derek would do it if Chase asked. The reality was the people that lived down here were exactly like my parents had been. School dropouts with too much time and too little skill. They were the product of the generation before them and the one before that. That mentality was learned. It was passed on like a hereditary disease that spread with each newborn. There were always exceptions to the rule, like I'd been or tried to be.

I didn't want to live in a one-bedroom place, one cigarette away from burning down around you, if you weren't shot by a stray bullet coming through your window first. I hadn't wanted to live in a spot like this where I worried about my girl traveling at night, and you had roaches for neighbors.

My brow furrowed, and I glanced at my friend picking the lock. Okay, I still had a roach, but still.

I became what my parents had brought me up to be. A prison rat who ended up bringing home the biggest fucking roach of them all.

The door clicked, and Roach pushed open the door. The smell of mold and stale cigarettes was the first to assault me. Stepping inside, Roach closed and re-locked the door. We stood there and stared at one another.

"Do you hear that?" He asked.

"Yeah, I do." There was the soft sound of rhythmical thumping and groaning from above our heads. Someone was getting lucky. No wonder he was late opening the shop. I nodded toward a door at the far right-hand side of the small building. "That way."

We walked through the tattoo parlor that had certainly seen brighter days. The leather chair was ripped to the point that it looked like a rat had tried to eat it, and only with the help of the magic silver tape was it not in pieces on the floor. Boards hung on the walls with pictures of people that had come in over the years sporting ink.

"Hold up a sec," I whispered.

Stepping around a few boxes, I reached the front of the shop where once upon a time, I'd spotted the tattoo that was now on my hand. My eyes bounced from one image to the other until I found it. Yanking the old and now faded photograph from the board, I stared at the artwork, the anger beginning to rise. It was just a hand image, and I needed to know who it belonged to.

"Let's go," I snarled as I marched for the stairs. The headboard was banging so loud that it masked the sound of our boots on the rickety wooden stairs. I thought my place was bad, but this place was falling apart at the seams. There were a few closed doors, but there was only one that was slightly open and sounded like a porno was being filmed.

Was it sick of me to like that I was catching this guy with his pants down physically and figuratively speaking? Maybe, but I didn't give a fuck. Pulling my gun, I lifted my foot and kicked the door. There was enough force that when it smashed open, the handle stuck into the shitty drywall.

A woman's scream echoed in the practically empty room as the man of the hour unceremoniously pulled the sheet up to his own chin, leaving her exposed. So much for chivalry, I guess.

"Well, isn't this cozy," I growled as Nick cowered. My eyes fixed on the woman's face, and low and behold, there was Mrs. Collins. In a blink, I was transported back in time, and my stomach rolled a little, thinking about my time between her legs.

"Long time no see, Irene. Seems your habits of fucking around on your husband haven't changed."

"Get the fuck out of my place, man," Nick yelled, sounding way too much like he'd just stepped out of the sixties and reefed one too many times. "I was kinda busy here."

"I noticed. We're not deaf," I drawled. "The difference is, I don't give a fuck."

"Kai, is that you?" Irene asked, her eyes blinking quickly. What the fuck was up with that? Was she trying to wish me away?

"No, it's Santa Claus, and he's the Easter Bunny," I nodded toward Roach.

Nick's face paled a little, and I could tell the lightbulb had just switched on in his brain. He stupidly reached for his cell phone, and I pointed my gun at him.

"I wouldn't do that if I were you. I have amazing aim, and I will blow your cock off." Nick's hand froze, and then he slowly pulled it back. "Smart choice."

"What are you doing here, Kai? I didn't even know you were out of prison," Irene said, then shrank back into the bed as I glared at her.

"Yeah, no thanks to you, I hear," I said, propping my boot on the bed to lean on my knee.

Nick's eyes went to my boot and then up to my face, and I looked away from Irene long enough to see if Nick was going to be stupid enough to say something. Her eyes grew wide, and she swallowed hard.

"I don't know what you're talking about," she said right on cue.

I didn't actually expect her to be honest with me. Liars didn't know how to be honest until their backs were against the wall.

Roach paced around the room, and I knew that Nick was thinking of making a run for it.

"You know, Nick, your skill for making smart decisions has certainly diminished. If you bolt for the door, you'll end up with two in the back and one in the head for good measure." Flicking my gaze away from the shifty man, I gave Irene my best don't-fuck-with-me look. "Then I will assume you haven't spoken to your husband?"

"We aren't together anymore," she said.

"Shocking. The point is, I've had some very interesting conversations in the last couple of days. The first one was with Raine," I said, and let that piece of knowledge seep into her brain. I tapped the gun off my knee. "It was amazing what she told me. How the police were told I'd threatened you to have sex with me." I raised my eyebrows at her. "And how you were the one who said it. Didn't exactly paint me in the best light, now did it?"

"I don't know how she got that mistaken. I...ah..." She licked her lips. "I mean, can you really believe anything that little bitch says?" she said.

A growl left me, and I stomped the short distance around to her side of the bed and grabbed her as she tried to scamper over Nick to get away.

Hand wrapped firmly around her neck, I shoved her down onto the mattress and stuffed the barrel of my gun into her screaming mouth. "First, don't ever call Raine a bitch unless you want me to cut out your tongue. Second, don't fucking lie to me."

I got low to her face, so our noses were almost touching. She shivered in my hold. Roach moved close to Nick's side of the bed, so he couldn't take off without me even asking. I appreciated that.

"Third, and this one is the most important. My patience after spending ten fucking years in prison is really like skating on thin ice with hungry alligators waiting underneath. So, here is what's going to happen... I want to know why you said the shit you did. I want to know now, and if you lie, I will kill you nice and slow. Understood?"

Irene nodded slightly.

"Perfect." Pulling the gun from her mouth, I laid it against her cheek. "Start talking."

"Dave found out about us. He'd put one of those nanny cams in the bedroom and caught us on camera. I didn't want to lose my relationship, so I told him that you threatened me to have sex with you," she spit out in a single breath.

"So you decided to tell the cops when I was arrested?" I asked, the gun pushing a little harder into her cheek.

Nick chose that moment to make a run for it, and a child-like screech could be heard as Roach clothes-lined him. Coughing ensued, and Nick let out a loud breath as Roach slammed his foot down onto the guy's stomach.

Roach waggled his finger at Nick. "Tut tut, Nick. Now I get to cut off a finger for fun." Roach pulled a switchblade from his back pocket. He began to scream as Roach stepped on his hand with his other boot.

"Hold up. If Nick here can provide good information, I'll let him keep his fingers. See Nick, I'm a generous guy, but don't try anything that stupid again."

He shook his head hard, and Roach released the parasite from under his boots.

"Dave was more pissed than I thought and ordered me to do it, or he'd divorce me and leave me penniless without a home. I'd committed adultery, and he had it on film. What else was I supposed to do?"

"Exactly how pissed off was Dave?" I asked.

"Oh, livid. He stomped out of the house, swearing and spouting off that he was going to kill you."

A shiver traveled down my spine.

"What did he do?"

Irene shrugged.

"Don't fucking lie to me, Irene."

"I'm not, I swear. He stormed off and was back a few hours later and was calmer, but said he wanted you to move out. That he couldn't to live under the same roof as you."

"When did the cops arrive?"

Irene screwed up her face as she thought. "I don't know. I was asleep by then and was groggy, but say, two hours. I don't know, Kai. It was a long time ago."

"Funny how prison will make it feel like it was just yesterday," I drawled. "Anything else you think I should know?"

"The only other thing I can think of is that when the cops came, Dave was all too happy to start telling them how terrible you were to me and how he was planning on throwing you out."

I stood up straight and fixed my gaze on Nick. "Your turn."

I walked over to where Nick was pathetically cowering against the bed. I stuffed my hand in my jacket pocket and pulled out the old image. I held it up to show Irene and Nick, who was whimpering more than Irene. This guy was a putz, and I'd quickly figured out there was no way he was one of the guys who raped Raine unless he had an entire personality overhaul in ten years. A guy who could rape a teenage girl was a different kind of animal than the piece of shit cowering in a ball in front of me.

Nick's eyes were shifty as he looked at the image and then away again. "You know what I want to know, don't you? That's why you're so scared."

A sheen of sweat broke out on Nick's forehead that had nothing to do with the workout he'd been getting a few minutes earlier.

"Before you try to lie, let me ask you a question. Between whoever you are covering for and me, who do you think will mess you up more? Who do you think will make your death more painful?"

Nick rubbed at his eyes, the quaking in his muscles making it very obvious just how terrified he was. "Fine, yeah, I know."

"Nick..." Irene started to say but shut her mouth when I looked her way.

"Keep going, Nick, or I'm going to let Roach here slowly saw off each one of your fingers and toes, one at a time, and if you pass out from the pain, we'll just wait until you wake up to continue."

"I only ever sold two more of those other than yours." He held up his hand. "And mine." He ran his hand through his hair. "The one dude was some random guy traveling through Florida and stopped at my tattoo shop on a whim. I never saw the guy again."

"And the other?" I prompted.

"The other is a guy named Frank, but he goes by Father Frank. He's a real whack job and has his own cult or something. Anyway, he is a friend of Dave's." My lip pulled up in a snarl, and Nick stumbled through the rest of his words. "That's his hand in the photo. He was the first one that chose that image, maybe a month before you came into the shop," Nick managed to stammer out. I looked at the artwork on the guy's right hand and knew this had to be the fucker I was after. Why couldn't I have chosen something like a fucking unicorn?

"How exactly does Dave know this Father Frank?"

"I don't know, man. Some bar, some random conversation, and the next thing you know, Dave is talking about him like he's the next messiah."

"You seem like a man who's in the know, Nick. One of those, like the local barber shop where everyone comes in and tells you their secrets." I squatted down to stare Nick in the eyes. "Tell me, Nick, did anyone happen to wander through your doors and spout off about who all put me in jail or, better yet, who raped Raine Eastman?"

Nick looked down at the floor. "Fuck, man. Yeah, someone might have come in and bragged a little."

"You're going to get us killed," Irene yelled at Nick.

"Well, I'll certainly kill you, and I'm in the same room." I smiled at Irene, but it didn't reach my eyes.

"Talk, Nick."

The man reminded me of a ferret with his narrow features and how he scrunched up his nose and wiggled it.

"His name is Jim, but everyone calls him Jumbo 'cause he always eats those massive hotdogs."

I knew exactly who Nick meant. I'd sat in the garage and chatted with Jim all the time. He might have been Dave's trucking friend, but he was around so much that he felt like family. The betrayal was thick as I thought about what had happened to Raine. About how many times she'd brought him a beer or his dinner when he was over. The more I thought, the angrier I became, until my knuckles cracked. I now understood the looks he'd given Raine and how his eyes would linger on her ass when she walked away.

I was pretty sure Raine had been collateral damage because I hadn't shown up at the fights that night. The fact that I had anything to do with what happened sat like acid in my stomach and burned the back of my throat.

My eyes slowly rose to meet Roach's, and he pulled his gun from the back of his jeans.

"What the hell? What is he doing?" Nick and Irene asked as Roach screwed on the silencer. Nick crawled onto the bed and jumped off the other side as if he could feel the walls closing in.

"We told you everything we know," Irene blubbered.

"I know. Kill them," I said and marched for the door as the sound of soft popping was accompanied by short-lived screams.

I was going to find those three men, and I was going to kill them. They'd signed their death warrants the night they attacked Raine. No one hurt Raine but me. She was Mine.

Raine

Chapter 33

Raine

I was shocked when I got Avro to agree to hold off a day in telling him what happened. I said I needed to sleep and think and that I would tell him the next night, but I needed the time to collect myself.

The issue was, I didn't sleep well. I cleaned up the rest of the mess, paced my room, tossed and turned, then read a little. The entire time, I worried about what their reaction to my story was going to be. I also couldn't help wondering if Kai was going to show up again. Now here I was having to pay the piper.

Avro had insisted that I tell both him and Jace at the same time. I argued, but I had realized that arguing with Avro was like yelling at the sky, telling it not to rain. He said the three of us were a unit—if wanted in—that meant we shared everything, the uncomfortable and the great.

I agreed with the idea in theory, but Jace's stare made me more nervous than if it had just been Avro. I paced Avro's living room and hated that they were watching me like I was a ball in a tennis match. It was fairly accurate. I felt like a ball bouncing around from one emotion to the next. Worry, then anger and frustration. I stopped and pinched the bridge of my nose.

If I told them and they both decided to bolt, I guess it was better now than later. I'd never told anyone what happened except the police and Kai the other night.

"Okay, I'll start with this. Jace, you asked the other night where I got my scars. I said it was a long story and didn't want to talk about it." The two of them nodded in unison. "I got them the night I was...." I licked my lips and stared at the ocean picture above the couch. "I got them the night I was raped," I said, and my shoulders slumped. It was like a fifty-pound weight lifted from my chest to get the words out.

The guys didn't move or even blink, which was eerie.

"Why are you staring at me like that?"

"Just didn't want to interrupt you. I know that took a lot to get out," Avro said. "I know it was like that for me, anyway."

I nodded and took a steadying breath. "I was just shy of sixteen. My friend and I have birthdays a week and two days apart, which made him eighteen. Anyway, I was attacked at this place that had underground fights." I waved my hand to dismiss that part. "The point is, I was attacked in an alley, and I thought that it was my friend who attacked me."

"Shit friend, if that was your first thought. But that doesn't explain the bruises now," Jace said, his eyebrow shooting up.

I chewed on my lip, angry at myself for wanting to defend Kai.

"I'm getting to that." I wet my lips to get some moisture into my dry mouth. "The friend that I went to see was supposed to be fighting at this club thing. When I was attacked, I mistakenly thought the attacker was my friend."

Avro crossed his arms. "Jace is right. That was some friend, if you thought that about him."

I glared at Avro. "Please don't interject like that. You have no idea what we went through together that led to that moment."

They looked at one another, silently communicating, before turning to stare at me. "You're right. I'm sorry," Avro said.

"The point is I was wrong, but I didn't think I was wrong, and he got a raw deal and was sent to prison for ten years." I sighed and looked up at the ceiling. "I sent my best friend to prison for something he didn't do." The words sunk in more now than the night I realized my error, and I fought back the tears forming all over again. I needed to keep myself together to get through this. "I have all this guilt over it, and I should. It was a shit thing to do to someone I cared about."

They shifted closer to the edge of the couch at the same time.

"Okay, stop doing that. It's weird."

"Doing what?" they asked together.

"That. Stop being so in sync. It's creepy."

They smiled at the exact same time, which I was sure they did to freak me out. Giving up, I started pacing again. The nervous energy was still thrumming through my body, and it didn't seem to want to let up any time soon.

"Okay, we will try to tone down the creep factor. So, tell us exactly what happened?" Avro asked.

This part was the worst. I knew what they would want to do, and I didn't know how to stop them. "My friend...he got out of prison a little while ago and...um. Well, he found me, and he was pretty pissed off about having to go to jail for something he didn't do and that I was the one who put him there for ten years."

Jace's eyes went wide. "So he beat the shit out of you?" His voice was a deep growl that made me shiver.

He leaned back, a scowl on his face as he crossed his arms over his chest. I could leave out what really happened, but with my luck, that would blow up in my face. I figured this entire thing would blow up in my face, anyway. Why the hell would they want to stay with me and the truckload of baggage I dragged around? If I were caught lying by omission, that would make it worse. At least this way, it was all out there, and if they kicked me out of the relationship, they did. Yeah, it was better to know now than months from now.

"He did more than that. He kind of...did what he was put into jail for," I said, and the room went silent.

I stopped near the window and stared out at the ocean across the road, but I could see their reflections in the glass. They looked like they'd been frozen between shocked and furious and couldn't decide which they wanted to be. I turned and leaned against the wall, crossing my arms over my chest as I waited for them to say something.

"I just want to make sure I heard you right," Jace said, slowly standing from the couch. I swallowed hard at the dark look in his eyes and was terrified to see what would happen with him and Kai in the same room. "This guy, this supposed friend, showed up at your house, assaulted you physically, and then raped you?"

"When you say it like that, it sounds really bad," I said.

Avro stood and placed a hand on his shoulder. Jace looked like he was getting ready to have a meltdown. His silver eyes bored holes into mine.

"Raine, that's because it is bad. I mean, who does that to someone who was once a friend? And you said he was in prison. Do you even know what he's been doing or has done? Could he be putting us all at risk?"

"I'd never let that happen," I said.

"How can you be so sure?" Jace asked, his eyes narrowing.

I swallowed hard. "Because I tracked him down and spoke to him first thing yesterday morning."

"That's where you were coming from? You went to go visit your rapist alone?" Avro asked, then shook his head and walked over to the bar. He poured himself a drink and chugged it back. My heart pounded harder at the thought of them wanting to end things. It would be exactly what I deserved.

"Yes, I needed to speak with him for a couple of reasons, and to make sure he was clean was one of them." Avro rubbed at his eyes as Jace paced the floor. "Guys, I need you to understand that I deserved it."

That was the wrong thing to say. Both of them whipped around to face me so fast that I wished I hadn't opened my mouth at all.

"Don't fucking say that," Jace growled. "No one deserves that. We're calling the cops," he said, taking out his phone.

Panic gripped my throat, and I pushed away from the wall. "No. No cops."

"What do you mean, no cops? He fucking assaulted you. Have you seen yourself? Go look in a mirror. You look like you were used as a human punching bag," Jace fumed and unlocked his phone.

I walked over and grabbed the phone out of his hand, glaring at Jace.

"I said no, Jace. This is my life, and if you do call, I'll deny everything," I said, then held the phone out to him. As he took his phone back, I realized he was shaking. "Just listen to me. I put him in prison. I did that. He did nothing wrong and was sent to a place with terrible people for ten years." I put a hand on my chest. "I named him and swore up and down that it was him. We were foster kids with no real family for help. He'd just turned eighteen and ended up spending all that time behind bars with only my face to blame. The one face he trusted most."

"That still doesn't give him the right to do what he did," Jace argued.

I could see Avro moving closer like he was worried Jace was going to Hulk out.

"You're right, it was an asshole thing to do, and I'm not denying that, but I also get it. I was his best friend, and he was mine, and I never even spoke to him after the attack to find out for sure that it was him. I was fifteen, scared, and felt betrayed. Between my foster father and the police, I felt pressured into naming him, so I did. What would you be like if Avro sent you to prison for doing something you never did?"

They looked at one another, and the anger in the room simmered down but only slightly.

"Fine, I can concede that maybe I'd be pissed. I can't say I would do what your 'friend' did, but I can at least say I'd be angry."

"Try furious. Your singing career—gone. Your name—tarnished and forever with the label of rapist of a minor hanging around your neck. I'm sure that you would've spent all that time fighting not to be assaulted in prison. Avro would become the object of all that rage. I was the object of all his rage." Jace still didn't look convinced. "This doesn't mean I forgive him. I'm just saying I understand his side."

I reached out to touch Jace, but he pulled his hands away as my fingers touched his. Turning around, he walked to the far side of the room like he needed space from me, and it hurt. I didn't think it would, with us barely knowing one another, but the sting was there.

Avro touched my shoulder, and I looked up into his eyes. "Tell me, how is it that after all this time, you're so certain it wasn't him?"

I nibbled my lip. "When he was...." I stopped, trying to frame my words, so they didn't sound any worse.

"Fucking you," Jace said from his spot, his eyes flashing with anger.

It was way too hot in here, and not for a good reason. My body temperature was going through the roof.

"Yes. When he was fucking me, he held me in a similar position, and I realized that the tattoo I'd seen on my attacker's hand was on the other hand. I also realized that the guy felt like a man, had man hands." Avro arched a brow at me. "I mean, when I was attacked, I realized it was all men, but as I said, my friend was eighteen, and I knew what his body looked like and felt like. From hugs and stuff, and it was no eighteen-year-old who had me. There were three of them, and I was scared with a cloth bag on my head, so I wasn't paying attention to details like that. The tattoo was all I could see well. It was what I remembered."

"And you're one hundred percent positive it was on the other hand," Avro asked.

"Yes, I'm more than a hundred percent positive. The memory of it is burned into my brain."

"I still don't like this. He should be punished for what he did, and how do we know he won't try it again?" Jace argued and shook his head.

Avro answered before I could. "None of us are innocent. We need to remember that."

"What do you mean?" I asked.

"That is a story for another time. Jace does make an excellent point, though. How do we know he's not going to keep coming back?"

"We don't, but I don't think he will. When I saw him this morning, he wanted me to leave him alone." I walked over to the couch and flopped down, suddenly exhausted.

"How did you find him? I'm sure he didn't leave behind a business card," Jace said, the sarcasm dripping from every word.

"Jace, I don't need your attitude. I spent most of my life since that moment living like a terrified hermit. Do you think I don't see that attack like it happened yesterday when I close my eyes? You think I can't feel their hands on my skin or the sharp blade piercing my skin? You think I don't still feel helpless all the damn time?" My anger was stirring, and I clutched my hands into fists on my knees. "It happened to me, not you. And you're not the one who thought for eleven years that your best friend turned on you, only to find out that you fucked up and sent the wrong person to prison. So now not just two of my attackers have been walking around free all this time, all of them have."

I stared at my hands and the faint scars lining my wrists, remembering the white zip ties cutting in and making me bleed. The way the blood ran down my arms.

"They've been dancing all this time, thinking they got away with what they did while my friend rotted in a cell. This is my pain and my cross to bear, and it is also my body and my choice. So, no cops, not ever. If you want me to stay in this relationship with you, no one can ever know what happened."

He ran a hand through his hair and looked down at the ground. I took it as a small victory that he didn't continue to argue.

"As for finding him...he happens to be part of one of the largest motorcycle clubs in the area. It was easy to hunt him down."

Jace threw his hands in the air.

"Oh, this just keeps getting better and better."

He stomped out of the room, and I heard his heavy footfalls on the stairs. I slumped into the couch as the defeated feeling washed over me. My head hurt. The headache that had threatened all day now took hold as the rest of my muscles screamed from everything that had happened.

Avro refilled his drink and wandered over to sit down beside me. He held the glass out for me to take some. It was probably the last thing I needed, but I sipped some of the concoction, anyway.

"Hmm, this one is different. I'm going to say crème de menthe,

Kahlua, and coffee mixed with chocolate," I said and then peeked at the counter to see the chocolate milk sitting out. "Not bad."

Avro smirked and took his drink back. "Jace wants to protect everything, and the more he cares, the angrier he becomes. When I told him about my attack, I knew he'd lose his mind and want to protect me. It's who he is. He just needs a minute to calm down."

He picked up my hand and linked our fingers together. I leaned my head against his shoulder. "Does that mean you're not planning on tossing me out the door?"

"Are you crazy?" Avro tightened his grip on my hand and brought it to his lips. The fear I had bottled up inside my chest let go, and I whimpered, letting the tears fall.

"Shh, it's okay." He kissed my forehead, but that only made the crying worse. I didn't deserve his kindness. Chaos loved me, and I was worried that I would only ruin what they had built.

"I know you think I should turn him in, but I can't, not this time. I understand him. I always have. It's like how you and I became friends, that instant connection, and now we finish each other's sentences. I had that with him. I knew him. I knew his heart and his soul, and I never spoke to him, never gave him a chance." I covered my mouth as a sob wracked my body. "I did the same thing everyone else did when they looked at him. I thought the worst. That ache will stay with me forever, and I can't add him going back to prison to the list. The weight of that happening will crush my soul," I said.

"So you still care for him that much?" Avro asked, his voice soft and soothing.

I loved how warm he was. It was like I could curl up in his lap and go to sleep, and he'd make me feel better no matter what was wrong.

"Yeah, I do. I know I shouldn't, and it's stupid, but I do. I saw genuine hurt under the anger. No matter what he did, I can't turn him in."

We sat quietly for a long time before Avro sighed and stood, bringing me to my feet with him. "Then we will respect your wishes. But, Raine, he can't hurt you like that again. Forget Jace. I'll hunt him down and kill him first."

There was something oddly calming about that statement, and I wrapped my arms around Avro's waist and held on tight.

Raine

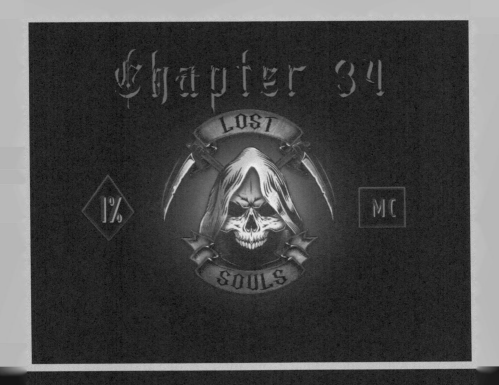

Chapter 34

Raine

As we neared the bottom of the stairs, I heard a piano. We silently climbed up the stairs, the music getting progressively louder with each step. Jace was amazing. I didn't even know he could play an instrument. I'd only ever seen him sing in the glimpses I got of him on television or even the nights at the bar.

Avro led me toward the music and the door that had been closed on my tour. The haunting sound stirred a complex blend of emotions whipping around inside of me. We didn't go in but stood in the hall listening as Jace's fingers flew over the keys. He looked like he was in some otherworldly movie. His back was to us. The piano in the middle of the room faced the ocean on the other side of the dark tinted glass. The lights were dimmed and had a fake flame effect that flickered off all the silver in the room, including the piano. It glittered like a silver lake as the flames danced over the shiny surface. The man at the keys was just as captivating.

Jace wasn't wearing a shirt, and the tattoos that stretched the width of his shoulders stood out in the low light. I hadn't paid much attention to them until now, but for whatever reason, I couldn't stop staring.

"I think the two of you need to spend some time together alone," Avro whispered in my ear. "He only plays this song when he's stressing over something." His soft voice was as intoxicating as the music, and I felt like swaying.

"I don't think he wants to see me right now," I whispered back, and Avro gave me a smile that warmed me to my toes. My eyes were drawn to his amber depths that always seemed to sparkle even in the dim light, like the mischief glowed from inside of him.

"Trust me. Do you think you're up for it, though?"

I peered through the gap in the partially open door and then back up at Avro. I knew what he meant. I nodded and bit my lip. "You don't want to join?"

He cupped my face, and we shared a kiss that was so light, yet held more weight than any other.

"No, you two need to find your path on your own. Besides, I think I had my fair share yesterday," he teased, and my cheeks warmed until I wanted to fan my face. The multiple rounds in the office had been incredible, but the shower afterward was hotter. Avro had some serious skills and played my body like he knew every button to push.

I had to admit that I was a little achy from all the new activities, but as my eyes drifted back to the man playing the piano like he was possessed, I didn't care. The old nervousness still hadn't surfaced, and I didn't know if it was gone forever or if it would suddenly come back, but I was taking all I could get while it lasted.

Avro kissed my hand, which he seemed to love doing, then turned and sauntered down the hall toward the bedroom.

I couldn't do anything but stare as I stepped into the room. Jace's fingers flew over keys, and his messy hair hung in his eyes as he hunched slightly over the piano. But it was the shirtless back and the tight muscles that had my mouth running completely dry.

Stepping up behind him, I tentatively reached for his shoulder. Jace stopped playing and spun around so quickly that I didn't even have time to react before his hand gripped my wrist. The soft silvery light in the room reflected off his eyes and made them look as liquid as the piano behind him. His eyes were hooded, and I held still as if caught in a trap.

He lifted one leg at a time over the bench he was sitting on as he turned fully in my direction. The walls in the room shrunk down around me as my pulse pounded hard in my veins. He pulled my wrist to his nose, and I shivered when he sniffed, as if scenting the blood underneath like a vampire. All he needed was a pair of fangs to complete the look.

"You always smell like peaches. Why is that?" Jace asked, his voice deep but smooth like an aged scotch.

"I don't know," I whispered.

"I like it," he said, and with a tug, I was standing between his legs.

His head was right at my breasts, and he playfully nipped at the zipper, but I couldn't take my eyes off the tongue ring that flicked out. I remembered all too well what his tongue could do and how that piercing felt. If Avro had been doing this, I would've said he looked cute, but there was nothing cute about Jace. He was sexy and rugged in a way that was more personality than his overall appearance, yet he oozed an intensity that reminded me of Kai before prison.

"Were you wanting something?" Jace asked, but as he stood, his body rubbed against mine, and all logical thoughts dove out the three-story window.

I squealed as he gripped my waist. With a single fluid movement, Jace lifted me and sat me down on top of the piano, the lid falling shut with a bang. His hands left my waist to grip the piano on either side of my legs like I was in a cage, and that was almost worse than if he'd touched me. I was suddenly terrified to move.

"I came in to see if you were okay and if we were going to find a way through this," I said.

He leaned in, and my heart sputtered with the sizzling energy he naturally ignited. I didn't know what he would do, and that was part of the thrill. He could kiss me or push me off the piano, and I could see both happening as surely as him fucking me on top of it. There was very little need for clothes in this house with these two around. All they had to do was look at me, and I turned into a puddle at their feet. My hand went to his chest, and he stared at it. I swallowed the lump in my throat as his silver orbs traced the line of my arm all the way up to my eyes. There was something so sexy and yet terrifying about the act.

"You planning on pushing me away, Peaches?" he asked, daring me to say no. I shook my head. "That's very good."

My heart stopped as his teeth nipped at my lower lip and sucked it into his mouth. The jitters in my stomach started, but they were different from before. I didn't fear him, but the anticipation of what he would do next and his ability to amp up every situation caused all my muscles to quake.

Fanning my fingers, I took in the feel of his hard chest and shuddered as Jace groaned when my pinkie finger ran over his nipple with the little bar.

"You seem different, Peaches," he said, and licked a line down the side of my neck.

"I feel different," I moaned, my voice no more than a whisper.

"Why?"

Jace pulled back, and I was forced to stare into those unnerving eyes. "I don't know. After what happened, I should feel worse, more scared maybe, but instead, I feel...calmer."

Jace lifted an eyebrow, and his lip curled up like he was laughing at me. "Interesting. Not the way I would've handled it, but it seems your friend did you a favor."

"I don't think it has anything to do with him," I said, not liking what he was insinuating.

"Oh, we may have already had you on the right path, but your friend literally forced you to relive and face your trauma in an almost identical fashion, I assume." I swallowed. "Not exactly a great recipe for therapy and could've gone wildly wrong, but then again, you're different. Aren't you, Peaches? You like it when Avro touches you with his sweet touch, but there is more to you."

I licked my lips, not wanting to hear what he would say next, and yet I knew he would say it, anyway.

Jace stepped in close to my body, and I shivered, but when he growled against my skin and nipped at my neck, I couldn't deny that I wanted him and was ready to strip my clothes off. Pulling back, he held my chin in his hand, and it felt like he was trying to look right through me with the intensity of his stare.

"You like it rough, Peaches. Whether it was always in you or caused by your first time being so traumatic, maybe. It's hard to say. This could simply be new, but you get off on the fear. I can see it in your eyes."

I looked away and clenched my jaw tight. "I do not," I said. Jace laughed.

"Oh, you can deny it all you want, but tell me something honestly. Did he make you cum?"

I wiggled on the piano, not wanting to answer this question.

"I'm going to guess more than once."

I knew my face was bright red as the tips of my ears burned. Jace moved enough that I was forced to look at him. Was closing my eyes an option?

"I'm going to go out on a limb and say that you screamed for him to stop, begged for it to be over, but there was a part of you that loved his hands holding you down, and that was even more terrifying to you than the sex. At least twice. But my guess is you came at least three times."

I crossed my arms over my chest. "Even if I did, it doesn't mean anything."

"See, I knew I was right 'cause I don't hear a denial." He smirked, and I wanted to smack the look off his face. "It's fine. I don't care that you got off. I probably would've while watching the show," he said, and my mouth fell open. "Don't look so shocked. There are a lot of kinks out there, Peaches, and we will explore them all until we find out what makes you so wet that you beg to be fucked. 'Cause you see, that is one of mine. I want to hear you beg for my cock from these sweet lips of yours."

I was fully clothed, yet I felt completely naked in front of him. He had just put his hand into my soul and ripped it open. I hadn't wanted to face my feelings about my time with Kai. Had I been scared? Hell yes. Had I not wanted it at first? Also, yes. But I couldn't deny that fighting with him in my bedroom had turned me on, and the fear of what I knew he would do intensified every touch. The moment Kai groaned in my ear and slipped into my body, something that I thought was disgusting took over inside of me—something that wanted the adrenaline and to feed off his anger and my terror.

"I don't want to talk about this," I said, and pulled my chin out of Jace's grasp.

"We don't need to talk about it, but it doesn't change facts, Peaches. You're fucked up, but in all the most delicious ways."

He smiled and stepped around the piano bench, out of my reach, which was good because I was liable to hit him. The voice inside my head warned that everything I said I didn't like or want would happen if I did it. My stomach tightened into knots as the thought had me squeezing my thighs together.

He was right. I really was messed in the head.

Jace grabbed his discarded T-shirt off the plush black chair in the corner and pulled it over his head. My eyes traced every movement of his reverse striptease, and even that was fucking hot.

"If you're done staring, I'd like to take you somewhere," he said with a teasing tint to his words.

"Where?" I asked, my eyes darting up to his.

"That's a surprise."

He walked toward me like a model as he ran his hands through his shock-white hair that, when you were up close, had strips of silver. I'd learned his hair color was similar to my platinum blonde, and I badly wanted to see his natural shade. My brain was still in a fog when he wrapped his arm around my waist, and as easily as he'd put me on the piano, he lifted me down.

"I could've gotten down," I said.

"Yes, but then I wouldn't have had your hard nipples pressing into my chest." Of course, I had to look down, and Jace snickered when I could see the evidence for myself. "Come on. I'll make this adventure worth your while."

"Wait a second." I tugged back on his hand as he grabbed mine. "That's it. You're no longer angry with me for not wanting to call the police?"

"Oh no. I'm still livid about that, but I want to show you something before we talk more."

I nibbled my bottom lip, and in the span of a breath, his lips were on mine. My head spun, and the earlier fog returned. Jace didn't just kiss me. He commanded my attention and took what he wanted, how he liked it. I gripped the white T-shirt and held on like it was the only thing holding me up.

Breaking away, Jace stared into my eyes. "Please," he whispered. A word I just knew he rarely ever said. I nodded, not trusting my voice.

Holding my hand, he marched out the door, and I was practically jogging to keep up with his long strides.

"Yo, Avro," Jace called out when we reached the top of the stairs.

"Yeah." Avro poked his head out of the bedroom door.

"I'm taking Peaches for a drive. We'll be back in a few hours," he said, and even though I knew they had a unique relationship, it wasn't until Avro smiled that I truly understood how complicated the layering was.

"Sounds good. I'm watching sappy rom coms, anyway," Avro said and laughed. "Are you going to be near Terri's Place?"

"Yeah, you want anything?"

"Couple pounds of spicy dill pickle and garlic wings with loaded fries and a banana milkshake."

"I swear to fuck you're pregnant, 'cause that is disgusting." Jace made a gagging face, and I laughed. It was pretty gross, but I'd seen Avro eat worse.

"If I am, it's yours, so we're fucked," Avro called back, making us laugh harder.

"Where are the keys?"

"Jacket pocket, and don't have too much fun without me," he called out as he disappeared into the bedroom.

"We're going to have all the fun without him, but don't tell him," Jace said, looking down at me.

"I fucking heard that," Avro yelled, making us both laugh as he jogged down the stairs.

When had I ever felt so free or at ease? Hell, I didn't even think feeling anything like this was possible. It was all fantasy and made up by those who wanted to convince little girls that there were perfect happily ever after stories out there. It was all bullshit, or at least I thought. Watching how Avro and Jace maneuvered through their conversations, the push and pull that was so natural, had my jaw dropping regularly. Score for communication. I'd never seen anything even close to the trust they shared, and it gave me so much hope.

Stopping at the door, Jace grabbed a baseball hat and pulled on a hoodie. "Don't you ever get sick of it?"

"What?"

"This." I held my hands out to what he was doing. "The constant hiding of your face and being unable to do normal things like go to a store in a mall or eat at a restaurant without a million pictures taken or people screaming and running up to you?"

Jace shrugged and put a pair of sunglasses on, even though it was dark outside. "It's part of the gig. If you don't want the success, don't fucking put yourself out there and act like you do."

"That's a pretty harsh way to look at it," I said.

"Not really. It's just the truth that no one wants to say out loud. We all grow up seeing what it is like to be in the spotlight. It's not like it's a shock that you're invited to fancy events and your moves are scrutinized, or your manager does shit to get your face in the news. It's all part of the game. Now if I'd been a kid, that's different, but I was twenty when my first video went viral, and two years later, I was offered a record deal and a five-year contract to travel."

We opened the back door, and Jace stepped out and looked up and down the street like we were getting ready to break into it, never mind leave the house. Convinced the way was clear, we walked to Avro's car and hopped in.

"The thing is, Peaches," Jace said as he removed the glasses and tossed the expensive rims in the cup holder like they were from a dollar store and didn't cost a fortune. "I never intended for it to go viral. I was just having some fun and posted the videos on the right platform, at the right time, with the right song. It was mostly luck."

He started the car and backed out of the driveway. "And as much as I love to sing and, of course, the money, I prefer to be here with Avro writing songs. So that's my goal and dream once my contract is up."

We pulled out onto the main road, and I let what he said sink in. It was true. You didn't know what was going on inside someone. Because Jace Everly, the frontman for Grimhead Crew, wanting a simple life—I never would've guessed it.

Jace

Chapter 35

Jace

Raine was growing on me. Fucking Avro. He knew she was exactly my type. Sweet and sexy, with a vixen hiding under her big blue eyes and a whole lot damaged, just like we were. I glanced at her, perched in the seat next to me, and took a deep breath to calm my mind.

If I didn't fucking love Avro so much, I would've walked out the door the moment he broke our promise. I thought about it, but the pain was too much, and now...Raine was crawling under my skin. I wanted to scream and fuck them both at the same time.

My hand tightened on the steering wheel as I created new colorful sentences with the word fuck. The other thing that had been weighing on me was that my writing was stale, and the only time I felt like myself and creative was when I was home with Avro. It hadn't felt like that during the first couple of years traveling. It had been invigorating to see the world and sing on stages with fans screaming our songs, but this past year had been tough. The fact that Avro felt the same way shouldn't have been a surprise. We were always on the same wavelength.

Since I got back, I'd managed to write three brand new kick-ass songs, which was the only reason Allen wasn't riding my ass to leave town. We needed new material, and nothing from other producers or writers felt like the band or me. Of course, the new stuff was killer, and the guys were keen to sing and get in the studio. I sent Allen two completed songs with melodies this morning, and my phone had been blowing up with how much everyone loved them. He was tempted to cancel the next few concerts so I could finish a whole album. Maybe I would tell him I wanted to go country just to watch him faint.

Raine's hands were in her lap as she played with the cuffs of her hoodie, and I wondered if it was a nervous habit. I filed the information away.

I was going to ease her into the questions, but it wasn't my style. I tended to go for the jugular. So why stop now?

"Do you love Avro?" I asked. Raine's head snapped in my direction, eyes wide and mouth open. "You heard me. Do you love him?"

"I...I...I...."

I lifted my brows. "It's a simple yes or no question. No need to make it complicated," I said, and she fixed me with a glare that had my blood warming.

"I don't know," she said, and crossed her arms over her chest. She definitely didn't like talking about herself or her emotions, but that was going to fucking stop. There was a lot of shit that I wasn't good at, but my communication was A-1.

"Hiding behind indifference doesn't make emotions magically disappear," I drawled, knowing how much it would annoy her. "I mean, you've managed to get away with it for years, but that's why you were a fucking disaster when I met you."

"Wow, way to just toss that shit out there, Jace. I thought you said you were going to make this trip fun?"

"Hmm, did I, though? I said I'd make it worth your while, but that is completely different. It's your fault you didn't get clarification before we left." I smiled at her and loved that she pressed her lips together in a hard line as she shot daggers at me with her pretty blue eyes.

That's it, Peaches. Let the tiger out to play.

"Besides, what good does it do us if we sugar-coat shit? All it ever does is create half-truths, hurt feelings, or misunderstandings, and honestly, I don't have time for that shit. If I like you, I like you. If I don't, you fucking know it. So, I will ask you one more time. Do you love Avro?"

Raine licked her lips, and I was so fucking tempted to grab her face and scare the shit out of her as I kissed her while driving, but the highway was too busy to do that tonight. Scaring the shit out of her was one thing. Driving head-on into another car was not on my bucket list.

Raine sighed and leaned her elbow on the door as she rubbed at her forehead. "This is all new."

"But you've known him for four years. Are you saying you have no idea how you feel after all that time? I find that hard to believe. And if you're just leading him on, I will leave your ass right here on the side of the road," I growled.

Raine turned in her seat and hit me with a glare that went straight to my cock and had it swelling. The way her brows drew together and those bright blue eyes sparkled with anger...Even the way she bit her bottom lip like she was trying to bite it off rather than say what she really wanted. Fuck, that look was hot.

"You can't force me to say something I don't fully understand.

Feelings don't exactly work that way, Jace," she said, her voice venomous as she said my name, and my cock twitched a little more. If she kept looking at me like that, I was going to pull over right here on the highway. It would make a great headline for the tabloids when the state police came knocking on the rocking car window.

"Tell me what you do feel. Spit it out, Peaches. Let go of all the doubt and wonder and worry and what ifs and just speak," I said, my voice holding as much heat as her gaze.

"Fuck, you're irritating," she groaned. I smirked. "I think so, but I'm not sure, and before you spout off again, I'll tell you why. I've spent our entire time together as friends. Did I want him? Sure, but I wasn't stupid enough to pine over something I thought would never happen. I shut down any inappropriate feelings before they got a chance to get rolling."

She held out her hands toward me. "You're asking me to describe how I feel when I've barely got my head wrapped around the ludicrous idea he even wants me. Then with the shit that happened with my ex-friend, I'm just not in the right head space to say yes, I love him, or no, I'm not as a definitive answer."

She moved her hands in two circles in front of her chest. "There is so much going on right now that I don't know which end is up, but if you are asking if I have strong feelings, then yes. He makes me smile and feel safe. He makes me feel things that I thought were only in fairy tales. So if you want to kick me out on the side of the road for that, go for it."

"Fine. Do you think you could?"

She nodded, but the softness in her eyes and the way her shoulders relaxed said she was all up in her feels, even if she didn't recognize it.

"Yeah, I do." She cocked her head. "Why aren't you asking about yourself?"

I tapped my finger on the top of the steering wheel and pulled out to pass a long line of cars that decided tonight was Sunday drive time. "Because I don't care if you love me or not." I gave her the full weight of my stare. "At least not yet."

"If you care so much about what Avro wants, why were you so upset when he wanted to change the arrangement you two have?" she asked.

"Had."

"What?"

"Had, as in past tense. Did you not pay attention in English class?" I snipped and bit the inside of my cheek to keep from laughing as she went as red as any cherry I'd ever seen. "Don't worry about answering. I don't really care. I grudgingly already agreed to his new idea, or I'm going to try for as long as I can." I shrugged, loving this game of poking at her way more than I should.

I still wasn't sure I could hold off having sex with anyone other than my hand for that long, but for Avro, I'd fucking give it my all. Not damaging our relationship was the most important thing to me. Not even my music career meant as much.

"So what does that mean? You just going to start cheating on him when you decide you've had enough?" Raine fumed, and my mouth curled up in a smile. Good, she was protective already, and that boded well for us.

"Do I strike you as an asshole?"

She turned her head like a bird as she stared at me with a 'are you fucking stupid' look on her face. "Is this a trick question?"

"Fine, I'm an asshole. Do I strike you as a cheating asshole?" I asked.

"How am I supposed to know that? We've spent less than a week together. I had a goldfish I knew better than you," she said.

I barked out a laugh and then smiled wide. "I like this side of you, Peaches. You have a fire that you've been keeping buried for far too long."

"Yeah, well, you seem to bring out the colorful side of me," Raine mumbled.

"To answer your question, no, I'm not a cheater. Despite whatever the tabloids, social media, or entertainment shows say, I don't do anything that is not a media stunt or is discussed and approved with Avro. I knew about you for a long time."

"You did?"

"Of course. Avro told me the moment he met you and felt a connection. I knew he'd want to bring you into the fold at some point. I was just sick of hearing him go on about you without meeting you, so I forced his hand. He needs that now and then."

"Oh," she said, and nibbled her lip. "So you actually do media stunts?"

"Yes, that happens. Not everyone does, but I find it works for me and what Avro and I wanted for our private life."

I ran my hand through my hair as I thought about the last time Allen made me do one of those fake shoots and play the role of the jerk boyfriend for ratings. He made a deal with the father of a Princess from some country I couldn't even pronounce. We made it look like we were living together in a fancy hotel suite in Paris.

We were in the same hotel for a month, but other than the staged photos, we never spoke or touched or anything else. The images circulating of us on a balcony, half-naked in a hot tub for the paparazzi went viral overnight. Fans started calling me Rock Prince, which I hated with a passion. I had no idea what she and her father got out of it, but I had a million more downloads than anticipated of the band's newest release in just two days.

"How does this work, then? You feel the urge to get yourself off with someone else and ask Avro for permission?"

"You and Avro," I stated. "If you're serious about being in this with us, then it's an 'us' thing. Not a 'you and him' thing, not a 'him and me' thing, an 'us' thing. Get it?" I pulled off the highway that led toward my old stomping grounds.

"I guess I get it," she said. "This is all very strange. I went from not having a boyfriend ever to two very different ones overnight." She made a little exasperated noise that was fucking adorable.

It made me so damn hard how she was sweet and naïve in many ways and yet so much more. I really wanted to draw that out of her, and the thought had my cock stirring again.

"Did you know Avro wants me to move in? I mean, isn't that a little soon? It seems a whole lot soon to me." She crossed her arms. "He blurted it out while we were at work today. Took me completely off guard."

I laughed hard. "Gee, I wonder what that feels like?" I said, and Raine blushed. "Look, Avro is an all-in kind of guy. He wants you to be with us, so he pushes all his chips to the center of the table. My suggestion is to compromise," I said.

"How?"

"What bothers you the most about moving in with us?" I asked, and she sucked in her bottom lip as she thought.

"I guess losing my own place," she said, her voice soft.

"Then don't. That's an easy fix." Putting on the turn signal, I pulled into the driveway of Terri's Place. This was the best chicken and pizza place for miles. It was a hidden gem far outside the city limits, but Avro and I used to come here at least once a week before I started to tour.

"You mean keep my house but still move in for now," Raine asked and tapped her chin.

"Why not? When Avro gets an idea in his head, he will chase that shit down and bug the fuck out of you until you agree, and good luck saying no. So you might as well give it a shot unless you want him harassing you every day." I swung my eyes to hers as I put the car in park. "And you know he will. Have you ever been able to say no to an idea of his?" I cocked an eyebrow and picked up my phone to put in my order. "Besides, you could rent it out after a couple of months of feeling comfortable and earn another income. If things go really well, you can then sell and put the money away or buy a different house when it's a good buying market. Many options."

Terri and the manager knew us by name and would bring the food out to the car, so I didn't run the risk of being spotted.

"Now that you mention it...No, I don't think I've ever said no to Avro. That's a little terrifying," she said, and I laughed.

"It's worth it, though. Trust me, he will fill you, and I don't mean with his cock, although that will happen too."

Raine laughed and gripped her stomach. The sound was as cute as she was.

"He does have a knack for making you feel like everything will be okay." Raine looked at me while I typed in the text message to Terri.

"Yeah, he really does." I held up the phone to show her the message. "Do you want anything, or would you like to share my pizza with me?"

"What are you getting on it?"

"Spicy buffalo chicken with barbecue sauce." Raine scrunched up her nose. "Trust me, you try it once, and you'll wonder how you ever lived without this in your life."

"Then sure, I'll share with you."

I finished typing in the message and waited for the thumbs up before setting the phone down. We lapsed into silence as we waited for the food. I took the time to gather my thoughts about what I was going to show her.

"How much farther do we have to go?" Raine asked as Terri pushed out the door with bags and a cooler. The man was always thinking.

"Not far," I said and then hit unlock on the car doors. Terri opened the back door, a dance we'd done many times in the last three years.

"Jace, it is good to see you," Terri said as he arranged the food that made my stomach growl. He still looked the same. Terri's dark hair was now going grey, but aside from that, the same smile was always on his face.

"You two, man. Terri, this is Raine." I nodded in her direction. "She is staying with Avro and me. So if you get a message from her, could you do the same thing?"

"For my best customer? Of course." He held out his hand for Raine to shake.

"Nice to meet you, Raine."

"Likewise." Raine shook his hand and offered a very business-like smile, and I picked up on the change even though most never would.

"Oh, Jace, I put the milkshakes in this cooler and packed it with ice for you."

"See, this is why I love you. Thanks, and the money is sent," I said.

"You're always way too generous, mon ami," Terri said, shaking his head as he backed away.

"To keep you in business, it's worth it. Who else is going to make my pizza the way you do and then deliver it to my car?"

Terri laughed. "Given how you're now a fancy rock star, I'm sure every restaurant in the state, but I appreciate your loyalty. Have a good night, and nice to meet you, Raine." Terri closed the door and was heading to the front doors before we could even say goodbye. He'd treated me in the same friendly and efficient manner the first time Avro and I walked through his doors.

"You're a conundrum to me, Jace," Raine said as I pulled out of the parking lot.

I smiled at the comment. "I like to keep you on your toes."

The last few miles felt like a chain slowly tightening around my throat. The memories flashing before my eyes had my heart pounding hard and my hands squeezing the life out of the steering wheel just so I didn't whip the car around and say fuck it.

Raine touched my shoulder, and I was startled by the soft contact.

"You okay?" she asked, her eyes filled with worry.

"Yeah, totally fine."

"Now who is lying?" she quipped.

"I'm so going to fuck that sauce right out of you later," I said, and I meant it.

If this unknown friend and Avro got a taste, then I sure as fuck wasn't standing on the sidelines with my cock in my hand like a good little boy. I'd never been one, so if the shoe fit, as they say.

She cleared her throat and mumbled something I was sure would've turned me on if I wasn't so distracted by the house we were approaching. I shut the car off on the quiet street, so we didn't draw attention, and I sat there trying to control my galloping pulse.

"Where are we?" Raine asked and looked out her window at the dark and boarded-up home. The caution tape was faded and torn but still hung on and flapped in the breeze like a warning sign that something evil had happened inside.

I wet my lips and looked straight ahead, not daring to glance at the house. "This was my home," I said. "Avro lived just down there, the second house on the left." I pointed to the house lit up with pretty little lights, the yellow garage door practically glowing in the dark. "His family is no longer there, though. They moved a while back and never gave us a forwarding address." I rolled my eyes. "We told them we were more than friends. Let's say it didn't go very well."

"Shit, poor Avro. I didn't know."

"He doesn't like to talk about it, but he will if you ask him to."

My leg started to bounce, and I couldn't sit there for another second. I started the car and pulled away from the curb. I could feel Raine's eyes as she silently asked what had happened.

"I just need a minute," I said through the pain constricting my throat.

In reality, I needed a lot more than a minute. It had been six years since my family was taken from me, and the only two things that got me through it were Avro and my music.

There were just some things you were never meant to forget.

Jace

Chapter 36

J ace

A last-minute decision made me pull into the big old cemetery and follow the driveway to the back. Killing the lights, reached into the back and grabbed our pizza.

"You want to eat here?" Raine looked out at the tombstones that were illuminated by the bright moon. "In the cemetery?"

"Yeah, I do." Pushing open my door, I got out before she could question me any further.

Her movements were tentative, like she expected a zombie to reach up and grab her from the ground. I made a growling noise at her, and she jumped and yelped.

"You're an asshole," Raine said as I laughed at her.

"They're dead, Peaches, and trust me, even when you want them to, they don't come back," I said and held her gaze that softened

"Come on, over here." I tugged on her hand and led the way to where my family was buried. Well, the family I loved, anyway.

I pulled her to a stop in front of the black granite wall. Lifting my hand, I ran my finger over the three names, and Raine followed it as I did.

"Janice Everly, my mother. Everly was her maiden name, and I was named after her. My father was a dick, and my stepfather was worse, so I took her name. Chad, my fifteen-year-old brother, and Shannon, my twelve-year-old sister." My hand dropped from the wall, and I walked over to the low crypt beside it. I placed the pizza box on top before turning to Raine. "Do you need a hand to get up?"

"You want to sit on that?" she asked, her voice low and horrified.

"Do you really think whoever this dude was cares? Besides, I sit here all the time, and no one has struck me with lightning. Come on, up you go," I said and held out my hands like a step.

Raine stared around as if someone would come down the dark path screaming that we were going to hell. She tentatively stepped up and placed her hands on the top of the flat roof of the crypt. With a push, she jumped up and sat down with her legs swinging over the edge. I took a few steps back and jumped, using the tomb on the right to push off and up, and landed on the roof of the one Raine was sitting on.

"Holy shit! How did you do that?"

I laughed as I sat down beside her and flipped open the pizza box. It was so quiet here, and I loved coming and just letting my mind wander. I wrote two number-one hits in this cemetery.

"I used to dabble in parkour. I was pretty good, but Avro made it look easy." I nudged the box in her direction. "Try it."

She picked up a piece and stared at it like it might bite before taking a tiny little nibble off the end. I smirked as her features lifted into a smile, and she took another bite. Soon she was eating it and letting out little moans with each mouthful.

"Told ya. The man is a genius with his flavors."

"This is incredible," she smiled and then looked around. "Can I ask what exactly we are doing here, Jace?"

I ate another slice of pizza and stared at the lines of names I could no longer make out from here, but I knew exactly where my family's names were.

"I'm going to tell you why I was so angry earlier." I glanced at Raine from the corner of my eye. Taking a deep breath, I started telling the story that seemed so unbelievable that it had been aired across the country, so I relived it in every time zone.

"As I said, my dad was a dick—my biological father, I mean. He had a boatload of money but took off on my mom when I was seven with his secretary. Do you get any more cliché than that?"

"Oh wow. I'm sorry, Jace."

I smiled and looked over at Raine. "Oh, Peaches, that's not even the main course. That's the appetizer to the appetizer, so you may want to hold off on your sympathy until I'm done."

She bit into her slice of pizza and narrowed her eyes like she was tempted to say something but held her tongue. I was mentally daring her. Not that I needed a reason to fuck her right here on the crypt, but I should finish the story first. Then...we'd see.

"Anyway, it was just as well. He liked to smack us around when he was in one of his moods. It didn't happen all the time, but it happened, and my mom was terrified. He had her so scared that she breathed a sigh of relief when he took off and sent her divorce papers. She'd joke with her friends on the phone when she didn't know that I was listening that she'd never signed something so fast in her life."

A car driving past the cemetery blared its horn at someone else, but we couldn't see what was happening, just heard the loud, *fuck you*. That's kind of how I felt all the time, like I was trapped inside a large area while the rest of the world revolved around me, except with Avro.

"Sometimes I wonder if that prior relationship with my bio-dad tainted how she saw people. Like she couldn't judge who was good anymore, so she decided just to be really nice to everyone. She was always nice, but I think her asshole meter was broken. Then again, so was mine."

I closed my eyes and let the memories I never wanted to think about race to the surface.

"My mom was the best. She was this amazing, warm, caring person and just a little too good. She was the type who never missed helping with homework and would kiss 'booboos' better." I chuckled. "I can still hear her voice and how ridiculous she sounded when she'd say that. She made the best cookies and never made you feel bad for your dreams. She was always telling me I could be whatever I wanted, and she'd support me all the way. My mom meant it too. It wasn't lip service. She'd take extra shifts if it meant I could play sports and would go without new clothes or eating dinner." I paused and bit at my lip as I pictured her beautiful smile that lit up any room.

"She was the type of mom every kid dreams of having, and she saw the best in others, even when there was no good in them to see." Tossing the rest of my crust in the cardboard box, I leaned back on my hands and stared up at the night sky.

It was rare that it was so clear out. There wasn't a single cloud to block out the stars. I used to wish I could be one of those stars, and I ended up a rock star instead. The universe worked in weird ways.

"When I was eight, my mom started dating Lyle, and they decided to marry after she got pregnant with Chad, and then along came Shannon. My stepfather, Lyle, was fine enough, or I thought he was, but I never really saw him as a dad." I shrugged. "I can't say why. He didn't treat me any different from how he treated Chad or Shannon, but it never felt right."

I turned my head to look at Raine, and she looked like one of the statues placed around the cemetery. She wasn't moving or blinking, and for a moment, I wasn't even sure if she was breathing.

"You okay?"

"Yeah, I'm good." She shifted position, so she was staring directly at me, and I didn't know if that was better or if more of her intense focus was worse.

I pinched the bridge of my nose and swallowed as the pizza churned from the tension building in my gut.

"I don't know what I would've done without Avro. His real name is Alex, in case he never told you," I said and let my mind float back to the fight that I didn't know would be the beginning of the end of my family.

Alex and I wandered along the sidewalk toward my house. I didn't get home from Duke as much as I liked. Between the full course load, playing on the basketball team that had brought me there with a full scholarship, and trying to promote my music, it didn't leave much time for family visits.

I glanced at Alex and wished he'd change his mind and move to North Carolina with me. I knew he had dreams of his own, but I missed him. We went from spending every day together to swapping every other weekend. He made the twelve-hour drive two weekends ago and stayed with me from Thursday night until Sunday morning, and this was my weekend to drive back home. I loved the school, my team, and the entire experience, including meeting people to jam with, and yet it felt like something was always missing until Alex was there.

"What do you want to do tomorrow?" I asked and then froze. I

grabbed Alex's arm as shouting from inside my house could be heard from where we were on the sidewalk.

"What the fuck?"

"Is that your parents?"

"Sounds like it." I jogged up the driveway with Alex beside me. My mom never fought with anyone, and I couldn't even remember her ever fighting with Lyle, but it was definitely his voice I heard as we neared the front door.

The door was locked, and I slammed into it as I tried to push it open. "Dammit."

Whipping my backpack off my shoulder, I rummaged around in my bag until I found my keys. My hand shook as I tried to get the key into the lock, then something inside smashed.

I looked at Alex, and he had the same horrified expression to match the anger and fear forcing me to break out in a sweat. Pushing open the door, I didn't understand what I was walking in on. My mother was sitting on the floor dabbing a tissue on Chad's head while Shannon stood in the archway to the kitchen, crying.

Lyle was pacing the living room, yelling about something to do with bills and money and where it was going. The sentences were choppy. As soon as he spotted us, he stopped and pointed at me.

"What the fuck are you staring at?" Lyle yelled. His hair was a mess, and his eyes were bloodshot with either lack of sleep or alcohol. I got my answer a moment later when he walked in my direction and looked like he was trying and failing a sobriety test.

"Lyle, did you fucking hit Chad?" I asked, my hands balling into fists.

I stepped toward him with my fists clenching tight and ready for a fight when my mom jumped in my way. She put her hand on my chest and shook her head no.

"Mom," I said, the anger over being held back clear in my voice. Before she could answer, a knock sounded on the open front door, and I looked over to see two officers standing in the doorway.

"You called the cops?" Lyle fumed at my mom.

"No. I did, Dad," Shannon said, the tears rolling down her face. "You're acting crazy," she said through her sobs. "You hit Chad and said you hate us," she wailed.

"You traitorous little bitch!" I pulled my mom into my side as the officers entered the room, their eyes focused on Lyle. My mom was liable to get in their way, but the fact he hit Chad and everyone else was in tears was enough for me to want to kick his ass.

"Sir, we're going to need you to come with us to give you time to calm down," the older of the two officers said.

"I don't need to fucking calm down," Lyle said, squaring off with the officers.

My mom covered her face and cried like I'd never seen before. I hugged her tight and watched Alex check in with Chad before wrapping Shannon in his arms. Chad seemed more pissed than hurt, but Shannon's heart looked like it was breaking. What the hell had caused this?

"Fucking little bitch!" Lyle yelled as the officers got the cuffs on him and escorted him out of the house.

"Mom, what the hell happened? I've never seen Lyle like that." I asked the moment the front door closed.

With Lyle gone, I realized I was breathing easier, and the room felt safer. His eyes held so much hatred, and I couldn't even imagine my mom doing anything to inspire that level of anger.

My mom waited until Alex had herded Shannon and Chad into the kitchen before answering.

"I'm sorry, Jace," she whispered. "I didn't want to tell you and have you worry while you were away at school, but I caught Lyle in a few lies and confronted him last month." She wrung her hands together. "There were these unexplained expenses from a city a couple of hours away when he said he was on the other side of the country for business. He was gone two weeks, got home, and acted like that was where he'd been the whole time." She took a shuddering breath, her lower lip trembling. I hated *seeing her like this. "We fought, but I wasn't letting it go, and he finally blurted out that he has a whole other family." She broke down into full-on sobs, and I held her tight, not even sure I heard her correctly.*

"I'm sorry, what? How is that even possible?"

She sniffed and pulled tissues out from the pocket of the knit sweater she was wearing. "He has two kids with her, Jace. They're eight and five. For more than eight years, he's been lying to us, all of us. Lyle came over because I had him served with divorce papers, and that was when Chad walked in. Lyle was going to hit me, and Chad took the swing." She wrung her hands. "I feel like such a fool. How often did I wonder why he didn't have the right amount of money going into the bank for me to pay bills?" She put a hand over her eyes. "How was I so stupid? How did I not see what was happening?"

I pulled her into another hug and held her until she said she was tired and needed to lie down.

When eleven o'clock came around, and everyone was asleep, I flopped down on the couch with Alex by my side. He picked up my hand and kissed my knuckles.

"What the hell am I supposed to do, Alex?" I looked over at the one person who had never changed and had always been the calm rock in my turbulent mind. "Mom said she's filed for divorce, and she wants me to go back to college, but how do I leave? I'm the man of the house now. Chad shouldn't have to take on the responsibility. And what about bills?"

"I don't know. Whether you decide to stay is not my call, but I think you need to do what will make everyone's life easier. If that's staying, see if you can get a temporary leave from the program. If your mom really doesn't want you to stay and ruin your scholarship, you need to decide how much you want to push back. One thing I can say is that if you drop out now, you'll never get the same ride, and if you got back, you could walk out of Duke with a six-figure job to help your family. Just things to consider, but I'm here no matter what you decide."

Laying my head back on the couch, I sighed. "Why is this so difficult?"

"Because you want to do the right thing, but you're not sure what that is."

Alex kissed me, his lips soft and warm, and I hung onto him like he was the only thing keeping me afloat.

"Lie down and rest. You can figure it out tomorrow," Alex said.

He gave my hand a gentle tug. I followed his lead and lay down on my side on the couch, facing him. Alex grabbed the blanket off the back and tossed it over us, and as he turned out the light, I shifted closer to the warmth of his body and the scent of the ocean that followed him around. Fuck, I missed that scent.

"Thank you," I said softly.

I hated to be weak. Maybe it was because my dad took off when I was so young, or perhaps it was always me, but I never showed any weakness to anyone other than Alex. He held me without judgment or pity and always made me feel better.

Mom refused to let me stay. She was in hysterical tears when I said I thought I should drop out to help the family until we could figure something out. Ultimately, I decided to go because it was causing her more stress, and that was the last thing I wanted.

"I hate this. I know she said it's what she wants, but why do I feel like such an asshole for leaving?" I growled and peeled my eyes away from the passing trees to look at Alex.

"Because you love your family."

"I can't even wrap my head around Lyle having another family. Mom blames herself, but I never had a clue that something was wrong. Was I the one that was blind?" Alex didn't say anything. He knew I just needed to vent everything I had going on in my head. "Lyle taught me how to ride a bike and helped me fix up my first car. We barbequed together, and he came to all my games. What the hell was I not seeing?"

"He's obviously a very good liar. You can't put this on yourself. I didn't see anything, and I was over all the time," Alex said.

"I guess you're right. What would that make him? A sociopath? A narcissist, maybe?" I turned my head to the scenery, and with each passing mile marker, I felt angrier about the entire situation. How dare he do this to my mom? He didn't want to be a dad to me, then fine, but don't hurt my mom. She didn't deserve that.

We pulled off the interstate at the service station. "You mind pumping the gas? I'll go in and prepay, but I need to take a piss, bad," Alex said as we hopped out.

"Sure."

"You want anything?"

"You know what I like. Just grab me something," I said.

I stared off into space, listening to the sound of the cars zipping along the highway when Alex came back out.

"You good?" I asked, taking in his ashen face and wide-eyed expression. He looked like he was in shock. He didn't say anything and climbed behind the wheel. Poking my head in the door, I stared at Alex. "Dude, what's up?"

"Get in," he ordered, his voice eerily calm and flat. He wouldn't even look at me. "Get in, Jace," he said again, completely freaked out.

I slipped into the passenger seat. I'd never seen him act like this before. He looked like he was in shock or frozen like a mannequin. I was worried something had happened inside the service station. Had someone done something to him? I'd fucking break their legs if they had.

"Okay, I'm in. Now tell me what the hell is going on," I said as Alex pulled out of the lot and onto the overpass. I looked back at the exit he was supposed to take and frowned as he pulled onto the interstate, going back the way we'd just come. He still hadn't said a word or looked over at me. "Dude, you're freaking me the fuck out."

He swallowed and didn't look over but gripped the steering wheel so hard that his knuckles were white and his hands shook.

"Alex, look at me," I said. He slowly turned his head, and it was like watching a horror movie where the person was possessed. "Answer me. What the fuck is going on?"

"Um…" I wanted to reach out and smack him out of it. "You, ah, need to open your phone." His voice was shaking as much as his hands.

"My phone?"

"Yeah."

"Okay, what for?" I asked, pulling the phone from my pocket.

"You need to find the news for our area. Like from home." Alex suddenly grabbed my arm, and I stared at his fingers as they gripped me hard. "Jace…I…Fuck, I'm sorry."

"For what? Besides freaking me the fuck out."

His bottom lip trembled, but he let go of my arm and gripped the steering wheel again.

Terrified now of what I would find, I unlocked my phone and scrolled to the news station from home. There was a live feed streaming. I turned it on and had no idea what I was watching. It was an aerial view from a helicopter as it hovered over a house I didn't recognize. The house was surrounded by police like in a movie.

"Turn on the volume," Alex said. I swallowed and wasn't sure I wanted to know what this was.

"The terrifying standoff is still underway.
Police have been trying to negotiate with the hostage taker for over thirty minutes.
The man, believed to be Lyle Winston, was tracked down here through a neighbor who saw his image on the news earlier today."

Lyle Winston? What was my stepfather doing at that house? Was this the other family's place? Was this the same Lyle Winston? It could be a coincidence.

My mind raced as my heart pounded out of my chest, but I couldn't look away. A cold dread seeped into every part of my body.

Suddenly, three pictures flashed across the screen, and I sucked in a strangled gasp as I stared at my mom's face and two blacked-out rectangles with my brother's and sister's names underneath. Under their names were the words deceased victim.

"No, this can't be real." My hand went to my throat as I tried to get air into my lungs, but I couldn't breathe.

"Police say they have no motive at this time,
but our crews on the ground say that the three victims
he allegedly killed were his wife and two children.
Police are still trying to find the oldest son.
Bang, Bang, Bang...Bang
Four shots have been fired inside the home,
and as you can see, the police are storming the house now."

I couldn't tear my eyes away. The world had become the small screen, the tiny thumbnail images of my family. Minutes ticked on, and the police slowly walked out of the house but didn't bring anyone with them. Switching the screen over to my cell, I tried my mom's phone, but no one answered.

"No, no, no." Hands shaking, I hung up and tried my brother. "Come on, Chad, pick up, pick up, dammit." Tears blurred my vision as I tried my sister.

"This is Shannon."

"Oh, thank god—" I started to say but was cut off.

"You know what to do." Beep.

My body trembled as I pulled the phone away from my ear and stared at the screen, counting down the seconds I had to leave a message.

"Shan, it's me. Um, I saw this thing on the news. Look, can you just call me? Please, it's important."

A pain-filled roar ripped from my body as the tears poured down my cheeks. Alex grabbed my hand as he sped down the Interstate, but it wouldn't matter. We'd always be too late.

I wiped away a tear and rubbed it into my jeans like that could scrub away the memories. Raine let out a soft sob, and my eyes flicked over to see her covering her mouth as tears streamed down her face.

"I told you. Look, the point is, I don't trust people often, and the only reason Lyle wasn't behind bars was that my mom dropped the charges. She felt bad. Why? I have no idea, but they should still be alive. Raine, I don't want to see you make the same mistake, and I definitely don't want Avro dragged into whatever you have going on."

She wiped at her eyes and shook her head. "It's not like that. I'm sorry for your loss, but this is completely different."

"Yeah, sure it is. Just another guy from prison assaulting his...

what exactly were you before he went to jail? Friend, crush? Doesn't matter, he's a dick, and I don't want to see the same thing happen to you."

"Is this why you brought me out here, to see if you could convince me to turn my friend in? Unbelievable. I thought you wanted to connect. All you wanted to do was change my mind."

Raine jumped down from the crypt and began marching away. Fuck, that didn't go the way I hoped.

Raine

Chapter 37

Raine

     I should've known better. Jace didn't have any interest in understanding me or supporting my decision. He wanted what he wanted and decided to pull on my heartstrings to get it.

"Peaches, hold up. That's not what I was doing," he said. I could hear the gravel crunching under his feet as he gained on me. Grabbing my arm, he pulled me to a halt.

"Let go, Jace. I don't want to hear it."

"Oh, you'll hear out the asshole who, 'did the crime he was charge for', but not me?" he growled.

"Stop saying that." I knew it was what happened, but I hated hearing the word repeatedly. It was like a lance to my heart each time.

"What? Rape? Don't like that word? It's what happened, you know."

"I know that, and I explained why," I fumed and tugged on my arm. Here I was once more with the dilemma of kicking him in the crotch or not.

"So, as long as the guy has a good reason, it's okay?" Jace's eyes flashed with anger, and my old fears slowly began to creep in as I realized just how isolated we were. Would anyone hear me scream? Where the hell did I go once I got out of here?

"I said let go of me," I yanked on my arm again, but it had the same effect as one of those little finger traps that the more you pulled, the tighter it became.

Jace gripped both my arms as he glared down at me. "Why? This is what you like. You like it when a guy gets rough with you and terrifies you." His hands didn't hurt, but his words did.

"Jace, I'm warning you to back the hell off," I said, and pulled back hard. I didn't want to hurt him, but I was on the verge of a panic attack and needed him to let go of me.

"I said let go," I yelled and lashed out, catching him in the shin with my foot.

"Fuck," Jace said, and sucked in a deep breath.

I yanked away and stared at him, doubled over, rubbing his leg. His eyes flicked up to mine, and they were full of anger. Oh shit. With a burst of adrenaline, I turned and sprinted along the path to...I didn't know where. How the hell had I gotten so turned around?

"Not smart, Peaches," Jace called out. "Not smart at all."

Oh god, I could hear him coming. I looked over my shoulder, and even in the dark, the moonlight lit enough of the trail to see him chasing me down and gaining. A flutter of excitement had my stomach in knots, but I pushed it away. I hated that my body had that reaction at all.

MALICE 415

Veering off the path, I weaved through the stones as I raced for the taller crypts, hoping to hide. I looked over my shoulder, but Jace was gone. Not seeing him was worse than knowing where he was.

"Ah," I cried out as my left knee clipped a tall tombstone. I sucked in a sharp breath as the pain lanced through my leg and hobbled my stride. A flicker of movement caught my eye, and I looked to my left, staring at the long shadows cast by the moon and the tall crypts.

"Oh fuck," I whispered as I spotted Jace's shadow and quickly looked up.

"Where do you think you're going, Peaches?" he asked, and even though I couldn't see his face, I could feel the smirk. A shiver shot down my spine while the rest of my body heated with words that weren't a threat but sounded like one.

"Leave me alone, Jace," I panted out and darted away from the shadow of the crypts.

I didn't make it three strides before I was hoisted off the ground like I weighed nothing. My back pressed into his hard chest, and my brain and body fought for control, each wanting very different things.

"Is that what you really want?" he growled in my ear as he hauled back into the dark shadows.

His arm felt like an iron vise squeezing the air out of my chest, and my brain screamed to fight, but the feeble smacks at his arm and wiggling were doing nothing. I needed to get mean if I wanted to get free. The question then became, why was I not fighting for my life?

With a spin and a hard shove, I was pressed against the cold wall of the crypt with my hands pinned above my head. Breathing heavily, I glared into Jace's silver, seductive, and terrifying eyes that glinted in the moonlight. His other hand clamped over my mouth when I opened it to scream, and he shook his head.

"I don't think you really want to do that, Peaches," he said, his body pressing into mine and setting it on fire. I nipped at his finger, fully intending to bite him hard, but only hung on as his teeth grazed the soft skin on my neck, and I quivered in his hold.

I reluctantly let go of the finger, and he removed his hand. His lips hovered over mine, and the heat of his body pressing into me was a stark contrast to the cool wall at my back.

"You going to bite me if I kiss you, Peaches?" The tip of his tongue flicked out and ran across my bottom lip, and my eyes narrowed.

"Try it and see what happens," I threatened.

His response was to rub his body against mine, and the desire I'd managed to kick down pushed my efforts aside. My eyes closed with a soft moan as he thrust forward with his hips, and I could feel the bulge of his cock pressing into me through his jeans. I knew exactly what he looked like with that silver ring pierced through the tip, and I still hadn't gotten a taste. I'd watched Avro play with it, and my mouth was once more watering with the thought.

What the hell was wrong with me?

I tried to pull my arms away again, but he didn't budge, and the only way out was to really hurt him.

"Fuck off, Jace."

Jace didn't even flinch as I tried again to free myself. Instead, he grabbed my lower lip with his teeth, and the aching between my thighs intensified.

"Let go, Jace," I mumbled, sounding pathetic even to my ears.

Releasing my lip, he smirked. "Oh no, Peaches. I know you don't really want that. You want me to rip these jeans off of you and fuck you right here. It's morbid and sick, and you fucking love it."

"No, I don't," I said, turning my head away so he couldn't see the truth of his words lying bare in my eyes. "You're the liar," I spit out, using the only bullet I had.

"Oh really, and why is that?" he asked, seeming genuinely amused.

"You say that you don't care about me, that you didn't want any of this, and Avro is forcing it on you." I turned my head to glare at him.

"That is what happened," Jace drawled, cocking his eyebrow.

"I call bullshit. I've only been around you a few days, and I can tell you don't want to go. You don't want to leave Avro, but more than that, you're different. Do you think I haven't done my research on you? I've watched you at these fancy award shows and the social media posts. I've listened to the last few songs you've released, and they all have one thing in common."

His eyes narrowed. "Oh, yeah, and what is that, Peaches?"

"They're uninspiring," I snarled. "They scream that you want out."

Jace's hands tightened on my wrists, and he made a growling sound that had a shudder ripping throughout my body.

"You don't know anything."

It was my turn to give him a cocky grin. "Oh, but I do. You're not the only one who people-watches, Jace. I've spent my entire life sitting away from others with my eyes and ears open. Everything you do when you're around Avro is different. You don't want to travel the world. Maybe you never did. Deep down, you knew that Avro would break away from you. You knew he would do exactly what you told him not to."

I paused and stared into his silver eyes, filling with rage, and he didn't look so confident now. "I'd go so far as to say that you hoped he would because then you'd have an excuse to stay. You want us to work. You want us to work, and you're terrified that if we don't, Avro will be devastated because we're already building a bond, and you can see it."

"Are you threatening to try to take Avro from me?" Jace asked, his voice low and sinister as his fingers dug painfully into my wrists. "Because I didn't get that vibe from you, but now I'm starting to wonder."

"No, don't be an idiot. Of course, I wouldn't do that. I'm saying that I'm not the only one hiding something, so stop acting like a paragon of fucking virtue."

"Oh, that's rich coming from you. Would you have even told Avro about your special friend if he hadn't seen the bruising? What was your plan, Peaches?"

I ground my teeth together as once more he pointed out how I wouldn't be truthful. Jace dropped his head, so our noses lightly touched, and my heart galloped hard in my chest. "Maybe you do see me, Peaches, but remember that I see you too."

Before I could think of something to say, he dropped his mouth to mine, and all the pent-up anger and desire erupted into something explosive. Hands ripped at my shirt as I yanked at his. We were like two animals that had been set loose, and in the back of my mind, there was a tiny little voice yelling that we shouldn't be doing this, but I already knew that I would. Nothing was stopping this now. I didn't want it to.

Jace

I hated that she saw through my act. No one did except for Avro, but he accepted it for what it needed to be. Raine didn't care about pointing out how unhappy I'd been, and I wanted to punish her for it.

Grabbing the zipper on the front of her hoodie, I yanked it down and pulled up the top she was wearing. I groaned as her perky tits came into view.

"No bra, you rebel. I fucking love it," I groaned.

Her nipples were already hard and begging to be sucked, further proof that she'd been lying about not wanting me or her dark needs. Needs she may not want to face, but I was about to prove to her once and for all that she was wrong.

Dropping my head, I sucked on her hard nipple and made her cry out as my teeth bit down enough to cause a touch of pain.

"Oh god," Raine moaned, her hands touching my hair.

I could still feel her trying to fight what her body craved. Switching to the other nipple, I ripped open the button and zipper on her jeans, confident I'd torn the material from the force.

Raine gasped and tried to wiggle away as she fought her mind, but I was quicker with my hand and slipped it down the front of her jeans to find her soaking wet.

"Oh fuck," I groaned as my fingers easily pushed the material aside and slid into her pussy.

"Ah, oh god," Raine cried as her body went limp in my hold like she'd finally given up the battle.

"Yeah, that's it, Peaches. Rub yourself on my fingers. You want to cum all over them." I left a wet trail along the side of her neck and sucked her earlobe into my mouth as Raine slowly moved her hips. "That's it. You're nasty, and you like it. Fuck my fingers. I'll even give you three," I cooed in her ear as I shoved a third finger inside her wet pussy.

My cock was so hard, it felt like I was about to cum in my jeans. I was so ready to bury myself deep inside of her. She'd been right about one thing. I'd hoped that Avro would pick well. I always knew it would be him to choose. My taste was whatever the fuck he wanted, and he hadn't disappointed.

"I'm going to fuck this tight pussy, Peaches. I'm going to cum in you and claim you as ours, and you'll let me, won't you?"

She bucked her hips harder, but only incoherent noises passed through her lips. The walls of her pussy tightened as she fucked herself harder. She was fucking sexy, and I couldn't get enough. I suddenly wanted to make her and Avro cum simultaneously. The thought was so potent that I groaned as my cock kicked behind the fly of my jeans. She was so close, but she wouldn't get to cum that easy.

I released Raine and took a step back. Her body slumped against the crypt wall as she panted hard. Her eyes filled with passion as she stared up at me. I could see her wondering what I would do next, but she wasn't asking, and I didn't plan on saying.

Lifting the fingers that had been buried inside of her, I stuck them in my mouth one at a time and cleaned them off. I groaned at her taste on my tongue and savored the look in her eyes. She was feral, alright. She'd starved her body for so long that now that she'd let the beast out to play, she couldn't get enough. Something else she tried to deny, but I could see it burning in her pretty blue eyes.

"Do you want me to fuck you, Peaches?"

She shook her head, but she avidly watched my hands as I undid the button on my jeans.

"Are you sure about that," I asked and slid the zipper down.

She licked her lips as my cock came into view, the silver ring glinting in the dull light.

"What's the matter, Peaches? I thought you didn't want my cock inside of you?" I spread my jeans open, and my cock was all too happy to be free of the confines.

I knew I was blessed and didn't take it for granted for even a single day. Gripping my shaft, I stroked my cock, groaning loud enough that Raine's eyes were trained on the head that now had multiple drops of precum sitting on the tip.

"Fuck, that feels good."

She shifted and rubbed her legs together as she stared at the prize.

"You don't want to taste it, do you?"

Her tongue ran across her lips.

"That's not something a good girl like you would want to do."

My hand picked up the pace, and I sucked in an exaggerated breath that ended with a moan. Raine shivered and took a small step forward.

"What are you, Peaches? Are you a good girl, or are you a nasty one who's going to let me fuck you right here so hard that you scream my name?"

Raine's eyes flicked up to mine. "I...."

"I, what?"

"I...." She wet her lips again. "I want you to fuck me," she said, and I was tempted to shove my cock back in my jeans and say I told you so, but even I wasn't that much of a fucking ass. At least not tonight.

"Then get over here and get on your knees. You're sucking my cock first for kicking me. That was a bitch move."

She nodded far more quickly than I thought she would, and I wondered if this was punishment at all with the way she dropped to her knees.

Her hand was cool as it wrapped around my heated cock, and I shivered as her soft fingers took the place of my hand. She was staring at it like it might bite, and I smirked because I planned on leaving my own mark. This ex-friend of hers had another thing coming if he thought he could swoop in and just take Raine. I had no doubt in my mind that this guy wouldn't be able to keep away, and as she drew her tongue along the underside of my sensitive head, I knew for sure that this time he was going to have to go through me.

My head fell back as she explored the ring and gently wiggled it with the tip of her tongue. Raine was tentative as she finally slipped my cock into her mouth, and I was nice enough to wait until she had a rhythm and a little bit of confidence before I grabbed her head and forced her to go deeper.

The shrill little noise of fear she made had a direct line to my cock as it vibrated up my shaft. I pushed my hips forward and forced it a little deeper before I released her head.

Raine pulled my cock out of her mouth and glared up at me. "What the hell?"

"What? It's a big cock, Peaches. You'll have to do better than that if you want to get me to come. Avro can take it all, and it would be pretty disappointing if you couldn't."

Her eyes flared as I cocked my brow at her, and I would've sworn she growled at me from under her breath. But it worked. She liked challenges.

A character trait that the two of us had in common. She sucked me into her mouth, taking a solid two inches more before she gagged and pulled out. She made another attempt and sucked hard while she did, and I had to force myself not to grab the back of her head and force the last few inches down her throat.

The temptation was real, and my fingers and cock both tingled with the thought, but I knew she wasn't ready.

"Fuck, Peaches, you know how to suck," I praised instead and was rewarded with it sliding a little deeper.

"Yeah, you like that?" she asked.

"It's what I said, isn't it?" As the words came out of my mouth, I knew that this would not end well, and a second later, I hissed as she gripped my cock ring in her teeth and tugged.

"Oh shit," I swore as the pain of the sharp jerk lanced down my cock. She continued to pull, and I was forced to take a step with her like I was a fucking bull with a nose ring. "Fuck, Peaches, that's not very nice."

"You're an asshole," she mumbled around the ring.

"You're right, I am," I agreed and bit my lip hard as she tugged again and hard enough that I worried she might actually pull it out. The combination of pain and anger was burning brighter than anything I'd experienced before, and I glared down at her, not even sure what I would do if she went that far.

"Are you going to stop?" she asked.

"Yes," I said through my clenched teeth.

She released the ring, and as soon as I was free, I snatched her by the neck and forced her to stand. Slamming her against the crypt, I glared into her wide, terrified eyes.

"Don't ask such stupid questions, Peaches. I'll never stop being an asshole. The nice part of me was sucked into the grave with my family when they were murdered, and it's never coming back."

Each breath I took hurt my chest, and my heart ached even after all this time, and I hated that Raine had forced me to look at it. We stared at one another, the tension still so thick in the air it felt like we were pulling on a rubber band, waiting for it to break.

"Fuck this. I'm out of here," I growled and pushed away from the crypt wall.

I didn't expect her to kiss me. The fear and anger in Raine's eyes fooled me. She wrapped her arms around my neck and crushed our lips together. My body reacted even if my brain was reeling. Nothing mattered other than getting inside of her now. All the different parts of my brain switched off as the need to take her overwhelmed my senses.

I realized there was so much more to Raine, and her ability to reach inside my chest and make my heart beat hard was just one of them. The way she looked at me was enough to make me shudder, but when her blue eyes burned with passion, I knew I was in trouble. Avro was right. She fit me as well as she did him, and I wanted her. I wanted all of her.

Deepening the kiss, I gripped her ass and lifted her so she could wrap her legs around my waist. I didn't need to see where I was going. The single light glowing on this side of the cemetery was all the beacon I needed to find the car. My strides ate up the ground, our lips never parting with the urgency that had broken free.

I dropped Raine to her feet, and she stumbled with the sudden change, but the car was behind her, and she leaned against the hood, looking like a sexy calendar model with her swollen lips and eyes hooded with desire.

Hooking my fingers into her jeans and thong, I pulled them down in a single hard tug and spun her around.

"You think you're ready for this?" I asked as I bit the side of her neck.

Her breath hissed out. "Would it matter?"

"Not really. Now bend over," I said, but she glared over her shoulder at me. Her elbow came for the side of my face. I snatched the arm out of the air and shoved her hard, forcing her to bend over. "You want to struggle, Peaches? Then you can do it with my cock in you."

Gripping her ass and holding her still, I lined up to her soaking wet pussy and thrust into her tight opening.

"Ahh," Raine screamed, her fingers clawing at the hood of the car as I forced the last inch into her body.

My cock was twitching and ready to cum already. Pulling almost all the way out, I thrust into Raine again, and I shuddered as she yelled again, but this time it was my name. It was as beautiful a sound as any song I'd ever written.

With each thrust, the little whimpering noises got louder. The sound traveled over my skin like a warm breeze.

"That's it. Scream for me," I said and picked up the pace.

I was lost to the pleasure flooding my system and was only vaguely aware of Raine cumming and soaking my cock with her release. Her body smacked into the car with each powerful thrust as I pushed us to the goal. Reaching around her body, my hand slipped to her clit. I pinched and felt it swell between my fingers.

"Scream for me, Peaches. Scream my name, or I'll stop fucking you right now," I growled. Lifting my foot up to the bumper, I changed positions, and Raine let out the first strangled yell with the new angle.

"Fuck, Jace!" she finally roared as I slammed my cock into her and pushed deeper than before. "Ahh."

"Do you want me to stop?" I asked, the sound of slapping skin and Raine's yells loud in my ears.

"No," she wailed, even as tears and sweat trickled down her cheeks.

"Rub your clit. Cum all over me again," I said, and watched her hand slip from the hood of the car to between her legs.

"Oh, fuck yes," I yelled, as I felt her hand rubbing vigorously at herself, and then she wrapped her fingers around my cock. They didn't even fit all the way, but it was still better than any fucking cock ring. "Fuck, Peaches, yes. You're going to make me cum."

"Jace," she screamed loudly.

Her body shuddered, and the walls of her sweet pussy gripped me hard as she came. There was no faking or denying it as she froze, and once more, my cock was flooded with the warmth of her orgasm. That was all it took, and a thrust later, my release gripped me in a chokehold. I opened my mouth to yell, but no sound came out. Pulling back, I slammed home hard, and more came out, so I did it again and again.

My breathing was ragged as I collapsed onto her body, and all I could hear was our panting and the drumming of my pulse inside my head.

Raine nodded, her eyes glazed over. "I really love the feel of that ring," she mumbled, making me smirk.

"That's good because as soon as I catch my breath, I'm fucking you again." The corner of her mouth pulled up in a grin, and my heart pounded a little harder for a totally different reason. Stretching my hands along her arms, I linked our fingers together. "You're ours now, Peaches, and no one is taking you away."

Snake

Chapter 38

Kaivan

"You know you're making me miss the sweetbut party?" Roach groaned. "I thought we'd be done by now."

I rolled my eyes at him. "You sound like you're going to miss a game show, you old man." I smirked as Roach swore at me. "I can't take the chance that Jim gets tipped off before I get what I need from him."

"Fine. You sure you don't want me to come in with you?" Roach asked as he lit a smoke, the little end glowing brightly.

"Naw, this piece of shit is all mine. If the fat fuck makes it out here, lasso his ass and drag him down the road."

"Dude, I'm riding a motorcycle, not a horse. How about I just run him over?" Roach said as he leaned forward on his bike. "Still not sure why I couldn't bring the truck. At least I could've had a nap."

"Stop bitching. You sound like Mannix when he misses the next episode of *The Young and the Restless*."

"Yo, no one is that bad, except maybe Naomi."

We snickered as I gave the area a once over and wondered if I should've brought Wilder too. The cabin home was set way back from the road in the middle of the swap. This was not my usual hunting ground, and I preferred the concrete and crack houses to chase my prey. On the plus side, there were no neighbors for miles. The smell of wet foliage and rotting undergrowth mixed with the typical humid stench made me think of Louisiana. I'd had to venture out that way a few times this past year on missions for Chase or Beast since I never saw our Prez. I just couldn't get used to the brackish smell that permeated everything around the Mancini Mansion. I had to give it to the Mafia family, though. They sure did know how to treat a guy right.

Cracking my neck, I revved my bike and wheeled into the driveway. I could have walked in, and that would've been a fuck load quieter, but I wanted to take him by surprise in a different way.

As I suspected, the sound of the bike drew Jim out of the house with a large rifle in hand. I pulled up beside his truck and cut the loud engine. My eyes skimmed over the shitty cottage-style home and any possible security system. There were no cameras that I could see and only a light on his porch.

"Who the fuck are you?" Jim called out as soon as the engine died.

A smile spread across my face. "Fuck, it is good to see your face, Jim. It's me, Kai," I said, leaning on the handlebars. I really could have a career in acting because all I could picture was ripping his balls off with my bare hands.

My gun was inches from my fingers, and they flexed and tingled, ready to grab it and shoot Jim where he stood. It would be quick, clean, and easy, but I wanted more than his death. I wanted answers. The rifle remained trained on me, but when I continued to smile, Jim turned the gun up.

"Kai? As in Kai, who used to be at Dave's?" he asked, a sheen of sweat breaking out on his forehead. His hands gripped the rifle tight enough to see the slight shaking from where I sat. The look of shock on his face told me he didn't know about Nick and Irene yet. That was good, very good.

You're going to be more than nervous before this night is through.

"Yeah, man. Took me forever to find you." I looked around at the surrounding trees and swamp. "No idea how you like to live out here with all these gators."

"What are you doing here?" Jim asked.

I let my smile fall and replaced the look on my face with shock.

"Jim, I came to have a beer like old times. It's been forever, but our talks in the garage are some of my best memories." Lifting my leg over the back of the bike, I kept my eyes trained on his hands. Walking over to the six stairs that led up to the porch, I stopped with my hand on the railing. "I can go if you want. I honestly thought you'd be happy to see me," I said and rounded my shoulders, hoping that I gave off a disappointed look.

The sound of the gun's safety being kicked into place was music to my ears, and the part of me that loved to kill smiled in the back of my mind.

"Wow, Kai. Sorry, man, I'm a little jumpy living out here. I don't get many visitors, and you're the last person I expected to see."

Jim smiled, and it was like being transported back in time. He had the same dopey expression that had always set everyone's mind at ease. It was the look that had sat in the garage, told stories, and let me have a beer even when I was underage. At the time, it felt like he was a cool uncle and the type of man I could've told anything, including my biggest fears. Ending up just like my father had always been at the top of my list.

I walked up the steps, and Jim did the same stupid dance he had when I was a teen. He got low and wiggled back and forth as he held his arms like a linebacker. The fucker wanted a hug, and I mirrored his pose and laughed as we embraced. The moment he touched me, the anger burning inside me rose, and I had to force myself to keep the smile on my face. My mind screamed that he'd touched Raine. He'd touched what was mine. He'd put his filthy cock in her. I planned to take it off.

"What the hell are you doing here?" Jim asked, pulling back and squeezing my arms as if he hadn't been involved in sending me to jail. Like he hadn't attacked Raine. My jaw twitched with the images my mind kept replaying on a loop, but I managed to hold the smile.

"I came to visit. I got out a little while ago, but it's been tough getting back on my feet," I lied and stuffed my hands in my jeans pockets. "I'm just getting around to reconnecting with the few people that I considered family," I said, laying it on thick.

He swallowed, and I saw a glimmer of something in his eyes. Regret, maybe. He could regret all he wanted, but it hadn't stopped him from doing what he'd done or ever coming forward to have my name cleared.

"Yeah, man...Listen, I'm really sorry I didn't visit you in prison," Jim said, rubbing the back of his neck.

"I won't lie. That hurt. Dave and Irene washed their hands of me, and I had no one. I thought you might visit, but I gave up hope after the first year," I said. That wasn't a lie. I hadn't known Jim was involved, and I'd kept hoping someone I thought was a friend would show up to see me.

Lifting a shoulder, I let it drop. "I'm hoping to reconnect, have a beer, and then head out. I'm leaving Florida. There are too many bad memories."

"Fuck, man. I'm so sorry. Come on in. Let's have a beer," Jim said, turning to the screen door and yanking it open.

I stalked him inside, my eyes searching every corner of the small home. There was a mounted gator head on one wall and pictures of Jim fishing and holding up a huge fish he'd caught. There was a particular picture that caught my eye as Jim stepped into the kitchen. The wall heading into the living room had a framed photo of Jim, Dave, and a guy I didn't know on a hunting excursion. It looked to be somewhere like Africa, based on how they were dressed and the boar at their feet. It wasn't the boar that held my attention. It was the face of the man with the same tattoo on his hand. There he was in a color photo, as he held a gun and smirked for the camera. This had to be Frank.

"Here you go," Jim said, handing me one of the bottles.

"Thanks. Cheers," I said, tapping his bottle as I pretended to take a swig. I didn't trust him any further than I could throw his ass. "This looks like an amazing trip," I said, pointing to the image. "I recognize Dave, but who's this?" I tapped the photo.

"It was a great time. That's Frank. I'm not sure if you ever met him."

I nodded and pretended to take another sip of my beer.

"Come on in and have a seat."

Jim flopped down in one of the two camo recliners facing the television. His taste in décor certainly was consistent. There wasn't a spot in the home that didn't have either a dead and very stuffed animal or pictures of killing them.

"I want to ask how things have been, but that seems like a terrible question to ask," Jim said, and had the decency to look a little remorseful.

"Yeah, what can I say? I went to prison for a crime I didn't commit, and it ruined my life. I planned on college and a good career, maybe one day having a family, and now I'm forever an outcast. A thug and ex-con. Just someone else for people to turn their nose up at. Getting a job was the hardest, and I had to stay at a men's shelter for a while." That was a load of lies, but I knew more than one guy who'd gotten out and that was their life.

"Sorry to hear all that. I wasn't sure what to think about the charges, and Dave talked like he was so sure it had been you who hurt Little Rainy. I was torn as to what the right thing was to do."

My hand twitched and flexed around the bottle at the mention of the nickname Jim had called Raine. I imagined wrapping my hand around his throat as I nodded and imitated taking another swig.

"You talk to Dave much?"

Jim squirmed in his seat, which told me he had.

"Not in some time," Jim said, and looked away. So Dave had warned him that I was out. Good to know. "You?"

"I saw him the other day. We ran into one another at a gas station. It was kinda fucked seeing him again. He was real aggressive. I mean, sure, I was fucking his wife, but it was over eleven years ago, man, and I paid my dues. Let it go already." I wanted to sound like I was being transparent, lull Jim in a little more. "He looked like shit. I would've placed a bet that he just crawled out of a dumpster. What the hell has he been up to?"

Jim's shoulders relaxed. He was obviously waiting to see if Dave had said anything about him. The more loose-lipped I could keep Jim, the better. I had no qualms about torture, and Jim would find that out, but I wanted him to have just enough rope to hang himself with first.

"His old lady left him a couple of years back, and she's been dragging him through the mud with the divorce."

I snickered, and Jim's brows rose in question. "I just find it funny. I mean, I was fucking Irene back in the day. You'd think that once Dave knew that, he would've left her long before now," I said, and Jim's hand stilled, the beer halfway to his mouth. I gave him a crooked smile. "What? Did you think I didn't know Dave found out and wanted to punish me?"

Jim swallowed hard, his Adam's apple bobbing as he did.

"Why do you look so freaked out, Jim? I mean, it's not like you had anything to do with me going to prison, right?" I drew out the last word and cocked my brow in his direction.

I loved this part of the game. I didn't get to do it often. Most of my interactions with those that I hunted were get in and get out, but make it as messy as possible. You'd think messy was easier than neat and clean, but that was a misconception. It was far harder to make things look like a slasher film and keep your DNA out of the shit. Knifes slipped, and blood was all over everything. It was actually a pain in my ass.

"No, no, of course not. I just thought you'd be a lot more pissed," Jim said, stumbling over his words.

He didn't know the half of it. Pissed was like saying I was mildly annoyed. I tilted my head and stared Jim in the eyes. "Why exactly would I be pissed, Jim? What did I have to be pissed about?" I asked, allowing my web to close around him.

"Um...I...ah...I just meant that..." Whatever Jim was about to say was interrupted by his phone ringing on the coffee table and making him jump.

We both looked at the phone and saw Dave's name. As Jim reached for the phone, I pulled my gun and pointed it at him.

"I wouldn't touch that if I were you." I allowed the full extent of my anger to shine through, and the man winced as I glared into his eyes. "Sit the fuck back."

Jim raised his hand in the air and slowly slid back into the recliner. "Kai, my man, I don't know what you've been told, but I swear to you on my mama's grave that I didn't have anything to do with you going to prison."

I smiled at him. "Splitting hairs, I see. How convenient that you can actually tell the truth and lie all at the same time."

"I don't know what you mean." He smiled, but the worry in his eyes was evident.

"Tell me, Jim. How does it feel to be invaded? To have the place you thought was safe turn into a jail? Or for the person you thought you knew to hurt you and rip your life away?" I leaned forward and let my forearms rest on my knees as the gun dangled between my legs.

Sweat was traveling in a steady stream down the side of Jim's face. The moisture showed on his upper lip as his body produced adrenaline and screamed to run, but he knew he couldn't.

"Tell me, Jim, was getting the chance to rape Raine worth your life," I asked, my voice coming out as a growl as I focused all my hatred on this man, someone I had trusted, someone Raine had trusted. Someone who was going to die. I'd trusted this man around Raine; a mistake I wouldn't make twice.

"He forced me to," Jim blurted, then bolted for the door and the rifle he had sitting beside it. He reminded me of a mouse that finally got its tail free from the trap, only to realize there was still a cat. Unfortunately for Jim, I was the cat waiting. Lifting my gun, I fired and got him in the back of the thigh. He yelled as he crashed to the floor in a blubbering heap.

Rolling out my shoulders, I slowly stood as Jim's phone rang again. "Apparently, Dave's worried about you. Isn't that sweet? Did you know your 'friend' had already given you up?"

Jim gripped his leg as he rolled around on the floor like a turtle on its back. His continuous begging for forgiveness was getting old quick.

Picking up his phone, I marched over, and before he knew what was happening, I held it in front of his face, and the thing unlocked. God bless modern technology.

"Please don't hurt me, please."

"Why shouldn't I? Dave already told me that you were the one who came up with the plan to get even with me. That it was all your idea to rape Raine," I said, once more lying my ass off.

"No, no, that's not true," he said as I flicked through his contacts and photos. I sent everything useful to the burner phone I'd purchased for this occasion and laid the phone on the tiny dining table. "I'll tell you what happened. Just please don't kill me."

I tapped my chin with the gun and watched the blood pool around Jim's leg. Walking into the kitchen, I grabbed a hand towel and tossed it at Jim. "Tie off your wound and tell me the truth. And, Jim, don't fucking lie to me, or I'll blow your kneecap off next."

He bellowed as I looked around for what I needed next and spotted his fishing equipment in the corner. That would work. Going over to Jim's boots by the door, I quickly pulled out the long black laces.

"What are you doing?" Jim asked, his eyes going wide.

"You said don't kill you. You didn't say don't secure you." His face relaxed. Such a stupid fuck. "Can't have you thinking you can grab your gun."

As soon as he had his leg tied off, so he didn't die before I wanted him to, I grabbed his wrists and tied them together, then dragged Jim across the floor to a crescendo of swearing.

"So nice of you to have this old-fashioned stove here," I drawled. I glanced at Jim's face, which was contorted in pain. "You better start talking before I even up your legs."

"It was all Frank," Jim said as I walked to the far side of the room and grabbed the tackle box I'd seen. That was not the answer I'd been expecting to hear.

"Why would your hunting buddy want me to go to prison?" I asked, pulling out the heavy fishing line. This shit was meant to hold a gator, so it would definitely hold Jim. Stuffing the gun in my jeans, I spun the round wire reel on my finger as I strolled toward my prey.

"He had Dave all fired up about you fucking his wife and how that was disrespectful and how you needed to be taught a lesson if he was a real man."

I lifted a brow at Jim as I squatted down and used the line to secure his hands to the heavy cast-iron stove. This was something you would see in a hunting camp way up north. Why the fuck he had one was beyond me, and I didn't care enough to ask.

"So you taught Raine a lesson instead?" I asked as I tied the knot in place and slit the line with my switchblade.

"Sorta. That wasn't part of the original deal, Kai. I swear to you. We were just supposed to rough you up a little. You know, teach you a lesson for messing around with another man's wife." He licked his lips as I moved to his feet and decided that the two recliners would have to do.

"Keep talking, Jim," I said, pushing the first chair across the floor.

"We went down to the fights and were going to wait for you to come out after you were done and jump you. Frank was the lookout guy. He was in the fights watching for you, but you never showed, and then there was a shoot-out."

My hands paused. I'd forgotten about the gunshots. What if she'd been shot that night? A cold dread spread throughout my body.

"Raine was there, and for whatever fucked up reason, she thought Frank was you and came racing down the alley where we were. Frank said this would be even better when Dave mentioned who Raine was. I swear to you. I didn't want to hurt her. Raine had always been nice to me," Jim said, lifting his head to look at me as I tied his first foot to the chair.

"So what you're saying is that you were forced to put your cock inside her and then frame me for it?" His chair scraped ominously across the floor as I pushed it toward Jim. "Or maybe you randomly ended up naked and fell on her, and then why not? You were already there."

"Man, look, I had sex with her, but you have to understand that Frank is scary. I didn't know what he would do if I refused."

I smiled wide as I tied Jim's second leg. "Psst, Jim," I whispered. "Guess who's scarier."

"Kai, believe me, I argued with them and begged them to let her go, but Frank wouldn't listen. He told Dave that this way, you'd be locked up for life."

"Oh, that must have been such a sad day when I took the plea deal for ten," I drawled, the sarcasm dripping off every word. Finished with my securing, I pulled out my knife, and Jim screeched like I'd already done something to him. Shaking my head, I slit the jeans on both legs and cut up the middle, so the material fell open.

"What the hell are you doing?" Jim cried, but I ignored him.

It figures this guy would be wearing tighty-whities. I really didn't want to see this, but I gripped the elastic band and pulled it up, so the knife slid through the material easily.

"I told you everything I know. I was scared, and that's the truth. I did what I was ordered to do," he said, his voice full of conviction.

"Did you come?" Walking to the gun case, I pulled out my leather gloves and stuffed my hands inside before gripping the rifle and fifty-caliber shells.

"What?"

"You heard me. Did you cum? Did you hate it so much that you were repulsed by her young ass, or did you cum?"

"Fuck, man...." Jim looked away from my hard gaze.

"Yeah, that's what I thought." Opening the ammunition box, I loaded the cartridge and marched toward Jim.

"What the hell are you doing with my gun?" He squirmed on the floor and pulled on his restraints, but everything held firm.

"Well, Jim, I believe in karma. That shit is my best friend, and today you're getting the chance to meet," I said and knelt between his legs. "Tell me something. Why the warehouse?"

"Frank busted open the door." His voice was shaking along with the rest of his body.

"Okay, one more question, and we're going to think of this as the bonus question. If you answer this one to my satisfaction, I'll let you go." Jim nodded. "Did she scream? Did she scream when you hurt her?" Tears filled Jim's eyes. "Did she?" I bellowed, and he jerked.

"Yes," Jim mumbled under his breath. "She kept begging for you to stop, but I swear I didn't want to hurt her."

I didn't think anything could infuriate me more, but I'd been wrong. To hear confirmation that Raine thought it was me. That she screamed and begged me to stop. That she was terrified out of her mind, snapped the last of my control.

"Well, tonight you're going to understand that pain, Jim. This is your night of reckoning," I said, and lined the end of the rifle up with Jim's asshole.

"No, no, no, please. Please don't do this!"

He fought the bindings, but he was already weak and secure, so all he was doing was wearing himself down further. The moment he stilled to catch his breath, I struck and shoved the end of the rifle up his ass to the sound of high-pitched shrieking. Jim's body bowed off the ground as the dry, cold metal penetrated farther up his shitter.

I held the gun still and let the wails die down to rambling that made no sense.

"You know, Jim, the sad thing is that I saw you as family. I thought of you as an uncle and one of the only people I could trust, but you destroyed that. So when you're on the slide down to meet the devil, I want you to remember that you would've been better off dying in that warehouse years ago."

"But you promised," he cried.

"So did you. You promised to always be there for me. Do you

remember that?" I pulled on the gun until it was almost out of his ass and shoved it back inside. He screamed again, his wails mixed with tears and the stench of regret. "I want you to remember how you hit my knuckles and said I would always be family. How does it feel to be lied to?"

When no logical answer was forthcoming, I shook my head. "I'd say it was a pleasure, but that would be a lie. Thanks for the info, Jim."

"No, wait. I—"

Bang

The sound of the rifle rang out as I pulled the trigger, and I was shocked when the two recliners were dragged a few inches from the force of the shot before it blew off part of Jim's head. The bullet exploded out of his skull and hit the far wall. I smirked as I stared at the hair stuck to the shitty wood panel siding before it slid down, leaving a red streak in its wake. Smiling, I glanced at the half-missing face and the remaining eye staring back at me. I'd always wondered what would happen if I did this. This was definitely up there in my most favorites. Heck it might have even taken over the number one spot.

"That was fucking cool. Too bad I didn't have two of you. I'd love to have tried a different angle."

The door slammed open, and Roach stepped in, holding his gun out as his eyes searched for a threat before he looked down at the man on the floor. His brows knit together with a mix of disgust and horror in his eyes.

"Dude, that's fucked up. I'm never helping you again," Roach grumbled and left, the door slamming closed with a bang. Standing, I stared down at Jim to take in and appreciate this moment before I cleaned up anything I'd touched.

Jim's phone rang again as I stepped outside, and this time, I hit the answer button.

"Jim? Jim, you there?"

I breathed heavily into the phone.

"Man, seriously, you need to answer. This is no time for your stupid games."

A wicked grin pulled at my mouth. "I'm coming for you," I growled low into the phone and hit 'end.'

Snake

Chapter 39

Kaivan

I learned very quickly you should never kill a man, go home, and drink like a fish while you lied to yourself about why you did it. I did want revenge for being sent to prison for something that Dave, Frank, and Jim had done, but it wasn't the driving force.

Raine. I couldn't stop thinking about Raine, even though I'd sworn her off forever. She was a fucking plague on my mind that was only getting worse. The harder I tried to stop thinking about her, the more I saw her shy smile and the fire burning in her eyes when I pissed her off.

Putting the whiskey bottle to my lips, I took a swig and stared out my living room window. It was dark in the house, and the spirits that haunted this place kept me company. Fuck, maybe I was one of those spirits now.

What did I have to show for my life? My cut was beside me on the couch, and I ran my hand over the soft material, tracing The Lost Souls logo as gently as a lover would. I had nothing besides the club and what I did for them.

Roach, Hollywood, Mannix, and in some strange fucked up way, Wilder, were my family. They were each part of the small circle I'd die for, but there had always been something missing. Someone....

"You look sad," Wilder said quietly.

"What in the ever-loving fuck!" I swore as I jumped to my feet.

My eyes searched the darkness behind me, and a shiver raced down my spine as Wilder stepped away from the wall a few feet away. My hand clenched into a fist on instinct before I could draw a decent breath. I grabbed at my chest.

"I swear your goal is to give me a fucking heart attack. You'd think I'd be used to this by now," I grumbled.

"Why would I want to give you a heart attack?" he asked as I stomped past him to the kitchen to clean off the whiskey that had spilled all over my hand and arm. "There are far easier ways to kill someone. I could've slit your throat or shot you in the head. I guess if I wanted it to be slow, I could poison you by slipping something in your drink," he said.

I stared at the bottle and then down the hall where I'd left Wilder.

"Yeah, definitely not finishing that now," I mumbled, and turned the bottle upside down in the sink before washing my hands.

I went back into the living room and used some rags to mop up what I'd spilled. Despite the house falling down around me, I liked to keep it neat and orderly. Some habits died harder than others, and the ones from prison hardly faded.

"What are you doing in here, Wilder?"

He didn't answer, just sat down in the recliner and stared out the window.

"Why are you sad?" he asked, and I glared at him. "You are sad, aren't you? Or do I have the emotion wrong?"

I cocked my head and stared into Wilder's eyes. Even though he had black and grey makeup on, like he was trying to blend in with the concrete and asphalt, I could see the confusion in his eyes. I'd always wondered why Wilder was so strange and why he asked the most fucked up questions, but a light had just gone on. He didn't have the same emotions as the rest of us. That was why he was always so curious. He was some kind of path. My best guess was psychopath, and I was suddenly more relieved than ever that Wilder didn't want to slit my throat, as he put it. He could've done it a hundred times by now, and I would never have felt a thing.

"Yes, the emotion was sorta sad," I said, flopping down on the couch. It was going to reek like whiskey in here for days.

"What do you mean by sorta?"

I rubbed my face and tried to put into words what I had going on inside of me. "It's hard to explain. There are things I wish for that can never be," I finally said. "Some of those things make me sad, others angry and frustrated."

Wilder rubbed at his chin. "Can you fix what is making you sad?"

"I don't know. Maybe, no, yes, it's hard to know. I kinda fucked up, and I'm not sure I want to fix it."

"But you can't stop thinking about it and wondering if you should fix it," Wilder asked.

"What the fuck, Wilder? Are you trying to be my shrink or what?" I growled and crossed my arms.

"Do you need a shrink?" he asked.

"I may need one shortly." His brow furrowed, and I knew he didn't understand my sarcasm. "Okay, yes. I may want to somehow repair what I fucked up," I said, hating that he'd gotten me to admit out loud that I still wanted Raine. Even after all these years of anger and hatred, she could stir up so much emotion with a single look. I wanted her. The thought of her moving on with the guy from the bar had my blood boiling.

"Then, if you want my opinion, you should fix it." Wilder nodded and resumed looking outside.

"Can I ask you a question?"

"Yeah, why couldn't you ask me a question?"

I wanted to smack my hand to my forehead. This guy made my brain feel like it was trying to walk along the floor of a fun house as it moved around.

"Why do you always dress like this?" I asked.

Wilder looked down at the matching black and grey camo fatigues he was wearing. "Why not?"

"'Cause it's not exactly normal. Do you see me or anyone else walking down the street dressed in camo or like a swamp thing or a garbage bin dude?" If he were going to kill me for insulting him, at least I'd see him coming.

"I don't wear this out," he finally said. "Well, I do, but only when I need to."

I wish I hadn't dumped out the rest of my whiskey. I'd rather take my chances with the possible poison. "Fine. Why are you wearing it now?"

Wilder leaned forward, his arms resting on his thighs. "To blend in. I thought that would be obvious."

Okay, forget the poison. I was going to pull my gun and shoot myself at this rate. "Wilder. Why do you want to blend in right now?"

Talking to him was like being at the top of a staircase with no recollection of how I got there. It felt like I needed to back up one step at a time until I figured out why I climbed them in the first place.

His steely gaze found mine, and I could feel him assessing me like I was one of the freak show exhibits from his dilapidated park.

"Can I trust you?" Wilder asked, his eyes narrowing and his voice dropping to a level that made the hair stand on the back of my neck.

"If you mean, will I tell anyone what you say? Then you can trust me to keep it to myself. I'll go to my grave with it," I said.

"Even if it puts you in danger?"

"Even better. I like living on the edge." I leaned forward. To finally learn the mysteries of Wilder was too good to pass up.

The corner of Wilder's mouth turned up as if what I'd said amused him. If he could be amused.

"I was ordered to do something but was set up, and now one particular person is after me, but they have the strength of many men like me looking for me." It was hard to tell if this was a wild truth or if this was just another twisted mess inside Wilder's mind. "That's why I was keeping tabs on your girl's fuck friend."

My nostrils flared at the mention of the bartender.

"Oh, really? And why is that?"

"He's related to the man who is after me. I keep an eye on all his family."

That had me sitting up straight. "Is she in danger? Are you planning something I should know about?"

I had no idea if I could get to my gun before Wilder killed me, but if he was planning to go after Raine, we were about to have an issue.

"No, the guy seems checkered for different reasons but has nothing to do with that side of his family. He seems to be estranged from most of his family. They don't like his life choices."

I had no idea what that meant, but I relaxed as Wilder said he had no intentions of attacking them.

"So these people who are after you, are you planning on eradicating them?" I asked.

"Killing them like rodents. I like that. Yes, if they come for me."

I leaned back and stared at Wilder. "I think you should take the fight to their door. Not that you don't look great in all your blending-in outfits, but wouldn't it be nice to be free of the worry?"

"I don't worry. There is no place for fear in my life." He turned his head and stared out the dark window. "But I do understand your meaning. Maybe you should take your advice as well. Better to know if you can fix what you fucked up than not try at all."

Crossing my arms, I stared at the side of his face and couldn't help wondering what it would've been like to have Wilder in prison with me. I had the protection of Mannix and the crew he'd gathered, and that was how I met Roach and Hollywood, but there was something about Wilder that made you want him on your team even if he made your brain do backward somersaults.

"Maybe I should. So, did you come over because you saw I was sad or to ask another question?"

"No, I just wanted to borrow some flour," Wilder said, and stood.

"Flour?"

"Yes, I'm baking cookies." He smiled, and I could only shake my head.

"Sure, I have a bag in the cupboard across from the stove. Help yourself."

"I know. You just purchased it last Tuesday." He walked out of the room like that wasn't the creepiest thing to date he'd said to me. I bet he also wrote down somewhere how many times I jerked off in a day. I didn't even want to fucking think about that.

Wisely or not, I decided to visit Raine. Pushing myself off the couch, I grabbed my leather jacket and called down the hall. "Hey, Wilder, I'm heading out. Can you lock up?"

"Yup, I always do." And there it was, the line that was creepier than the one before.

"How in the hell did I get talked into leaving the wet pussy I was fucking for this?" Roach grumbled as we pulled up to Raine's house.

"Because you still owe me," I said, eyes trained on the dark windows.

"For what?"

I turned my head to look at Roach. "You know for what."

He shook his head and lit up a smoke. "You're a prick. I paid that debt back a hundred times by now."

"Keep dreaming," I mumbled.

Hopping out of the truck, I jogged up the few steps and tried the door, but I wasn't surprised to find it locked. Now that I knew the locks in her home, I made quick work of it and stepped inside. Not much had changed. The coffee table was gone, but it hadn't been replaced. The closet door had a dent, and I could still feel her shoulders as I slammed her up against it. Running my fingers over the little mark, I felt a flicker of guilt.

Taking a deep breath, I walked away from the door and took the stairs two at a time. The room had been tidied just like downstairs. The bed was made and not slept in, and the door to the bathroom had been removed. Other than that, there was no sign of Raine or that she'd been here since that night.

My hand balled into a fist. There was a ninety-nine-point-nine percent chance that I knew exactly where she was, and I should stay away. I should head back to my house and let this be a fucking sign, but before I made it out the front door, I knew that wouldn't happen.

"Head to Eclipse. I'll give you directions from there," I barked out.

"Are we killing someone? I just need to know what we're getting into." Roach turned the truck around and pulled off the residential street and onto the main road that led to the beach. The place Raine worked was closed tonight, but as we got close, my eyes scanned the parking lot for the plain black sedan. Not seeing it only made the rage brewing in my gut rise to dangerous levels.

"That way," I said, pointing. The closer we got to the house I'd followed Raine to, the harder I ground my teeth. "Pull over here," I growled out. Roach did as I asked, and I stared at the three-story home. The lights were on, but I couldn't see anyone moving around inside, and that made me anxious and enraged.

When I grabbed the door handle, Roach gripped my biceps. "As your friend, you need to calm the fuck down before you go over there."

I glared at his hand, but he held firm. "I fucking mean it. This is not a job, and Raine and whoever she's in there with haven't done shit to anyone or anything to do with the club or you. Other than pissing you off by proximity to something you want. You've never been one to kill casually, but I know that look on your face, and you're close to murderous. Take a deep fucking breath, man. I mean it."

He let go of my arm, and I knew he was right. Every logical part of my being told me I should tell Roach to drive away, but I opened the door and got out. I wasn't letting Raine go without a fight.

Chapter 40

R aine

"I still can't believe you got food first," Avro complained as he poured his once-upon-a-time milkshake into a glass. It looked like yellow milk, and I covered my mouth not to gag.

"You ordered more, and it will be here soon. What's the big deal?" Jace argued and earned an 'are you fucking kidding me?' glare.

I snickered as I watched the two of them together. It was easy to tell that they'd known one another for years. They were the embodiment of an old married couple, and it was hard to keep the smile off my face. Jace was still a total asshole, but we now had this weird connection, or maybe it was more of an understanding between us. It was a start. He certainly could make my blood race and made me squirm with just a look.

"And then you had hot sex without me in a cemetery. You know that's on my bucket list." Avro continued to sulk, but it seemed directed toward his now cold and melted food.

"Oh, my god. Do you want to go right now? I can fuck you in a cemetery on a tomb of your choice," Jace muttered, and rolled his eyes.

I couldn't hold back any longer and burst out laughing. Avro shot a glare my way.

"Sorry." I covered my mouth but bit my finger to avoid making noise.

"I thought you wanted Peaches and me to get closer," Jace asked.

He pulled a small dish of grapes from the refrigerator and popped one into his mouth. His eyes found mine, and the look he gave me made me warm all over as they danced with mischief that bordered on something darker. We hadn't been back very long, and the memories of what we'd done and the feel of his body were still very fresh in my mind. I'd officially decided I might be addicted to his piercings, because I could still feel them on my tongue and in other places.

"It is what I want." Avro leaned against the counter. "I'm just hangry. Ignore me."

"I need to hit the head. I'll be back." Jace left the kitchen, and I took the opportunity to go to Avro. He was quick to pull me close to his body.

"You sure you're okay with Jace and me...you know?"

Avro smiled widely. "Totally." He leaned in close to my ear. "I just love giving Jace a hard time. He gets extra spicy when he's riled up," he whispered, making me laugh. The doorbell rang, and Avro smiled even wider. "About time. I'm starved."

I was going to mention that the rest of the food was fine, and it was just a milkshake, but I figured that would set him off on another rant. I picked up the glass of liquid milkshake to try a sip as Avro opened the door. I looked up when Avro asked who the person at the door was, and the smile fell from my face.

"Fuck," Avro yelled as Kai punched him square in the face.

Blood thrummed through my veins, and the world slowed down as Avro stumbled back and Kai stepped into the house. I could hear the thump of his boots, and they echoed in my mind like a movie. I thought he'd leave me alone. I was so stupid.

My stomach flipped and then tied itself into knots at the sight of him with his hands clenched into fists, and his lip pulled up like he was snarling. My heart pounded harder with each step he took, but when those enraged eyes found mine, the world narrowed in on just him. I sucked in a shuddering breath and felt paralyzed, like his eyes alone could hold me in place.

Kai was almost at the kitchen doorway when Jace came out of nowhere and tackled Kai. I sucked in a breath as Kai and Jace disappeared. They crashed into the front sitting room so loudly that it jerked me out of my shocked state. The noise around me came crashing back as loudly as the sound of the two men swearing and growling like a pair of animals.

I forgot I was holding the glass until it slipped from my fingers and shattered on the tile floor, sending little shards and banana milkshake in all directions. I blinked as a flash of my childhood hit me. I could see the blood on my hands and remembered the feeling of the glass cutting my feet. I shook my head and closed my eyes to rid myself of the image.

Leaving the mess in my wake, I ran from the kitchen and rounded the corner to the sitting area. In those few seconds, it looked like a cyclone had taken the room in its grip. Kai and Jace rolled around on the floor, exchanging and taking blows with even measure. Neither seemed to have the upper hand, and I stood there feeling useless as I tried to figure out how to help.

"Kai!" I screamed, but he didn't glance my way.

If he heard, he ignored me, but it seemed more like he was so focused that a car could have driven through the window and he wouldn't have cared.

They rolled again, and this time Jace was on top, but Kai used his feet in a wrestling maneuver that tossed Jace over his head. Jace crashed down on top of the large glass coffee table, and it shattered on impact. He groaned, his face grimacing in pain.

"Kai!" I screamed again and ran at him as he lifted his arm to punch Jace. Slamming into his side only knocked him off balance. He glared but then looked away like I was a pesky insect.

Avro jumped into the fray as Kai got to his feet, blood dripping from his split lip. Avro wasn't as skilled as Jace, but he held his own as he and Kai took turns swiping at one another like a pair of boxers in a ring. They were saying something to one another, but I couldn't hear over the roaring in my head.

Darting around the two, I knelt by Jace, who rolled onto his side. "Are you okay?"

"Yeah, I will be. I'm going to kill this fucker." He shook off my hand as he stood up.

"Jace, don't. I'll get him to leave."

"Fuck that. This asshole is mine," Jace snarled, the glass shards falling off him as he stepped away from the table.

My heart leaped into my throat as Kai pulled a switchblade. I screamed like a banshee when he slashed at Avro. Jace charged, and as Kai turned to face the attack, he kicked the blade from Kai's hand with an impressive move and sent it spinning through the air until it stuck into the couch.

It was two-on-one, yet Kai looked like a feral dog in a fight to the death, and it terrified me. They all terrified me, and there was way too much testosterone and not enough brains between the three of them. I suddenly knew what it felt like to be the bone all the dogs were fighting over, and I didn't like it.

Avro gripped Kai from behind but got two hard elbows to the gut. The blows made him let go, and he was doubled over as he tried to breathe.

Jumping in, I tried once more to stop Kai. My hands gripped his leather jacket, but I was no more effective than a flea as he lunged for Jace, and the material was ripped from my hands.

The two men collided like bears. Kai and Jace gripped each other and pushed one other around the room. I had to dance out of the way as they ran sideways at me and crashed into the wall with a thud. A very sick and twisted part of me loved the ferocity of the moment and wished this was just for fun, but there was nothing fun or amusing about their intent.

"Enough!" I tried again and marched toward them, but Avro charged Kai again and gripped him around the waist before I got there. They managed to destroy everything they touched as it fell from the walls or clattered off tables. Avro and Jace picked Kai up and slammed him down hard on the floor like wrestlers I'd seen on television with a tag team maneuver.

Kai wouldn't stay down, and blood flew as his elbow cracked Avro across the jaw. Kai jumped up, but before he and Jace could go another round, he pulled a gun.

"I'm going to fucking kill you," Kai growled, his voice as threatening as the night he'd been in my home.

Jace gripped Avro's shoulder and pulled him back before holding his hands up.

"No, Kai, don't you dare!" I yelled, jumping in front of Jace and holding my arms out in my pathetic attempt to block the shot. "Kai."

"Get out of my way, Tink," he snarled, wiping at the blood trickling from his chin, his eyes focused on the men behind me.

I could see Jace in the glass, moving to grab me out of the way.

"Don't touch me, Jace," I said and glanced over my shoulder.

He was going to have a black eye. It was already swelling, and blood was flowing from his nose. My heart broke as our eyes locked. At that moment, I knew that Jace was right, Kai would always keep coming unless I locked him back up, and I couldn't do it.

Even now, I knew I couldn't put him back in the cage that had turned him into this. I loved Avro, and my feelings for Jace were wild and new and would eventually turn into love, and I couldn't put them at risk. This needed to end.

When I was sure Jace wouldn't try to yank me out of the way, I turned my head to look at Kai again.

"Don't you dare hurt them. They've never done anything to you. It's me you're after." I took a small step forward, and Kai's eyes flicked to mine. "Isn't that the truth? I'm the one who hurt you. I'm the one you hate. I'm the one you want to kill and end whatever fucked up war you have inside your mind," I said.

All the bubbling emotion was pushed aside with the urgency of the situation. There was time for fear later.

Kai licked the blood from his lip, but it was the slight tremor in his hand that told me he heard me.

"Look at me, Snake," I yelled, and he stepped back. I'd never used his fighting name, but I did now. It had divided us then and had the effect I was after now. Kai's eyes grew large as he stared at me. "You're not Kai, not right now, not like this. I don't even recognize you." I looked him up and down and tried hard not to remember the teen who had made my heart beat as if it would pound out of my ribcage.

"Don't call me that," he said, his voice soft and horrified.

"Why not? You want me dead anyway, right? That's what Snake wants. To destroy the person who made you this angry." I spoke like he was two different people. That was what it seemed like to me. Kai could be sweet, caring, and romantic, but then there was Snake, who was only out for blood and pain.

"Well, I'm right here. Do it. Take the shot and end this, because

I'm not living in fear of you anymore." A tear slipped from my eye, and he watched it trickle down my cheek. "I know now that it wasn't you back then, but I've lived the last eleven years a shell of who I was because of what was done to me, and I won't hide in my closet anymore. I won't triple lock my door and stay up all night with a knife by my bed. I won't close my eyes and see your face hurting me." I shook my head. "Not anymore." I stepped forward as my anger rose higher.

"Raine, stay back," Avro said, but this was no longer about them.

Kai was here for me because of our past. I was the only one that could stop this.

Kai's eyes flicked to the ground. But I wasn't having any of that bullshit. He came here, and he was finishing it one way or another.

"Look at me," I growled. Marching the last few steps forward, I stopped when the barrel of his gun touched me, and I gripped the end so he couldn't simply pull away.

"Let go, Tink," he said. "I don't have a fucking safety. Let go." Kai's voice was panicked as I pushed the barrel, so it was over my heart.

"Do it."

"No."

"Do it!" I screamed at him, the tears breaking free and sliding down my face. "I've wasted so much of my life being scared. I can't be that person again. So do it, 'cause I'm done. My heart was ripped from my chest in that warehouse. You might as well destroy my soul too." Tears poured in a steady stream down my cheeks. "Do it," I whispered.

"No, Tink. Just let go. I won't shoot them," he said, but I didn't believe him.

The images of my attack flooded my mind. My hands clawed at the dusty old couch as my clothes were ripped from my body. My screams were never heard, and no one cared. The pain that they caused as they violated me over and over and shoved my face into the cushion so I couldn't breathe. My hand shook, and my body trembled. I wouldn't go back to being that girl, but I couldn't turn him in. I was fucked either way.

"I think everyone needs to take a breath," a new voice said.

I glanced over to see the man who was at Kai's house the day I went to speak to him.

He slowly stepped around the room, wisely keeping his distance with his hands in the air. "Neither of you wants to do this."

"And how would you know what I want?" I asked, never taking my eyes off Kai.

"Because you don't look like someone who wants to die. It's Raine, right?"

I looked at him but kept my hand clenched tight around the gun barrel.

"I'm Roach. Snake and I met in prison. Kai never stopped talking about you. He always loved you. He tried to convince me that he hated you, but no hate burns that bright."

"Shut up, man. You don't know what you're talking about," Kai said, but there was no conviction in his tone, and I hated that my chest clenched a little tighter for a man I should want to forget forever.

"Really? So you want to kill her? Then I'm with her. Do it. Get it over with. Otherwise, this is a lot of drama for nothing."

Kai turned his head and looked at Roach as he crossed his arms over his chest, possibly bored, I didn't know.

"Don't look at me like that. Do you want her dead or not?"

"No, of course, I fucking don't. Them, on the other hand..." Kai growled. "I'd happily see them bleeding all over the floor."

"For what?" I yelled, and my hand shook violently.

"Whoa, Tink, don't be doing that," Kai said like he was trying to soothe me, his eyes wide as he stared at the shaking barrel of the gun.

"Or what? It might go off. Let it. Avro and Jace are the first people to make me feel human and myself again in years. You want to come in here and destroy that, rip away the slice of happiness I've carved for myself? Fuck you, Snake." I pressed harder into the metal until it hurt. "I won't let you tear me down anymore, and I won't let you hurt them."

"Let go of the gun, Snake," Roach ordered, and Kai immediately let go.

My lower lip trembled as the last remaining bits of the girl I'd once been crumbled to dust around me. Flipping the gun around, I quickly popped the magazine, and it fell to the floor with a thud. I uncocked it, and the loaded bullet dropped to the floor. I tossed the gun at Kai, and he caught it. I'd never liked guns, but I'd gone to the range and learned how to use one. Fear makes you do things you never thought you would.

"Get out. I never want to see you again. If you ever loved me at all, leave me alone," I said, my heart breaking with each word.

"Tink...." I could see the remorse in his eyes now that he'd calmed down, but it didn't matter. The damage was done. In one single act of jealousy, he'd destroyed my life all over again.

"Don't call me that, and get out," I said, my chin held high.

"Come on. Let's go," Roach coaxed.

The way Kai hesitated, I wasn't sure if he would go. He looked at me, then glanced at Avro and Jace before letting Roach herd him out the door. I stood and watched from the window as the two of them got into a truck and drove away, and still, I didn't move.

As soon as I did, I knew what would happen. Encasing my heart in the walls it needed, I turned to face Jace and Avro. Jace was, of course, the first to speak.

He dabbed at his nose with the hoodie he was wearing. "Let me guess, that's your friend, and you still don't want me to call the fucking cops." I didn't say anything, and he shook his head. "Fuck me," he snarled and stomped off.

"I'll talk to him," Avro said, and I held up my hand.

"No, let him cool off." I lifted a shoulder. "He has every right to be angry, and so do you. I need to go home and spend the night there to clear my head." I took in the destroyed room. "I'm so sorry," I said. "I'll help with cleanup, but I just can't right now."

"Let me drive you home." He stepped toward me, and I held up my hand to stop him. I couldn't let him touch me, or I'd lose all the courage I needed for what was next.

I shook my head and grabbed my purse and hoodie. "I could use the fresh air. I'll be fine."

"But Snake could be waiting. I really should drive you."

I shook my head. "No, he won't stick around. He knows this was a huge fuck up. Trust me. I know that look in his eyes. He won't be back."

Avro's eyes held the same sad and hooded expression as my heart did. I stepped up to the front door and gave him a small smile as I tried to alleviate the worry I saw on his face.

"I'm so sorry for all of this. I really am. Can you tell Jace I'm sorry too?"

"You can tell him tomorrow. It will be better coming from you," he said, and I nodded. "You'll be at work tomorrow, won't you? Do you want me to pick you up? Jace flies out the following morning, so we can talk after work," Avro blurted out. He would make a terrible poker player. He was worried that this would drive a wedge between us, and he was right, which was why I couldn't let that happen.

"Yeah, that works. Pick me up at the normal time."

"You sure you're okay? It's no problem to take you home," he offered for the third time.

"No, I need the space at the moment." Swallowing down the

emotions churning inside me, I sucked in a deep breath to help steady myself. "I love you, Avro," I said and heard him say it back as I closed the door. I couldn't stay for even another second, or he would tempt me to stay.

The walk was forty minutes to my house, and with each footstep, the tears fell a little more until there was nothing left to cry out. My life had been one blow after the other, and I wasn't sure how I was still standing, but I was, which meant that I was stronger than I'd realized.

Stepping into the little house I'd called home for the last six years, I ran up the stairs and didn't bother to look at my reflection in the mirror over my dresser. I knew I looked like hell warmed over. Stripping off the hoodie I had on, I tossed it into the pile of laundry that would never be washed and pulled on my favorite one and a jacket before grabbing my go bag. I swapped out my runners for the short leather boots and went to my nightstand to take the only other two personal items I had in the house: my journal and my V.C. Andrews book.

Tearing a page from the journal, I quickly wrote a note to Avro and Jace, and my lower lip quivered the entire time. Tears dripped onto the paper as I read it over, folded it, and put it in an envelope. Pushing the journal into the bag, I gave the room one more sweep before jogging down the stairs and locking the door.

There were some things in life you just couldn't fix, and this was one of them. Love or hate, Kai was filled with a toxic amount and would never be able to stay away. I'd seen it in his eyes tonight. That meant Avro and Jace would never be safe from his wrath. One of those rages would end up with me, or one of them killed, and I wouldn't have that. Avro had been my only friend for so long. He saw past the scars and cared enough to get to know me, and now he was the single piece of happiness and good in my life. If he died because of me...

I shook my head, unable to contemplate that thought. The look of fear and sadness on their faces was enough to crush me, but the dark bruises, blood, and cuts were just too much. This was for the best, and it was the only card I had left. The ace of spades was in my hand, and it was time to use it.

I put the envelope in my mailbox and walked to the bus stop. Pulling up the map on my phone, I thought about all the places I'd wanted to see in person. This wasn't how I thought it would happen, but it was time. The universe was giving me the boot like the Collinses had when I got out of the hospital. I had survived then, and I would survive now.

Chapter 41

Avro

Jace wheeled the rest of his luggage toward the door, and my heart sank. He didn't say we were done. The words never left his mouth, but that was how it felt. I'd never seen Jace so angry after Raine left. He fumed and paced as we argued all night about what to do.

I understood why Jace was adamant that he couldn't be part of the relationship if Raine wouldn't call the police, and yet I knew she wouldn't. The look on her face said how bad she felt about everything, but under that was the same look she gave me when she said she couldn't turn Kai in. Weirdly, I understood her and her reasoning more now than before I saw Kai.

Despite my broken nose and bruised side, the look on his face made me think of Jace and how he would've ended up. I was scared to think about what would've happened without his mom when she was alive and me after she died. We kept him on the path whenever he started to wander off. He was just as stubborn and ambitious, but it didn't lead him down dark alleys and into fistfights.

The way Jace and Kai had gone at it, I knew that one of them was going to die. They were too similar to give in, and only Raine could've stopped that. Fuck, what she did was so brave. I was terrified he was going to do it, or that gun would accidentally go off.

"You don't have to leave this morning. I can take you to the plane tomorrow like we planned," I said.

"No, I need some space from all of this. I don't want to argue with you. I've always hated fighting with you, but I'm telling you, that guy will not stop. He is going to be back, and next time, he will probably pull the trigger the moment you open the door." Jace finished tying his boots and stood. "I'm surprised he didn't, and when I think about that." He shook his head. "I can't. I can't live through that again."

I pushed myself to my feet and faced the one person I'd loved almost my whole life, and it felt like I was being torn in two. Jace grabbed my face and kissed me hard. It was so Jace, so demanding, so all-consuming that I forgot he was leaving and this could be our last goodbye.

"I can't lose you that way, and if I spend any more time here, I'm going to fall in love with her 'cause the fucking tug is there already, and I can't. I just can't. Call me a fucking chicken all you want, but I already had to bury three people I loved because of an unhinged man." His hands dropped from my face. "I won't put myself in that position willingly again. If Raine won't do what she needs to, to make us all safe...." He grabbed the bomber jacket and shrugged it on. "If she calls the cops, then I'm all in. If you decide we find a different third, I'm all in." Jace paused in his rant and sighed. "But this? Always worrying when that fucker will come to the door with a gun? No. No. No. No."

"That's a lot of 'no's. Are you sure?" I teased and earned a glare. "Okay, bad timing. Look, Jace..." I grabbed his shoulders and searched his face. "Just give me time to get something worked out."

"I am. We're not done. I love you too fucking much, but you need to get Raine to see reason, and I can't be here for it 'cause I know that I'm just going to fight with her, and that will make it worse." A horn blew outside, and Jace walked over and opened the door to show off the long black limo. "I have three concerts over the next week, then three days off. I'll come home, and we can talk more."

"I hate this," I grumbled.

"So do I." He grabbed his bags and the suitcase and wheeled it to the open door before looking back at me. "I do want things to work out, Avro. You were right. She is unique and...I just wish it had worked out. Please be safe. That guy is not right. I saw it in his eyes."

With that, Jace walked out the door, and a minute later, the limo was gone. I stared at the living room, which was still a complete disaster, and knew it looked how I felt. My world had imploded. I had no one to blame but myself for falling in love with Raine, but I did and wouldn't change a moment. Every touch, glance, and laugh we'd shared over the last five years were tiny building blocks in our relationship.

I couldn't wait until work tonight. I needed to see her now. Locking the front door, I grabbed my keys and ran to my car. My chest felt like it was being stepped on. Raine left, Jace left, and I was the ribbon in the middle of a game of tug-of-war.

Hitting Jace's number on my phone, I tried calling him, but as usual, when he was pissed and wanted space, he had it turned off. It was a habit I hated.

"Jace, it's me. Look, I'm sorry. I know we said we would talk soon, but I just...Fuck, I love you. Call me back."

Racing down the street, it didn't take long to reach Raine's house, and I jumped out and ran to the front door. I knocked, but no one answered, and I didn't hear anyone moving around inside. I knocked again when I spotted an envelope sticking out of the mailbox, and feeling compelled to do it, I grabbed it.

My hands shook as I stared at the name scrolled across the front.

Avro and Jace

I tore open the envelope and pulled out the small handwritten letter.

I don't even know what to say. I have all these emotions and thoughts, and they are all jumbled up and barely make sense to me.

Avro, I want you to know that I really do love you. You have a special heart, and you took the time that no one else did to understand me. You made me feel like I wasn't a walking scar that everyone would see and pity. I cannot even explain to you what that means to me.

And I'm sorry to go like this, but I had to. I just couldn't look you in the eye and do what I needed to.

Jace, I hate to say it, but you were right about one thing. Kai is never going to stop. I'm not sure what it would take to stop him, but no matter what, I would never put the two of you at risk. I did hear you.

Please know our time, as short as it was, was very special to me.

I love you so much, Avro, and I know in time I would've loved you too, Jace.

The issue is that I still love Kai, even all these years later. I'm responsible for destroying his life and turning him into the enraged man who drove off the rails. He used to be so different and was someone the two of you would've liked. Now I don't recognize him, and that scares me.

It's time I start a new adventure, and maybe one day, our stars will realign.

Raine

I read the letter for a second time, my body shaking. No, this is not happening. I wasn't allowing that asshole to run her off. Letter in hand, I stomped down the steps to the car and flipped through the web search engine until I found what I needed—the dilapidated amusement park that sat next door to the motorcycle club.

Putting the car in gear, I drove to the old amusement park I'd been to many times as a kid. It used to be a huge attraction, and I had great memories of making out with Jace in a few dark corners. The top of the Ferris wheel had been highly entertaining. I felt free up there, with no one around to see or judge us.

I wasn't letting this guy destroy my life. I'd paid my dues on the wheel of fucked up. My hands clenched the steering wheel as I pushed the car much faster than I should on these streets, but I had one mission, and the blue-eyed motorcycle-riding fuckpot was it.

I pulled into the Lost Souls driveway as the gates were opening. Four bikes were getting ready to leave. They all had their hands behind their backs, waiting to see if the black car with tinted windows was a threat.

Putting my window down, I yelled. "Don't shoot. I'm just here to see Kai."

"Who the fuck is Kai?" one guy asked. I couldn't see who said it, but someone shouted back.

"Snake, you idiot. Get going. I'll meet you soon."

The three bikes peeled out. I took that as a good sign and slowly got out of the car.

"Roach, right?" I asked the guy as he cut the engine on his bike.

He leaned forward and looked me up and down. "Yeah, you got the name right. Are you fucking stupid, lost, or do you have a death wish?" Roach asked, and my back bristled.

"I need to speak to Kai."

Roach's eyebrow cocked upward. "Death wish, it is." Roach sat up and pointed toward the amusement park. "He has a house on the other side of that. Good luck. You're going to need it." Roach waited until I got back in my car and pulled out before starting his bike.

It was easy enough to find the long driveway with the weed-covered overgrowth he called a lawn.

Pulling up to the house, I got out and jogged up the porch. My fist banged hard on the door as I yelled Kai's name.

The door whipped open, and we glared at one another. He looked like he was ready for bed with jogging pants on. It was nice to see that his face looked as beat up as ours did.

"What the fuck do you want?" His hand flexed into a fist, and I pointedly looked at it.

"You gonna hit me?"

"Depends on why you're here," he said. "How exactly did you find my place?"

"Wouldn't you like to know?"

Kai's eyes narrowed as he glared.

"She's gone, and it's your fucking fault," I said before he could argue some more.

His eyebrows shot up. "What?"

I pulled the letter from my pocket and tossed it at Kai. He snatched it out of the air and slowly unfolded it. I waited until he had time to read it all before I spoke.

"She's gone, and it's your fault. What are you going to do about it?"

"Me? Why am I the one having to do something?" Kai asked and leaned against the doorjamb as he sneered at me. He looked me up and down like I wasn't worth his time, and I didn't like it. Like Raine, it took me a long time to figure out that I was worth someone's time, and my anger burned a little brighter.

"Are you hard of hearing? You and that fucking stunt last night chased her out of town. First, you almost killed her, then you assaulted her. As if that wasn't bad enough, you almost shot her after you tracked her down to my home. She was happy. We were fucking happy."

"Aw, did I ruin your little family?"

My fist flew before I had time to think about it. I gave him the same courtesy as he had with me last night and caught him in the middle of his face, completely off guard.

"Fuck," Kai yelled and stumbled backward. "I'm going to kill you."

"Then fucking kill me, but find her first, then fucking apologize and find a way to make her come back. I don't care what you have to do, but don't fuck this up. Remember, she's only gone because of you. So much for loving her." I shook my head as Snake's glare darkened. "Then if you want to kill me, you can, asshole." Snatching the letter from his hand, I marched down the stairs and got behind the wheel of my car.

There was no way he was going to be able to resist the thought of losing Raine. I'd seen it in his eyes just now when I said she was gone. His whole body twitched like he was ready to run out the door and find her that second. I would let him do the hard part. I was pretty sure he would find a way to hunt her down, and when he did, I would follow.

Everyone thought I was the nice guy, and most of the time, I was, but even nice guys could be pushed too far.

Jace

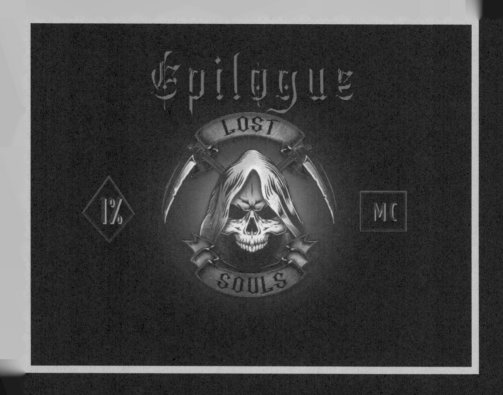

Epilogue

J ace

The plane's engine roared, and I sat back as the jet took off down the runway. I was able to get the pilot to come in early. I would've been too tempted to stay if I had to spend the night on the plane.

As the plane rose, I stared at the water and the state I called home. Even though I knew I was too far away, it didn't stop me from looking for Avro's house. My chest tightened with the thought of him. Then the memories of Raine and our time at the cemetery was like a movie behind my eyes.

"Fuck," I grumbled as we reached cruising altitude. The little light for the seatbelt turned off, and I connected my phone to the plane Wi-Fi. As soon as I did, it began to ding with notifications and

I was going to ignore them, but I couldn't resist when I saw Avro as one of the callers. The first message was from Allen.

"Hey, I hear you're flying in early. That is great news. I'm going to set up an interview with the EN broadcast. They've been bugging me for months to have you come for an interview." I rubbed my forehead, not wanting to deal with all of this right now. "Also, things are too quiet lately. We need to stir up the hornet's nest, so think about what you want to do. All right, that's all I've got. See you in a few hours." Oh, I could give him a scandal.

I moved on to the next message.

"Jace, it's me. Look, I'm sorry. I know we said we would talk soon, but I just... Fuck, I love you. Call me back."

The phone beeped, and I saved the message. I saved as many messages as I could from Avro. It was silly, but I loved listening to his voice when we couldn't talk.

The next message clicked on.

"Jace...Shit, she's gone. Raine left. I couldn't resist and went to see her, and she was gone. This is all that guy Kai's fault. I need to go see him." The line clicked, and my heart pounded hard as I pulled the phone away from my ear. I stared at the screen expecting another message, but there wasn't one.

He couldn't see Kai alone. What the hell was he thinking? Did he have a death wish? I quickly hit redial on the phone, but it just rang and rang before clicking over to voicemail.

It's Avro. Leave a message unless you're selling something. Beep.

"Hey, it's me. What the hell are you doing going to see a motorcycle gang member on your own? Call me back." I tapped the phone off my bouncing knee. "Shit, shit, shit!" I tried Avro again, and it went straight to voicemail. Karma. It was fucking karma for turning off my phone.

Unable to sit still, I stood and paced. Raine was gone and probably in danger, since Avro was going to go tell Kai that she was missing. Avro would probably get himself shot in the head before Kai took off after Raine to finish killing her. All the worst scenarios raced around in my brain like a merry-go-round with no off switch. Meanwhile, the fear over them getting injured, or worse, gripped my throat.

Stop it. You're getting yourself worked up over nothing.

But it wasn't nothing. This was the same feeling I had when I left home and my family ended up dead. That wasn't happening again.

"Fuck this," I grumbled, and marched for the front of the plane and knocked on the door. "Marco?"

The door opened, and the co-pilot stared out at me.

"We need to turn around."

If you liked Book 1 then be sure to keep an eye out for
Surrender
Book 2
Releasing May 16

THANK YOU

Thank you to all those that decided to pick up this book and read it. It is only with readers continued support that Indie Authors, such as myself, are able to keep writing which is why your reviews mean so much to us. If you enjoyed this book, please consider leaving me a review.

ABOUT THE AUTHOR

Writing is not just a passion for me. It is a lifeline to my sanity.

I have always loved writing but suffer from severe dyslexia and short-term memory retention issues. I struggled in school while I worked every night on re-training my brain.

I was frequently treated like I would never succeed, and I found myself putting my love for writing on a shelf.

Even at the age of six, I found it easier to communicate with animals than people, which was a big reason why I was drawn to dressage horseback riding. I remained focused on my passion for riding until I had to step away from the competition world for personal reasons.

Today, my desire for writing and storytelling has been rekindled. I have published multiple books and will never let anyone or anything hold me back again.
I am a proud romance author who offers my readers morally grey heroes, a ton of spice, epic journeys, and redemption stories.

-Follow Your Dreams-   *Brooklyn Cross*

Below are the links that you can use to find me if you'd like to follow me on my social media platforms.

Book Bub: <u>Brooklyn Cross Books - BookBub</u>
Goodreads: <u>Brooklyn Cross (Author of Dark Side of the Cloth) |
Goodreads</u>
TikTok: <u>Author Brooklyn Cross (@authorbrooklyncross) TikTok |
Watch Author Brooklyn Cross's Newest TikTok Videos</u>
IG: <u>Brooklyn Cross (@author_brooklyncross) • Instagram photos
and videos</u>
FB Group: <u>Crossfire - A Brooklyn Cross Reader Group | Facebook</u>